The TUSCAN SECRET

ANGELA PETCH

TUSCAN SECRET

bookouture

Published by Bookouture in 2019

An imprint of StoryFire Ltd.

Carmelite House
50 Victoria Embankment
London EC4Y 0DZ

www.bookouture.com

ISBN: 978-1-78681-959-8
eBook ISBN: 978-1-78681-958-1

Quant'è bella giovinezza
che si fugge tuttavia!
Chi vuol esser lieto, sia:
del doman non c'è certezza.

Lorenzo de' Medici (1449–92)

How lovely is youth
Which is over far too soon!
Grab your happiness while you may:
There is no certainty in tomorrow.
(*Author's translation*)

In memory of Paul Francis Sutor

PROLOGUE

An owl hoots, and in the distance I hear wolves howling from the Mountain of the Moon. I picture them huddled together on the ridge, their muzzles raised to bay their melancholy song, stars blinking in the blue-black of night behind them. I know no matter how hard I try to sink back to sleep, the memories will attack me. It's a pattern I can't break.

There was only one teacher for our village school, and so all thirty-three of us, every age together, packed ourselves into that single classroom. In winter a wood-burning stove warmed us, and in summer all the windows, built high in the walls to banish distraction, were flung wide to let in the mountain breeze.

I am an only son; I'd always longed for a younger brother, but my mother's belly never swelled again. And so I befriended the younger boy who shared my desk, guiding his hand to form letters on the slate, protecting him from the bullies in the school yard. We shared our simple *merende* – snacks of dried pears or a heel of yesterday's bread.

When he was older, when school was finished, we'd camp together in a cave, where salamanders hid on cool walls that glistened in the night. We rose early to catch the birds migrating over Friars' Peaks, treading softly to avoid our feet crunching on the rust-gold leaves and chestnuts. And now that we were brothers in arms, it stood us in good stead in our present danger. The fight against evil.

Years later, as sleep eludes me, I remember how I climbed to the cave that night, careful to skirt the sentries' posts. I passed so close I could hear their guttural whisperings. I wanted to find him seated on a rock, waiting for the sun to rise above the splendour of our purple mountains. Was it madness to hope for a single day of peace? We'd read in school about the Great War: how Germans and British called a truce on Christmas Day and played football, their trenches forming the makeshift boundaries of their pitch. I prayed he was up there, gazing over the mist enveloping our hills, concealing the brutality beneath. Was it too much to hope?

Keeping to the track, I stopped beside a huge boulder, a stench of rotting flesh causing me to gag. A body lay face down across my path, half hidden in the foliage, hands pillowing its head as if in slumber. I turned it over, dread in my heart, but even with half the face blown away, I saw it wasn't him.

As I turned back towards our occupied village, where our simple houses had been converted into barracks and gun emplacements, I heard his cries. The sound of his agony will never be erased from my head. It came from the village school. Light spilled from a barred window high in the wall. How often as a boy had I stared up at this scene from the classroom, gazing at the tips of two cypress trees swaying freely in the breeze, wishing I could be outside on the grassy slopes. I climbed onto a pail to look inside and my foot slipped, the metal container clattering in the night, setting the dogs barking.

The guards who rushed out to restrain me were from my own people, making it a thousand times worse. Men and boys I'd grown up with, tainted by misguided politics, dressed in militia uniforms. They dragged me inside as I kicked, swore and spat in their traitorous faces.

They had tortured him. Tied by wire to a chair too small for a grown man, knees hunched up, exposing what they'd done to his most private parts. I lunged towards him, but they held me fast. Mercifully he'd passed out, his bloodied head sagging forward as if in prayer.

But the worst betrayal was the man who leered over me, telling me I was next. I couldn't believe his treachery. And as I sat at the table and he swung a hammer to nail down my fingers, I screamed in agony and stared through the window, averting my eyes from his blood-spattered, black shirt. Clenching my teeth against the pain, I watched the cypress trees and refused to believe I would never be free again to go hunting with my young friend or hold my girl in my arms.

CHAPTER ONE

February 1999

On a dingy February afternoon in North London, Anna is having a duvet day after two bad nights. She listens to commuters scurrying home from work on the street below, half gloating at not having to join the bustle.

Life feels wobbly. She's lost her job; her mother has recently died. They say things happen in threes, and she wonders what will come next.

Just as she's nodding off, her doorbell rings. Sighing, muttering, 'I'm coming, I'm coming,' she untangles herself from her nest of bedding and opens the front door of her second-floor flat.

'Parcel for you, miss.' The young delivery man smirks and looks her over with a grin as she wraps her dressing gown tighter. Taking the parcel, she shuts the door firmly in his face, slaps across the kitchen floor in her slippers, flicks the kettle switch.

The package is bulky. It's something she's been expecting but relegated to the back of her mind. At the reading of her mother's will last week, the solicitor had mentioned that, as well as fifty thousand pounds, she'd been left a file of assorted papers. Harry and Jane, her brother and sister, had been given everything else. While Peregrine Smythe of Smythe & Sons, in crumpled Savile Row pinstripe, droned on, Anna had watched a trapped fly batting against the windowpane. From time to time she glanced at her older brother and sister sitting opposite, thinking how fat and bald Harry had become, how dated and middle-aged Jane looked, with her immaculate hairdo sprayed stiff and crisp. She'd never felt close to them. They'd been old enough to be parents themselves when she was born, a surprise child arriving when her mother was almost forty, upsetting the family dynamics.

She makes herself a mug of Earl Grey, taking it back to bed with the package. Inside the paper wrapper is a cardboard box, the lid tied down with an old shoelace, which she pulls open. A brown envelope bears her name, written in her mother's flowery handwriting, and there are notebooks, bundles of papers rolled up in a perished elastic band and a piece of folded fabric.

She withdraws a sheet of lined notepaper from the envelope, cheap and old-fashioned, with a spray of violets printed in the top left corner. Her mother has written in English, which she spoke with a strong accent but wrote well.

Willow's End,
16 August 1997

My darling Anna,
As you read this you will have already been to my funeral. Maybe there were tears shed, but I hope it was also a happy occasion, with some of my favourite Italian music played in church and a spaghettata *afterwards, my favourite traditional meal of spaghetti with a simple sauce. I imagine there were stories shared. Maybe the family will have recalled my quick temper and my dreadful mistakes with English. If people were kind about me or harsh, then so be it.* Pazienza! *as we say. It was hard for me to learn to be patient.*

I have so much to tell you. Maybe this is a coward's way out – to write it all down instead of telling you face to face. It was hard to know what was for the best. If I had told my own story of what I went through during the war, the results might have been cataclysmic. Cataclismico, disastroso… *They are nearly the same words in Italian. There are many similarities, but oh so many differences between the English and Italians, as I discovered when I first came over here.*

When the doctors told me my cancer was inoperable, I decided to sort out my papers and gather together all my untidy scraps of memories, jotted here and there whenever I'd felt the need. Let us call it a kind of diary. At the reading of the will, my solicitor will have mentioned these would be coming your way. Maybe you felt you were being left out. Apart from the money, Harry has Willow's End – I know he will cope with the draughty old place, he always loved it and it will go with his new status as company director. Jane has my jewellery. She always loved dressing up with it when she was a little girl.

And you have this box containing my scribblings. My memory pearls, from me to you. I hope by the time you finish reading, you will understand that I never intended to make you feel left out, my darling. Maybe some details have been forgotten over the years. I didn't write a journal from day to day, so there are a few gaps. I've never been able to talk openly about my life, but now I feel a duty to do so. And the only way to do that is through this diary.

Read it when you have time. Do with it what you will. It is my inheritance to you.

Your loving Mamma

Anna leans back against her pillows, intrigued but at the same time angry at her mother for being so enigmatic. Theirs had always been a difficult relationship. Her mother was fiery, inclined to be dramatic. Sometimes she'd be folded into her arms, but on other occasions Mamma was distant, undemonstrative: the two sides of a coin. It was typical of her to hint at 'cataclysmic' events.

Anna remembers one occasion when she must have been about six years old. Pushing open the door to the living room, where Ines, her mother, sat writing at her desk, she'd asked, 'When are you having another baby? I've got nobody to play with.' Ines had snapped shut the journal she was writing in and turned to pull her little girl into her arms. 'Mamma's too old now for all that,' she said, kissing Anna's cheeks, 'and where would I find more love to share out? You have it all, my little *tesoro*.'

She remembers this vividly because endearments from her mother were few and far between, especially when Harry and Jane were around.

Her siblings did their own thing. They were much older than her, and unaware of their insensitivity when they teased. 'You were an accident, one big mistake,' Jane said once in a throwaway comment, and Anna had taken it to heart. She'd grown up feeling less loved than them, and nothing but a nuisance most of the time, alone for long spells while her grown-up siblings were out dancing or at the cinema with friends.

Strangely, she had felt a closer bond with her mother when she was in the Claremont rest home, where she died. When Ines was confused, Anna knew how to soothe her.

'Tell me about your life in Italy before you came to England, Mamma,' she would prompt, partly out of curiosity for a side of her life she knew little about, and partly because she'd discovered it calmed her mother down to talk about her Italian side.

Sometimes Ines would oblige, although Anna couldn't follow most of her ramblings. Other times she refused to talk, content to sit staring out of the windows at the gardens and the sea. On one of the last visits before Ines died, she was tired, lapsing into a dialect which Anna couldn't follow. She didn't mind when her mother was quiet. There was room enough for both of them in her silence and the pair would sit holding hands, Anna giving her mother space to wander through her thoughts. Sometimes a sound or a smell seemed to spark a memory and she would talk as if an event had just happened. Perhaps a motorbike would zoom by on the promenade, and then it was as if she was plunged into the past.

'The others have gone down to the city today. It's too hot to dance, but the Germans are in the next valley now. They've been clearing the hamlets…'

Anna would humour her, treat her accounts as everyday occurrences. 'Really, Mamma? And what happened next?'

But there were times when she felt like an intruder, listening to what should have been private moments.

'If they find out I'll be in such trouble, but it was so hot. My blouse clung to my body, my hair floated on the water like weed. He held me tight…'

Anna didn't respond. She'd change the subject or fetch her mother's box of photos from her bedside cupboard and they'd look at family snaps together.

There were afternoons when her mother sat with tears flowing down her cheeks and Anna gently wiped them away. Ines clung to her daughter. 'He came back, Anna, he came back. But I'll never leave you. You're a good girl. My special gift.'

It had been hard to understand what was going on in her mother's befuddled mind when she came out with those strange sentences, Anna recalls as she flicks through the batch of papers. And what a shame her mother seemed to feel so much more love for her at the end of her life, almost as if her bottled-up emotions couldn't be contained any longer. Emotions Anna could have done with knowing about in her early years.

The shrill ring of her mobile makes her jump from the past to the present.

'Anna! I'm sorry I didn't phone you last night – I was up to my eyes in work. But why didn't you wait for me?'

She can't be bothered to calm her lover down. Right now she doesn't feel like telling Will how, yet again, she'd grown tired of waiting for him at the restaurant, hating the way waiters cast pitying looks as she sipped her wine, trying to make one glass last until he eventually turned up.

'Can I come over now?' he says. 'I'm in a taxi. Be there in, say, fifteen minutes?'

She glances at her watch. Five thirty in the afternoon. A few weeks ago she'd have said yes, but she's no longer satisfied with snatched evenings with Will or these last-minute arrangements, as if squeezing in time with her is an afterthought.

He lowers his voice. The cabbie is probably eavesdropping on his famous passenger whose distinguished features are regularly seen on Channel 4 News.

'I could stay the whole night, darling.'

'I'm not feeling great today, Will, I've got a bad migraine,' she fibs. 'I'll call you soon.'

She has no energy for an argument, and before he has a chance to persuade her otherwise, she snaps her mobile shut and switches it off, tossing it onto the bed next to her mother's thick bundle of papers. She doesn't know if she can really face reading through the mysterious documents. Mamma had never wanted to talk much about her Italian life when she was alive. It seems late to be doing so from the grave, with this diary and her enigmatic notes. Is there some skeleton in the cupboard Anna should know about?

She pulls out the top sheet from the pile. Her mother has written copiously, the handwriting smudged and difficult to read in places. Stapled to the front is another note written in English.

Anna, I kept a diary for a short while during the war. It was something I shouldn't have done. If discovered by the wrong people, there would have been reprisals. I've not looked at it for years, and reading it now, I can hardly believe I was the young author. I hope you'll be able to understand, because some of the Italian is old-fashioned. You have to remember this all happened half a century ago. How times have changed!

Skimming through the first few lines of Italian written in her mother's untidy hand, Anna knows she will struggle. Mamma had taught her a smattering of basic Italian, but all three children were brought up with English as their main language. She makes a start, labouring over every other phrase, but it's soon apparent that she'll need to get hold of a good dictionary. She only has a tiny pocket edition, and she guesses at several words.

She can't think straight. Her head is spinning with the task her mother has presented. Pages and pages of Italian to translate, and for what purpose?

As she slips under her warm duvet, she thinks sadly of how much less puzzling it would have been if Mamma had talked to her more when she was alive. But she hadn't, and now she's gone, leaving a bigger hole than Anna could ever have imagined. It takes her a while to fall asleep, and when she does, she dreams her mother is still near her, screened by a billowing gauze curtain, mouthing words Anna can't understand.

CHAPTER TWO

It's dark when Anna is woken by the long bellow of a car horn. She glances blearily at her alarm clock. To her amazement, she's slept for almost twenty-four hours.

Yesterday's package has fallen to the floor from her bed. An assortment of papers, notebooks and envelopes has spilled out – some of them numbered with red crayon. Number one is a large brown envelope. Number two is a scuffed school exercise book. Instead of lines, the pages are segmented into little squares, like graph paper. She remembers Mamma explaining how different types of copybooks were used by different school years in Italy, laughing when Mamma described the overalls and huge bows they wore to primary school – even the boys. Ines taught her a few simple words in Italian when she was little, but never when Father was around. He went berserk if he heard her speaking anything but English.

'You'll confuse them. How many times do I have to spell it out, woman?' he'd shout, his face turning purple.

Then there would be a row. There was always lots of shouting. Anna would retreat to the bottom of the garden and climb the copper beech, or hide under the stairs clutching her teddy bear to her chest.

Sitting cross-legged on her bed, she resumes her attempt at translating her mother's words.

Rofelle, 8 September 1944

He's still in the stable. Mamma made up an extra plate of pasta with *zucchini* we bottled last spring and, when it was dark, she told me to put on my scarf and take a bucket of feed for the chickens with me in case anybody should be watching and ask what I was doing out at that time of night. I know she's terrified somebody will find out we're hiding an *inglese* but she said we must, for he will die otherwise.

We are all terrified. Last week we heard they shot the Benuccis because they wouldn't vacate their house. The Germans only gave them a day's notice. Poor old souls, they refused to go; they had nowhere to go to anyway, and the old signora was riddled with rheumatism and couldn't walk far.

They are cruel, these *tedeschi*. We're scared, but Capriolo says they won't break our spirits. We use this name for him because we have been told again and again by the *Resistenza* not to call him by his real name. His family will be executed if they discover his identity. He's named himself after the mountain deer, nimble and fast as they scamper up high. Capriolo comes automatically to my tongue now, but he would skin me if he knew I was writing this. If I don't tell someone I shall burst – so I'm telling my diary, which I hide behind the loose stone in the niche in my room. Nobody will ever find it. And if they do, they will think it's my old schoolbook.

It takes Anna over an hour to translate this section. And she is not sure if she's really grasped the full meaning of it, or what to think. Try as she might, she can't imagine her mother as this young country girl, or identify her with this voice from the past. Who is Capriolo? And the Englishman they are hiding? Could he possibly be her own father? There are so many questions, just from this one small section. She wonders what else she might discover from her mother's diary.

There are many pages to tackle. Flicking through, she finds a few sections dated post-war in her mother's writing, but she'd prefer to read everything in the correct order. If she's going to find out more about her parents, it will be important not to tangle up events. Eventually she comes to the conclusion that the Italian will have to be translated by somebody else.

Inside a hard-backed vellum ledger, she finds a further couple of pages written in English. As she opens it, a slip of paper falls from between the covers, written in her mother's hand.

Anna,

These few pages in here are a small part of your father's story. I found them in his shed when I was sorting out his effects. Do you remember how it was a no-go area for us all? Your father's sacred den!

I never knew he spent his time writing in there. I thought he was simply escaping from us, with the excuse of mending something or other.

I have read it through and I think he must have written it after the war. Your dadda never kept a journal, like me. He moved around a lot and he never talked much about what he endured. It wasn't an easy time for either of us.

I decided to add this to my own record, to fill in the missing bits of our story. They say everybody has a book inside them but what you'll read isn't fiction, it was the truth. And I believe our story deserves to be told. The war still casts its long shadow over our lives even though more than fifty years have gone by.

It made me sad to read your father's words. For a while they transported me back to the time when we fell in love. How things change. What a lot of rubbish life throws our way.

Mamma

Anna finds it strange to read those words, 'when we fell in love'. She can only remember her parents fighting, and if she's honest, she was always a little afraid of her father. She has a vivid childhood memory that haunted her: another type of occupation in Dadda's shed, besides writing and mending second-hand furniture. She was about nine years old. Unusually, he had left the shed door unlocked that afternoon and she'd slipped in to have a nose. A magazine lay open on his workbench, revealing a photo of a woman's legs spread wide, her breasts naked. She didn't understand the 'rude pictures' and it didn't feel right to gawp. Backing out of the shed, she tripped and grazed her knee, crying out in pain. Her father, hoeing in the vegetable garden, looked up and rushed over, shouting, twisting her ear, 'I thought I told you never to go in there.' He'd slapped her hard on the back of her sore leg and she'd run up the path and into the kitchen, sobbing. Mamma was ironing while listening to music on the radio.

'Darling, whatever is the matter?' She unplugged the iron, resting it on the side of the kitchen table.

'Did you fall? Show me.'

'I hate him, I hate him.'

Her mother pulled her onto her lap, wiping her tears with the corner of her pinafore.

'Now, tell me what happened, *tesoro*. Stop crying, I can't understand anything if you make that noise.'

Her father stormed in, reached for the tin on the dresser where spare coins were kept.

'You spoil that brat. Next time I find her in my shed, I'll give her such a hiding she won't be able to sit down for a week.' He pulled on his jacket. 'And you needn't wait for me for supper. I'm going out, and I'll be back late.'

The door slammed.

They listened to him stamping down the front path and Ines sighed, pulling Anna closer. 'Never mind, we'll wash that poorly knee and then have a special supper – just you and me on our own with spaghetti and *gelato* for afters.'

She held her daughter close and safe and Anna listened to the kitchen clock ticking as her mother rocked her.

'I meant it,' Anna sobbed. 'I *hate* him. He's always so *cross*. I think he hates me too.'

'*Shh*, don't talk about hate.' Ines undid Anna's plaits, redoing them neatly as she searched for words. 'Your dadda doesn't hate you. Not one little bit. Sometimes it's life he hates… how can I explain? Now, be a big girl and listen to what I'm going to tell you and try to understand.'

She lifted Anna from her lap and fetched onions, celery and carrots to chop up for the meat sauce.

'Come and help me with supper. We'll have a little talk.'

Together they prepared the traditional sauce and now, whenever Anna eats pasta and *ragù*, she always associates this meal with the strange conversation of that evening. Afterwards, she felt less of a child, as if her mother had been trying to give her a glimpse into what it was like to be a grown-up.

'Dadda wasn't always such a crosspatch. But the war changed him, you see. Horrible things happen in wars. It was difficult for everybody, but the young soldiers saw cruel things that people do in times of war. We must make allowances for his tempers. Now, lay the table and we'll eat.'

'What cruel things, Mamma?' Anna asked.

'Too cruel to talk about, my darling.'

And as far as mention of her father's time in the war was concerned, that had been that. Her mother never spoke about those years to her again.

Anna's childhood was filled with shouting, the slamming of doors, stormy arguments and her parents' constant bickering. There were moody silences at mealtimes and then snatched moments, when her mother would suddenly scoop her into her arms, cuddle her, pouring out Italian as if she could no longer keep the words inside. But that happened rarely, and only when her father wasn't around.

Once, she'd picked a bunch of red flowers off his runner beans for Mamma and arranged them in a vase on the kitchen table. Dadda was furious. 'Stupid, stupid child,' he'd shouted, smacking her and sending her to bed early, 'now, because of you, they won't fruit. There'll be no beans this year.'

He was never there to play with, like other children's fathers; there were no games of cricket on the back lawn or rough and tumble on the sitting room carpet. When he was home after long spells away, he would complain about the noise.

'I can't hear myself think in this place! What about a bit of hush?' was his constant refrain.

Her father died suddenly of a heart attack when she was ten and she wasn't allowed to attend his funeral. He disappeared from their lives, and not long afterwards they moved to Willow's End.

'We'll start afresh,' Mamma had said, packing away his photo from where it stood on the piano and dusting the surface. It was as if she'd wiped him from her mind.

The writing in the mildewed book is clear, precise, with tiny script and very upright letters, unlike her mother's artistic scrawl. Her father was a meticulous man, rebuking his family whenever they left possessions around the house.

'You're not in the army now, Jim,' her mother would snap at him as he squared up cutlery and glasses on the supper table, or passed a finger over the top of the door to inspect for dust.

Her mother's memories are stirring up her own pictures from childhood, with all the emotions she hasn't touched on for a long while. Anna picks up the papers and, with a deep sigh, resumes reading.

Campo Fontanellato, near Parma
2 September 1943

My injured leg is still playing up, but Bob says the climb onto the top bunk is good physiotherapy. I need to get strength back into the bloody thing for when we leave this place. It's siesta time and there's quiet for a couple of hours. Although it's early September, it's still hot and the cicadas in the fields are kicking up an almighty racket. Lying up here on the scratchy blanket, I examine the frescoes on the ceiling of this villa where we're confined. Naked cherubs stare back at me, and bare-breasted virgins with harps surrounded by garlands of fresh fruit, puffy white clouds and trails of ribbons. Tantalising decor for a dormitory of frustrated men who've been banged up together for months.

This place is better than the last dump. Here, the Italian *Comandante* speaks some English, and he allows us our Red Cross parcels.

There are bars at the windows. My last escape was short-lived. I'd faked sickness for three weeks with delirium and was escorted to the local hospital. As one of my imaginary symptoms was diarrhoea, I made several trips to the toilet each night and the guards eventually grew used to my staggering back and forth from the ward. One night, I climbed out of the toilet window, not banking on the crumbling masonry on the ledge, and fell awkwardly to the street below. I gained one night's freedom in a drain culvert, dreaming of rejoining my platoon. It was an uncomfortable night, but proved escape was possible. My souvenir is this gammy right leg. Understandably the *Comandante* hadn't wanted to send me back to hospital and I reckon the bugger's set wrong now.

'What's the first thing you'll do once you're free?' I ask Bob.

He grunts at me from below. His nose is stuck in a book, as usual. There are a few dog-eared books in the camp we pass around in some kind of fair system. Bob has read them all three times over.

He's an academic type, a daydreamer with an edu-cated brain who wears round, glinting specs. He's been planning our next escape and teaching us German phrases. Out of here, we reckon we can pass as Germans as most of us have blond hair and fair skin like the Teds.

(That's Fritz to you and me – the Eyeties call them *tedeschi*.) No point in trying to pass off as Eyeties. We're generally too tall.

'Bob!' I go again. 'What's the first thing you'll do once you get back to Blighty?'

He puts down his volume. Lately we have more of these daft conflabs – probably because of the rumours. A couple of months ago we heard whooping and cheering coming from the guards' quarters. Then one of them, called Joey, though Giuseppe's his real name, tells us, 'Mussolini's been deposed. *Il Duce* is no longer our leader.' He makes an obscene gesture with his arm. 'The *fascisti* are *finiti*.'

That was around 21 July, and ever since we've not heard a dicky bird. The escape plan is on hold.

The Senior British Officer (SBO) calls us to meetings regularly. 'We have to stick together in an orderly fashion,' is how he puts it. 'We don't want escaped POWs all over the shop, struggling around the Italian countryside.'

There's a different atmosphere in the camp now. The Italians have painted over all the fascist slogans. They're friendlier, and the SBO has told us we'll soon be free. We're waiting for the Eyeties to sign the Armistice. Until then, we're still prisoners of war. The waiting game is frustrating.

I ask old Bob again, 'Go on, what are you going to do?'

'I'll have a clean set of clothes and a plate of bangers and mash with thick onion gravy. And a hot bath, deeper than the rationed five inches of water, hopefully.'

I agree. 'A clean set of clothes and no more frigging lice.'

We've grown expert at getting rid of the buggers during the siesta. When we complained to the *Coman-*

dante, he shrugged his shoulders in the way the Eyeties do. His hands went palms up and he told us all his men suffered from the same trouble and to stop complaining. 'There is nothing I can do about it, signori. *Niente*. It is *normale*. My men also bear this discomfort.'

'Clean clothes and a soft, curvy woman,' I say.

Bob throws down a dirty sock. 'Don't start, Jim!'

We are interrupted by a stampede of feet up the stairs to our dormitory and in burst the Eyeties brandishing rifles. *'Fuori, fuori, fuori tutti…* Everybody out!'

Mutters and groans all round from the men resting on their bunks.

'Pipe down, you chaps!'

'Can't a man get a decent kip around here?'

Bob's talking to the guards. He speaks passable Italian as well as German.

The Eyeties are even more excitable than usual, gesticulating and shouting away.

'What's up, Bob?'

'It seems they've signed up to the Allies, at last. We're no longer prisoners. They're opening the doors and cutting the wire at the back of the exercise ground. We're free to go.'

Then there's shaking of hands all round with our guards and they're off again, clattering down the stairs with much excited yelling.

At first there's euphoria, then stunned silence and then somebody tries the door. It isn't a trick. It really is open. Somebody else finds keys to the kitchen and we have an impromptu feast of fresh bread and cheese, washed down with vinegary wine. It's like Christmas in September, even if the wine is foul.

Our SBO thumps on the table as he stands up. He's a good sort, although he likes to use big words to show off his education.

'Gentlemen! Now is the time to put our plans into action. There's risk of an imminent German attack on the camp. None of us wants to be transported to Germany. Although the Italians should defend us, I envisage a stronger German counter-attack. I therefore propose to delegate guard duty from the roof terrace. At the first sight of a German approach, the bugler will sound the alarm and we shall march out in good order to a point south of the village.

'The *Comandante* has provided me with a sketch, and I need six volunteers to accompany me in reconnaissance.

'In the meantime, gentlemen, I recommend we have our wits about us. Tap these bottles of foul wine and prepare for departure. Pack one small bag of essentials. We must travel light and fast. Our route is north along the Apennines to Switzerland. And the going will be tough.'

I hobble up the stairs, with Bob taking the steps three at a time. We quickly gather together just a few necessary items.

Our food parcels from the Red Cross are received sporadically but the Eyeties always pierce the lids of canned goods, knowing that preserved food is useful for escape. Bob and I devised a recipe for vital protein and vitamins. It tastes grim. We mixed bacon fat with raisins, cocoa, marge and condensed milk and melted it into bars. Inside tins of Germolene antiseptic cream, we've hidden money wrapped in cellophane. The money came from guards who bought our fags. A few of the vitamin bars go into my knapsack, plus knitted socks.

Folks back home would be surprised to know that in Italy the temperature drops well below zero in the hills. I shove in my regulation jumper. At the last minute I pack a notebook and slip in a photo of my girl, Phyllis. Absence makes the heart grow fonder and I could do with her company right now. It's a pity Ma and Pa don't like her. Bob's made a compass from an old button and a magnetised safety pin which will come in useful for navigating our way back to our outfits. We've both had it up to here with prison and enforced inactivity and can't wait to do our bit again. No doubt it will feel strange to be out on the open road, after being cooped up with a bunch of men, but we've yearned for freedom and whatever comes our way, so be it. Bring it on, as the Yankees say.

CHAPTER THREE

Anna searches for more of her father's accounts but finds nothing, thinking it's a pity it was all he wrote and wondering why. He was a complicated man, and it might have filled in some gaps and maybe helped her understand him better.

She sits for a while staring at the ruled sheets, written neatly in pen, the ink faded but not the events his words conjure. Children have a boundless imagination, she thinks, but not the experience of life to understand what adults have to wade through. She only remembers her father from a child's perspective. She wonders what more she might learn about him, if anything. And what Pandora's box of memories she is in danger of unlocking. She knows her father was an escaped POW when he met Mamma, but that period in her parents' lives was never discussed. Instead, they used to describe the war shortages and make their children finish everything on their plates, reminding them how lucky they were.

'You couldn't afford to be fussy when I was a girl,' Mamma would say after Anna turned her nose up again at liver and bacon. 'If you didn't eat what was on your plate, somebody would and there was nothing else until the next meal.'

They told them about coupons and ration books, and how they registered Harry as vegetarian when he was a toddler so they could receive bigger cheese portions, but she never heard any talk of fighting.

Although her father's account reads like an adventure comic, her heart is pounding because she knows she's reading about real events. The troubled, reclusive father she recalls, dressed in his baggy cardigan, smelling of cigarettes, is totally opposite to the picture of the cheeky young POW in his notes.

She considers how the young believe they will be young forever, and the old have always been old. She knows it's a ridiculous notion, but she has never imagined her parents as young people. Now that she's glimpsed their past, a period she's heard so little about, her curiosity is piqued. What really went on during those war years?

If the events her mother and father have written about in these papers are not to be talked about, are too cataclysmic, as Mamma has described, then why leave them to her to read? Anna gathers the collection of papers together, determined to find out more. She wonders if her brother and sister might fill in some more details – being a lot older, they're bound to remember something.

She dials Jane's number, letting it ring to allow time for her sister to come to the phone in her vast house.

'Anna, how are you? This *is* a surprise. To what do I owe this honour? Twice in the same month, what with the funeral and that ghastly solicitor's meeting. *So* depressing!'

She ignores her sister's typical sarcasm. She can hear the clattering of dishes as she moves about in her kitchen, picturing her emptying her dishwasher with pink Marigold-encased hands, phone lodged under her chin, shoulder hunched up to support it. She is irritated Jane cannot be bothered to concentrate properly on their conversation, but there is no point starting an argument; she will never win. Instead, she explains about the papers.

'I've started dipping into Mamma's diaries. The first part is in Italian and quite beyond me, I'm afraid, but—'

Jane interrupts. 'But I thought she was *always* rattling on at you in Italian – you should be almost fluent, I would have thought. It was very rude once you two got going – I used to feel quite left out.'

'I can only speak basic Italian, so her diaries are more than I can manage. I'm going to have them translated.'

'Can you really be bothered? They're probably mad ramblings. You know what Mamma was like at the end. Whenever I went to visit her in that ghastly, smelly old people's home I could never get any sense out of her, and Harry told me it was a *complete* waste of time his going. She never recognised him and it used to take him a whole day with that awful traffic on the M25. He was always fed up with the faff of it all. It makes my blood boil the more I think about it. So unfair! That he should inherit Willow's End, and you and I just end up with a pile of old papers and tatty, worthless jewellery…'

Anna holds the phone away from her ear as her sister's sentences grow longer and louder, and decides not to retaliate. Jane hardly ever visited Mamma in the home, but she isn't going to pursue that one.

'Anna! Are you still there?'

'Yes, Jane. I was only calling to find out if they ever talked to you about the war. Mamma included a couple of pages Dad wrote too. About his time as a POW. They're amazing, like a *Boy's Own* adventure. And if I've translated correctly, I think Mamma may have been involved with the partisans.'

Jane's laugh is more a snort of derision. Anna realises the conversation is going nowhere and wonders if she might get more sense out of her brother, Harry. But he is always hard to track down, always busy with property investment deals and often abroad. From the way his girth is spreading, she reckons he dines out frequently on company expenses. In the background, Jane's doorbell rings and her sister brings their frustrating conversation to an end.

'I've got to go. Come for dinner this Saturday – stay the night. Harry and Cynthia are coming too. You can talk to your darling brother about Italy, and I won't have to talk so much to ghastly Cynthia. Got to dash, people are arriving for bridge.'

She thumps the phone down and, for a while, Anna listens to the empty whir at the other end before clicking her mobile shut. There must be more to her parents' story than they know.

The next day, she is sitting in front of a mirror at the salon for her six-weekly appointment, explaining to André that she's sick of her hair. 'Just do something with it, please. Anything. I want a change.'

He runs his fingers through her dark brown tangles and she watches him pulling faces in the mirror, which does nothing for her morale.

'I've been trying to get you to chop this off for yonks, Anna. It's pulling your features down, hiding your gorgeous sparkling eyes. You need to accentuate those cheekbones, too. How about I put a few lowlights in? A hint of copper and auburn. And shape it here, at the back? You'll love it.'

'Go for it!' she says.

He starts up his usual patter. 'Got anything planned for the weekend? Hols booked yet?' Then he stops and looks at her in the mirror. 'What's up, darling? You look mis.'

She usually hides herself in a magazine stuffed with articles about the latest celebrity wedding, but today she welcomes the chance to talk to André.

'Is it that obvious? Sorry.'

'Yes. Go on, Anna, spit it out. Treat me as a punch bag, so to speak. Everybody else does. Do you know, I could write the next blockbuster, complete with details of suburban bonking, gossip and titbits you could only dream about. Trouble is, I can't write.'

She laughs and he picks up his scissors and starts to cut into her long hair. 'That's better. A smile! Now, tell Daddy all about it. A problem shared, yada yada…'

'My mother died a couple of weeks ago, and now I've lost my job and my love life's one big mess,' she blurts out.

'Oh, sweetie! No wonder your hair's looking dull and lifeless.'

He looks at her with genuine concern. 'When my darling mum died, I didn't know what to do with myself. If it hadn't been for Marcus, I would have thrown myself off a cliff, I kid you not.'

As she tells him about the diary bequest and how she's started to read it, he stops snipping and shaping and, hands on hips, gazes at her in the mirror. 'Wow. That's absolutely *brill*, darling. How *exciting*!'

He stands back, surveying his handiwork, frowning slightly at one or two straggly hairs at the nape of her neck, then he starts chopping again.

'And are you going out to Italy to see where all this happened? How *fascinating* – a mother in the partisan movement! It's like one of those old movies on telly they dig out for winter afternoons. Love it.'

'To be honest, I hadn't thought about going to Italy.'

'But why on earth not? What are you waiting for? You're not working at the moment. You're not married, are you? No kids, no ties… go for it, woman. You'd be mad not to. I'd be *aching* to find out more about it all. You wouldn't see me for dust. Ooh, lucky you, all those handsome men and scrummy clothes. Gucci, Versace… And the food! To *die* for.'

All the while he talks, he continues to shape and snip away faster than ever, her dark brown hair falling to the salon floor. She hopes he is concentrating.

'You could go there for a kind of… what do you call them?' He waves his scissors around while he thinks of the word. 'A sabbatical, or whatever. Nice little pad in the Tuscan countryside. All that wine and those gorgeous colours – burnt umber, Tuscan terracotta…'

He holds up the mirror to reveal her new look, angles it so she can see her hair from all sides. 'There we are, madam! What do we think?'

He is right. The haircut has taken years off her and she looks more twenty than thirty-three. Before, her hair had hung below her shoulders and she stuck it up in a chignon for work. Now it's shaped into a bob, shorter at the back. She loves it. Standing up, she flings her arms around him and plants a kiss on his cheek.

'You're a miracle worker, André. You don't know how much you've helped.'

She's not talking about the new hairstyle. He's planted a gem of an idea in her head. There really is no reason why she can't go and spend time in Italy. She rents the flat where she lives at the moment, so she only has to hand in her notice and ask Jane very nicely if she will store her few possessions in one of her spare rooms. She has her inheritance from Mamma: fifty thousand pounds, a little less after tax, and can happily live off that until she finds another job. Blowing André another kiss as she leaves the salon, her heart lighter, she hurries down the steps to the Underground, a new sense of purpose filling her as she walks.

Sitting on the train, she plans what to say to Will when she sees him later.

When Anna started work at the estate agency it was only going to be temporary. Then she'd plan to sort out her career once and for all, maybe apply again for the teacher training she'd started years ago and abandoned. Since then she had flitted from job to job in an effort to find out what it was she really wanted to do.

But then she met Will, and before she knew it one month at the agency had extended to two years, because the job made it easy to stay in London to be near him.

They'd met within three weeks of her starting. He'd walked into the office, and, although she thought she might have seen him somewhere before – there was something familiar about his craggy looks, salt-and-pepper hair, mesmerisingly blue, blue eyes – she couldn't quite place him. She never watched Channel 4 News, otherwise it would have clicked. That was one of the first things that appealed to him, he'd told her later; the fact she hadn't realised he was famous was refreshing. To be liked for *who* he was and not *what* he was. It was a novelty for him.

She'd shown him round a top-floor flat in an Edwardian villa on the edge of Clapham Common and she'd liked him straight away, their age difference somehow making him even more appealing.

'Let's talk this sale through at dinner tonight,' he'd said.

But they hadn't talked about the house. Instead he'd told her about his tired marriage and subsequent divorce after their three children had flown the nest. He was preparing for the next stage in his life: retirement, and he was nervous about growing old.

In turn, she'd found herself telling him about her near escape from marriage in her early twenties, how she'd almost made it to the altar: the church and reception organised, only a few details about flowers and seating arrangements to be finalised. Her fiancé had let her know, in a letter stuffed under her door, that he had changed his mind, how he wasn't ready for marriage, might never be ready. She'd had boyfriends since then, but as soon as any relationship threatened to turn serious, she would end it. 'Once bitten, twice shy,' she would explain, 'I don't do promises.'

Months would pass without a man on the scene, and she was happy enough in her own space. But Will filled a need in her.

She enjoyed their occasional meals out and trips to concerts. He was always the gentleman: opening doors for her, pulling out her chair in restaurants. Through his job at Channel 4 he'd met loads of interesting people, and he knew how to spin a good story. All infinitely more interesting than her own company and microwaved dinners on her lap in front of the television.

It was an uncomplicated partnership. Every now and again she would experience a niggling doubt that she was being lazy by sticking with someone she wasn't head over heels in love with, simply because he was a charmer and good in bed, but she was adept at pushing any concerns to the back of her mind. One day she'd seen a photo of him with a glamorous woman in a magazine. When she'd asked about her, he'd explained it was his ex-wife, Tricia, how he still saw her to catch up with news of the children and to help with her finances. She'd been surprised at how elegant his beautiful silver-haired ex was. And, if she was honest, it made her jealous that he still felt the need to see her.

Will has booked their usual table at Chez Nous, tucked discreetly away in an alcove. She is slightly early and orders a glass of chilled Pouilly Fumé. She sits waiting, nibbling on a roll, wondering how late Will is going be tonight. The restaurant is quite full for a Tuesday. If she kept a tally, she wonders, how much time would his keeping her waiting amount to?

'Sorry, Sooty.' He stoops to plant a kiss on her lips. 'Had a report to finish. Big news story about to break on Blair.' He'd named her Sooty after one of their first dinner dates together. Her mascara had run when they were dashing from the restaurant in the pouring rain to a waiting taxi, leaving dark smudges under her eyes.

She wonders how many different excuses she could add to his 'lateness record' she's been mentally compiling. Tonight, she finds it irritating that he takes her for granted. And the irritation is largely directed at herself, for putting up with him so long.

'You look different,' he says as he takes off his coat, arranging himself opposite her. 'It's your hair. Yum, yum! It's much shorter, isn't it?'

She pats the back of her head. 'I like it,' she says. 'It's sort of liberating. I felt in need of a change.'

'Oh dear, that sounds rather ominous.' He laughs and picks up the menu. 'Have you ordered yet?'

'No!' she says pointedly. 'I was waiting for you.'

He sweeps a cursory glance over the menu and then calls the waiter over.

'What's the special today?'

'We have some very nice veal. Or the mussels are very good... and the *boeuf bourgignon*.'

'Veal, we'll have the veal.' Will snaps the menu shut. 'And bring us the usual bottle of Châteauneuf.'

Normally she is happy for Will to take control and place the order, but not tonight.

'No veal for me. Just *poussin* and a salad,' she says.

If Will is surprised, he doesn't comment.

They sit in silence, sipping the excellent wine, dipping into the bowl of black olives that have appeared while they wait for their meal.

She looks around the room. A young couple are draped over each other, sitting side by side instead of opposite like she and Will. The young man has his arm around the girl and they share a plate of starters. Every now and again he whispers something in her ear and she laughs, her eyes wide with... wide with what? Anna wonders. Excitement, or delighted shock at what he is proposing? The girl feeds him a piece of squid from her own fork and he nibbles on it, staring all the while into her eyes. Anna looks away. It's too intimate. How long will their lustful stage last? she asks herself. How well will they connect after their first few passionate weeks? Or are they simply a perfect couple? Do perfect couples exist?

Will is fiddling with his wine glass. 'What's up, Anna? You're miles away. Are you cross with me for being late?'

'I'm used to that,' she says, turning her attention back to the man she used to desire so much. 'I told you. I'm out of sorts and I've got a few things on my mind.'

'Is it the time of the month? Tricia was always very niggly when she was on.'

'I'm not premenstrual, if that's what you mean, and I do wish you wouldn't compare me with your ex.'

He flinches, puzzled at her reaction.

'It's losing your mother, isn't it? Poor Sooty, you should give yourself time to grieve.'

How is it possible, Anna thinks, *for the same person to be both sensitive and thoughtless at the same time*? She makes an effort to be more civil.

'Mamma left me some diaries. They arrived from the solicitors the other day and I've started to read them. My mind's on all that, I suppose.'

'I could take a look and cast my journalist's eye over them. You never know, you might get a publishing deal.'

'Thanks, Will, but no, they're not publishable. They are masses of bits of paper in no particular order. There's even a tatty piece of cloth she's written on. And it's in Italian.'

'Are you sure it's not something your mum scribbled down when she went loopy? She was in that home for a while, wasn't she? Old people do daft things. I'll be like that soon.'

He laughs nervously and Anna wonders if he's hoping she'll contradict him.

'Anyway, you ravishing young thing with your sexy new hair-style.' He lowers his voice. 'I feel I've got to get to know you all over again… from top to toe. I can't wait to get back to your flat.'

She leans back in her chair. 'Not tonight, Will.'

There's a pause while the waiter sets down their orders and pours more wine into their glasses before disappearing in the direction of the kitchen.

'I'm in the doghouse, aren't I?' Will asks.

'I'm thinking of going to Italy for a while,' she says abruptly.

'What a splendid idea. You need a break. Perhaps I could pop out for a couple of days and join you. I could do with some winter sunshine myself. Eat up, old thing. Aren't you hungry?'

She toys with her *poussin*, her appetite non-existent.

'If you're not going to eat that,' he says, pointing his fork at her plate, 'I'll have it. I'm starving. Waste not, want not, eh?'

'I'm not going for a holiday, Will,' she persists. 'I'm going for a couple of months. To see where my mother came from. I've never been. And…' She pauses, not knowing how to explain.

He pushes his plate away and takes her hand, finishing her sentence. '… You need some time on your own.'

She looks at him, wishing he wasn't being so understanding. It would be far easier if they were shouting at each other.

'I've been expecting this for some time, if I'm honest,' he says, stroking her fingers. 'I've often wondered what a beautiful girl like you sees in an old codger like me.'

She doesn't comment on this last remark either, and he lets go of her hand and knocks back the rest of his wine. It dribbles onto his shirt, and she watches the red stain spread.

'When are you going?' he asks.

'Quite soon. The contract on my flat comes up for renewal in a month. I'm jobless. Now seems right.'

'Bit of a shock,' he says.

'We can keep in touch from time to time, Will. But I've got to do this.'

'I suppose a girl's gotta do what a girl's gotta do, as they say, but I don't want you to disappear completely.'

The silence between them is awkward now. He asks for the bill and insists on calling a taxi and accompanying her to her flat.

They sit apart on the back seat, and she's thankful there's not much traffic so the drive takes only fifteen minutes. Even so, it amazes her how, once upon a time, there was always something to say to each other.

'Let's say good night here,' she tells him at the main door to her building. 'I'm tired, Will.'

'Good night, or goodbye?'

She pauses. 'Both, I suppose.'

They stand opposite each other for a few seconds on the pavement and then he moves forward to drop a kiss on the top of her head.

'Keep in touch, dear girl,' he says, as he turns to climb back into the waiting taxi.

She lifts her hand in a half-salute as the black cab pulls away from the kerb.

Climbing the stairs to her flat, she thinks that explaining to Will was far easier than it probably should have been.

CHAPTER FOUR

Jane lives alone in a five-bedroom mock-Tudor house in a part of Surrey that estate agents' parlance would describe as 'Purley. A most desirable location'.

When Jane's husband, Charlie, left nearly ten years previously for another man, Anna hadn't been surprised. She'd often wondered about their marriage, what gentle Charlie saw in her domineering sister. Jane had returned alone from a family holiday in Madeira, announcing that Charlie was researching a new enterprise abroad. Charlie, however, had no qualms about being open and coming out. He sent all his relatives a cheerful round-robin letter at Christmas, explaining how he had met the love of his life and had decided to stay on in Madeira to help Santos run a fabulous boutique hotel in Funchal. He was ecstatically happy (if they would pardon the phrase). As their sons, Stephen and Julian, were almost through university and practically independent, he felt it was time to start living his own life now, and had separated from Jane. Everybody was very welcome to come and visit whenever they wanted. Anna took him up on his offer and had one of the best holidays of her life, but Jane and Harry had erased him from their radar.

Anna hires a taxi to take her from the station to Jane's house. Two stone lions guard the porch, together with a matching pair of clipped laurel obelisks. No weed dares lift its head in any flower bed. The family house is large for one person, but Jane is reluctant to move. Her bridge-playing friends live nearby, and there is a parade of exclusive boutiques and a popular delicatessen within walking distance. She can easily afford help in the house and garden on the generous allowance that Charlie provides.

'Come in, come in, you're letting in the cold. We're having drinks in the sitting room.' Her sister pulls her into the hall, whispering, 'Thank God you're here! It's impossible to have an intelligent conversation with that woman. And Harry's obviously had a dram or two before arriving.'

Harry and his third wife, Cynthia, sit at opposite ends of the chintzy sitting room. She has her legs crossed and is turning the pages of a glossy *House and County* magazine. She is a good twenty-five years younger than Harry's fifty-two, but her make-up is so heavy it disguises her age. Anna wonders if there is anything real about her at all. Even her breasts seem disproportionately large for her small frame. She glances at Anna entering the room, barely raising a manicured hand in acknowledgment. Harry heaves himself up from an uncomfortable armchair covered by Colefax & Fowler, splashing gin and tonic from his glass onto the pale carpet. He seems relieved to see Anna. There is a frosty atmosphere, and Anna wonders what their argument is about this time.

'Let me take that from you, Harry.' Jane swoops on him, plucking up his drink and depositing it on a mat on a side table beyond his reach.

Jane has inherited their father's lanky Anglo-Saxon looks, although her waistline is not as slim as it used to be, but Harry and Anna are more like Mamma facially. Harry could have been very good-looking with his dark Latin features, but he has put on weight in the last few years and is a little too fond of his wine.

'Come here, little sister. Give your old brother a hug.'

As he crushes her to his belly, the smell of alcohol on his breath is overpowering. 'We've just been talking about Willow's End, having a little discussion.'

He indicates Cynthia, and pronounces his words slowly and carefully, in the way of someone trying hard not to show that one too many has been downed. 'She doesn't like the place, doesn't like it at all. What's to do? I see battles looming.'

Cynthia uncrosses her legs, pulls her tiny skirt down as far as she can and crosses her legs again. 'There are umpteen rooms and it's poky and draughty,' she says. 'More of a liability than an asset. It needs so much work doing to it, a total revamp, in my opinion. I think Harry should knock it down and start again, but he's got some hare-brained idea about *living* in the dump.'

Anna could never see Cynthia living in a draughty, rambling 1930s house and she is surprised Harry wants to. She's already imagined him bulldozing the place and squeezing in half a dozen executive houses on the back lawn.

'Well, I'm getting tired of the flat up in town. All that glass and open-plan living. A man's got no privacy at all. It's like being in a ruddy great goldfish bowl.'

He looks around for his drink and makes his way to the nest of tables.

'I just thought it would be a splendid idea to do up the old ancestral seat and try living in a proper house again, with rooms how they should be. A snug and a breakfast room. A nursery, maybe.'

He beams at Cynthia, swaying a little. 'How about it, Cyn? Pattering of tiny feet appeal to you?'

'Dream on, Harry!' Cynthia throws the magazine onto the coffee table. 'I need the loo,' she announces, and leaves the room, making it clear that any discussion about children is over. Harry watches her totter out in her high heels and attempts to lighten the atmosphere with a joke.

'Mind you, the only pattering of tiny feet at Willow's End at the moment is from the mice, ha, ha! More's the pity!'

Anna feels momentarily sorry for her brother. She knows he misses his daughters. His second wife, Melissa, has custody of their twin girls, but they are away at boarding school and he rarely sees them. In their school holidays they are booked in for tennis lessons or away on adventure holidays to keep them from under Melissa's feet.

Jane returns to the sitting room carrying a platter of meat just in time to prevent Anna from having to comment. She does not feel qualified to offer advice on Harry's marriage, thinking wryly that none of them has been particularly successful in the relationship department.

'Where's Cynthia gone?' Jane looks at the armchair where Cynthia has been sitting. 'Lunch is ready. It's nothing much, but it will go cold if we don't eat now. Let's move into the dining room.'

Anna knows about Jane's 'nothing much' meals. She is a cordon bleu cook and likes to show off her efforts. They are treated to a home-made terrine of pâté, followed by stuffed loin of pork and roasted vegetables. Cynthia picks at her food, pushing a slice of aubergine round her plate, and Anna wonders what new diet she is on. The meal helps Harry sober up and while Jane is in the kitchen, Anna picks his brains.

'Do you know anything about where Mamma came from in Italy? I've started reading those papers she left me and I realise I know absolutely nothing about her background – or Dad's, for that matter.'

'Rofelle, you mean?' he asks, leaning back in his chair, wiping his mouth clean with a damask napkin. 'Haven't been back since before you were born. I must have been a teenager – let's think, over thirty years ago. God! Where does the time go?'

Cynthia sighs, raises her eyebrows and excuses herself from the table. 'I'm going outside for a smoke. I don't want any pud.'

Anna watches Cynthia open the French windows and sit on a wrought-iron bench on the patio. She rummages in her

Mulberry handbag and produces a mobile phone, nails flashing bright red as she begins to text, cigarette smoke spiralling into the winter sunshine.

Harry stares wistfully at her through the window. 'She's always on some diet or other. She'll waste away one of these days.'

He reaches for the bottle of wine and pours himself another glass, offering some to Anna, who covers her own with her hand. 'None for me, thanks, Harry. Tell me about Rofelle.'

'Absolute dump of a place. Primitive! I'm sure Dad didn't like it very much either and I don't think we ever went back on holiday – I remember their godawful rows about spending time there. It was around the time he had his breakdown.'

'I never knew he'd had a breakdown.' Anna looks up.

'Oh yes, it was a *ghastly* time. He had a spell in hospital, but Mamma never wanted anybody to know. That was the way they were, their generation. They didn't talk about things, open up, not like nowadays.'

'He was in a POW camp for a while,' Anna says. 'His breakdown may well have been something to do with that… and he was injured just before the Armistice, and that slowed him down when he was on the run. All really stressful events…'

'Poor old boy,' Harry says, draining his glass. 'Sounds like an old war film to me. *The Italian Escape*. Rather him than me.'

'My goodness, Anna, it's a good thing you're not working at the moment,' Jane says, coming back into the dining room. 'Your head is absolutely stuffed full of this story. How could you possibly concentrate on a job?'

She fetches a crystal bowl containing *tiramisù* from the sideboard and places it on a serving mat, then glances through the window. 'Do let's change the subject. Harking back to the war is too depressing for words,' she says absently, and then tuts when she sees Cynthia.

'What *is* she doing out there? She'll catch her death in that skimpy outfit.'

She knocks on the window, beckoning to Cynthia to come in. Cynthia holds up her hand, indicating she will be five minutes longer. As she serves dessert, Jane asks, 'Talking of Rofelle, do you remember, Harry, there was only *one* single bed in that hole of a room we had to share?'

'Yes. *You* made me sleep on the floor. How could I forget?'

'It was quite disgusting, their expecting us to share. I mean, you must have been nineteen, because I was definitely sixteen. I know that for certain because I distinctly remember feeling very left out when I went back to school that September. All the girls were going on and on about the fab times they'd had in their summer hols, and all I could think about was "sweet sixteen and never been kissed". There was nobody in Rofelle I'd have let come near me with a bargepole. I was so glad we never returned.'

Anna listens to her brother and sister reminiscing about a time when they were young, before she was born, as if she's listening to the history of another family – one she doesn't belong to. Anecdotes about awful Italian plumbing; an old lady they were convinced was a witch who used an old broom as a walking stick; a little boy who came to the bar each day, his hair crawling with nits. The comments swing back and forth between Harry and Jane. It's interesting enough, but Anna wants to learn more about their parents. When Jane starts clearing away the dishes, she helps gather the cutlery. 'Don't you both find it at all strange that they didn't go back? Didn't Mamma even return on her own?' she asks, touching her sister's arm, as if to delay her from ending the conversation.

'Not that I'm aware of,' Jane replies. 'I don't even know if there is any family left there. To be quite honest, I'm not that bothered.

It was dreadfully boring for us teenagers, not the sort of place I would ever have chosen for a holiday for youngsters of that age.'

Harry reaches for the wine again.

'There's water on the table,' admonishes Jane.

He ignores her and pours a full glass of Merlot, draining the bottle.

'To accompany the cheese, old thing. That is, if the cheese-board is ever going to put in an appearance.' He winks at Anna while Jane moves Stilton and mature Cheddar from the sideboard, placing it just within reach of her brother.

'No wonder you've got gout. I don't know how Cynthia puts up with you, really I don't.'

Anna thinks that maybe Cynthia might not be putting up with him for much longer. She is still outside, texting.

She decides to tell her brother and sister about her plans. 'I'm going to Italy for a couple of months or so, as soon as I've packed up the flat. I was going to ask you, Jane, if you could hang onto my stuff for a while. I want to spend some time looking up the locations in Mamma's diaries.'

Both Jane and Harry look at their younger sister as if she is mad. Harry is the first to speak. 'What on earth will you do there? How will you manage?'

'I haven't totally finalised that part yet, but I've got some redundancy pay from the agency... and then there's the fifty thousand Mamma left each of us.'

'That won't last forever. I would have thought you'd be better off putting a deposit down on a property instead of swanning off to Italy. I could help you if you like.' Harry helps himself to a generous chunk of ripe Stilton.

'No thanks. I've made up my mind to go.'

'Come on, Anna! What's the real reason? Things not working out between you and lover boy?'

Anna thinks Harry is the last person to be commenting on this. She bites back a sarcastic comment, but she's still indignant. 'Will has got nothing to do with it… or with *you*, for that matter.'

Jane intervenes. 'I wouldn't set too much store by those diaries, if I were you. Mamma wasn't exactly all there at the end, you know. I think it will be a complete waste of your time.'

'Quite apart from the diaries. I mean, even if they had never existed,' Anna tries to explain, 'aren't you at all curious about Mamma and Dad's past in Italy? When all's said and done, we're half Italian. Aren't you interested in our Tuscan roots? Mamma refers to some huge events that she never wanted to talk about – something that happened in the war. Don't you want to know?'

'No!' Harry's reply is immediate. 'Absolutely not. And I, for one, feel British through and through. We've been brought up here, educated here, we spoke English at home.'

'I really can't see the point,' adds Jane. 'All I remember are the almighty rows when Father was alive whenever the subject of Italy was brought up. Maybe it's slightly different for you. At least Mother taught you some Italian, but we couldn't speak any, and all the relatives used to natter away nineteen to the dozen. We couldn't understand a damn word. There was nothing to do in Rofelle except eat vast quantities of fattening pasta and cool down in the river, which was full of tadpoles, snakes and God knows what else.' She pulls a face at the memory. 'I'll never go back. I don't feel Italian at all. I'm not interested.'

It is fruitless trying to explain her need to go to Italy and Anna realises there's not much more she can discover about Rofelle from her brother and sister. She will just have to go to Italy and find out for herself.

CHAPTER FIVE

April 1999

The plane touches down in early-morning sunshine at Perugia. The tiny airport is surrounded by fields dotted with a forlorn scattering of last year's drooping sunflowers. On the tarmac by the modest arrivals hangar, two men in bright orange overalls wave their hands about as they discuss something which might be vitally important but could equally be a description of what they had for dinner last night. They break off to watch a pretty Italian girl descend the steps of the plane in front of Anna. As they look her up and down, Anna imagines she wiggles her bottom just a little more as she struts over the tarmac in skintight jeans and a leather jacket.

It is as though Anna has been thrown onto a stage set, with mountains in the distance forming a scenic backdrop. The contrast between busy Stansted Airport and this sleepy place is stark. How much easier would it have been with her mother at her side, she thinks, to travel in her company and ask questions about the partisans. Then again, would it have made any difference? Would Ines have opened up? It seems her diary was the only place her mother was able to speak freely.

She has booked a hire car to drive to San Patrignano, the village near to where her mother was born and where she has found, via the Internet, a room in a little *agriturismo*, a country guest house. It feels good to be behind the wheel of an Italian car, pretending to be Italian: a step towards merging into the local culture. Fiddling with the radio dial, she finds a station playing Italian ballads, but there are so many interruptions for adverts, she switches off the radio and lets the scenery provide the entertainment instead.

Just over one hour later, she leaves the busy dual carriageway that cuts its way through tobacco fields sprouting green shoots and takes a mountain road joining Sansepolcro to Rimini. On the lower slopes, farmers have been pruning olive trees. Piles of silver-grey foliage have been left around the knotty trunks like discarded petticoats. The road climbs steadily, and at the Viamaggio Pass she parks the hire car in a lay-by and takes photos of the valley with a large lake glistening below in the sunshine. These might well be the mountains where her father had hidden and fought during the war, where each fold of land or clump of forest held danger and death. She feels a tingle of excitement as she stands there, the wind whispering through the flattened grass on the slopes dropping away from where she stands. In the deep ditch next to the car, there are patches of lingering snow, and daisies open their faces to the sunshine that is trying its best to warm up the hills.

She sets off again and soon uses her Italian for the first time, stopping to ask the way from an old man sorting logs into piles by the side of the road. He peers at her suspiciously, looks at the number plate and then gives directions to the *agriturismo*. She is delighted to have managed to communicate in her mother's language. Her father had forbidden Italian to be spoken in the home because he had a theory, one quite prevalent in the 1950s and '60s, that it was confusing for his children to learn two languages, that they would end up speaking neither language well. It strikes Anna now how hard it must have been for her mother not to be allowed to sing her babies Italian lullabies or tell them stories in her own language, and she resolves to learn as much Italian as possible during her stay. She feels she owes it to her mother.

*

The owner of the Agriturismo Casalone is Teresa Starnucci, who is about Anna's age with elfin features and cropped black hair. She ushers Anna in. 'Welcome to our family guest house,' she says in halting English.

Anna replies in Italian. 'Please speak in Italian. I'm trying to improve.'

A smile of relief lights up Teresa's striking face. She shakes hands and switches to Italian. 'Phew! Thank goodness. We studied English at school, but it was difficult for me. When Francesco comes later, you'll see he speaks excellent English. So, if we have problems, he can help interpret. Let me show you around. Tell me if I speak too fast.'

Anna is pleased she understands most of Teresa's tour round the beautiful old farm building, and she feels easy in her company, even though they've only just met. She learns that Teresa's father was born in the house and that it has been in the family for over a hundred years. Two years ago, they decided to restore the place before it fell down. Nobody had lived in it for over thirty years, as Teresa's mother, once married, preferred to live up in the village in a modern apartment. Many families from this hamlet did the same, and until recently there was just one elderly couple living here permanently.

'But our generation feels it's important to rescue a part of our history before it's too late,' continues Teresa. 'Our parents thought we were mad at first, to want to live in an old building. Then when they saw the way we were modernising, with central heating and bathrooms, they could appreciate what we were doing. We hope more young people will follow our example and bring the village back to life again.'

The farmhouse has thick stone walls to keep the house warm in winter and cool during July and August, when sun bakes the countryside. A main feature of the dining room is the huge fireplace, large enough to stand in, where in the past all the cooking was done by Teresa's grandmother. On the walls hang old metal cooking pots and utensils.

She follows her guide through the dining room and up some stairs to a landing, where everything is gleaming, the walls whitewashed and spotless. Teresa stops at the first door. 'And this is your bedroom, with its own bathroom.'

On the door is a wooden plaque bearing the name '*Ortica*'. 'It's a plant grown everywhere,' she explains. 'We even use it in some of our recipes.'

She points to a picture of a stinging nettle, telling Anna how they have themed the bedrooms according to plants growing around and about in the woods.

'I'll leave you to unpack and make yourself at home. If you need anything at all, come and find me. I won't be far away.'

Anna is more than delighted with her Internet find. The whole place has been restored with great taste and attention to detail. At the little windows of her room hang simple linen curtains, decorated by hand with lace worked locally, Teresa has explained. A wrought-iron double bed, made at the forge in the little town of Badia Tedalda, further up the hill, is positioned on a compact mezzanine level. The view from the tiny window of the soaring mountains surrounding the hamlet is breathtaking. The lower slopes are thickly forested, with intermittent lighter green strips of meadow. Higher up, she can make out the outline of a village perched precariously on a peak, its roofs poking above the mist like the funnels of a liner at sea. Throwing open the shutters, Anna takes in deep breaths of clean air and looks forward to waking up and starting her day with this view of lush countryside: the place where her mother grew up. She wonders if she'll be able to track down the stable and other places mentioned in the diary. Will they still exist after all this time?

The dinner table in front of the fire is laid for five with a white cloth, gleaming cutlery and simple posies of primroses.

'Is it okay if we sit with you tonight, Anna?' Teresa comes through from the kitchen carrying a basket of bread. 'You're our only guest, and we hoped you wouldn't mind.'

She is tired, and would really have preferred a quick supper and an early night, but she likes the informality of the little guest house and doesn't want to offend her host. 'That's fine. But don't expect me to keep up with you. My Italian is *very* poor.'

'Two weeks here with us and you will be practically bilingual. Your accent is already quite good.'

'My mother was Italian.'

'Ah, that explains your dark hair. You could almost pass for an Italian woman.'

'Until I open my mouth…'

'Don't exaggerate!' Teresa laughs.

A man enters the dining room carrying a couple of bottles of wine. He is wiry, a little taller than Anna, with a shock of black hair peppered with grey. A little girl trails after him.

'Teresa, I've brought up these bottles of Sangiovese. I think they will go with tonight's menu.' He greets Anna with a slight formal bow before placing the bottles on a side table.

'Anna, this is Francesco,' says Teresa.

He grasps her hand firmly and then gently pulls the little girl from her hiding place behind him. 'And this little monkey is my daughter, Alba,' he says.

Francesco's English is good, and Anna detects a slight American twang. She wonders at the use of 'my daughter', thinking he might be a bit of a chauvinist, the way he's left Teresa out of his introduction. The little girl slips behind her father again, her eyes cast down. She is thin and her complexion is very pale. It is hard to tell her exact age, but she looks about eight. Her thumb goes straight into her mouth and she remains behind Francesco, clutching hold of his shirt.

'Ciao, Alba,' says Anna, bending down to her height, but the child does not respond. She decides not to pay her too much attention, thinking she will come out of her shell when she wants, but Alba stays silent throughout the whole of the meal, taking tiny bites of her food, only nodding or shaking her head when Francesco and Teresa speak to her.

The plate of starters could have come straight from a still-life painting. Stuffed *zucchini* flowers; little squares of *crostini* topped with spicy tomatoes; liver pâté; a creamy relish made from dandelion flowers; roasted bay leaves topped with ovals of melted cheese. It has all been delicately and painstakingly prepared using locally sourced ingredients. The main course, a luscious pink colour, is a blackcurrant risotto. Anna has never tasted anything like it.

'It's like a meal from a fairy tale,' she says. 'Thank you! *Grazie!*'

'What made you decide to spend a holiday in this area?' Francesco asks as they finish off supper with a dish of *pannacotta* topped with fruits of the forest. 'We don't usually have foreign tourists here, being somewhat off the beaten track.' He speaks English with confidence, his use of idiom far beyond the level of the usual learner.

Anna explains a little about her parents and the diaries, and her determination to find out more about her mother's past. Francesco listens intently as he pours *limoncello* into three liqueur glasses.

'What was her name before she married? Everybody knows each other in a place like this.'

'Ines. Ines Santini.'

Teresa gasps. 'But that is *such* a common name around here. There are lots of Santinis in our neighbourhood.' She leaves the dining room momentarily and returns with a telephone directory, thumbing through the pages until she finds a long list of Santinis.

'If you go to the *Comune* you should be able to find out more about your mother's family. Maybe Francesco can take you tomorrow morning. I've asked him to collect some guest forms for me.'

'Oh, I forgot to tell you, Teresa,' Francesco interrupts. 'I can't tomorrow. They've asked me to pop into work – I have to give a lecture for Professor Tosti.'

'*Again?*' Teresa thumps the table. 'You're *always* being asked to step in for him. I hope you're being paid this time.'

'Teresa!' There is warning in his tone. 'Don't start up again. I haven't the energy right now. You don't understand, anyway. The man's ill.'

'The man's incompetent. He should have been given the push ages ago.'

He stands up, his chair scraping across the *cotto* floor. Anna feels embarrassed listening to the pair of them having what is clearly a familiar squabble, and gets up to leave. 'I'll say good night now. I'm very tired, and it's been a long day.'

Francesco makes a move as well. 'It's time for Alba to go to bed, too. School tomorrow, young lady!'

He scoops her up and leaves without saying anything to Teresa: no thank you for the meal, no see you later or good night. *A typical spoilt Italian male*, Anna thinks as she undresses for bed back in her room. It was obvious he didn't want her tagging along with him to the town hall, either. She doesn't believe his work excuse.

But she doesn't dwell on the evening for long, save for a flutter of excitement at the discovery that Ines' surname is still common in the area. Maybe she'll come across some relatives to talk to about Mamma. It has been a long day. There is no London traffic noise to disturb her, no music thumping from the flat below. All she can hear as her head touches the crisp linen pillowcase is the gentle sound of wind playing around the old stone building. She falls asleep immediately.

CHAPTER SIX

Anna forgot to close the bedroom shutters the night before, so the sun streaming through the window wakes her early. The view of the hills, zigzagging against the sky like the spiny ridge of a sleeping dinosaur, is too inviting for dawdling in bed. She pulls on jeans and a fleece, runs her fingers through her short, newly styled hair and lets herself out quietly so as not to wake anyone.

She follows a narrow, well-trodden path dropping down in front of the guest house. Later on there will be blackberries to pick from the thorny bushes, but for now cyclamens peep between rocks studding the path's edges, their leaves patterned in marbled white. The morning air is fresh and she is pleased she put on her warm fleece. The mountain ridges above are sprinkled with a dusting of snow, reminding her it is still early in the season. There is the sound of running water, and as she rounds the bend, a river comes into view, splashing noisily over a weir under a bridge.

She isn't the only early riser after all, for Francesco is fishing from the weir. Not far away, Alba is crouched by a little pool, stirring the water with a stick.

So much for the feeble excuse of an early lecture, Anna thinks to herself; *he could simply have said he had no time to come with me.*

Raising his hand in greeting, he calls her over. Alba ignores her and continues with her game. She wonders what explanation Francesco will have up his sleeve this morning. She would actually prefer to continue her walk, but doesn't want to appear rude.

'Didn't you sleep well?' he asks as Anna approaches.

'Like a log,' she replies in Italian.

'We say "like a dormouse" in Italian,' he laughs and translates the expression into English. She is peeved he doesn't seem to want to make an effort to listen to her attempts at Italian, and watches as he expertly reels in his fishing line and casts it out again into a deeper part of the pool.

'It's a beautiful morning,' he says. 'I thought I would help Teresa's menu along. These little fish are delicious deep-fried, served with garlic and chopped parsley. If I'm lucky I'll catch her some trout too.'

She gives up speaking in Italian and comments on Alba, playing at the water's edge. 'Obviously she doesn't like staying in bed either, in the mornings.'

The little girl is building a tower of stones, carefully balancing one on top of the other in decreasing sizes.

Francesco glances at his daughter. 'It's something we do. She likes to be with me for half an hour before breakfast. If it's not raining we go for a walk or come down here to the river and then the school bus arrives to fetch her.'

'She's a very quiet child,' Anna says, thinking back to last night's meal.

He gives a wry laugh. 'Yes, very quiet. What I would give to hear some noise from her.'

She looks at him questioningly.

'Alba has decided not to talk,' he tells her. 'Diagnosed as elective mutism. She's kept it up for nearly half a year now. She's as stubborn as a mule.'

The noise of the water rushing over the weir prevents their voices from carrying over to the child, who has wandered a little further downriver, so she asks why Alba has decided not to talk, trying to imagine how difficult it must be to keep quiet for so long. Years ago, when she was still at convent school, the nuns had made all the girls go on a silent retreat, but she hadn't managed even one afternoon of not speaking. Six months of silence is quite another thing.

'We don't understand for certain why she does it,' he replies, 'but what we do know is, she hasn't uttered a word since her mother died.'

'But I thought Teresa was her mother,' she says in surprise.

'Teresa is my sister. I'm staying with her here in the family home in the hope that the peace and quiet of the place will help Alba. Maybe by being away from Bologna, where we usually live, she can begin to forget. I've taken time away from my work at the university there.'

Anna feels awkward. She's jumped to the wrong conclusions, assuming Francesco and Teresa to be a couple and Alba their moody, spoilt child.

'I'm sorry. I feel so clumsy.'

'Why? It's not your fault. You English are always saying sorry!'

He bends down to open a plastic container of worms, selects one and attaches it to the hook on another rod. 'You know, it's good to be able to talk. Everybody tiptoes round me as if I'm some kind of precious piece of porcelain about to break into fragments if they mention anything about the past.'

He casts his second rod, the line cutting the water, the float settling as ripples extend across the surface. Anna waits, feeling there is something more he wants to tell her.

'My wife, Silvana, was killed in a car accident. Alba was in the car too but she escaped without a scratch. Or at least, without any visible scratches.'

'Poor kid. Who knows what must be going on in her little head?'

'Exactly! Who knows? It doesn't take much to understand why she's retreated the way she has. What I need is something magic to unlock her silence and break her suffering. I thought coming here would help, but we've been here since Christmas and nothing has changed. The irony is that Silvana would have known exactly what to do. She was a wonderful mother.'

He starts packing away his rods and fetches a basket resting in the shallows. There are half a dozen fish trapped in it but he throws them gently into the current. 'Better to let them go. They won't make any type of feast.' He calls over to his little girl, switching into Italian. 'Come, Alba. Time to get ready for school.'

She stands up and with a piece of driftwood knocks over the tower of stones she has been carefully constructing. Hopping from stepping stone to stepping stone, she comes over to join them by the weir, her curls bouncing as she moves.

'We'll have to get you out of those wet tights in time for the bus. I hope Teresa has some clean ones ready.'

She puts her hand into her father's. She still hasn't acknowledged Anna in any way, not even with a smile. It's as if her father is the only other person present.

'Let me take the rods,' Anna says, 'then you can concentrate on Alba.'

He smiles at her as he passes up the fishing paraphernalia. A smile which completely alters his face that, up until now, seemed to Anna to be permanently fixed in a scowl. Then he hoists his little daughter onto his back and they return up the path to the *agriturismo*.

Early sunshine has now been replaced by a mist that suddenly swirls down the mountains without warning. It sticks halfway, tangling in the branches of firs in cotton wool wisps. The temperature drops, too. Yesterday it was over fifteen degrees, but it feels about four degrees today with the sun gone in.

'It's freezing,' Anna says as they walk up the footpath. 'I'll need to buy warmer clothes.'

'We're in the mountains, don't forget. The weather can change quite suddenly.'

'My father mentions that in something he wrote. I think it had an impact on the fighting around here, too.'

'For sure it did. And I think that was another reason why our *partigiani* were so useful – they knew this area and the weather conditions. When we go to the tourist office, maybe you will find out more. They're trying to record as much detail as they can for an exhibition.'

'But I thought you had to give a lecture this morning.'

'It's been cancelled. I'm free now.'

Anna wonders if the lecture has really been cancelled or if he has simply changed his mind.

'If you really don't mind,' she continues, 'it would be a great help. My Italian is still not up to much beyond the basics of shopping and asking the way. And...' She hesitates, wondering if it is too soon to ask this man for help. 'I really want to understand what my parents went through.'

'I said I am free.'

She cannot make him out: so prickly one moment, and charming the next. She had been going to ask him for help with translating the diaries, but she's not sure. They are silent on the way back, and Anna drinks in the scenery. She cannot imagine such a beautiful spot brutalised by war. She wonders if soldiers had ever come down to the river and walked along the same path they are following. The place is already having an effect on her. She feels a deep sense of history, and for the first time in her life, a kind of belonging.

Egidio, the manager of the tourist office, has twinkling brown eyes and a weathered face that might tell a story or two. He is delighted to have a visitor showing interest in the collection of records written by old people from the town. He explains how they are being gathered together by the children at the middle school to mark the millennium. At first he speaks slowly, but then he gradually gathers speed until she has to ask him to repeat himself. Francesco fills in the details she misses.

'It's so important they know about their past,' Anna says to Francesco. 'Can you tell him how much I regret my own mother not telling me more before she died? I feel as if a chunk of myself is missing by not knowing her background. Can you also explain that I'm grateful he's sharing all this information with me, and say I don't want to come over as nosy or intrusive.'

Francesco relays her fears and the old man takes hold of her hand, turning to include Francesco in what he has to say.

'From what you have told us about your mother and father, I would never say you were an intruder. You are practically one of us. Wouldn't you say, Francesco?'

Francesco nods agreement and explains to Anna, 'Egidio has collated all these accounts because he firmly believes the stories should never be taken for granted, and I agree with him totally. And you have a right to know about your own family. Now come and see Egidio's exhibits. He's very proud of this tourist office, run by himself and other volunteers.'

They wander into a side room. There is a glass case containing a stuffed wild boar, and a wolf's head is mounted on the wall. Shelves display snakes pickled in large jars that once contained olives, and in smaller glass cases there are intricate fossils discovered in rocks in the hills or along the river. In a far corner, war memorabilia take up space: an old tin helmet, an ammunition belt, a row of medals pinned to a board. Francesco points out a board mounted with sepia photos of the town as it was both during and after the war. She peers into the grainy faces, wondering if she could possibly be related to any of the figures in the square: women with long woollen skirts, scarves on their heads; men with bandy legs and long whiskers, some with hunting guns slung over their shoulders, all looking very stern for the photographer.

'Have you got time to grab some lunch and come on a mystery tour?' Francesco asks. 'There's a place I want to show you. We can go and buy picnic ingredients first.'

'What about the weather? It was very misty before.'

He points out of the museum window. 'Look now.'

The sun has come out again and the sky is cloudless, blue and inviting.

'But won't it change again?'

'We'll be fine,' he reassures her.

She bows to his local knowledge, delighted she is making a start in the company of somebody who knows the area, and they say goodbye to Egidio, Anna thanking him again for showing her his precious papers.

They cross the square to a tiny supermarket, where one forlorn trolley is parked outside. The shop isn't big enough to fit any trolleys in or even more than four customers at a time, and she wonders about its purpose. Francesco explains that it is for delivering purchases to old people who can't manage to go shopping for themselves. She smiles at the thought of the contrast with the supermarket delivery vans back in England. When she enters the shop, her nose is assaulted by a mixture of smells: ham, salami, soap powder, cheese. Francesco introduces her to the shopkeeper, perched on a high stool behind the counter. When she moves to fetch a large cheese from the shelf behind her, Anna sees that she is frail and needs the stool for support. *The trolley outside is probably also used as a walking aid*, Anna thinks. Fresh ciabatta, a paper twist of black olives, a couple of slices of pecorino cheese, two apples and a bottle of wine make up her first picnic lunch in Italy.

*

Francesco's Fiat Panda bounces over a dirt track higher and higher into the mountains facing Badia Tedalda.

'We call this area "L'Alpe della Luna" – the Mountain of the Moon. Few people live here now, and there are many fables and ghost stories about the place. For me it has a special atmosphere.'

He tells the story he learned at elementary school. In the Middle Ages, young Count Manfredi of Montedoglio and a beautiful peasant girl, Rosalia, had fallen madly in love, much to the disapproval of the Count's family. One evening when they were alone together, whispering words of love to each other on a balcony, Rosalia told him that if they were to climb the mountains facing them and touch the moon, all their wishes would be granted. They set off, never to be seen again. And now, at full moon, it is sometimes possible to hear the galloping of two horses on the peaks and to see shadows with hands extended to the silvery night.

She laughs, delighted with the romance of Francesco's story. 'Well, whether that story is true or not, I love it. And folklore often holds a grain of truth, otherwise such stories wouldn't still be told after all this time.'

'Indeed!' He smiles at her, a smile that transforms his pinched face, and she wants to tell him he should smile more often but stops herself. Pulling on the handbrake, he parks and points at the view and she appreciates the derivation of the name, Mountain of the Moon. Tracts of impenetrable woodland are interrupted by masses of grey-brown rock, rising like craters. He points out two peaks that are over fourteen hundred metres high, covered with fresh snow. The scene is dramatically beautiful yet sinister. She takes a photograph and then peers at the image on her new digital camera.

'I can see why you think it's a special place, but it's hard to capture the atmosphere in a picture.'

'It's a place to store in the memory. Now hop back in the car and I'll take you to a restaurant the like of which you've never visited.'

'Where did you learn these English expressions? Not all from a textbook, I'm sure.'

'I'll tell you over lunch.'

With the car back in gear, they climb higher still up the mountain. Anna is mesmerised by the views. Throughout the trip, they haven't seen another soul, and it feels as if they are the only people in the world. But when Francesco parks the car in a clearing, a fenced-off picnic area proves there've been other visitors. Leading her towards rocks opposite the picnic site, he pulls aside slender branches to reveal a narrow opening to a cave. They slip through, entering a wide chamber high enough to stand up in. Her eyes adjust to the gloom; only a thin finger of daylight penetrates an opening in the cave roof, circled in black. He explains it was caused by smoke from fires made by people seeking shelter. Built into the side of the cave is a man-made trough collecting a trickle of water that seeps through the rock. She gasps when he shines his torchlight on fantastic stalactites twisted into elaborate patterns, hanging down like glass chandeliers.

'This place has been used by woodcutters and peasants working on the land, but during the war partisans sheltered here, too. I remember my father telling me he had to sleep here once,' Francesco says. 'Last year, when *il corpo forestale*, the forestry workers, were coppicing in this area, they discovered a stash of ammunition hidden further back in the chamber. Then they decided to tidy up the place and make it into a tourist venue, but it's too far off the road for most people to venture. I thought it would be of interest to you. Who knows? Your father might even have sheltered here.'

'That's exactly what I was thinking. It's given me goose pimples. This place is alive, full of ghosts from the past.' She shivers and touches the wall with one finger, trying to picture her father hiding in the far corner, behind the water trough. Would he have been alone? How far away were the enemy? Was he scared?

'Let's have our picnic at the tables outside,' he suggests, guiding her out of the gloom. 'I think we need sunshine.'

'Too right,' she says, grateful he seems to understand, without commenting or intruding on her emotions.

They unpack their simple feast at a table with the best view and Francesco uncorks the wine, then raises his plastic beaker to the hills. 'I propose a toast to the mountains and the secrets they hold – and a toast to you too, Anna. Welcome to your mother's land!'

They touch beakers and while he cuts slices of ciabatta, Anna asks him where he learned to speak such good English.

'In Africa. After I finished university I travelled to Tanzania to help on a programme documenting wild dogs in the Serengeti. It was run by a young American couple.'

'I'm confused. An Italian in Africa working for Americans?'

He laughs. 'You will come across the system of *raccomandazione* sooner or later.'

She looks puzzled.

'It's a matter of survival, Anna. Often in this country it's *who* you know, not *what* you know! One of the Americans is a cousin and he more or less created some work experience for me. We Italians end up everywhere, you know. After the war there was mass emigration to find work, and that is how my uncle landed up in Boston.'

He cuts more pecorino, handing her a generous slice and continues, 'Tanzania was an unforgettable experience. Such an amazing country. I would love to go back one day and show Alba.'

'I've never been out of Europe. I used to have so many dreams about travelling. You know that feeling, when you're young?

When you believe the world belongs to you? That you can put your arms around it and embrace all the opportunities?'

He laughs. 'But you're still young. There's a world out there waiting for you, Anna.' He points to her head. 'It's what's up there that matters.'

She helps him pack up the remnants of the picnic and then walks to the edge of the picnic area, absorbing the view of the mountains.

All around her, in the deep folds and valleys, is a wealth of history, she feels. Francesco has whetted her appetite with his entertaining anecdotes. If only the hills could talk, or she could travel back in time to see with her own eyes what happened in this place. She's glad she came here, to her mother's birthplace. She can almost feel her young presence, picture her playing in the meadows or walking to school along one of the dusty tracks they've travelled. But now she's more frustrated than ever that she can't read the diaries. This afternoon has been very special; the wine has relaxed her and Francesco is not the bear she thought he was when she first met him. She admires the way he's trying his utmost for Alba. Plucking up her courage, she decides it feels right to ask him to collaborate with her quest. 'You toasted the hidden mysteries of the mountains, Francesco. I was wondering if you could help me with my own mystery... could you help me translate my mother's diaries?'

She looks into his eyes as she says this, needing to gauge his reaction. It's important that any involvement he has with her mother's story is done in the right spirit.

'I wanted to do it myself,' she says, 'but it would take me ages, and I'm frightened of missing something.'

'Of course! I would be very interested in helping you, when I have time – between looking after Alba and the occasional lecture I might have to give.'

'Thank you. I'd pay you.'

He looks at her, the scowl returning to his features. 'I don't want paying. It will be a challenging project.'

She is not sure about his use of the word 'project', but she's desperate to understand what her mother has written. There is no going back now.

'Can I give you the papers when we get back to Teresa's?'

'Of course.'

The return journey down the potholed tracks is spent in silence, but Anna is tired and enjoys not having to talk. All in all, it's been a good afternoon.

'I'll take good care of them,' Francesco says, when Anna runs in to fetch the diaries from her room in the *agriturismo*.

'I know you will. *Grazie*,' she says, out of breath with the exertion of running up the stairs. She hands them over, hesitating a little. 'This is the only copy. Do you think I…'

'Don't worry. There's no need to make a photocopy. I understand how precious these documents are to you.'

His grasp of her hand is firm as he reassures her, and she watches as he finds a folder and carefully writes *Anna's Story* on the outside. She wants to correct him, tell him it should read *Ines' Story*, but she lets it be.

CHAPTER SEVEN

A couple of days later, Francesco returns the first instalment, handing her an envelope at breakfast. Her coffee and toast seem to take an age that morning. Anna feels like a child waiting to open her Christmas presents. As soon as she can, after helping Teresa clear the table, she runs up to her room to read his typed translation.

Rofelle, 8 September 1944

The *inglese* was still asleep on the planks above the cows. The nights are chilly and the animal warmth and dry hay have made a comfortable bedroom, much better than mine. I have to share with Nonna, and she kicks and tosses at night. She snores like the pig we used to fatten for Christmas. There have been no pigs this year. The Germans have requisitioned ours and everybody else's in the area. 'Pigs eating pigs,' we mutter among ourselves.

'Signore,' I whispered.

There was no response. His face was long and pale. Blond curls fell over his forehead, which was bound with a dirty cloth. Blood had oozed and crusted onto the material. He was like a big baby.

'Signore!' I said it louder this time. There was still no response. I put the bowl of pasta down and gently shook him.

He opened his eyes, shouted and grabbed me round the neck. I pummelled him with my fists – I could hardly breathe. 'Let me go, leave me alone!' I shouted.

And then he recognised where he was and dropped his hands from my neck. '*Scusi, scusi*. Sorry, sorry, signorina.'

'You nearly knocked over the food.'

I was shaking and I rubbed my neck. His grip had hurt me. The cows below seemed to sense something was wrong and they mooed and stamped their hooves.

I pushed the dish nearer to him and he struggled into a sitting position. He looks very young to me, not much older than Capriolo, maybe in his early twenties. We lent him some of our clothes and burnt his uniform, but he still doesn't look like one of us. His hair is too blond. We talked about shaving it off or dyeing it with plants. Nonna has told me about a woman in the next village who used walnut shells and spindle berries to keep the grey from her hair. Her husband was not as old as her and so she was frightened he would run off with a younger woman. One day she was caught in the rain without her scarf and the dye ran down her face, the colour of dried blood. I thought of bringing the *inglese* one of Papà's cloth caps next time I come to the stable. He could pull it down to cover his hair. 'Eat, eat!' I mimed, my hand going to my mouth. 'You must get strong again.'

He repeated the words, '*Mangia, mangia.*'

I giggled. It would be best if he pretended to be a mute. If he opens his mouth to pronounce words in such a ridiculous accent, then that, together with his blond curls, will give him away immediately.

The door of the mill opened, casting a triangle of light onto the path leading to the stable. 'Ines, Ines,' Mother called. I had been gone too long, so I left the dish with the *inglese* and hurried back to the fireside.

They were sitting round the hearth in a semicircle – Mamma, Papà, Davide and Nonna. Their faces were sombre, the firelight enlarging their features, creating a grotesque group.

Mamma was the first to speak. 'We can't do this. It's too dangerous. There are too many Germans around.'

Davide piped up. 'It's not only Germans – we can't trust anybody. Giorgio told me at the bar there were ten women, children and old men butchered in Gattara in retaliation for the *partigiani* killing one German soldier. There's no telling who is spying on us at any one moment.'

'Giorgio is always in the bar,' said my father. 'The only truth he knows is at the bottom of a glass. How can *he* be the judge between what is true and what is tittle-tattle?'

'No, Papà, honestly – he's not the only one who knows,' my brother explained. 'The Germans put up a poster in the square yesterday offering a twelve hundred lire reward for information about prisoners of war on the run. You and I know only too well that many people would give their right arm for such a sum.'

The ashes hissed and spluttered, sending sparks up the tarry chimney.

Davide continued, 'Didn't you hear about Pippo, who was out herding the cattle? The Germans shot him, no questioning, nothing... They told his parents he was a partisan, that he would have no proper burial.

They were to leave his body up on the mountain for the wolves.'

'Stop your scaremongering, you young rascal,' my father said, raising his voice. 'Stop frightening your mother.'

'I know about it already,' our mother said quietly, putting down her mending and staring into the fire. 'When I was at the fountain two days ago, all the women were talking about it. When the Germans warned the priest not to conduct his funeral, the whole of Montefaggio turned out to attend. Padre Luca carried Pippo's body down from the ridge himself. One by one the people opened their doors and came out onto the track, following him down to the church. Everybody. The old, the sick, the young – everybody crowded into the church to give that poor boy a proper send-off. And the German soldiers stood there with their rifles aimed, shouting at them to return to their houses. Nobody obeyed, and there was not a thing they could do, save shooting the whole village. Those people were brave.'

Such events are rumoured among friends but seldom openly discussed. There's always the fear that the wrong person will overhear these conversations and report rebels to the militia. Even our neighbours cannot be trusted. But hearing such stories only strengthens my resolve to continue to help with the fight in any way I can.

'But I'm scared,' my mother said. 'I don't want the risk of that Englishman lying up there in the stable. I don't mind cooking, sending up medical supplies and clothing to the boys, but this is too close for comfort.' She lowered her voice as if the walls had ears.

'Capriolo will know what to do,' I said. 'He's coming later to see us.'

Davide teased me. 'See *you*, more like. Everybody knows he just comes down here for you.'

In return for that comment he received a cuff round the ear from our father.

I rounded on my brother. 'Capriolo and I are like brother and sister. We've known each other all our lives. Don't be so stupid. Your brain is stewed from this stupid war.'

Capriolo is two years older than me. We both had our lessons in the same classroom at the village school. We were considered star pupils by the old headmaster, who had a soft spot for us because we were eager to learn. He said we would go a long way, and that we understood there was a world beyond the mountain walls of our village. He coached us in mathematics and history after the other children had straggled home down the hill from our tiny elementary school.

Three months ago he came up to find me in the meadow where I was tending our Chianina cattle. I was sitting on a boulder, dressed in one of Davide's old coats, belted with a length of rope, one of Papà's hats pulled down over my dark curls and Nonno's boots on my feet. Mamma had warned me to keep away from *tedeschi* soldiers and had dressed me in shapeless rags to make me look as ugly as possible. I was half asleep. The spring sunshine was pleasantly warm and the tinkling of the bells round the necks of the cattle was like a lullaby, so I had undone the coat to feel the rays on my winter skin. A wolf whistle startled me from my snooze. Wrapping the scratchy coat tighter round my body, I

jumped up, terrified. I couldn't see anybody and I called
to Mimi, our Maremma shepherd dog. She wagged her
shaggy tail, not in the least bit alarmed. Then Capriolo
jumped down from the tree above me, knocking me
to the ground. I screamed and hammered at him with
my fists and he laughed.

'Whoa, Ines, quite the she-wolf! But not in sheep's
clothing, in scarecrow's clothing. *Not* a sight for sore eyes.'

I pulled off my cap and my hair tumbled down past
my shoulders. I don't know why I did that. I didn't
really care what he thought of me.

'Don't ever do that to me again. I nearly wet myself,'
I shouted.

'We couldn't have that, could we?' He laughed at me
again. 'It would take you three hours to take all those
garments off to change into dry ones. No, seriously, you
should be more vigilant, there are all sorts of people
wandering around in these hills at the moment.'

He looked me up and down and then sat with me
on the boulder. 'It's good you look as ugly as a tramp,
though. Remember, Ines – you are not only a woman,
you are also a communist.'

I laughed, but the smile had faded from his face and
his expression turned serious. 'Ines, I've been waiting for
the right moment to talk to you – we need your help.'

'What is it? What help?'

He spoke earnestly, warning me that what he was asking
me to do in our fight for freedom would be dangerous.
If we were caught, there would be repercussions, but as
I listened, there was no doubt in my mind: I wanted to
help in any way I could. And so began my initiation into
the *Resistenza*. I became a *staffetta*, running errands for

Capriolo and his band of *partigiani*. More times than I can remember, from that day on I've hidden medicines or food from my mother's kitchen, spare clothes beneath my bulky overcoat and left them in the ditch that runs alongside the track where I lead the cattle up to the summer pastures. Sometimes I pass on messages that my brother Davide asks me to relay. I don't understand them and I never ask where Capriolo takes all these things. It's best not to know too much, he told me.

An hour later, after we had argued back and forth about what to do with the *inglese*, Capriolo turned up. Four knocks on the door and a cough. His password. He came near to the fire, rubbing his hands. 'It's warm during the day but the nights are beginning to grow colder.'

My mother rose to pour him a cup of coffee, made from ground acorns these days. But it was the best we could manage.

'Capriolo,' my mother said, pouring the hot liquid into a little cup, 'we can't keep the *inglese* here. It's too danger-ous. Not only for us, but for all of you up there too.'

He touched her arm. 'I know, Signora Assunta. That's why I've come to talk to you. Can he be moved, do you think? Are his leg and head wounds healing?'

She shrugged. 'In normal times I would make him sleep and rest for another week or so, but these are not normal times.'

'Maybe I could take him up on the mule,' I suggested. 'If we planned the route along the edge of the forest, there would always be somewhere to hide, if necessary.'

He shook his head. 'The *tedeschi* have a machine gun station dug in just along that path where it forks. No good.'

Papà was sitting by the fire, making a new wooden sole for his work boots. He said quietly, 'Sometimes the obvious is not what it seems. Maybe we should try some kind of disguise.'

'You will need courage, Ines,' Capriolo said. 'But this family has plenty of that. And I think you are ready.'

As she finishes reading the last lines, Anna slumps back on her bed, hardly able to believe the life her mother led: harbouring prisoners of war, risking her own safety for the sake of the *partigiani*. She cannot square this account with how she remembers her mother later in life: a constant bustling presence in the kitchen, or later, an elderly, confused woman in a nursing home. She reaches for her phone to talk to Francesco, but there's no answer. So she goes downstairs to find Teresa.

Teresa is loading baskets into the back of her pick-up truck. She turns to smile at Anna.

'Hey, ciao! Fancy coming with me to the market? I need to pick up a few things for the house.'

'Gladly. *Volentieri,*' is Anna's response, thinking it will be good to share her thoughts about the diary with her new friend.

CHAPTER EIGHT

The monthly market in the piazza is only a small affair, a chance for villagers to meet up with friends and family living in hamlets scattered across the mountains. Teresa and Anna immediately make for the busiest stall. A round-faced storybook figure surrounded by squawking caged hens and baskets of eggs is keeping up a stream of good-natured banter with a queue of customers.

Teresa introduces Anna. 'Evalina, this is my English friend.'

The diminutive old lady holds out a work-weathered hand, thrusting a twist of newspaper containing half a dozen brown eggs at Anna. 'Taste these, signorina, and then tell me next week how good Italian eggs are.'

She refuses payment, and Teresa laughs at Anna's unsuccessful protests.

'She's a clever businesswoman. It's her way of luring you back. They are fresh eggs, and free-range, from *polli ruspanti*.'

Anna has seen plenty of these 'scratching about' hens in villagers' backyards: happy hens scavenging in the grass and dust. They move on to a colourful stall selling materials, and Teresa haggles for a length of linen edged with fine lace.

'I need to replace the curtains in one of the guest rooms,' she tells Anna, who listens to her arguing cheerily with the stallholder, laughing when he tries to sell her some towels as well. She follows the gist, but wonders if she will ever be able to rattle off her Italian at even half the speed. A tablecloth with a bright pattern of olives and grapes catches her eye, and she buys it to remind herself of the friendly market.

Next, they browse at a stall selling knick-knacks and old furniture. Teresa holds up a wood-framed contraption. 'We call these priests. And we put them in our beds in winter.'

Anna laughs at the irreverence. 'A priest in the bed! I can't imagine anything less cuddly!'

Teresa explains how the frame holds up the bedcovers and then a pot of hot ashes from the fire is placed underneath to heat up the bed. She smiles when she tells Anna the receptacle for the ashes is called a nun. She asks the price and then bargains hard again, finishing up with a handshake and a smile.

'Another antique for my city guests to admire,' she says.

Anna enjoys the way local people shop and decides to try and drive a bargain too. In the corner, under the shade of perfumed linden trees, she spies an old man in a wide-brimmed hat seated behind piled pyramids of golden jars of honey. When she tries out her Italian on him he stares at her for a few seconds, scratching his head, shrugging his shoulders, making no effort, it seems to her, to understand. And when he mutters something about *americani*, she retorts in her best Italian, '*Sono inglese, non americana.*'

At this he pulls a face and sits down to read his newspaper, even though Anna can see it is upside down. Teresa comes to her rescue, pouring on his head what Anna hopes is a stream of Italian curses. He scowls and holds up five fingers. '*Cinque mila lire,*' he pronounces slowly and deliberately, making Anna feel like the idiot he obviously thinks she is.

Retaliating and, equally as slowly, she replies, '*No grazie, troppo caro,*' (No thanks, too expensive), wishing she knew the expression for 'up yours' in Italian.

Teresa laughs and, putting her arm through Anna's, they wander over to the bar behind the honey stall.

'Don't take any notice of Danilo, Anna. He's an eccentric and used to his own company. He lives way up in that hamlet you can see from my house. The place is almost deserted, except at weekends and holidays. He's the only permanent resident. Deep down, he's a good man and held in high regard locally because he's a respected war veteran.'

'I'd love to pick his brains about the war, in that case. Maybe he even knew my mother. But talk about unfriendly – my Italian's not that bad, is it?'

'I'm sure he'd chat to you. Maybe you could take a walk up to his village some time. Montebotolino is a beautiful spot. Locally, it's known as the village in paradise – *il paese sul paradiso.*'

'I'll think about it. *Il paese sul paradiso,*' she repeats. 'Such a musical language. I need to become fluent, Teresa.'

'*Pazienza, pazienza.* You'll get there, slowly but surely.'

There's a pause while the two women sit and wait for their coffee. Anna gazes round the square, enjoying the theatre of market day. It is like having a seat at the opera, only a whole lot cheaper.

'I'm loving all this, Teresa.'

'What do you mean?'

'Being here. It's hard to explain, but… I feel a connection. And…' As she talks, her voice is animated, and she even starts to wave her hands about like a true Italian. 'Starting my mother's diary is like stepping into a new world for me… it's amazing to know she was writing it from this very place. I wish I'd been able to appreciate the life she left behind when she was alive. And understand *her*… she could be difficult, you know. In fact, both my parents were difficult.'

Teresa rests her hand on Anna's arm. 'If Francesco and I can help in any way, simply ask.'

'You're both doing so much already. I can't tell you how much. *Grazie, amica!*' Anna says.

'*Prego!* Now drink your coffee before it becomes tepid.'

She sips her cappuccino. Teresa knocks back her tiny cup of espresso, after commenting that she's noticed *stranieri* always seem to prefer cappuccino, even after a large meal, which Italians cannot understand.

Anna glances at the old honey seller, who is staring at her, but when he realises she is watching him, he hides behind his newspaper again.

The cantankerous old grump is soon forgotten as they look at each other's purchases and Teresa chatters away, slowing down every now and again when she sees Anna has been left behind in her stories about various village personalities. When Anna comments that she seems to know everybody, Teresa shrugs and says it's not surprising, as she's lived here all her life.

It is all so different from Anna's life back in London, where she doesn't even know the name of her neighbour in the flat across her landing. But here, in the heart of this bustling piazza, where her mother might even have shopped, handled goods on stalls and haggled over prices, there might be somebody who remembers her. Anna feels a bond with her mother she's never experienced before. And if reading the start of the diary has sparked this emotion, she wonders how she will feel by the end of it.

In the afternoon, she collects Alba for an informal English lesson that she had offered in exchange for Francesco's help with the diaries.

'Thanks so, so much for your translation, Francesco,' she says when he comes to the door. 'It's amazing. I can't wait for the next instalment. Hint, hint!'

'Slave driver,' he laughs. 'I'm actually enjoying seeing the past come to life. Our parents' generation certainly went through a lot.'

'I can hardly believe what I'm reading. I want to know what happens next, like in a soap opera, but of course it's real life… if you see what I mean. Sorry – didn't mean to harass you. I can wait... but not too long.' She grins.

'I'll see what I can do, madam.'

'Rather than stay indoors with Alba, I'd like to take her down to the river in the sunshine,' Anna says. 'Do you think she'll come?'

He talks to Alba, and it's obvious from her reaction she's not keen. Eventually, she shrugs her shoulders and pulls a face.

'I've bribed her with the promise of her favourite cartoon programmes,' Francesco explains. 'But I think we should make it a short session. I'll come and meet you down at the weir in about half an hour.'

Anna has suggested the river thinking it will be easier for Alba in the fresh air. Her silence will be less noticeable with the sounds of birdsong and water splashing over rocks in the river. Over the past couple of days Alba has become more accepting of her, smiling more and not averting her eyes so readily. There have been few guests in Teresa's *agriturismo*, as it's low season, and so they've fallen into the habit of sharing a table together in the evenings, like a family.

Anna had noticed Alba sketching in her notebooks and wondered if drawing might be a good start to the lesson.

'Can you draw me a cat like this, Alba?' she asks her now, in English, trying to engage the little girl by showing her a picture of a cat from a magazine.

But Alba pushes the sketch pad away and picks up a stick to stir water in a pool. Then she is distracted by tiny darting fish, and after that she finds a stone encrusted with quartz and starts to extract the white crystals by beating it against a rock. Anna gives up. There is no point in insisting, and in any case she doesn't have the patience today. So she sits on a boulder watching her play, immersed in her mystery world.

She reminds Anna of herself as a little girl. So often she'd been left to her own devices for long stretches of time. Harry and Jane would be busy with their studies or out with friends, and sometimes Mamma would leave her at home, asking her father to keep an eye on her. He would promptly disappear to his shed. As children, they were not allowed to sit in front of the television for hours, and Anna's imagination became her entertainment.

At the bottom of their garden was a huge beech tree. Its branches drooped down like the walls of a tent and the trunk was knotted with gargoyle joints and holes where she imagined a gang of miniature-sized friends lived.

One afternoon, when Jane came home earlier than expected from a cancelled piano lesson, she caught Anna talking aloud to her friends.

'Don't you know that mad people talk to themselves?' she teased her little sister, unaware of the effect it would have on Anna, who took her big sister so seriously. 'That's the first sign of madness… and the second is hairs growing on the palms of your hands.' And she laughed when Anna anxiously inspected her palms.

'Why am I so much younger than both of you?' she'd asked at the Christmas dinner table when she was four.

'Because you're adopted,' was her twenty-three-year-old brother's attempt at avoiding the subject of the birds and the bees.

'Don't fill the child's head with nonsense, Harry,' her mother had said.

For a long time, Anna believed him, staring at herself in the mirror, trying to find some resemblance to her siblings.

Small wonder she had felt an outsider in her own family, and created a fantasy family for herself. She appreciates how Alba feels more secure within her own silence.

*

As soon as the sun falls behind the ridge, the air turns chilly and Anna calls to her little pupil that the lesson is over for today. 'We'll try again another time, and anyway, here comes your daddy.'

She hopes that by talking to her in English most of the time Alba will learn something and, by attuning her ears to different sounds, she might pick up a word or two.

As Francesco approaches down the footpath, Alba runs to him and he swings her round and round. '*Babbo* has come, not Daddy,' he shouts, using the Italian translation. 'Who is this Daddy, Daddy, Daddy?'

She squeals with laughter. It's the only sound Anna ever hears her make. She wishes she could find a way to break her silence.

'How did it go?' he asks, setting Alba down as they begin the walk back together.

'*Così così* – so-so!' Anna replies, tilting her outstretched hand this way and that, palm downward, the way Teresa has taught her. 'I'm not giving up, though! Did you enjoy a peaceful half hour?'

'A *fascinating* half hour. I started work on the next instalment of your soap opera. I'll type it out when I have a free moment.'

Anna smiles at the description. 'That would be great. Thanks so much.'

'*Prego*, Anna.'

Alba has stopped walking. She is standing still, blocking the path, her arms crossed, an obstinate look on her face. Francesco speaks firmly to her, telling her she is too big to be carried and that they will be late for Teresa's supper. When Anna tries to help by suggesting they have a race back to the *agriturismo*, the child puts out her tongue at her and runs off in the opposite direction, back to the river.

'You go back by yourself, Anna,' Francesco calls as he goes in pursuit of Alba. 'Tell Teresa we won't be long.'

She continues up the mule track to the guest house. As she passes their vegetable plot with its neat rows of seedlings pushing through the soil, she glances up to the village of Montebotolino silhouetted on the peaks. She remembers her conversation with Teresa in the piazza about how the irascible old honey seller might be persuaded to talk about his war memories. She resolves to walk up there at the first opportunity to find him, but in the meantime Anna is intrigued to know what Francesco has translated.

CHAPTER NINE

At breakfast next morning, Alba is subdued and hardly touches anything, even though Teresa produces her favourite chocolate drink and biscuits for dunking. After Francesco has seen her onto the *scuolabus*, he comes into the kitchen where Anna is helping tidy up. He pours himself another espresso and Teresa warns him it will make him *nervoso*, tetchy, that he has already had too much caffeine this morning.

'Don't you think I am already *nervoso*?' He yawns and turns to Anna. 'I'm sorry, but I didn't find any time last night to work on your diary. It took me ages to put Alba to bed. I couldn't seem to do anything right. First she wanted to wear a different pair of pyjamas, but they were in the wash, then she insisted on me telling her another two stories. It was almost midnight when I turned off her light. If anything, she's growing even more demanding.'

Anna thinks the child might be ruling the roost and could do with firmer handling. But she doesn't comment, reminding herself she has never been a parent and that it is none of her business. 'Don't worry. I can wait,' she says.

Secretly she is disappointed. Teresa and Francesco talk away in Italian but she can't follow, their words spilling from their mouths faster and faster. Finally, Francesco raises his voice, leaving the kitchen abruptly and slamming the door behind him.

Teresa throws her dishcloth into the sink, turns round to lean against it and folds her arms. 'He is so tired, and worried about Alba. I'm sorry about the shouting.'

'I couldn't understand it anyway. My Italian still has a long way to go. Can I help at all?'

'Actually, it was about you.' She hesitates, obviously embarrassed.

'Go on, Teresa! *Dai! Forza!* Remember you taught me that expression the other day?' Anna tries to make light of the situation.

'Right, then. It's about your room. I have a long-standing booking at the weekend and I need all my rooms for five nights, and I didn't know how long you might be staying. Or if you would mind me moving you into a different room, one that still needs decorating. I'm sorry!'

'Why are you sorry? You're running a business, after all. In fact, I was going to chat to you soon anyway. I love my room, but I can't afford to stay in a guest house all the time I'm here. I need to save money for the future when I return to England and I was going to ask you for advice about finding somewhere else. Please don't worry, Teresa. You've been so good to me.'

'It's just that you are becoming such a friend. Francesco is angry with me as he says I should let you stay where you are, but he's not the one running the business, and—'

She takes Teresa's hands in hers. 'I'm *honestly* not offended and I *really* don't mind – what is the expression? *Non faccio complimenti.* And thank you for considering me a friend, because I feel the same way.'

Teresa smiles in relief. 'Thank you. Then, I have a suggestion. Come!'

She leads Anna around the corner from the front door of the *agriturismo* into a small square and up a flight of steps into a narrow house. They step over a couple of cement bags and Teresa moves aside a tin of paint standing at the entrance to what will eventually be a small kitchen. 'I was going to advertise this for a long let, but it's not quite finished, as you can see.'

It is already delightful, bearing the hallmarks of Teresa's tasteful restoration of the *agriturismo*. An original stone sink, far too low for modern use, is fixed below the window overlooking the square. Anna imagines a trough spilling with red geraniums or basil on the window ledge. There is a fireplace which Teresa assures her is functional, and a log burner waiting to be installed in the far corner of the room, where a dining table and four chairs are arranged.

'It used to be my aunt's house and she left it to me when she died. Some of the furniture was hers, too. I'd much prefer to have somebody I know living here. And if you like it, we can go on seeing each other and I can make sure you're practising your Italian.' She waggles her finger in pretend strictness. 'But it's not quite finished.'

'I don't care. I absolutely love it. Show me the rest.'

There are three storeys, each containing one room. The middle floor has been refurbished as a bathroom, with a shower, toilet, bidet and tiny bath fixed cleverly into a corner, the walls lined with hand-painted tiles. The top floor in the eaves is the bedroom, which is open-plan, with another small fireplace and a floor-to-ceiling window that frames a view of the spectacular mountaintops.

'When can I move in? And how much is the rent?' She cannot believe her luck, especially when Teresa tells her she only wants 400,000 lire a month, explaining that, in return for the low rent, she could help her out occasionally in the *agriturismo*, especially when the summer season starts.

'There's another thing that worries me,' Teresa continues. 'I haven't finished furnishing the place. It might be too sparse.'

'I prefer it this way. I was brought up in a home where we were always tripping over furniture. Our parents' generation was making up for a lack of possessions during the war. But there I go again, always talking about the war! My mother's diary has ignited a new interest, and I'm becoming so one-track-minded.'

'It's perfectly understandable, Anna. I would be the same, I'm sure. Family is so important.'

Later that day, Anna moves in to her new place. Teresa has left a basket of vegetables on the stone worktop, with a note:

A house-warming gift for you, fresh from the vegetable garden this morning. The first salad of the season, and spinach beet planted last autumn. Wait until the tomatoes start coming and I can teach you delicious recipes.

Everybody is so kind, and Anna doesn't know how she can ever repay them.

It doesn't take her long to unpack her few possessions. She decides she needs to buy more cooking utensils from the market and a warmer counterpane for the brass bed in the eaves. The bed takes up most of the room and she sits on it for a while, taking in the view. The bell tower of the chapel in Montebotolino sits atop the mountains, which are splashed yellow with the same *ginestra* she's seen sprouting everywhere along the roadsides and steep, stony banks. She decides to walk up to the village. The weather is dry and she's eager to talk to Danilo, the honey seller. She hopes to find him in a better mood than he was the other day in the market.

Teresa advises her to follow the path indicated by red and white markers that are fixed to the sides of the houses, tree trunks and rocks.

'It will take you a good half an hour to climb up there. Take your mobile phone with you, Anna. You never know what may happen with the weather at this time of year. There've been landslides this winter and the path may have changed, and it's easy to get lost if you don't know the mountains. Are you sure you want to go alone?'

'I'm a big girl now! Don't worry.'

She leaves straight after a lunch of bread and pecorino cheese. The path starts just beyond the cemetery at Rofelle and, after crossing a weir, climbs steadily. At first she walks under a canopy of pines, the wind moving gently through the branches, trunks swaying in the light breeze, her feet crunching over last year's fallen pine cones. After twenty minutes she stops in a clearing and gazes at the valley below. In the distance she can hear the tinny music of bells from a flock of sheep – toy models in a meadow sliced out of the forest. The houses of Montebotolino are above her, looming over the edge of the path. She thinks how difficult it must have been to build villages like these, in a time before machines and vehicles. Some of the houses are complete ruins; others are shells, with just the sky for a roof. One is obviously under reconstruction, a cement mixer and new roof tiles arranged beside the track.

Danilo's house is just off the village square. She works this out for herself, as it's the only building showing any real signs of life: a patch of earth in front has been planted with a few courgettes and tomatoes. There is a dish of pasta and milk by his front door, food for an animal, perhaps. A couple of strings of last year's onions and chilli peppers hang from rusty nails in the stonework, and a shirt flaps on a makeshift washing line slung between plum trees. The door is open.

'*Permesso?*' she calls, asking if it is all right to come in, waiting for the usual response of '*Avanti!*' But nobody answers.

She pokes her head round the open door and peers into the gloom, her eyes not immediately focusing after the bright daylight, and nearly jumps out of her skin when she is grabbed roughly by someone. She screams and tries to back out of the door to escape. A voice growls at her in Italian and she is so shocked she can barely understand, but she makes out the word 'thief'.

She can't think how to reply and shouts in English, 'Let me go!' She scrabbles for her mobile phone in her pocket, then, realising she doesn't know the number to punch in for the police, she screams, 'Take your filthy hands off me!'

The old honey seller scowls. He releases her and she stumbles backward, righting herself against the outside wall of the house. But he moves forward to grab her again. 'Who are you?' he shouts, peering at her more closely. 'I've seen you somewhere before, haven't I?'

She tries to calm herself down and think of the words she needs in Italian. 'The market, at the market. With Teresa. From the *agriturismo* at San Patrignano,' she stutters.

He nods recognition, gesturing to her to sit down on the wooden bench outside his door. He talks quickly – she doesn't recognise many of the words, thinking maybe he is speaking in dialect, so she asks him to slow down. '*Piano, piano, per favore.*'

He starts again, explaining he is suspicious of strangers, that there's been a burglary up here. When she says she doesn't understand, he throws up his hands in exasperation and then mimes until she does understand. Four houses were broken into – he holds up four fingers. '*Quattro case. Bastardi,*' he says, spitting onto the dirt. 'I have nothing valuable in my house,' he tells her, raising his voice again, 'I have no antiques to sell you, signorina. And my mill is not for sale either. Keep away!'

'I'm not interested in antiques or your mill, Signor—'

The only name she has for the old man is Danilo. It feels offensive to use only his Christian name.

'Just call me Danilo,' he says, as if reading her thoughts. 'That's what everybody calls me.' He pushes his cap back off his head and scratches. 'So, you are an *inglesina?*'

Feeling she might be gaining his trust, she broaches the subject of the war. 'Yes, I'm *inglese*,' she says. 'Would you tell me something about the occupation? And when the *inglesi* were here? Teresa told me you were a partisan.'

He stands up, the smile wiped from his face. 'That's all over and done with. Long gone. I never talk to anybody about that time. It's best forgotten.'

'Perhaps you knew my mother, Ines? Ines Santini? I have a photograph of her I can bring next time I come. She lived here during the war.'

The old man turns away to pick up an old pot. 'No need for a next time. I told you already. The war happened a long time ago. It's over and done with. Don't go poking your nose into other people's business. Now, signorina, I have to go and feed my hens and lock them up. There are wolves about.'

'Wolves?' Anna wonders if he is joking. 'Did you say wolves?'

'Some idiot outsider told me it's a stray dog abandoned by a city family, but I know better,' he says, throwing up his hands. 'I found its spoor. It's definitely a wolf. Nobody can teach me anything new about these mountains, what goes on and what doesn't go on up here.'

He taps the side of his nose and continues to chat, but she doesn't understand the rest of his diatribe and she is ready to leave anyway. He all but pushes her away from his patch of garden, directing her towards the track, his hand guiding her brusquely in the small of her back. '*Inglese*, are you?' He concludes his rant. 'Coming here to snap photographs of everyone and everything. I don't like the *inglesi*. They buy up our old houses, poke around and interfere with our ways... keep away. I have nothing to sell you.'

Anna decides she doesn't much like him either, and wonders why he is so reluctant to talk. She feels sure he could tell her more. She decides to persist and return to Montebotolino another time with her mother's photograph. Hopefully she will catch him in a better frame of mind.

The windows of the ruined houses stare at her, like empty sockets in dead faces, as she hurries past and down the track. The little hamlet is a mixture of spellbinding and spooky: a place hiding ghosts from the past.

CHAPTER TEN

The next morning, there is a loud rapping at Anna's door to the house in the little square. She's slept in late, and she drags herself out of bed to open the window.

Francesco is below, carrying a tray.

'Teresa sent me round with this. Coffee, fresh bread and home-made jam. Aren't you going to let me in?'

Dragging on her dressing gown, she hurries down the stairs and unbolts the heavy oak door.

'How wonderful! Thank you so much. But tell Teresa this has got to be the first and only time. I'm an independent woman now.'

'I was hoping you might invite me to join you. I've got something for you.'

He pulls a brown envelope from under the basket of bread rolls, waving it enticingly in front of her.

'Really? More translation? So soon? Francesco, you're kindness personified.'

Over breakfast he talks about the next section he's worked on.

'I found it fascinating. I won't give anything away, Anna, but after you've read it through, I plan to take you to some of the places mentioned. That is, if you don't mind.'

'Of course not. Why would I? But I hope it's not taking up too much of your time.'

'I'm enjoying it. It's pure history. When Alba went to sleep I burned the midnight oil, as you would say.'

'How is she?'

'Difficult! But I have to keep reminding myself that she's been through a hard time. Before I forget, there's a music festival at the weekend in a town not far from here, and I wondered if you'd like to come along with Alba and me.'

When she hesitates, he adds, 'There's music from all over the world performed in the street. It's a great event.'

'I'm sure it is, but I was thinking Alba might want to go alone with you.'

'She has to learn that grown-ups need to do what they want sometimes, too!'

Anna agrees but says nothing, and Francesco gets up from the table. 'Have a think about it, and in the meantime, enjoy your mother's diaries. I'll leave you in peace and go and see if Teresa needs any help. Ciao!'

Bounding up the stairs, she hopes she wasn't too abrupt with Francesco. Rude, even, in her haste to be on her own to read more of her mother's story.

What did they decide to do eventually with the *inglese*? she wonders. And if it was so risky to harbour POWs, where would they have hidden him next? Opening Francesco's folder, she reads on.

9 September 1944

This morning, a storm had turned the river outside the mill to the colour of milky coffee. Huge branches swept down with the current, transforming the river into a vicious, foaming flow. We had to shout above the roar of the water.

Papà held our mule as the *inglese* was helped onto the cart and into his makeshift bed. Mamma had killed a precious chicken and used its blood to soak rags to daub on our faces to resemble sores. Charcoal from the fire was rubbed into our skin to complete our appearance, for we were to pretend we were *carbonari*. These are the charcoal burners, whose faces are always stained from their grubby work. They keep themselves to themselves, labouring away for weeks in the clearings in the forest, far from habitation, slowly burning their wood within mounds of heaped-up branches covered in dirt. They camp out while they are working and feed on potatoes and whatever they can store for their time in the mountains. Nobody mixes with them, but we know of their presence because of the wisps of smoke that spiral up through the trees. Occasionally one of them will break into song and a chorus of voices will rise on the mountain air: ghostly voices, like long-lost souls lamenting.

'Keep still, Ines. Stop your wriggling.' My mother smeared my face with a piece of blackened wood from the hearth.

'Open wide, and I'll find you an evil-looking husband to match your ugliness.' She was trying to smile but she didn't want me to go. She blacked out my two front teeth and gave me her mirror to look at my reflection.

'If you are going to carry out this madness, I shall at least try my very best to make you look ugly like little old witch Befana on her broomstick in the sky, bringing coal to naughty children.'

The *inglese* and I were dressed in vile-smelling clothes trampled on overnight by the cattle in the stable.

Capriolo was hovering about, watching my mother complete my disguise. 'Don't forget, Ines,' he said, 'if the German soldiers stop you, act stupid. Pretend you are a halfwit. If they ask you something, just act dumb. I have instructed the *inglese* to lie completely still and not to talk to you at all during the journey. There are *tedeschi* all over the mountains. He must stay down. Let's hope this foul weather keeps the bastards in their ratholes.'

When we were ready, Mamma and Papà embraced me. My mother started her wailing again. 'I don't want you to go, Ines,' she cried. 'It's too dangerous. I'll be praying for you every minute until you come back.'

Capriolo caught hold of my mother's arm. 'Assunta, I have told you, we'll never be far from them, we'll be shadowing them from the woods. If it looks as if Ines is in any danger, then we'll be there. And I shall use this.'

He brought his rifle round from where it was slung over his back and at that, my mother started to wail again. She drew out her rosary beads from her pocket. 'Take these, Ines. And God and the angels protect you. I shall pray to the Madonna for your safekeeping.'

I pushed the rosary into the pocket of my tattered coat. Earlier Mamma had given me a cloth bag holding herbs for the *inglese*'s wounds: dried elderberries for the inflammation round his leg wound, calendula for his fever. My mother's distress was infectious, making me want to stay at home round the mill hearth, safe with my family. But at the same time, I wanted to go. I wanted to be of use in the fight that was destroying so many lives.

My heart was beating so loudly, I was sure everybody could hear. Capriolo sensed my hesitation. He pinched my cheek affectionately between his fingers and tucked a stray curl into my cap. 'Don't worry, little Ines, it will go well. You are doing what you have to, like a brave communist. This is the best way to get the *inglese* away from here.'

He slapped the mule's rump and we were away up the track.

The rain had stopped by the time we reached the ridge where the pines grew. Fat drops still splashed off the branches, trickling down my neck and onto the path. Here and there large snails emerged from their hiding places, leaving silver trails. Capriolo had suggested that if I began to panic, I should distract myself from my fear and think of ordinary things.

I couldn't talk to the *inglese*, so I talked to myself, in my head.

Look at you, you wonderful snails. Nonna would love you for her sauces. Should I take some of you back for her? No point. Who knows how long it will be before I come back down the mountain? Nonna loves you for the sauce she makes from you. She drops you in a bucket of cold water to clean out your insides overnight and then pops you in a pan of boiling water.

Further on I spied porcini mushrooms growing in a coppice of holm oak and I started off another silly conversation.

Mmm! I'll have you instead. Pull you up, shake off your spores so I can return and gather more. Clean you with a cloth, slice you thin as thin can be and fry you in butter. Eat you with a plate of Mamma's tagliatelle. Sell the rest at market, buy a headscarf for Sunday Mass.

I should have spoken these fantasies out loud, to make my village idiot act even more convincing. Who knew what the *inglese* would think of me then? As it was, my conversations with myself calmed me as we continued on our way and I urged the mule on with a thwack of my stick whenever he wanted to stop.

We approached a fork in the path. One route descended towards the River Marecchia, the other led to the town of Sansepolcro. Many villagers used this route to escape from the Germans when they carried out their *rastrallamenti*, clearing the hamlets for fighting. The Germans could only know about this route from fascist informers, for it wasn't on any map. In the evenings, round the fire at the mill, I would listen to Capriolo and the others talking and my narrow world stretched wide as I followed their discussions. He spoke of fortifications the Germans were building across from one coast to the other, and how they were turning our beautiful mountains into a big trap, with machine gun pillboxes and camouflaged pits. And they were everywhere. Our country was like a huge cauldron of *minestrone* with many different flavours. Each mouthful was different: some you wanted to spit out, some you could swallow and some you were not sure about, Capriolo said as he explained the situation. We had Germans, fascists, communists, Muslims, Christians, Slavs, Croats and Slovenes all dotted about the place in our mountains.

And it was hard to know whom to trust.

The sun came out and the path steamed as it warmed up. I was perspiring and trickles of sweat ran down my face. I hoped it wouldn't wash away the 'sores' and charcoal that Mamma had daubed on my face.

'*Halt!*' A young German soldier jumped onto the track. Another was crouched behind the rocks by a machine gun. I hadn't noticed them as I daydreamed. '*Documenti!*' he shouted.

My heart was pounding so much I thought it would burst through my ribcage. I stared at him blankly as Capriolo had instructed and then I gave an idiotic, toothless smile, showing off my blackened teeth to their best advantage. He shouted again, waving his gun at me, '*Documenti, documenti!*'

I reached into my pocket, wafting cow shit stench towards him in the process. He covered his face and stepped back, glancing at my papers, the standard Fascist Party documents that we'd all been issued with. He sneered at my photo and made a comment to the other soldier that met with laughter. Then he walked round behind the mule to the cart. My knees were trembling. It was just as well my coat was long and covered my lower limbs.

The *inglese* groaned and I stepped towards the soldier. '*Malato*,' I said, followed by, '*colera.*'

That was what Capriolo told me to say. I mimed vomiting and squatting down as if I were defecating. The German started to prod the sacking covering the *inglese* and I chose that moment to feign a violent coughing attack, making sure I spluttered over the *tedesco*. He shoved me away and waved me on and as I moved forward, the two young Germans roared with laughter, their words sounding hard and ugly.

It took all my self-control not to make the mule break into a trot to get as far away as quickly as we could.

'Above all, remain calm. Act stupid… think of other things than the situation you're in,' Capriolo's words of advice echoed in my head.

I tried to imagine a better time. A time without war and hunger and fear. A time when I could once again dress up on a Sunday and dance in the village square. But I couldn't. I was terrified.

We continued up the path for another hour or so. I was exhausted. My heart stopped its furious beating but my head was aching as I forced my feet to take one step after another. Just when I felt I would faint, there was a low whistle from among the trees and Capriolo jumped onto the track in front of us, together with Paolo and a man called Toni, to whom I was introduced later. I hadn't seen Paolo for some time. I thought he was dead, like so many of our friends. He looked like a man now, not the youngster I remembered from our schoolroom.

Capriolo swept me into his arms and then just as quickly dropped me. *'Porca miseria!* Bloody hell, but you stink. Let's get you out of those rags and washed as soon as possible.' He laughed. 'No wonder they wouldn't touch you. You've done well, Ines. Congratulations! You are one of us now.'

The *inglese* climbed slowly off the cart. He limped over to me, looked into my eyes, kissed my hand. *'Grazie,* signorina!' he said.

Then he collapsed.

CHAPTER ELEVEN

Anna takes a break to make a cup of tea, her head full of her parents' story, which is like an old film starring actors she knows personally. What a shame her parents never discussed all this with their children. She wonders why they hadn't. What possible results could have been so 'cataclysmic', as her mother insisted in her very first letter? The events she is reading about are enthralling, and compared to the memory of her parents' humdrum life, light years away.

She grabs a handful of Teresa's home-baked *cantuccini* biscuits and climbs the stairs to the bedroom, curling up against her pillows to resume reading.

September 1944

I remained in the camp for ten days, and during that time I began to understand more about the struggle, what it's like for Capriolo and his men. Spending evenings with my family and neighbours around our hearth is very different from sharing a piece of hard ground in the company of a bunch of fighting men. I think it has made me start to grow up.

My main job at the camp was to tend to our Englishman, applying the salves and ointments Mamma had recommended. As I nursed him, I began to learn more about the *inglese*. He slept a lot in the first few days, and while he did, I watched over him.

His name isn't too difficult to pronounce – 'Jim'. He told me it is Giacomo in Italian. He is so different from the men I know, with his long legs and blond hair. His skin is milky white. In the earliest days he wore a moustache, but Mamma shaved it off, because his fair whiskers would immediately give away that he wasn't Italian. He looked younger without it. Jim told me he is nearly thirty and that surprised me.

While he recovered, the men kept him inside a kind of shelter constructed from coppiced branches. It was meant to resemble a charcoal mound, like one of many constructed around the mountains by the *carbonari*. In the top of the roof was an opening, and in the centre of the wooded 'tent' a small fire had been lit and smoke spiralled through the hole above him. He lay on a typical mattress made from sacking and stuffed with dried maize leaves. It took a few days before his fever died and he was able to hobble about.

I started to help him learn Italian. He needed to know at least the basics, in case he was ever confronted by the militia. He couldn't stay hidden forever. At first it was difficult, but with the help of one of the group, we made progress. One of Capriolo's band is Toni, the man I met on arrival at the camp. He's fluent in English, and he acted as my interpreter. He told us his family had left for London after the Great War, to make a better life, and that he was born there. His dad is a barber. Toni told us he feels more English than Italian, but he has relatives in our area of Tuscany and his Italian is perfect.

'How did you end up here then?' I asked him.

'We were rounded up in London at the beginning of the war and shipped back to Italy. They didn't want us in England, and they bloody didn't want us back here either. They thought we were spies and banged us up in prison… but I escaped.'

He translated Jim's explanations for us, how he'd been in a camp the other side of Bologna called Fontanellato. When the guards set the British free after the Armistice, most of the other prisoners set off north for Switzerland, but Jim decided to head south to join the Allies who'd made their way up from Anzio, and he thought the terrain would be easier than crossing the Alps. But the route along the Apennines was just as tough and before long, he found himself in difficulties because of his injuries. He slept in barns and was sheltered by peasants and told us he would write a guidebook about Italy if he ever got back to England.

I hope he never makes it back. I'd miss him. Our lessons in the camp are fun. His accent makes me laugh but he's a quick learner – although sometimes he comes out with blasphemous words that the others teach him.

And, in return, he tries to teach me English. I think he chooses the most difficult words for me to learn and when I try to pronounce 'th', he grins. He tells me he likes to see me giggle. I understand almost everything he says, because he mimes for me. Words are not always important between two people, I am discovering.

'It's too difficult, your language,' I said. 'Why are there so many words with these stupid sounds? Italian is more musical.'

When he was able to put weight on his leg, we walked. And his face began to lose its pallor. We never strayed too far from the camp on our walks. If we left the shelter of the canopy of pine trees, any sniper on any one of the ridges in the surrounding hills could pick us off. I told him this exercise was to build up his muscles, but secretly it was because I wanted to be alone with him.

One evening by the fire, I listened as Toni told his story to the group. The men had been drinking wine that evening. Mamma warned me about what wine can do to a man, so I sat apart from the group, in the shadows, eavesdropping on their conversations.

Toni's story was the most shocking, and I didn't want to believe it.

'When I escaped from the concentration camp at Arezzo,' he began, 'I couldn't believe my luck.'

He kicked a log further into the embers and sparks flew up into the night sky.

'Originally my people are from these parts. So the idea of looking up my relatives came to me. On Good Friday I decided to go and find my pa's sister. I'd get a decent meal from her, she'd look after me. Anyway, it took me over a week to make my way through the hills. I had to sneak my way around fucking *tedeschi* machine gun posts and sleep in ditches. The weather wasn't too bad. Spring was in the air. It was wonderful to be free, to listen to owls, the rustlings at night in the open after months of being locked up. You know what I'm talking about.

'As I drew nearer Fragheto, I started to pinpoint landmarks. My parents had talked about the place often enough, so I recognised the narrow, wooded valley, the stream tumbling at the bottom.'

Lighting up another cigarette, he paused for a few seconds.

'I passed through a tiny hamlet and guessed I had another half hour's walk in front of me, so I rested for a bit. Suddenly there were gunshots and I dived for cover into a culvert. The shooting went on and on. When I was sure it was over, I crawled from my hiding place and continued up the hill. As far as possible, I kept to the fields, wary of using the road. But at a certain point it became impossible not to, and then I heard footsteps. Nearby was a thicket of trees and I hid in there.

'A family was hurrying down the road away from the village. One of them, a lad in his late teens, was carrying an old woman on his back. Another woman had a toddler by the hand. The kid was sobbing and the woman was dragging him along behind her. As she hurried past me I could see the little boy's knees scraping on the road. The woman didn't stop to soothe him, ignoring his screams and pulling him on. They were ordinary countryfolk, they weren't going to hurt me, so I came out from my hiding place in the trees and asked if I could help. But they were terrified and rushed past.

'Further up the hill there was a shrine by the side of the road. An old man leant against it, wrapped in a blanket, eyes closed, muttering to himself. I crouched down near him. He opened his eyes and started babbling even louder, "Shoot *me* instead, shoot me," he gabbled, half crazed. "Don't touch the babies."

'I didn't know what the hell had happened in this place, but I soon found out… I approached the houses with caution. Thick smoke filled the air. A dog scampered out of a building and scared the shit out of me. I went down an alleyway leading to a little piazza, and then I came across a scene I never, ever want to witness again.'

Toni paused and rubbed his eyes with the back of his hand.

'Heaped up against the side of the church was a pile of bodies. Blood ran over the cobbles, sticky underfoot. The smell of burning made me gag and I tied my handkerchief round my mouth and went nearer. A child of about two or three, I don't know how old exactly, lay on the ground. He looked asleep but the top of his head was blown off. A woman, most likely his mother, was slumped near him, a dead baby clasped in her arms.'

He broke off and then continued his grim story.

'I found out later my aunt and her two babies were among the dead. Maybe she was the woman I saw among the mangled bodies, I'll never know. I was too young when we left Italy to remember what she looked like. The bastard *tedeschi* and *fascisti* shot thirty-three civilians. There'd been a skirmish with the *partigiani* the day before, further down in the valley. A couple of *tedeschi* were shot and they found *one* wounded partisan in the village, so they decided to carry out a reprisal, the fucking bastards. Most of the dead were women and children. There was even an old man of seventy-four. What did *they* ever do to anybody? They weren't armed. They were just simple peasants.

'You asked me what I'm doing here. Well, that's my fucking reason for coming back here. Revenge! I want to do as much as I can, with my last dying breath if necessary, to avenge the death of my family. Talking about it is not enough.'

He spat into the fire.

My brother Davide got up to pat him on the shoulder, and after Toni had finished speaking, one by one the men moved to the places where they slept. I lay awake for a long time, filled with the horror of his story. How could men do this to women and children? The war was crazy. I could understand why Capriolo, Davide and the others were risking their lives to fight this oppression. I felt proud to be playing a small part in the campaign.

At the end of the ten days, although I didn't want to tear myself away, I had to return to the mill. My parents needed me to help and Capriolo said the camp was no place for a woman on her own. He sent me down with Davide and I moaned the whole way along the mountain track.

'You're beginning to sound like Nonna when she sits by the fire and grumbles in the kitchen,' he told me.

'I wish I were a man and could do what I wanted,' I snapped. 'It's all right for you.'

'And I wish I could sleep in a soft bed like you and sit by the hearth in the evenings. Accept, Ines, accept. You always have to kick against everything.'

'It's easy for you to talk like that. You get what you want without a fight. Try being me, and you wouldn't preach at me the way you do.'

'And that's why you nag so much. Because you're a woman,' he said.

I picked up a handful of pine cones and lobbed them at him. He laughed, ducking and protecting his face from my missiles.

'I suppose you're going to sneak in a visit with Carla while you're down here,' I teased. 'You always say you're off to check on the sheep, but there's no way your girlfriend is a sheep.'

I knew he crept away at home to spend time with her. I wondered what excuse he used for leaving the camp to come and see her.

He pulled off my headscarf and tied it on a branch out of my reach. 'That's what you get for being nosy. Were you spying on us?'

'Take it down, Davi. It's the only one I've got.'

We kept squabbling and laughing, until suddenly we heard footsteps behind us. Davide grabbed me, pulling me down into a ditch filled with dry leaves near to the path. He put his finger to his mouth, warning me to keep quiet.

A man walked by. It was Toni. Davide called to him and Toni sprang round, a pistol pointed at us.

'Hey, Toni! It's only us. Put that thing down,' Davide called, standing up, hands raised. I stayed where I was.

'Never do that to me again, fucking idiot,' Toni growled. 'I could have shot you.'

'Where are you off to?' Davide asked. 'I thought you were on guard duty today.'

'Someone is covering for me. I have business in Badia,' he replied.

'Walk part of the way with us,' Davide suggested.

'Us?'

I got up from the ditch, brushing leaves from the trousers Davide had given me to wear. 'Will somebody please get my headscarf down?'

They laughed, before Toni untied the scarf and presented it to me with an exaggerated bow. Then we all continued on our way. As we walked together, Davide asked a favour of Toni. 'You must have helped your dad in the barber's in London. I need a haircut.'

'For when he visits his Carla,' I chipped in.

'Ines, leave it out,' Davi said.

'I'll see what I can do,' Toni replied.

'Thanks, comrade,' Davide said. 'Can't remember the last time I had this trimmed.' He held up a long lock of his curly hair. 'I'm starting to look like a woman.'

CHAPTER TWELVE

October, 1944

Life down at the mill is so dull, so tedious in comparison with my days up at the camp.

How can I find an excuse to go up the mountain again? Mamma keeps giving me jobs and they fill my days. I spend whole afternoons sweeping dust from the milling machinery, cleaning out the hoppers for when we grind again, setting traps for mice. We are extra busy because we have to prepare for harvest time, at least for those few people who have any wheat to bring down to us for grinding. Papà says it will be a very lean harvest, and only a few old men have been available to work in the meadows.

Over the past days he's moaned on and on about the crops left to rot on the ground last year, when so many of the young men had to flee and hide in the hills to escape from being sent to work in Germany.

And this year the Germans took much of the grain to feed their horses.

'Bloody war, bloody Germans, bloody fascists,' he swore as he chopped up wood for our fire.

Mamma came rushing to find me as I was sweeping round the millstones.

'Quick, the finance guards are coming down the road, Ines. Go and tidy yourself, put on your new headscarf. Keep them busy.'

I hate oily Sergeant Ezio, the worst of all the guards. I hate the way his eyes slide up and down my body, undressing me. It makes me feel like one of the women who stand on the street corners down in Sansepolcro, keeping themselves warm by their fires. Davide has told me they call them *lucciole*, but I think it's a pity to call them fireflies. These little insects light up at mating time each June, flitting over our hayfield at night like twinkling stars, but one I caught in a jam jar last summer looked very ordinary in daylight, a disappointing, dirty little grub. Mamma has warned me about Anna Maria up in Badia and called her a *lucciola*. She said she's 'been' with a German soldier and that the women in the village are bound to punish her one day. They'll pin her down at the fountain where they do their washing and shave off her hair, she says, and then she will have to wear a headscarf for months until it grows again. I don't want Ezio thinking I am like Anna Maria.

'Don't worry, Ines, I won't leave you alone with him for long. I'll come and help you out,' Mamma continued. 'Papà caught a trout in the river yesterday. That'll keep him happy and stop him poking his nose into what we're doing.'

Mamma is worried too about the guards finding her hiding place in the woods. Strict rationing has been introduced, with severe penalties adding to all our other burdens. At the mill, we are meant to distribute 250 grams of grain per month, per person. But Mamma knows that many families and especially widows can't manage on this meagre ration. A lot of households have extra mouths to feed with evacuees from the cities or young men avoiding conscription.

I thought back to a conversation between my parents a couple of months before I took Jim up to the camp. 'Aldo,' Mamma had said to my father one evening, as we sat eating our polenta supper, 'I can't sit by and see our friends starve because of these mean rations.'

He looked up, a mushroom from the woods speared on his fork. 'And what do you suppose we can do about it? The police are always hanging around when we distribute flour.'

'We'll hide it for them.'

'Hah!' he grunted scornfully. 'And where do you plan to do that? Up a tree?'

'No, under the trees.'

'Now I know the war has really got to you, woman. You're even crazier than your mother.'

Nonna is deaf, so she couldn't hear my father's insult.

'You could dig a hole in the woods over there for me.' Mamma gestured to the window overlooking the trees on the other side of the river.

'And fill it with flour so that the animals in the forest can get into it, not to say rain and mud. What kind of an idea is that?' Papà finished off her sentence and snorted.

At that, my mother flew into a temper and stood up at the table. I was waiting for the usual argument to follow. My mother is a fiery woman. When she has an idea in her head, nobody can shift her.

'Aldo – if you don't dig it, I will. And then you can sleep in the stable with the cows. Where are all your principles now? You're good at spouting when you're with your drinking friends in the *osteria*, but here at home you sound like a defeated coward.'

She reached angrily for the bottle of red wine to stop my father drinking any more.

'I will not be spoken to like this in my own home,' Papà shouted. 'Stop your nonsense talk, woman.'

I tried to intervene.

'I'll help dig it, Papà. It's not such a bad idea.'

He looked at us and then threw up his hands in resignation. 'What can I do against the might of women? I'm surrounded by you – even Mimi is a woman,' he said. Then the old Papà I know chuckled. 'I'm sorry to fly off the handle. This war is getting to me. Thank you, Ines, for your kind offer to help me.' He looked over to Mamma, who shrugged her shoulders as if to say she knew he would climb down eventually.

I patted Papà's shoulder and went over to stroke Mimi.

'We could line the hole with wood, so the flour doesn't spoil,' I suggested from where I was crouching by the dog.

'Exactly what I was planning, before your father interrupted. And leave it in sacks there at night,' my mother continued, 'and our friends can collect it under cover of darkness, away from the mill.'

My father grudgingly agreed to the plan. 'We must all be careful, for if we're caught...' He dragged his hand in a cutting gesture across his throat.

And so, ever since that time, we have started leaving flour in the woods, and Papà has begun to think Ezio is growing suspicious. He has seen him loitering on the other side of the river too often. Maybe somebody up in the village opened his mouth in the *osteria*. We have to be so careful. Dreadful things have been happening all the time to people we know. Papà told us of the latest victims of the Germans – Gino and Tommasina, an elderly couple in their seventies who were shot because they hid a wounded partisan in their pigsty. The partisan was their nephew.

'You're looking very pretty today, Ines.'

Ezio leant against the stone wall of the millpond, twiddling his moustaches, his uniform too tight on his fat body. He smelt strongly of olive oil. He'd smeared it on his head in an attempt to smooth his few thin hairs over his bald patch. I wanted to giggle. He looked like a pig ready for the spit. I cast my eyes down demurely, hoping the laughter in my eyes wouldn't betray me.

'Are you coming to the dance on Sunday afternoon? The party is putting on a special celebration. There will be music, and the

Germans are providing plenty of food. A girl like you shouldn't be hiding herself away from the world down by the river. The Germans want company, and so do I.'

If only he knew, I thought to myself. *If only he knew about my escapes up the mountain, about the company I keep with his enemy.* Little did this fat, oily pig know.

'You know my parents won't allow me,' I mumbled, 'it wouldn't be right. Davide is away, and I wouldn't be allowed to come alone.'

'Leave it with me. I shall talk to your parents.' He pushed himself away from the wall towards me and I stepped back, increasing the distance between us. I couldn't retreat any further – I would have fallen in the river. His unwashed, greasy smell was strong in my nostrils as Mamma timed her appearance perfectly at the top of the steps. A second later and I would have slapped his stupid fat face, but it didn't do to anger the police, and especially vile Ezio.

'I have something for you, Ezio.' Mamma handed him a trout wrapped in wet sacking. 'Give it to your mother to cook tonight. It's freshly caught today.'

He had the grace at least to bow slightly to my mother. 'I want your permission to dance with Ines at the *festa* on Sunday,' he said. 'There will be a celebration for the arrival of a new German SS platoon in Badia. We're expecting as many people to turn out as possible.'

I was standing behind Ezio and I gave my mother a pleading look.

'I'm not sure we can spare her,' she said. 'There are too many jobs to be completed, and with so few hands to help…' She shrugged, a defeated look on her face.

'We have already noted your husband's absence from the party meetings lately, signora,' he said menacingly. 'You would all be wise to show your faces more often. A good start would be to come to the *festa*.'

'I will speak to my husband,' my mother replied. 'But if Ines goes, we will of course accompany her.'

Over our supper of bread and beans we talked and talked about what to do for the best.

'Please don't make me go,' I pleaded. 'If Ezio so much as lays a finger on me, I swear I shall scream and make a spectacle.'

Mamma backed me up. 'If Ines kicks up a fuss and refuses to dance with him, then it will make life even more difficult for us. At the moment we can give the guards bribes of fish from the river and distract them, but it wouldn't take much to make them turn nasty.'

Papà agreed. 'There is no way any fascist will walk out with a daughter of mine.'

There was silence in the kitchen, save for the occasional crackle from a burning twig and Nonna's sighs as she sat crocheting near the hearth.

At length, Papà sighed too. 'There's nothing for it. Ines will have to go up the mountain again for a while. We'll explain to Ezio that she's gone to stay with your sister in Pennabilli. We'll say she's ill and that Ines has to look after her Zia Elda.'

'What a good idea, Aldo. *Bravo!*' My mother rose from the table. 'Ines, help me get together some things for your stay. Davide will take care of you up there. You can take up more herbs and medicines for the men as well. And we have one spare pecorino cheese left that you can give them.'

'Give them the rest of the ham, too, Assunta. We can manage without it. Take Mimi to help protect you, and send her back down after you arrive. She knows the way and we need her down here to guard the animals.'

*

My parents want to avoid my having anything to do with Ezio and so do I. My honour is at stake, but they don't know of my growing feelings for Jim, although in truth, even Jim doesn't know. They are feelings I keep firmly inside my head and yearn about in bed at night. Of course I'm not going to tell anybody about it, especially not my parents, otherwise I shall be forbidden to go up to the camp. I am to leave at dawn tomorrow morning, and we worked into the night preparing a bundle of clothes for myself and food and medicines for the men.

I am excited and anxious, feeling my life is never going to be the same again. As I embraced Mamma and Papà in the fresh September morning, I clung to them and covered their faces with kisses. My mother was crying again as she tied the belt round my filthy coat and checked no curls were escaping from my brother's cap, which I'd pulled firmly down over my brow. My faithful disguise.

I avoided the route we took with Jim in the cart. Capriolo has told me of an alternative route but warned me I still had to be very careful as the Germans are always changing their guard posts. They continue to dig new trenches and use caves all over the mountains to house their machine guns and store ammunition.

The moon hung in the sky like a cold river pearl, and the leaves on the oak trees rustled like long skirts. The scent of dew-soaked pine needles was strong. A twig snapped somewhere in the woods and my heart hammered. The sound of deer galloping through the undergrowth nearly had me screaming with terror. I thought they were soldiers, but I saw a couple of stags scamper off deeper into the trees and my heartbeat slowed down. I was still an hour's

trek away from the camp, feeling very alone, very afraid, and I
didn't honestly know what I would have done if even oily Ezio
had appeared in front of me and offered to accompany me for
the rest of the journey. To my shame, I would probably have said
yes. Once again I used Capriolo's strategy, diverting myself from
descending into sheer panic by making pictures in my mind.

What if I made a life with Ezio – cooked for him, produced
his children? I would probably live in the village, stepping across
the square every morning to the grocer's store knowing I was
being stared at by old crones from behind shuttered windows.
At the fountain where women washed clothes, nobody would
talk to me and all my school friends would despise me for having
succumbed to his persuasions. But at least I would still be alive.

Then I pictured myself in the arms of Jim, living in a house
far away across the mountains and sea. In a house like those I've
seen in a couple of American movies flickering on a screen erected
in the piazza at *festa* time before the war. It would be a square
house, with flowers at the windows and a veranda at the front
with a swinging seat. I know Jim isn't American, he is English.
But he speaks the same language and, to my way of thinking, the
houses are bound to be the same. I wondered if we would have
children with blond curls. Or if they would have my dark looks.
Would they be tall? What would it be like to sleep in Jim's arms
night after night? What would it be like to lie with a man? He
hasn't kissed me. No man has ever kissed me properly – Capriolo's
childish, after-school kisses don't count. But I want to kiss Jim.

I asked myself how I could ever have even thought of compar-
ing Jim with loathsome Ezio.

At the base of the rock where I knew one of Capriolo's band
would be on guard, I threw up a handful of stones. And I whistled

the first line of the partisans' song, '*Ciao, bella, ciao…*' as he'd instructed. It was light now. Birds had started their morning greetings. I needn't have gone through the cloak-and-dagger routine because Mimi started to bark excitedly. She must have sensed Davide was around and, as luck would have it, he was coming to the end of his guard duties. His sleepy face appeared from above the rock, breaking into a grin when he recognised Mimi.

'Ines, what in God's name are you doing up here again?' Then a worried look came over his face. 'What is it? Not Papà? Mamma?'

'No, don't worry. Just come down and get me, and I'll explain later. And bring something to shut Mimi up. She'll be waking the whole of Tuscany before too long. And what on earth has happened to your hair, Davi? You look like a convict.'

His hair has been badly trimmed and there are cuts where I imagined the razor slipped.

'Let's just say that Toni obviously never helped out much in his father's barber shop.'

I grimaced. 'You look terrible. What will Carla think?'

He shrugged. 'It will grow again. Carla doesn't like me for my hair, anyway.'

I sniggered and sat down, exhausted from my trek.

Davide was joined by Capriolo and another two men I'd never seen before. They led us through a passage concealed by creepers into the heart of the camp and tied Mimi to a tree, throwing her a bone and placing a bowl of water nearby. Davide helped me with my heavy bundles.

'Careful with that sack,' I said. 'There are jars in there with Mamma's medicines, and Papà's sent you up the last of the *prosciutto*.'

Davide fetched me coffee and a hunk of bread and I told them about Ezio.

'He's getting worse. He hangs around too much, and is always bothering us about not attending fascist meetings. And yesterday he asked me to the dance, and I thought he was going to grab me but Mamma arrived just in time.'

Capriolo spat into the dust. 'He always was a little shit. Even at school he used to lift the girls' skirts in the playground. Wait until I get my hands on him…' He snapped a stick in half across his knee and threw it on the fire. Sparks flew up like ammunition.

'Well, Ines,' he said, wiping dust off his trousers, 'you will have to make yourself useful if you stay up here. We have an important project planned in the next few days. Davide is leaving tomorrow for Rimini with information needed for the next big assault.'

'Papà told us that Firenze was taken back from the Germans last month. Is that true?'

'Yes. And the British are heading this way. It will be Rimini next that falls. The way we are going, the war will be over before too long and we can return to normal life. We can settle down, reclaim our country and plant our crops again.'

'You're beginning to sound quite old and established!' I teased. I looked at my classmate, the boy who'd shared my childhood games. I pinched his cheek between my fingers and he grasped hold of my hand.

'Don't laugh at me, Ines. If you'd seen half of what we've seen, you would understand how sick we are of all this. We don't enjoy fighting, you know. It's not a game.' He looked into my eyes and I turned away, pulling my hand from his, puzzled at this young man I thought I knew so well.

I changed the subject. 'Where shall I sleep? I'm here for longer this time. Where shall I sort out my things?' I felt awkward in his company.

Something of his old sense of humour returned. 'Well, there is the double room with the view over the Apennines, or the single with its own terrace and view of the German trenches but no bathroom, I'm afraid.'

He gestured to a sheltered place under the rocks, a small hollow in the stone face where rain and sun wouldn't reach. I dumped my bundles and went to see if I could help in the kitchen area.

I didn't see Jim until later that evening. He, Toni and a couple of others were away all that day and returned to the camp tired and hot. A month of mountain air has built Jim up. He looks stronger, more handsome and taller than I remember, maybe because he isn't limping like before. His hair has grown longer, too, and he's caught the sun, losing that sick, sallow look of weeks ago. But there is still no way he could pass for an Italian. He smiled at me and I smiled back, my heart turning crazy somersaults.

'Have you learned that English tongue-twister yet, Ines?'

I made him laugh with my attempt at 'Sixty-six thick thistle sticks' and asked him to repeat an Italian saying I'd taught him a few weeks earlier.

We all ate by the fire. It was only lit at night, when darkness hid smoke from anybody searching for signs of partisan presence in the mountains. We were camped too far away from any *carbonari*, so couldn't use their fires as our cover. No flames or sparks would be seen in the night sky by anybody outside this camp as we were in a deep hollow. It was a kind of natural fortress.

Jim and I talked softly. My brother and Capriolo were further away, deep in discussion about the mission tomorrow.

'I've missed you, Ines. It's so good to see you again.' His Italian is much improved.

I explained why my parents had sent me up. 'I hope Ezio believes them and doesn't take it into his head to check my whereabouts in Pennabilli. It's not that far away from Badia,' I said.

'Maybe I should go looking for *him*. I can't stand the thought of him ogling you.'

I put my hand on his arm. 'Don't be foolish! You would be recognised straight away as an Englishman. There is a high price offered for prisoners of war, and plenty of starving people round here who would be pleased to claim the money.'

He caught hold of my hand, his fingers big and strong on mine. I felt myself blushing.

'Anyway,' I continued, reluctantly pulling my hand away, 'you will be gone soon. The English have won back Firenze, then it will be Rimini and then you will disappear back to *Inghilterra*. You will forget all about the war and Ezio… and me.'

I wanted to provoke him into denying this. I thought I knew what he felt about me but I wanted to hear it from his own lips, and wished we were alone.

'I'll be leaving here for a few days, Ines. I'm going away with Capriolo,' Jim told me. 'He needs me in case we meet up with other British prisoners of war. Toni is great but I know more about our forces, and can tell if any are Germans acting as spies. It happens, you know.'

My heart sank. Up here in the camp, the war seemed distant, despite the guns stacked inside the cave.

'You've all been so kind to me,' he said, 'but my leg is much better now. It's time for me to play my part.'

'Has the scar healed? Show me.' As I reached out to roll up his trouser leg, shy as my fingers moved across his skin, Capriolo's voice startled me and I jumped away from Jim, feeling guilty.

'Jim, I need to talk to you. I'm considering sending Davide over to Arezzo with new information tomorrow, to meet up with the *partigiani* there. Come, we have to discuss final plans.'

And to me he said, 'I think you should go and talk to your brother, wish him luck. He'll be gone for a while. And then, sleep. We need you up sharp tomorrow. This is not a holiday camp.'

I felt like answering 'Yes, Papà!' and sticking my tongue out at him. But I didn't.

Davide was sitting by the fire and I sank down beside him. He was staring into the flames and hardly noticed me. We sat for a while in silence. He looks so much younger than Jim, and so Italian with his dark hair and skin burnt by a summer of living outside on the mountains. Eventually he turned to me and I thought I read fear in his eyes.

'Ines, tomorrow I'm leaving here and going with Toni and the others. First to Arezzo and then down to Rimini. There's fierce fighting there. We have information needed by our Allies for the counter-attack. If anything happens, I want you to take this to our parents.' He handed me a folded piece of paper. 'Don't give it to them unless anything happens to me. And Ines, promise me you'll look after them.'

I put my arms round him and held him tight. 'Don't talk soft, little brother. Everything will be fine.'

But I dug deep into my overcoat pocket and pulled out Mamma's rosary beads she gave me when I brought Jim up the mountain. I wound them round my brother's hands.

'Take these. They've kept me safe and they'll keep you safe too.'

The next day dawned hot and sultry, the type of heavy weather that heralds a storm. The air had no breath, and the mountains seemed to close in and suffocate the land.

I was woken by a fierce argument between Davide and Capriolo. Davide was very upset.

'You treat me like a child, Capriolo. I need to come too. Yesterday you told me I was included.'

'There's a new plan, Davide. I need you to stay here and keep guard. You're more useful to me in camp.'

'But I've trained for this, and who was it that found the documents in the first place? I thought you were going to let me deliver them to Arezzo,' I heard my brother shout.

'Keep your voice down. I've changed my mind. Don't forget it was you who shot the German major on the motorbike on the Rimini road. Your face is known to the survivors and is on posters everywhere. Best to lie low for a while.'

'Well, why didn't you tell me this last night? Why spring it on me now?'

'I told you – I've changed my mind. There will be other occasions when I need you with me, but not today.'

'But—'

'No buts, Davide. I have the final say. You'd do well to remember our fight is not all about you.' Now it was Capriolo whose voice was raised. 'Let that be the last of it. Either obey my orders or leave.'

Listening to all this, I couldn't imagine my young brother killing a man. But of course, this is war. And people die all the time.

Then Capriolo came over to me with Jim. I watched Davide slump against a boulder, a scowl on his face. He looked so young.

'Can you take a look at Jim's leg, Ines?' Capriolo asked. 'It's flared up again in the night. I doubt he'll be joining us today either.'

'Of course,' I said, my heart singing at the thought that Jim and Davide would both be safe for today at least. Last night by the fire it felt as if I was saying goodbye to my brother forever.

I smiled at my patient and hoped nobody would see how my fingers trembled as I applied a poultice to his shin. Each touch on his body was like dipping my hands into warm water, my tummy turning over as I smoothed the cloth over the wound.

'He's in no fit state to walk far, Capriolo,' I said, concentrating intently on binding Jim's leg, willing my cheeks to stop burning.

The journey usually took two hours by road, but of course Capriolo and his band would not be in a vehicle. They would criss-cross the hills on foot, making their way stealthily down into the valley, no doubt coming across Germans dug in in their bunkers. I didn't want to think about it too much.

After they left, the camp was almost empty. Capriolo took Toni and most of the men and couldn't say when they would be back. The only people left were myself, Jim, Davide, now on guard duties, the old cook and a couple of lads recovering from wounds. They were pleased to have me there with Mamma's salves. One had been bitten by a viper and I used sunflower seeds to paste onto his swollen ankle and gave him wormwood for his fever. I did what I could for the other young lad, the butcher's son. I was more used to seeing him chop up meat, wrapping up parcels, whistling as he went about his work. But he lay there on his makeshift mattress of sacking, ashen-faced, suffering violent stomach cramps. I brewed him a drink from basil and boiled water and sat holding his hand until he dropped back to sleep. He was far too young to be fighting in a war, and I didn't imagine he would see the war end.

Tending to Jim was completely different, and as I prepared a poultice for his leg, I wondered where our conversation would lead us today.

CHAPTER THIRTEEN

Early June 1999

The ringing of Anna's mobile drags her back to the present, interrupting her mother's story.

'*Pronto!* Francesco again. Just checking you're all right.'

Anna shakes her head, trying to adjust her focus from the pictures in her mind of the young people in the forest to the cosy, everyday world of her bedroom, dust motes dancing in the fresh mountain air coming in at the open window. An image of Francesco springs to mind, dressed in raggedy clothes, surrounded by partisans, an ammunition belt slung around his shoulder. She hesitates over her response.

'I'm fine.'

'You don't sound too sure.'

'I've been immersed in 1944,' Anna says, rubbing her eyes. 'I can hardly believe what my mother went through. I wonder how you or I would have coped. They were so courageous, Francesco.'

'Nobody knows how they will react until they're in that situation. But I hope I'd have been part of their fight, like my own father. Anyway, let me drag you into the present – are you free tomorrow afternoon to come out with us? Remember I told you about Pennabilli and the *festa* of the street musicians?'

At first Anna is so dazed she doesn't realise why Pennabilli sounds familiar – and then the memories of what she's just read make the connection.

'That place rings a bell – wasn't it where Mamma was supposed to be staying, looking after her sick aunty instead of being at the camp? I'd love to come along and see what it's like.'

'It's a pretty town, and it will serve as an introduction to the locations you're reading about.'

'Great! And what about the mill where my mother lived?'

'It's a ruin. But I'll take you there very soon. Oh, and bring something warm to put on later when it's dark and the temperature drops.'

They take the road down towards Rimini, Alba sitting in the back, hunched in the corner, staring out of the window, ignoring Anna, who gives up trying to include her in the conversation. And anyway, turning to speak to her is making Anna carsick on the hairpin bends. Francesco knows the road well and she feels safe, despite the steep drops. The road winds down one side of the mountain range with the River Marecchia below. Rocky, impenetrable forested slopes snake up from the river valley. Every now and again they pass a cluster of ruined houses perched impossibly on crags high above them.

'Do you realise how beautiful all this is?' Anna says. 'And how lucky you are to live here? Or do you take it for granted?'

In her mind she compares it with the view from the train window on her commute to London, remembering how she used to gaze into gardens backing on to the tracks. A few were neat, with vegetable patches or patios, but most were unkempt dumping grounds. She'd count abandoned supermarket trolleys in the back yards and try to imagine what kind of people lived in each house.

Francesco shrugs his shoulders. 'I suppose we're used to it. Most of these hamlets in the mountains are uninhabited, with maybe a few of the houses used by weekenders.'

He points to a building on a ridge above the valley, towering over the countryside like a lone guard. 'See the crane up there? That farmhouse is being restored for an English family.'

'I can't begin to imagine how they built those houses in the past, or how they worked such steep land,' Anna says, peering out of the back window.

'They didn't have much choice. If you could have seen this countryside thirty, forty years ago, there were far fewer trees everywhere. People needed every bit of land they could use to grow food for their families. It was a hand-to-mouth existence. Many found it too hard, and after the war there was no work. Italy was on her knees. Some peasants went north to work in factories in Turin. Others went abroad, many to France. But their houses remained in the family... like that house with the steep outside staircase in our village. That belongs to another aunt of ours who speaks French just as well as she speaks Italian. She returns every August to live in it for a month. That same story is repeated all over Italy. Roots are very important to us – we need to return to them. We tend to say "I am Florentine", or "I am Roman". We rarely say "I'm Italian".'

'I've noticed that. But it makes it all the stranger to me that I know so little about my mother's roots.'

'I'm sure you'll find out more, Anna.'

They continue their journey in silence, and as she enjoys the spectacular mountain scenery, she thinks about her parents, imagining how they too might have used this same road in the past, wondering where they might have been going and why. She thinks about the passage of time, and how short a lifetime is in the scheme of things. As they pass another rocky outcrop, she cranes her neck to look up, picturing a soldier dug in, waiting to take a shot at the enemy, and she murmurs almost to herself, 'What a terrain to have to contend with!'

'What did you say?' Francesco asks, changing down a gear to negotiate a sharp bend.

'I was thinking about the partisans fighting in the hills, and I was trying to imagine them battling on these slopes. It could have been my father, or my uncle…'

'The Germans used these mountains to form a line of defence. It was known as the Gothic Line.'

'My mother mentions that.'

'Ready for a potted history now, Anna? The Apennines form a spine along our peninsula and they used the mountains as one part of a barrier. Then, in the plains on the east and west coasts, near Rimini and Pisa, they added man-made barriers.'

'You know a lot about it.'

'Sure! We're talking Italian history here, and don't forget, my father was a partisan too.'

'What was his name?'

'Dario.'

'Were you close?'

'Very. But he didn't talk about the war that often – he only told us one or two stories. For example, how they sabotaged the concrete the Germans ordered for their pillboxes. They made it so it wouldn't set. But there were repercussions. There were some who thought the partisans caused more harm than good when the Germans punished ordinary citizens in retaliation – but best not to go into detail.' He gestures discreetly to the back seat where Alba is staring out of the window.

'It's sad to be discovering about my mother's past now she's no longer alive. There are dozens of questions I would have put to her. In England we know a lot about the French Resistance, but don't hear about what went on in Italy.'

She sighs. 'Let's change the subject and have a break from the war. It's too sad to think about it all the time.'

'Okay! *Va bene!* We're nearly there, anyway.'

They take a right off the Rimini road and after a short drive up a narrow lane they enter a town after a sign announcing: PENNABILLI – THE CITY THAT WELCOMES ARTISTS.

As soon as the car stops, Alba clambers out, jumping up and down in excitement.

'This is one of her favourite places,' Francesco explains. 'You'll see why.'

After paying the 5,000 lire entrance fee to a barefoot youth with dreadlocks sitting cross-legged on a table blocking the alleyway, they stroll up a cobbled street closed to traffic. To Anna the place seems at first to be another typical picturesque medieval town, one of many found in Italy. Alba pulls her father up a narrow lane and they climb to an area at the top. In the walled gardens of a ruined house, unusual carved stone statues bearing inscriptions have been arranged to form 'a sanctuary of thoughts'. Francesco helps Anna decipher messages written for travellers bound for eastern shores. As they make their way back to the main square, he points out colourful sundials painted on the facades of certain buildings.

'This is Alba's favourite,' he says, resting his hand on his daughter's head. She has stopped beneath a bright blue and yellow image of a duck floating on choppy waters, and she leans up to trace the outlines with her finger.

'She used to call Pennabilli her picture-story place. When Silvana was alive, we came here often as a family. I thought she'd find it upsetting to return, but she never does.'

Anna watches Alba skip towards the next sundial. *Onlookers would never detect her problems*, she thinks to herself. *On the outside she seems like any ordinary eight-year-old.*

'I think she's a very artistic child,' she says. 'I love her paintings. She has talent and probably feels at home here amid the art. Perhaps you shouldn't analyse so much. Maybe it's simply a place she loves, a place of happy memories.'

'You're probably right. But if she would only talk, then maybe I'd stop trying to analyse. It's so hard.'

He looks sad, and she feels like squeezing his hand, hugging him. But she knows Alba would be jealous, so she says and does nothing. They walk down to the square, packed now. He explains how two years previously a young man had started up a festival for buskers and invited performers from as far away as South America to attend. As word has spread, it has grown in popularity.

They stop to listen to a group of Mongolian throat singers performing melancholy tunes. Alba crouches down near the only woman in the group. Her fingers coax plaintive chords from a zither and she's dressed in an elaborate beaded costume, long black plaits hanging below her bonnet. It is completely un-Italian music, but the sound drifts around the square and blends perfectly with the atmosphere.

After a while they move on to the source of jazzier music drifting from a turret on the old bastion walls. A group of English musicians, led by a diminutive female saxophonist, has everybody tapping their feet and a few couples jigging to the cheeky lyrics. Alba persuades Francesco to dance and Anna watches him bend his dark head down to hers and scoop her into his arms, whirling her round and round until she squeals.

'After all that, I need to sit for a while,' he says, laughing as he sets her down, watching her regain her balance from their dizzy dance. 'Let's go and sit quietly in the amphitheatre. I'll fetch us all a drink and we'll watch the mime artists.'

They find front-row seats. It's beginning to grow dark, and the town is filling up with people coming from work, looking forward to an evening of unusual entertainment. The two young mime artists on stage are talented. They juggle with coloured balls, pretending to be inept at first, dropping them into the audience, which serves to highlight their true skills when they transform themselves ingeniously into different characters and objects with nothing but a roll of masking tape. Alba claps her hands when they create dancing partners from the tape and perform an extravagant tango. Next, they don long black cloaks and become spooky giants, swooping down suddenly onto the audience of children in the front row, who shriek in terror and delight. As they wave goodbye at the end of their act, Francesco grabs Anna's arm. 'Where's Alba? Is she next to you?'

The little girl is nowhere to be seen, and Anna tries to reassure him. 'I don't think she liked it when they were in those cloaks. Maybe she moved further to the back?'

They can't find her in the amphitheatre. In the main square, Anna pounces on a little girl with the same bouncy curls but when she turns round, it isn't Alba.

'*Mi scusi!*' she says to the anxious mother, who pulls her child closer.

Francesco is growing more and more worried. 'I think we should go and look in the stone sanctuary, and if she isn't there, I'm going to the *carabinieri*,' he says.

They hurry up the alleys to the old town again, pushing people out of the way in their need to reach the top. Every band or performer they rush past on each corner plays a different kind of music, and now the sounds jar and jangle their nerves, like the soundtrack to a thriller movie.

When they reach the sanctuary, they search frantically behind the strange stones, calling Alba's name, but she isn't there either. Francesco pulls Anna by the hand. 'This way – there's a shortcut back to the square.'

They run up crooked steps to a grassy slope above the rooftops, where a Buddhist prayer wheel sits incongruously opposite a rusting metal cross, and they make for a narrow path leading down the opposite side. Right at the top of the climb is a ruined house fronted by a patch of overgrown garden. Anna almost trips over a shape in the gloom and stops still. 'Here, Francesco!'

At the edge of the garden, Alba is crouching by the railings.

Francesco grabs her. 'Are you hurt, *tesoro?*' he asks, covering her face with kisses, following this up with a severe scolding. 'But why did you run off like that? We've been so worried.'

She struggles in his arms, pointing at something below. They follow the line of her outstretched finger and approach the railings. On a ledge in the rocks is a tiny kitten in danger any minute of falling to its death. Without thinking, Anna pulls off her jacket, lies flat on the ground and pushes her arm through the rusting rails, grabbing the terrified, scratching little bundle of fur and pulling it to safety. Alba kneels next to her, stroking the trembling animal.

'Gently,' Anna says. 'You mustn't frighten it. Keep very, very still and quiet.'

After a while, she wraps the kitten in her jacket and places it in Alba's arms and she stares up at her father with imploring eyes, not needing words to convey what she is asking.

'I personally think it would be a good idea,' Anna intercedes before Francesco can refuse. 'She's clearly a stray, and I'm sure Teresa would be pleased to have a mouser around the *agriturismo.*'

But he disagrees. 'Teresa would not be at all pleased to have a dirty animal around her paying guests.'

Alba squeezes the kitten tighter to her chest, looking up at Anna, who suggests, without having thought it through, 'Why don't I keep it? Then Alba can come and visit and help look after it. How's that for an idea, Francesco?'

She looks meaningfully at him, willing him to agree, but she doesn't have to plead for long.

He leans over his daughter's head and strokes the tiny animal with gentle fingers. 'The first thing we shall do is call in at the vet's tomorrow morning.'

Turning to Alba, he says, 'And you must say a big thank you to Anna.'

They find a box beside an overflowing bin outside a bar and the kitten, newly christened Billi, after the hilltop city where he was found, scratches and mews in his cardboard prison all the way home. Anna wonders what on earth she has let herself in for, but one look in the mirror at the sight of Alba's happy little face reminds her why she offered. Alba beams her a huge thank you smile and Anna wishes the little girl could allow herself to say it in words.

'I have a suggestion,' Francesco says. 'Your hands will be full this evening with your new housemate, so how about I sort supper and bring it round to your place?'

Back at her house in the square, Anna decides to confine the kitten temporarily to the bathroom until after the visit to the vet. That way, it will be easier to clean up any messes. She showers quickly. Billi cowers in the corner, looking up at her with round, startled eyes after a watery christening. After changing into clean jeans and a red silk blouse, she lays the table for three in the corner of the living room, using the bright tablecloth she bought in the market at Badia. It's perfect, adding a touch of homeliness to the minimalist room. She guesses it won't look half as good back in England.

Francesco arrives as she searches for paper napkins. He wears a tailored white shirt and black jeans and looks stylish, in the way only Italian men can. He greets her with a kiss on each cheek. She likes the musky-scented aftershave he's splashed on his face and nearly asks him what it is.

'Where's Alba?' she asks.

'She is, how do you say it – zonked out. Teresa's put her to bed with the promise of missing school so she can come to the vet's in the morning. I think she worked out that if she went to bed early, then the morning would come sooner.' He chuckles.

Anna isn't disappointed. It will be good to have a chance to talk to him without feeling she almost has to ask Alba's permission.

With a flourish, he pulls a cloth from the tray he's carried in. 'We must eat this while it's still warm. Teresa gave me some extra restaurant food and I'm not going to tell you what anything is. You'll enjoy guessing. But first, try this.'

She picks up the glass of red wine he's poured, in the way she always does, cupping the bowl in her palm. He puts his hand over hers and lifts the glass until the stem is between her thumb and forefinger. His fingers feel warm and she doesn't want him to let go.

'Otherwise you will heat the wine,' he explains, removing his hands from hers. 'Now hold it to the light, swirl it around and look at the sides of the glass. Look for the arcs the wine leaves – they show its strength – the closer together, the stronger. Next, savour it in your mouth before swallowing it. Wait for the aftertaste.'

'History and wine-tasting lessons all in the same day! Is there no end to the man's talents?' she says jokingly. But she does as he instructs and the wine tastes good.

'Do you remember we were talking about how peasants scraped a living from the land?' he asks, holding up a plate of starters. 'Before the *agriturismo* opened, Teresa and I researched old documents and talked to older women for their recipes. These are some of the results.'

From a variety of starters, she can identify tomato *bruschetta* easily enough, with its added kick of chilli pepper. But she would never have guessed the identity of the deep-fried borage leaves or bladderwort if Francesco hadn't told her what they were. They have to look up words in her dictionary too specialised for his English vocabulary. With these unusual dishes, Teresa has made a reputation for the *agriturismo*, which is popular with people living on the coast without access to such plants. He slices portions from a cheese pie with added ingredients of tips of old man's beard, known as *vitalba*, and wild asparagus. Afterwards there is a salad made from poppy and dandelion leaves, nasturtium and borage flowers, harvested earlier that afternoon by Teresa.

Anna holds up her glass between thumb and forefinger in a toast. 'To the best last-minute supper I've ever tasted. Thank you, Francesco.'

'*Prego!* I told you our peasants had to be resourceful. You wait until I introduce you to edible *funghi*. I'm quite a dab hand when it comes to preparing wild mushrooms.'

'You'd make somebody a very good husband.' She realises what she's said and stammers, 'I'm sorry…'

'There you go again with your English *sorry*. I enjoy cooking. Silvana didn't, so that was fine by both of us. What about you, Anna? Have you ever been a wife?'

She picks up a piece of bread from the basket and breaks some off to mop up tomato spilled from her *bruschetta*. 'No, I've never been married, just almost married…' She pauses, not ready to share the details of how she was stood up practically at the altar.

'But there must be somebody in your life – someone important?'

His tone seems merely interested, but his eyes gaze into hers with a quiet intensity. She wonders whether all Italian males are taught the art of seduction by their mothers at the knee, and then silently rebukes herself for being cynical. She's loving his company.

When she hesitates with her answer, it's his turn to apologise. 'Forgive my nosiness, Anna.'

She throws a piece of bread at him. 'How come I'm not allowed to say sorry and you are?'

He ducks, laughing. Then, feeling she's embarrassed him somehow, she says hastily, 'You've every right to ask. There was somebody in London, until very recently actually, but not any more. It was complicated.'

'I see,' he says, his brown eyes still gazing at her. She suddenly feels the need to explain further.

'He was divorced, but he still seemed married.'

'Ah.' He picks up his wine glass and takes another sip. 'You deserve someone who will commit to be with you always. Did you love him?'

'I *did*. I mean, we got on very well. But it all changed…'

She pauses, trying to put into words an explanation she hasn't quite fathomed herself. Then looking at him she says, 'Lately, I've felt it wasn't enough, or that I needed to rethink my topsy-turvy life. Something like that.'

'Is that why you came here, Anna?'

She is uncomfortable with his questions, for which she has no real answers, but offers him the reason she's been telling herself.

'I came here to research my parents' story, and I can't wait to find out more.' She swallows another gulp of wine, forgetting his advice about how to hold her glass, cradling it once again in her palm.

'Anyway, this is boring,' she says. 'Let's change the subject. What about you? Were you married for long?'

'No. But we'd known each other since we were at school together.'

He stacks their plates, pushing them to the edge of the table, then leans back in his chair, folding his arms and watching Anna as he continues.

'We didn't believe in marriage. And then, two years ago, we decided it was the best thing to do for Alba. Silvana felt strongly about our daughter being labelled illegitimate. She thought it might cause problems for her in the future. So we had a big, fancy wedding, invited all our family and friends, booked an expensive restaurant in the centre of Bologna for the wedding breakfast. We even took Alba on honeymoon with us to Zanzibar.'

'I don't think I believe in marriage either. I seem to come from a family with an allergy to marital bliss.'

He raises an eyebrow and she explains.

'My sister is divorced, my brother's been married three times and it looks like he's heading for a third divorce, and let's just say my parents' marriage made in heaven turned out to be a disaster. They argued constantly. I've always said, though, that if I ever did marry, I'd like a quiet affair. No extended family, nothing fancy.'

'Very wise. Thinking back, I suppose Silvana and I were just papering over the cracks in our relationship. It was bizarre, but once we got married everything went downhill. We both felt... stifled, I suppose that's how I'd describe it. It was only Alba that was keeping us together.'

She is surprised to learn of his unhappy marriage. For some reason she'd imagined it to be good, had him summed up as the grieving widower. Finishing the last of the wine in her glass, she shrugs her shoulders, saying, 'Life is complicated.'

'I think people are complicated.'

The wine has gone to her head. He reaches across the table and takes her hand. Turning it over, he kisses her palm. 'Your ex-married man is a fool.'

She pulls her hand away.

'What are you so afraid of, Anna?'

They sit for a moment, watching each other. Anna doesn't know what to say and he is the first to break the silence. He is gentle, calm. 'I know we've not known each other for long but I'm growing very fond of you. I think you like me too.'

He rises from his side of the table, comes over and pulls her to her feet. They kiss tentatively. He pulls her closer and when she doesn't resist, their kisses grow more passionate.

A knock at the door makes them spring apart. Teresa calls urgently from outside. 'Francesco, I'm sorry but Alba's been very sick. She's crying.'

He smiles ruefully. 'Now I really *can* say sorry with good reason. I'd better go. Thank you for sharing supper with me, Anna. I'll see you tomorrow.'

He lets himself out, but not before blowing her a kiss. She is disappointed, but also faintly relieved he's left. It's simpler this way. She hadn't planned on falling in love when she left for Italy.

Next morning, waking early, she stretches luxuriously, reaching over to the other side of her lovely old bed. She wonders for an instant what it would be like to have Francesco next to her on the linen sheets, and then dismisses the idea quickly. Wrapping her dressing gown close, she goes downstairs to make a cup of tea. *Francesco is almost certainly a black coffee person first thing*, she thinks. Is he a morning person or a night owl, like her? They know so little about each other, but she feels comfortable in his company. Alba provided her with a lucky escape last night, because she knows they might well have ended up in bed. And it would have been too soon. Not her style. Her mobile rings and she grabs it eagerly.

'Anna, darling. At last! I tried to call you yesterday but your number was always unavailable.'

It takes her a moment to register the very English public school voice.

'Oh, Will. It's you. I didn't expect you to call.' Disappointment flattens her tone. 'Reception's not very good here up in the mountains. Er, how are you?' she asks.

'Well, you're about to find out, Sooty,' he says, using his pet name for her. 'How's this for a stroke of luck? They've put on a team-building exercise for us, in San Marino of all places. I've had a look on the map and it's a stone's throw from you. So tomorrow evening I plan to whisk you away for a romantic Tuscan dinner with all the works, and then you can fill me in on what you've been getting up to.'

'Listen, Will, I'm busy and… please don't talk about romantic dinners. I thought you understood, we talked before I left…'

'What?' he shouts. 'This line's really bad. I'll call you in the morning, Sooty.'

And before she can say anything else, the line goes dead.

CHAPTER FOURTEEN

June 1999

Supper with Francesco last night has stirred new feelings, but to embark on a new relationship so soon seems like jumping back into the fire.

And she's annoyed Will has called. He obviously hasn't computed the message that it's over, and she wonders what's going on in his head.

In the shower Anna tells herself not to be stupid. Francesco is simply another aspect to the romance of the place. It's a case of Italy's magic sweeping her off her feet. She chooses her outfit carefully: a coffee linen trouser suit and a cream blouse, which looks much better on her now she has more colour to her face. The mountain air is doing her good and, remarkably, despite the wonderful food she's been eating over the last few weeks, she's lost a couple of pounds. Her diet is more balanced, with none of the takeaways or calorie-laden pastries she snatched on her morning dashes to work. The reflection in the mirror tells her she's looking good.

But she doesn't feel good inside. Will's phone call has sent her into a spin. A knock at the door, and Francesco's face appears, almost hidden by a huge bunch of sweet-smelling yellow *ginestra*. Beaming, he hands the flowers to her, but Anna is immediately tongue-tied.

'I stopped off at the most expensive florist in the area to pick these off the mountains myself,' he says. 'And may I say how smart and beautiful you are looking this morning, signorina.'

He bends to kiss her and Anna flinches.

'Anna? Are you unwell? I hope I didn't poison you with my culinary delights last night?'

He laughs, nervously. She avoids his gaze and, shrugging her shoulders, says, 'No, of course not. How's Alba this morning?'

'Oh, she's fine now. But I have my suspicions… it's funny how she behaves like that when I go out in the evening. She's gone with Teresa to the vet, so we have a couple of hours to ourselves.'

Anna places the flowers on the table and he comes over to her, smoothing her hair back from her face. 'You seem distant this morning. What's up?'

He tilts her face so he can see her better. 'Something's happened. Tell me.'

'The man I was telling you about last night—'

'The *fool* you were telling me about last night,' Francesco interrupts.

'What you're really trying to say is that *I'm* the fool.' She pulls away, angry with herself, but sensing it comes over as anger against him. 'I'm in a hurry, so maybe you could drop by later?' she says, reaching up to the kitchen cupboard to find a vase. 'He's arriving early this afternoon and I've got a million and one things to do before I see him.'

He raises both his hands as if in surrender and turns for the door, his jacket catching the *ginestra* blooms on the table, sending them hurtling to the floor where they remain scattered on the *cotto* tiles.

'Don't worry,' he says, 'I know when I'm not wanted. I wouldn't want to get in the way of your *million* things to do.'

In dismay she watches him stride across the piazza, regretting her bluntness but at the same time reminding herself that she needs fewer complications in her life right now.

*

Will sticks out among the tables of smartly dressed Italians, his panama hat and cream linen suit screaming Englishman abroad. They've arranged to meet in a bar near his hotel in San Marino. The sophisticated atmosphere is completely different from the sleepy corner of Tuscany she's growing to love. She feels ill at ease, and realises how much she has changed in just a few weeks.

He shouts to her across the occupied tables as she enters the smart bar with its trendy chrome fittings and expensive orchid arrangements.

'Darling, over here. You look divine. Italy clearly suits.'

People look up as he welcomes her and she wishes he were more discreet. Bending to kiss him on both cheeks in the Italian way, she thinks how much older he seems. His face is flushed and there is an unattractive sweat stain on his pink shirt. One side of his collar is sticking up and she has to stop herself from adjusting it.

'My, my, how very formal! I was looking forward to a bit more than that, Sooty,' he says, pulling her closer and planting a wet kiss on her lips.

Today, her nickname jars.

She pulls away from his grasp and sits down. 'Will,' she hisses, 'I can see you've already had a drink or two. Everybody's looking. Keep your voice down, *please*.'

'So bloody what if I have? Nobody knows me here. The Prosecco's damn good. Damn cheap, too.'

People at the table next to them exchange knowing looks and, beckoning to the waiter, she suggests he has a strong espresso instead.

'Don't start bossing me about!' Will waves a finger, his voice booming above other people's conversations. 'God, I had enough of that from Tricia. No, I'll have another glass of this excellent vino.' He half rises from his seat and shouts to a waitress, 'Vino blanco over here, and bloody pronto!'

'Will! Let's go for a walk.'

'Oh, I see, darling. Changed your mind about dumping me? Can't wait to get me back into the bedroom? How long has it been? I'd say it's about two bloody months since we hit the sack. Old Will's willy's getting very rusty, ha ha!'

She cringes, rising to leave at the same time as Will, who knocks his glass off the table in the process. A waiter approaches and bends to mop up the mess. Anna thrusts a couple of notes into the young man's hand and guides Will to a bench outside under the shade of an umbrella, calling for a taxi to deposit him at his hotel.

Dusk is falling when she lets herself back into her house in the square. The lights are on in Teresa's guest house, and through the window she sees Francesco working in the full dining room. She closes her shutters and sits in the dark thinking about the events of the past few hours. She wonders, where men are concerned, why she always seems to make such a muddle of things.

When Will phones much later she is still awake, her mind too tangled for sleep.

'Sorry, Anna. Empty stomach and too much wine. Unforgivable. Please can we meet again tomorrow? My flight's not until the evening and I can skip the stupid sessions they've arranged. We could spend the day together. Let me make it up to you. Please!'

She hesitates. She should say no, but he sounds so contrite.

'You *were* rather awful tonight, Will. I've never seen you like that before.'

'Just give me a chance to explain. Please? For old times' sake?'

'Oh, you're impossible. Listen, I can manage a snatched hour tomorrow morning, but you'd have to come away from San Marino and meet me down in Sansepolcro. I've promised to collect some laundry there for my landlady. I'll meet you in the little bar in the corner of Piazza Torre di Berta at ten o'clock.'

Sansepolcro is bustling. It's Tuesday, when the inhabitants reconnoitre in cafés, exchanging news and gossip, and old men stand in huddles on corners, deeply involved in conversation, gesticulating and arguing about the latest political cock-ups. People are down from the towns and villages in the mountains, searching for bargains at market stalls that their village stores cannot afford to stock. Anna sips a cappuccino in the bar in the main square, watching and listening to the spectacle of market day.

Will is only five minutes late. He looks tired, preoccupied. He stoops down to kiss her on the cheek and orders a double espresso from the pretty girl who comes to take his order. 'You're looking so beautiful, Anna. So well.' He takes her hand and kisses it. 'I've missed you.'

She withdraws her hand and settles back into the easy chair while the waitress sets down Will's order. He's like a stranger to her, this man, who, over the last two years, has occasionally shared her bed.

He watches her nervously, knocks back his espresso in one gulp. 'You're cross about yesterday, aren't you?' he mutters.

The coffee leaves a dark stain on his upper lip like a badly drawn moustache. Shrugging her shoulders, she replies, 'I was embarrassed.'

'I'm one hundred per cent over Tricia,' he blurts, without preamble.

'What are you talking about, Will?'

'I've finally made up my mind. She's not the woman for me.'

He leans forward, looking at her again, trying to gauge her reaction. She frowns, confused that he seems to be talking about Tricia as if they are still married, confused that he doesn't seem to have taken on board that she has broken off their relationship. Before she can say anything, he continues. 'I've missed you more than I can say. As soon as it registered you were really gone, I realised what a fool I was.'

She tries to interrupt to prevent him from saying any more, but he's in full flow.

'I know we both said there were to be no strings, and you came over here to be on your own... but, I'm all yours now, Sooty.'

'Will, stop...'

He leans forward and grasps her hand, stopping her from saying anything.

'I've come to Italy to ask you to marry me. Naturally I'll have to sort out where to live, a few financial bits and pieces and whatnot, but we can marry as soon as that's over. I don't want to lose you again.'

She is reeling with surprise at his proposal. She might have been pleased to hear it in the past, right at the beginning of their relationship. But not now. Finding her voice at last, she shakes her head in disbelief. 'I can't marry you, Will. I'm sorry you had to come all the way here to understand. I thought you understood.'

'But why not?'

'Because I don't love you.'

He slumps back in his chair, winded, as though he's used up all of his strength. She thinks again how much older he looks, how he could almost be her father.

'I suppose it was always going to be a wild goose chase. Daft of me to think coming out here would make you change your mind...'

'You're not daft. We were good together, and it worked while it lasted, but you've totally misunderstood my feelings.'

She is amazed at how rational she sounds to herself, how clear everything suddenly appears. 'Maybe you're in a kind of panic, scared of what's coming your way, leaving television, divorcing, going into retirement. They say it's one of the most traumatic of times.'

He sits for a few seconds, stunned and silent, picking up his panama hat, fidgeting at it. Life continues around them. Coffees are ordered at the bar, teaspoons clatter onto saucers, stallholders exchange banter with housewives over prices. A scooter whines in a side street, its tinny echo bouncing off high palazzo walls, and she knows with absolute certainty that she could never share her life with Will.

'You loved me once, didn't you?' he continues. 'If I'd asked you to marry me earlier on, do you think you would have said yes?'

She pauses, searching for words that will not hurt this man she once adored. 'You made it plain you were recently divorced and weren't ready for another marriage. And that was fine by me, Will.'

'That evening in your flat – you told me you needed space. I suppose I did misread it … I got that you were dumping me, darling, but I thought you were really sending me the message that you were fed up waiting for me to commit.'

'You thought wrong then. I'm sorry.'

There really is nothing much else to say.

When Will returns from paying for their coffees inside the bar, he pulls her into a bear hug.

'Oh, well!' he says. 'Nothing ventured, and all that. We're still friends, aren't we?'

She kisses him soundly on the cheek. 'Of course, you idiot. But, you need to go home. I'm sorry.'

On the opposite side of the square, Francesco emerges from the stationer's to see Anna locked in an embrace with a man who could only be the English lover she's talked about. The lover she said she'd finished with. He stares at them for a while, angry at himself for feeling jealous, thinking it might be time to return to Bologna.

CHAPTER FIFTEEN

Anna finds a package with a curt note on her doorstep when she returns from Sansepolcro.

> *This is all I can manage.*
> *I'm returning the rest before we leave for Bologna.*
> *F.*

She isn't surprised. Last time they met she really messed up, but she hopes he'll return soon so they can talk.

After preparing a simple salad lunch for herself, she settles down to read Francesco's newly translated section of Ines' diary.

The last days of September 1944

It is still hot. Even up here at over a thousand metres, where the snow falls deep in the winter months. The cicadas keep up their noise, their monotonous, insistent song intensifying the heavy atmosphere. There is no breeze and the trees stand perfectly still, like sentinels guarding the cloggy air. The whole world dozes, but my senses are still wide awake as I write this, desperate to capture every moment of my afternoon with Jim.

I sat beneath the shade of a pine tree, trying to stay cool. My eyes traced the bark along the tree trunks – the crevasses, knots, the black ants marching in single file through dried leaves and pine needles. The wind purred through the feathers of a honey buzzard coiling on the thermals high above.

Most of all I was aware of Jim sitting opposite, leaning against a tree trunk. My eyes followed the contours of his mouth, the cleft in his chin, his Adam's apple, the hairs in the hollow at the base of his neck, the rising and falling of his chest as he breathed. I thought how fragile we were, how a sniper's bullet could still our breathing in the blinking of an eye. How fragile our time was together. When I'd tended his leg earlier, my hands shook as I rubbed calendula cream in and applied a fresh poultice, wondering if he could hear the beating of my heart or sense the feelings in the pit of my stomach as I touched his warm skin.

It didn't surprise me when he looked up and our eyes locked, my stare was so intense.

'Come for a walk, Ines.'

He pulled me to my feet and we started down the mule track. It was cooler here, in the shade of some beech trees. The track was narrow and we bumped against one another. Each time my body brushed his, I wanted to keep hold of him. I was a moth attracted to a candle flame, singed but compelled to return to its heat. We came to a pool where water for the camp was fetched and where we washed. There was nobody else about. We waded into the water together, my dress clinging to my thighs. He pulled me closer, looking into my eyes, his hand caressing my breasts through the thin material.

'You are so lovely,' he whispered.

I pressed myself against him and then I kissed him. His lips were gentle at first, and then I was surprised to feel his tongue inside my mouth. He groaned and his hands reached inside my dress, touching my breasts with the tips of his fingers, tracing circles round my nipples, which aroused wonderful, sinful sensations. He kissed my throat, pulling my dress buttons apart, and sucked at my breast. Sliding my wet dress up my thighs, his fingers felt for the button on my knickers.

And then a pheasant calling in the woods cut the air with its raucous cry and brought me back to where we were and what we were doing. What if somebody was to walk round the path to fetch water and find us, half undressed in the water? I pushed him away.

'No, Jim, not like this. I'm sorry, I shouldn't have let you.'

He seemed not to hear. He tried to kiss me again. I pushed at him harder, shouting, 'No!' He covered my mouth with his hand to stop my cries. Then he muttered under his breath and stepped away. 'I'm sorry. You're so lovely. You're driving me mad. I've spent too much time in the company of ugly men.'

I was embarrassed then, and went behind a tree to tidy myself. The buttons on my dress were pulled off their threads. He saw me fumbling, and took a safety pin from the waistband of his trousers. 'Here, use this,' he said.

'But how will you keep your trousers from falling down?'

He laughed. 'As long as you keep your distance, I shouldn't have any more trouble with my trousers.'

'Don't make fun of me, Jim.'

I felt confused, dirty, like Anna Maria who went with the German soldier. My mother talks about her often enough, warning me never to be alone with a man. But I want to be with him. I don't want him to think I am easy, but I like Jim kissing and fondling me like this. Does that mean I am a *puttana*? Even though I was brought up in the countryside and have seen couplings between bulls and cows, rams and ewes, I am still innocent about what goes on between a man and a woman. And I dare not ask anybody, not even my own mother. I would die of shame.

He pulled me to him again and this time I held myself away. 'I've fallen in love with you,' he said, 'and I want to marry you, but I can wait, if that's what you want.'

'Are you asking me to marry you because you want to make love to me?' I said, pushing him away. 'We don't truly know each other. Normally, the way it happens in the country is that two people grow to know one another over many months, years even. They visit each other's families. The man has to ask permission from the girl's father – and they're never allowed to be alone like we've been. I can't believe what you've asked me. You're crazy.'

I looked up at him in puzzlement, but he was smiling down at me. He kissed the tip of my nose. 'You said "normally", Ines. These are not normal times. And yes, I *am* crazy – crazy for you. But I'll do what you want and ask your father.'

I moved back into his arms, despite my misgivings. 'We mustn't be together like this. If Davide catches us, he'll kill me.'

I'd given Mamma's rosary beads to my brother, but now I wanted them back. I wanted to find myself a quiet corner in the camp and pray to Our Lady for forgiveness, ask her to calm my wild, sinful feelings by reciting the Ave Maria I've prayed with Mamma since I was little. The way Jim made me feel in the pool frightened me, and now I wished he was somewhere far away. But when I looked at him, the lovely, shameful feelings returned and I wanted him to kiss me again. I was so muddled.

Jim took my hands in his. 'So, will you marry me?' he asked. 'I haven't heard your answer. And you don't seem very happy about my proposal.'

'I've never been in love,' I said. 'I'm not sure how to behave.'

'You don't need to behave in a particular way, darling Ines,' he said, his blue eyes smiling.

'And now you're laughing at me again.'

'Do you love me, Ines Santini?'

'Yes,' I whispered, my heart fluttering like a caged bird.

'And will you change your name to Ines Swilland and marry me?'

He found a piece of creeper tangled in the briars, and kneeling down in front of me, he took my hand and wound a strand around my betrothal finger, promising to buy me a beautiful ring when the war was over.

'Yes,' I replied, stroking the top of his head as he knelt before me. 'Yes, yes I will.'

And now I am unofficially engaged.

CHAPTER SIXTEEN

Anna can't help thinking that her parents' love story is the stuff of old black and white movies shown on wet winter afternoons on television. And yet she knows that what she's reading is the truth, not fiction. She has never been one to believe in falling in love at first sight. Cynical it might be, but she believes her mother was swept up in the excitement of a first crush, literally carried away by a romantic notion. She was only eighteen, a country girl who'd never travelled further than the town in the valley. The war and its hardships had been grinding away for four long years, and a handsome young soldier from England must have been a wonderful distraction for a girl of her age. At the same time, Anna can imagine her father being delighted and flattered by the attentions of this innocent, beautiful country girl.

And she was very beautiful. When Anna visited her in the care home, she sometimes helped her sort through a box of old photographs. Her mother would peer at them and once again her Italian would take over as she described who was who. She would start in Italian and then her words melted into dialect and Anna was lost.

After her mother had passed away, and she'd cleared out her room, she'd kept the box, and had brought the photos with her to Italy. Now, she roots through until she finds what she's looking for: a photo of her parents as a young couple, her mother's flashing, mischievous eyes, her hair arranged round her face in shining sausage curls, as was the fashion in those days. Pencilled on the back is a date, June 1945, just after the end of the war, but Jim is still wearing uniform. The pair are standing, arms linked, in front of the town hall, and Anna realises they're outside the old *Comune* in Badia Tedalda. A group of villagers cluster round them. She wonders if any are still alive. There are a few scrawny children in the group, looking as if they need a good meal, which was most likely the case.

Her mobile rings. It's Francesco again.

'Hello, Anna. How's it going?'

'My mother's diary is incredible,' she answers. 'I can't put it down.'

'Does that mean you're not free this afternoon?'

She pauses.

'That's a shame,' Francesco says, 'Alba was really looking forward to being with you again. She's drawn you a picture.'

'Once I start reading, I'm hooked. I promise I'll make up for it tomorrow. Tell Alba I'll take her for a long walk by the river after school to look for fossils. I'm sorry, Francesco. Catch up with you tomorrow?'

'Tomorrow I have to be in Bologna for a faculty meeting, but Alba will be waiting for you.'

He hangs up on her abruptly before she has the chance to thank him for all the work he's done. Once again, she's puzzled by his mood swings. *It's his being a stereotypical Italian male who likes to have his own way*, she thinks to herself, and settles down to continue with her mother's story.

Wednesday, September 20 1944

Jim and I have to be careful with our snatched moments. Somebody is bound to guess what's going on sooner or later. At least Davide hasn't been lurking around us for a few days. Jim nicknamed him the Gooseberry. Apparently this is what the English call a type of chaperone.

I laughed, for our phrase *uva spina*, or prickly grape, is fitting.

I use the excuse that I'm teaching Jim Italian, and he is wicked sometimes. Other than Toni, nobody else understands English, so he comes out with outrageous sentences.

'I dream about you at night,' he said one time, 'with your long hair covering your breasts.'

'Shhh! Jim,' I scolded. 'I'll stop these lessons if you don't behave.'

Of course I didn't mean a word of it.

'Tell me in Italian what it's like in England,' I said, to bring him back on course, 'and what you will do after the war.'

'I'll take you back and make babies with you.' He smiled.

And when I laughed, one of the men commented that our lessons seemed fun and he wanted to join in too.

'It's because he makes foolish mistakes,' I explained in Italian, glaring at Jim and hissing at him to be sensible or else we would be discovered.

We are always careful not to sit too near Toni. Aside from speaking fluent English, he also has the habit of turning up unexpectedly. One afternoon Jim and I walked deeper into the pine forest. He pulled me down with him on the needles, kissing and fondling me. It was only the snapping of a branch that caused me to break away, fearful a wild boar was lurking nearby, snuffling for truffles in the roots of trees. I sat up and straightened my blouse. There was no boar in sight. But Toni was leaning against a fallen boulder barely three metres from us. He laughed when I looked at him, my cheeks flaring in embarrassment; he winked and lit a cigarette before walking away through the shadows. Jim and I walked back to camp, keeping a lookout for Toni or anybody else who might see us. Jim turned serious.

'Our King was near us in July, Ines, and I didn't know. And then he came to visit the dragoons in Viamaggio. That's really nearby, isn't it?'

I nodded and asked him about these dragoons.

'The King's own soldiers,' was his explanation. He was quiet for a few seconds and then he tried to take hold of my hand, but I didn't let him. Capriolo and Toni were seated nearby, discussing something in earnest.

'Ines. I need to get away from here. It's wrong that I'm not with my own men,' Jim said.

I bit my lip to stop my tears. 'And you'll go away and forget all about me. You asked me to marry you, I said yes and now you want to leave,' I hissed, trying hard not to be overheard.

'How can you believe I'd forget about you? I've never been happier in my life, but you have to understand, I can't stay here forever. It's my duty to return to fight with my own people. I promise I'll talk to your father before I leave.'

'Your own people? I thought I was enough for you, Jim.' Even to my own ears I sounded petulant, but that is how I felt. I'd found my love and now I was going to lose him. 'You're mad to try to travel alone,' I continued. 'Take me with you. I know the paths you need.'

'You only know the paths in this part of the world, my sweet. Capriolo has given me advice on a route into Umbria.'

'I thought you were useful to him here.'

'He understands my need to leave.'

'And what is this advice he's given you?' I mumbled.

'Not to say I'm English if anybody stops me, in case they're fascist sympathisers escaped from the towns. He's told me to say I'm a soldier from the Italian Fourth Army, trying to return to Trieste. Many of them are blond. He says they're crazy, too, like me.'

'Please don't go, Jim. I have a bad feeling about this.'

'I have to go.' This time I let him take hold of my hand.

'I'm too happy. It feels wrong,' he half whispered. 'There's a war going on and I must get back to my men.'

Then Capriolo approached and I snatched my hand away.

'Ines, have you seen Davide?' he asked. 'Any message from your parents?'

'No – how could I hear from them? I've been up here two weeks.'

'I just wondered.'

'Why?'

'He's missing, and I'm concerned.'

Anna sits for a while, staring through the window at the darkening mountains, listening to twilight birdsong. It's peaceful, sweet, and she wishes she could pick up the phone and talk to her mother.

The picture of her parents so much in love is such a contrast to her memories of them as a little girl. The nightmares she suffers even to this day stem from that time, she's sure. She would wake up to the sound of her father's temper as he crashed about in the kitchen beneath her bedroom, yelling at her mother. To block the sounds of arguing, she'd hide her head beneath the covers, only to wake up later, hot and sticky in the night, her pillow suffocating her.

It's nearly dinner time and she should be hungry, but she isn't. Instead of eating, she slips downstairs to fetch a glass of chilled white Grechetto and takes it back upstairs to resume reading the remaining pages.

Sunday, October 8, 1944

Mamma and Papà sent word for me to come down from the camp. Nobody has had any contact with Davide for ten days, and my parents want me near them while we wait for news. We are all beside ourselves with worry. I try to put on a brave face, and whenever Mamma asks me where he could possibly be, I make up some reason, like he is lying low, spying on the *tedeschi* and that he will be back as soon as he can. But I know she doesn't believe me, and I don't believe myself either. He's never been away for this long.

The first night I was back at the mill, I crept into his tiny bedroom. The scarf I knitted him last Christmas hung over his bedstead and my eyes traced the shape left by his head on the pillow. When we were small, we'd sleep top to tail in this bed until he grew taller and I complained about his kicking, so Mamma moved me into Nonna's room. All his annoying brotherly ways are forgotten with the ache I feel in my heart. I miss him so much. The room was chilly and I pulled the window to.

In one sense, I am relieved to be home. The last few weeks on the mountain have been intense, the mood in camp sombre. The men returned without Capriolo. Toni had disappeared in a skirmish along the Rimini road, apparently, and Capriolo stayed in the valley to find out what had become of Davide.

When Capriolo eventually turned up alone, five days later, he was badly wounded. He'd aged about twenty years in those few days; his face was gaunt, one eye was closed and black and his right hand was swaddled in a filthy sling made from a torn shirt. He wouldn't let me near him when I offered to tend to him. He was drunk and shouted at me to get lost. That evening, by the fire, I watched him swallow wine as if it were water and eventually he had to be helped to his bed in the cave. I heard him raving and shouting.

'*Porca vacca*,' he swore, 'I'm a useless specimen, no good to anybody. And how can I hold a gun with this paw?'

The men tried to calm him. It was unlike him to be so out of control, but everybody has a breaking point. I kept my distance that night.

I wanted to remain with Jim in the camp, and at the same time I was scared to be near him. Surely my mother has an inkling that I am in love, for I feel she can see into my mind and picture me with him at the pool. She is constantly short-tempered: 'I knew we shouldn't have sent you up there. Just look at the state of you – all thin and wasted. You can't do anything properly at the minute either, Ines! What have you done to this polenta? I shall have to throw it to the hens! What a wicked waste.'

If Mamma had slapped me at that moment I wouldn't have been surprised, even though I have never seen her raise a hand to anybody. My father used to, but never my mother. She was right to chide me, and I understood her worry for Davide was driving her short temper.

Sitting by the hearth, I had been stirring and stirring, not noticing that the polenta in the cauldron hanging over the flames was catching. My mother smelled it scorching while I was daydreaming – wondering what Jim was doing up in camp, when Davide would return and if he was safe, and what would happen between Jim and me in the future. He hasn't talked to Papà yet, and I worry about that too. Was he telling the truth when he said he loved me, or was he saying sweet things to me so we could kiss and cuddle? At night I cry myself to sleep, wishing I'd given myself to him. Maybe by now we would be officially betrothed and I wouldn't feel so unsettled. This business of love is so mysterious.

Friday, October 13, 1944

We've had so many days of watery sunshine. This morning, the sky was leaden and the trees drooped with rain-sodden foliage. I needed to be outside, and I called to Mamma that I was going to look for mushrooms in the meadow and wouldn't be long. The ground was muddy and my boots were soon clogged underfoot with sticky lumps of clay.

Early-morning mist was pinned in the fir trees on the lower slopes of the mountain like a shawl draped round a woman's shoulders. I made my way up the path, never intending to go as far as the camp but I felt a need to be nearer Jim, near the woods where we walked together. Halfway up, I stopped to sit on a rock. The valley below was still shrouded in mist. Nothing in my life seems clear any more, and there is so much unhappiness around.

Tears trickled down my cheeks as I thought of what my father told us last night at our fireside. Another school companion of mine, Silvestro, had been simply minding the pigs, but the Germans were convinced he was a partisan pretending to be a swineherd. He was only a boy, fifteen years old. He knew even less about life than I did. The soldiers beat him up. They beat him with their rifle butts until his face was unrecognisable – the sweet face of a boy who hadn't even started to shave. There was blood everywhere, and they threw him to the pigs to finish him off. But next morning when the cowards returned, he was still alive. The pigs hadn't touched him. Papà said that speaks volumes; animals are less savage than men. Then the *tedeschi* made the poor boy crawl on his hands and knees while they kicked and spat on him, forcing him to dig his own grave. And afterwards they shot him.

I want this craziness to end. Papà used to rebuke Davide for talking about acts of slaughter, but now even he drops these brutal stories into conversation as if they are routine. I want to run far away and start my life afresh.

Suddenly the mist lifted, as if a giant had puffed up his cheeks and given an almighty blow, and then I knew I had to hurry home. It wasn't safe to perch on a rock, thinking. The *tedeschi* might spy on me through their binoculars and wonder what a lone girl was doing on the mountainside without cattle or sheep to tend. I ran home down the path, and only when I reached the steps to the mill did I remember that I hadn't searched for a single mushroom. Now there would be even more reason for my mother to nag. From the kitchen I heard people talking, and I wondered who was calling at such an early hour.

Jim and Capriolo were sitting at the kitchen table with my father. My heart missed a beat and I felt a deep blush starting in my cheeks. Turning round to cover my confusion, I knocked a glass over with the corner of my shawl. As I stooped to pick up the pieces, my mother, busy at the hearth making *piadine*, shouted at me to be careful not to cut myself. An open bottle of Vin Santo sat on the table. 'Have you found Davide?' I blurted, thinking this to be the cause of their celebration.

Jim rose from the table, offering me his chair. 'That's not why we're here, Ines. I promised I'd talk to your father, and here I am.'

Mamma came over to stand behind Papà, who looked at me very seriously and asked, 'Is it true you love this Englishman?'

I nodded shyly and Jim smiled his encouragement. 'I've asked your father's permission for your hand.'

Then Capriolo interrupted, 'But your boyfriend is leaving today. Think very carefully, Ines. Now is not the time to be making plans for the future.'

I was angry with him for interfering. 'What has it to do with you? We love each other. That's all that matters.'

Jim took my hand. 'He's right to make you think, Ines. I *am* leaving today, and while I'm away you'll have time to think again about us.'

'But why do you have to go? I don't understand why you're leaving now. It's too dangerous.'

My father broke into my outburst. 'Capriolo is right. It's wiser to wait. If Signor Jim returns and you both still feel the same way, then I shall give my blessing. I've seen he is a brave man. It would be an honour to have an *inglese* as a son-in-law. But you are very young, Ines, and time will tell you what to do for the best.'

'May I take your daughter for a walk before I leave?' Jim asked my father.

Papà made Capriolo chaperone us, as was the custom. Once we were outside, Capriolo told us he'd give us a few moments alone. He spoke to me in dialect so Jim wouldn't understand, and I thought that was very discourteous, but I was too excited to say anything.

'Be sure you know what you're doing, girl,' he muttered, and then he added something which I didn't understand at the time, 'the grass is not always greener.'

He sat down on the stone bench near my parents' vegetable garden and waved us away, telling us to be five minutes at the most.

I can barely remember everything Jim said to me this morning. I felt so overwhelmed. On the one hand I am happy he wants to marry me, but on the other I am distraught that he is leaving. I'm angry, too, with Capriolo for not approving of our engagement, and I can't understand why, if Jim loves me so much, he can think of going away. He explained he was going to try and join up with British soldiers on the Viamaggio Pass. He said he'd come back when he could, and in the meantime he asked me to wait for him.

'If it weren't for the war, Ines, I could buy you a diamond ring. I could put it on your finger and you would be my *fidanzata*.'

'If it weren't for the war, we wouldn't have met,' I replied.

'I'll come back, and if you still want me, we'll marry.'

'Of course I will still want you. Do you think I'm so fickle that I would change my mind? I know what's in my heart. Let me come with you! You have no idea how to find the paths over the pass. I'm frightened this is the last time I'll see you.'

He kissed away my tears and gave me a rag he'd been using as a handkerchief. I dried my face as best I could. After a while, Capriolo coughed and I untangled myself from Jim's arms. We returned to the kitchen and Papà handed us all a glass of Vin Santo, toasting us and wishing Jim a safe return. Then Capriolo and Jim left, and I felt as if love had walked out of my life.

CHAPTER SEVENTEEN

Anna spends the next morning pottering – planting up an animal feed trough outside her front door with basil and parsley, hand-washing a silk blouse – but all the time her mind is on the diary and her father's romantic marriage proposal. With no further mention of her uncle Davide, she wonders what became of him. She wishes her Italian was better and she didn't have to rely on Francesco's kindness. He was awkward on the phone last time they spoke, making it hard to ask him for more help. Once he and Alba return to Bologna, it will become harder still. Teresa might be able to help a little, but her English is about as good as Anna's Italian and, between them, it will take ages. Despite her difficult behaviour, she'll miss Alba when she goes. And Anna admits she'll feel disappointed about Francesco leaving.

Her thoughts are interrupted by the arrival of a worried Alba at the door, with Billi clasped in her arms. As far as Alba is concerned, Anna has become an unofficial vet and cat counsellor, and she holds up Billi for inspection. The cat's tail is wrapped in a bloodstained handkerchief.

'Oh, poor little thing!' Anna says, bending down to stroke the cat. 'Is he in the wars again? Come in and we'll bathe his tail. Has he been back in the woodpile, looking for mice?'

She has grown expert at this one-way conversation with Alba, feeling instinctively that she shouldn't force her into talking. One day, when she's ready, she'll rediscover her words.

'It's not a deep cut,' she tells the little girl. 'Maybe his tail got pecked by the hens – perhaps the silly things thought it was a fat, juicy worm.'

Alba giggles and helps bathe Billi's tail in boiled, salted water, holding fast to the wriggling bundle of fur.

'How about another English lesson later today, before you leave for Bologna?' she suggests when they've finished with Billi. 'We could learn more words as we walk along the river. It's a sunny day, and I want to be outside too.'

Alba nods and Anna tells her in English what time they should meet, asking her if she has understood. Alba holds up three fingers and Anna smiles her approval. 'Well done. Three o'clock. See you later, alligator!'

Francesco drops her at Anna's front door just before three, hovering on the threshold. The last time they spoke, he hung up on her abruptly. She wonders if she will ever have the chance to tell him what went on with Will. She misses Francesco's company and regrets the frosty atmosphere hanging between them, but doesn't know how to break it. She daren't ask him if he'll do some more work on the diary, with him in this strange, distant mood.

'I've got to go to Bologna to finalise plans for our move back,' Francesco says, abruptly handing over Alba's rucksack. He looks tired and refuses Anna's offer of coffee. 'No thanks, I'm late enough already, and I heard on the radio that the traffic is bad. There's been a major accident on the main road and I don't know what time I'll be back. Teresa says she'll look after Alba this evening. She's expecting her about five.'

'We'll be finished well before then.' She wants to tell him to drive safely and come back in one piece, but he's already climbing into his car. They wave him goodbye as his Fiat Panda disappears down the dirt track.

'Come on then, Alba. I've packed us a picnic. We're going further down the river today. New words need new places, and

we're going to find a little chapel downstream that your daddy
told me about. Then we'll find a big rock to sit on and have our
English afternoon tea. I've even baked you special buns which
we call rock cakes.'

Alba laughs and carefully pulls her rucksack onto her back.
The bag wriggles.

'Oh no, Alba, Billi can't come. He'll be a distraction and he
won't want to get wet. Cats don't like water.'

She wonders if the little girl has taken on board that she will
be returning to Bologna soon, and if Francesco will let her keep
Billi when they're back in their town apartment.

Each day now the weather is improving, and the June sunshine
is warm enough for dips in the river. The little girl squeals when
Anna points out long necklaces of toad spawn tangled in the
pools. Disturbed by their approach, a pair of fishing egrets rise
from the shallows, their wingspans casting graceful shadows over
the stones.

'Let's see how many heart-shaped stones we can find, and some
flat ones to paint and write words on in English.'

A pleasant half hour later, they reach the path leading to an
abandoned chapel, a humble stone building with a corrugated
metal roof. Inside is an altar and a gaudy image of the Madonna.
Artificial flowers are arranged in jars on a darned altar cloth and
outside, on an enamel plaque, is a simple inscription, which
Anna roughly translates:

> *In this little church where on Sundays Eliseio used to listen*
> *to the walnuts falling onto the roof, he kept his wife company*
> *as she came to clean and arrange plastic flowers in jam jars*
> *on the altar. Now that he has passed away, the words he used*

*to say to me about the existence of God remain hanging in
the air: 'To say that God exists may be a lie, but to say that
He does not exist may be an even bigger lie.'
Tonino Guerra, poet and raconteur.*

Anna likes the sound of this poet who freely leaves his
thoughts scattered about the countryside for people to discover.

She was brought up to keep her feelings hidden. It wasn't easy
to confide in her mother, and Jane and Harry, being so much
older, were wrapped up in their own lives and studies. During
these past weeks she's noticed how gregarious Italians are, and
once again she marvels at the loneliness her mother must have
endured, having crossed such a great cultural divide to live among
the reserved English.

A huge clap of thunder echoing from the next valley makes
them both jump. They'd started their walk in brilliant sunshine,
but now the sky is overcast and the temperature has dropped
several degrees.

'Quick, Alba. Run for shelter! We're going to be soaked
through any minute now.'

Glancing at the menacing clouds, she grabs the little girl's
hand and they make for a ruined barn. Half the roof has caved
in, but there is a dry corner where the timbers above still bear a
few cracked tiles, offering a little shelter. Alba is shivering in her
skimpy clothes and she pulls the trembling child into her arms.

'It's only thunder, nothing to be scared about,' she whispers.
'It'll be over soon, and then we can go home. We'll have our
picnic here and pretend it's our house. I'll be the farmer's wife
and you can be my little girl, and we'll pretend we're having a
rest before milking our goats.'

Alba smiles and runs into a corner where a woodworm-riddled
stool lies discarded on its side. She rights it, brushing off most

of the dust with her hands, arranging cakes and plastic beakers on her makeshift table. Rain is falling heavily now, curtains of water blocking the view outside the barn. Fat drops occasionally fall on them between the broken tiles as they eat their picnic. *Rock cakes in Tuscany – now there's a cultural divide well and truly crossed*, Anna thinks to herself.

Alba tugs at her arm, pointing at something on the wall beneath a half-rotten manger and smiles. Inside a heart, crudely scratched into the crumbling plaster, are four intertwined letters and a date:

DS & IS, agosto 1966

'One day,' Anna tells her, 'somebody will write your name like that when you fall in love.'

The little girl covers her mouth with her hands and laughs out loud.

'Come on, Mrs Mamma Cat,' Anna continues, using the name that always makes Alba giggle. 'Let's clear up and go home. The rain's stopped, and if we don't start back now we'll be very late and your Aunty Teresa will be wondering where we've disappeared to.'

They retrace their steps along the river, Alba hopping from stone to stone. The level has risen slightly and the water has turned murky after the recent deluge. They are almost at the bridge, the point where they should clamber up from the riverbed to join the road, when a sudden roar causes Anna to look up. A wall of muddy water is gushing towards them, funnelling through the arches of the bridge.

She has to shout to make herself heard above the water's furious approach. 'Alba! Run up the bank as fast as you can. Get out of the riverbed.' But the storm surge is upon them sooner than Anna anticipates.

The river boils, crashing over boulders, dragging tree trunks and branches in a crazy helter-skelter of water. Any moment now the flood will catch them up and knock them over. Alba is already halfway up the bank and Anna throws off her rucksack to lighten the load. She struggles to catch up, but the little girl loses her footing on an unsteady rock and slides into the churning river. Without thinking twice, Anna jumps in and grabs her, and, fighting against the current with all her strength, she pushes Alba up the bank to safety. The torrent flows on, and Anna is dragged further down. For what seem like minutes but are only seconds, she's held beneath the water, stones and debris crashing into her, knocking her breath away. Each time she thinks she will surface, logs catch her as they career past, bruising her, stopping her from regaining control. Then at last her hand grasps a willow sprouting from the bank and she clings on, pulling herself up with both hands, bracing her body against the racing water. She is only yards away from the dam, and if she doesn't hang onto the tree she'll surely be tossed over the twenty-foot-high wall and onto the rocks below. And then she remembers how she's shoved Alba up onto the bank and fears the rising water will have pulled her under.

'Alba, *Alba!*' she shrieks, but the crazy river whips away her words. Clawing her way along a thicker branch of her perch, her heart in her mouth in case it snaps under the pressure of the storm water, her left foot finally makes contact with the bank and she gains a foothold. When she puts weight on her right foot she yelps with pain, almost losing her grip. It takes a few seconds for her to compose herself before attempting to climbing again, but her right leg is useless.

Then she hears her name and looks up to see Alba, eyes huge in her ash-white face.

'Anna, Anna!' the little girl cries over and over.

Never has her name sounded so sweet to Anna's ears.

'Alba, thank God you're safe,' she shouts.

Her arms are sore from hanging on against the fast-flowing current and she doesn't know how much longer she can hold. She's cold, near to panic, but she tries to keep her voice calm so as not to frighten the little girl.

'Alba, run back along the bank, look for my rucksack and mobile. Phone Teresa! Tell her what's happened. Tell her to be quick.'

She can't remember much about her rescue. Later on, when she's sitting beside the stove wrapped in Teresa's bathrobe with Alba snuggled next to her on the sofa, Teresa explains how she had grabbed the gardener working on her vegetable plot. Together they had jumped into his truck and sped down to the river. It had taken Arnaldo no time to attach a length of thick rope to the back of the vehicle, tie the other end round his waist and scramble down to rescue Anna from the freezing water. A few minutes later, and they reckoned it would have been too late. Anna had fainted just as Arnaldo reached her and he had to jump into the water to carry her out.

'I was so frightened, I thought you were going to drown,' Alba is bubbling with words long unspoken. 'I'm so glad now we didn't take Billi with us.'

She starts to cry and Anna pulls her close, kissing the top of her head, wincing as she moves.

Teresa gently pulls her niece away. 'Come and sit over here, Alba. Anna is very sore.'

'I am a little sore,' Anna says, 'but it's like medicine for me just listening to Alba speak.'

'When I answered my phone, I didn't recognise you at first, Alba,' Teresa says as she pulls her onto her knee. 'You were fantastic. What a brave little girl you are.'

'I'm going to find Billi and tell him all about it.' Alba struggles from her aunt's arms. 'Can I go and find him upstairs, Anna?'

'Of course. He's probably under my bed.'

When they are alone, Anna tells Teresa how frightened she was for Alba's safety. 'I would never have forgiven myself if anything had happened to her.'

'Don't worry, it wasn't your fault. You weren't to know. When it rains hard further up the valley, the river turns like that almost without warning.'

'It's an awful thing to say, but it's almost been worth it to hear her talk again. I can't wait for Francesco to hear her.' She shuffles her bottom to find a more comfortable position and grimaces as pain shoots up her right side.

'I phoned him about the accident,' Teresa says.

Two beams of light stroke the room from outside and there is the sound of a car drawing to a halt on the gravel.

'Speak of the devil. He must have driven really fast.'

Turning back to Anna, she says, 'I don't like the look of that leg, and you're covered in bruises. I think we should call for the doctor tomorrow.'

'I'm sure it's nothing serious—' Anna starts to say, but before she can finish, the door is flung open and Francesco bursts in, shouting in Italian. Anna hears Alba's name mentioned, but she can't understand what he's saying, or Teresa as she responds. A heated, rapid exchange follows, Francesco waving his hands about as he shouts.

Then he turns to Anna and says in English, 'What the hell were you thinking of, woman? Taking my daughter down to the river in a storm like that?'

Hearing him, Alba comes rushing into the sitting room, flinging herself into his arms. 'Babbo, we've had an adventure. I fell in the river and Anna jumped in after me and I had to find her mobile and call Teresa, and then Arnaldo came and rescued us and we've had hot chocolate and cake, and I can't find Billi. Let go of me, Babbo, you're squeezing me too tight, it hurts!'

His voice is gentle now and he kisses his child over and over. 'Alba, *tesoro*, you've found your voice.'

'Don't be silly, Babbo, what do you mean? I never lost my voice, I just put it away for a while. Anyway, I was bored with not talking. Can I have another piece of chocolate cake now, Zia Teresa?'

Francesco and Teresa laugh. Anna watches the three of them, still feeling upset by Francesco's outburst. Suddenly she feels she doesn't belong. If she could walk, she would quietly leave the room and let the family be on their own. But she is marooned on the sofa.

Without further acknowledging Anna's presence, Francesco picks Alba up and nuzzles her. 'I think you've had quite enough chocolate cake and excitement for one day, young lady. It's bedtime! Maybe you can miss school again tomorrow, and Teresa will let you have a slice for breakfast.'

There is another exchange in Italian with Teresa, too fast for Anna to follow, although she knows he is talking about her again, and then he and Alba leave.

'He's really angry with me,' Anna says after they have gone.

'Take no notice, he'll calm down. I told him how you saved her. He doesn't know whether to be angry or happy that Alba's speaking again.'

'He blames the accident on me. He's furious I took her there in the first place. But I didn't know a river could change from one minute to the next like that. I've never seen a storm surge in my life.' She shudders and covers her face with her hands. 'Oh, Teresa, she could have died.'

'But she didn't.' Teresa sits on the arm of the sofa next to Anna. 'He's had a lot of worrying and thinking to do since Silvana's death, and I think he's exhausted. Sometimes he overreacts. I was trying to point out to him that nothing happened to Alba and that he should simply be pleased she's speaking again. And I also lost my temper with him for not caring about what happened to you.'

'I think it would be better for everyone if I left.'

'Anna, don't be ridiculous. Look, it's been a long day. Get some sleep and everything will seem better in the morning.' She laughs at herself. 'I sound like my mother. Will you be all right, sleeping where you are on the sofa? Can I get you another pillow, or a glass of water?'

'No thanks, Teresa. You've been an angel. Just put the light out for me when you leave.'

Teresa bends to kiss her friend. '*Sogni d'oro.* Sweet dreams. See you in the morning, but call me if you need anything. Anything at all.'

She closes the door gently behind her. A tear rolls down Anna's cheek. She tells herself it is exhaustion and the effects of shock after the day's dramatic events.

CHAPTER EIGHTEEN

Anna is sore and stiff the next morning. Trying to walk upstairs to the bathroom, she can't put weight on her leg and resorts to calling Teresa on her mobile.

'You poor thing,' she says when she comes over. 'Look, I'm calling the doctor to check you over and, in the meantime, you can't possibly stay by yourself in this house with the bathroom upstairs.'

She tries to protest, but Teresa is adamant and Anna knows it makes sense. Teresa reminds her about the little apartment opposite the *agriturismo* that she's modified for disabled guests, where Anna will be much more comfortable.

'Stop protesting, Anna! I've made up my mind. Tell me what I can pack for you and we'll get you sorted in no time.'

She bustles round collecting toiletries, clean underwear and a comfortable tracksuit. 'Shall I pack these too?' she asks, holding up the diaries.

'Please! Then I can translate them while I'm immobile.'

'I thought Francesco was doing it for you.'

'I don't want to bother him any more. He's so angry with me, it doesn't seem right to ask. And anyway, he's going back to Bologna, so it'll be problematic.'

Teresa frowns. 'That's news to me about Bologna.' She shrugs her shoulders. 'I'll ask Arnaldo to come and carry you over to the apartment.'

'I'm being such a nuisance. You all have better things to do than run around after me.'

Hands on hips, Teresa retorts, 'Wouldn't you do the same for us?'

'Of course, but…'

'No buts. End of. See you in a while – I'm off to make a phone call to the clinic.'

Scooping up Anna's bundle of possessions, she hurries out. Anna flops back against the sofa cushions, letting out a huge sigh of frustration as she looks around the little house where she has started to enjoy her independence. She's anxious to pick up on the next section of the diaries, and wonders how she will find a replacement for Francesco. The phone directory might be the first place to search, but she knows it won't be easy. She really needs to be able to chat to someone, to ensure she gets the right person. Her Italian is improving all the time, but it will be hard to find anybody like Francesco. He's ideal. She sighs again and throws her phone down onto the bedcovers in frustration. *Italians would say* pazienza, she thinks, and wonders how long she will have to be patient.

It is Francesco who comes to fetch her for the move. 'Arnaldo's busy ploughing a neighbour's field, so Teresa sent me instead. Are you ready?'

'I think so. Thank you.'

He bends down to pick her up, neither of them looking at each other. 'Put your hands round my neck,' he says, 'otherwise I can't lift you properly.'

She leans away from him as he carries her but he strengthens his grip. 'Relax, Anna, then it will be easier for both of us.'

He's strong, despite his lean build. She smells his familiar aftershave, sees a mole beneath his right ear she hadn't noticed before, wonders if he thinks she's heavy. She might have made a joke about it if she weren't feeling so awkward.

'Here we are,' he says, nudging the apartment door open as they arrive. 'I'll put you down here for the time being. Teresa is coming over to make up the bed for you.'

He helps her into a leather armchair in the lounge area. Stepping back, he leans against the kitchen counter that divides the two living spaces and folds his arms. They both start to speak at the same time.

'I'm sorry I'm being such a nuisance,' she says.

'I'm sorry I lost it last night,' he says.

She laughs nervously and he continues, 'I was out of my mind with worry. Alba is my world, but I shouldn't have shouted at you like that. You were very brave to jump in that river.'

'How could I not? Anybody would have done the same. Please don't apologise. I completely understand.'

'She hasn't stopped talking about yesterday.' He smiles. 'In fact, she hasn't stopped talking, full stop. It's amazing, listening to her. Teresa has told me off because I keep asking her questions so I can hear her answers.' He pauses. 'To be honest, Teresa also told me off for being objectionable to you last night.'

Anna doesn't comment. 'She's also persuaded me not to leave quite yet for Bologna. I think the saying is "Don't upset the apple cart"?'

'In what sense?'

'She thinks it's best to keep living here for a while, for Alba's sake. Now that she's talking again, Teresa reckons we should stay put. Another change might upset her again.'

'She has a point, I suppose, but what do *you* think? She's your daughter, after all. You know best.'

He shakes his head. 'If only that were true. Anyway, the faculty are being good to me and letting me do my research from here. I think we'll be here for another month or so.'

'I'm pleased.' She smiles at him but he doesn't reciprocate. Instead he asks her rather coldly what her plans are for the future, and Anna wonders if they will ever get back to their easy companionship.

After the doctor has gone, prescribing rest for a couple of days for bruising and a sprained ankle, Teresa carries in fresh sheets to make up a folding bed for Anna.

'Dottor Negri told me to feed you with chicken broth and good red wine,' she giggles. 'The old remedies are the best.'

'It's a relief it's nothing serious. But I meant what I said last night, Teresa. Maybe it's best if I find somewhere else once I'm on my feet again.'

Teresa sits down in the leather armchair opposite Anna. 'Why are you continuing to talk such rubbish? I thought we were supposed to be friends.'

'But I feel like I've outstayed my welcome.'

When Teresa begins to protest, Anna adds, 'It's not you. It's Francesco. I think he'd be glad to see the back of me.'

Teresa tuts. 'You're too sensitive. You shouldn't take things to heart so. And anyway, what about your project? What will happen to that if you leave?'

'My Italian needs to improve before I can finish the diary. I've looked for a translator, but I don't know if I want to entrust my mother's story to a complete stranger. Actually, I thought about continuing with it myself, with the help of a good dictionary. Do you have one I could borrow until I can buy one?'

'Well, there you are, that proves it. You can't leave. You need Francesco to help you.'

'I don't think he will.'

'He's not going back to Bologna yet, so he has plenty of time now and no excuses.'

'Please, Teresa, just leave it.'

Teresa looks at her for a long moment. 'I thought you two were getting on so well.'

'I thought so too, but…'

Anna explains briefly about Will and how Francesco thought she was stupid to meet up with him again, and how he'd stormed out on her. It's a relief to talk about it, a lot easier than she thought it would be. Anna can't help wishing Teresa could have been her sister rather than Jane.

'Do you want *me* to talk to Francesco, and tell him you and your friend are finished and that he has gone back to England?' Teresa asks when Anna has finished telling her about Will's proposal.

'No. I want to find the right moment myself.'

Teresa looks at her, pausing before asking, 'Do you like my brother?'

Anna looks up. 'A lot.'

'I thought so. Well then' – Teresa gets out of her chair and comes over to hug Anna – 'you must make sure you find the right moment before it's too late,' she says, as if it were the easiest thing in the world. 'Now, I'm going to go and make some lunch and you must rest, like the doctor ordered. But ten o'clock in the morning is too early for good Tuscan wine,' she says, checking her watch and grinning. 'Afterwards I'll go and hunt for my school dictionary.'

Anna dozes on and off for the rest of the day, and it's almost dark when she wakes to Alba's chatter. She switches on the table light and the little girl runs over to her bed carrying a picture of the stormy river and chatting nineteen to the dozen in a stream of Italian. Although Anna's Italian is improving, she can only catch a few words, 'Billi' and 'Teresa' and '*fiume*' (the river) being just some of them. She is followed by Teresa and Francesco, who is carrying a huge wicker basket covered in a white cloth. Anna feels dopy after her long sleep. She rubs her eyes, saying, 'Whoa, Alba – you can talk for Italy!'

'Alba, slow down a little so Anna can follow what you're saying,' Francesco says.

He helps Teresa carry a table into the room and she spreads the cloth, laying four places, asking Francesco to fetch another basket they've left outside the door containing more food and wine.

'Hey, are we having a party?' Anna asks, pulling herself up in the bed.

Teresa straightens her pillows and Anna catches hold of her wrist. 'You're spoiling me,' she says. 'I'm sorry I can't get up to help.'

Alba climbs up beside her. 'That's exactly what this is. It's a party for you and me, to celebrate. I love parties, don't you? Usually we buy a new dress for a party, but this is a different kind of party. Babbo said it was to be spon… spon…'

'Spontaneous.' Francesco helps his daughter.

'That's right,' she continues with her chatter, 'a party that you don't have to plan too much, a party without balloons or presents.'

Anna understands the drift and replies in halting Italian, 'The best present for this party is your voice, Alba.'

The timely sound of a bottle of Prosecco being uncorked and Alba's begging for a glass, 'Me, me, me too. It's my party too,' makes them all laugh.

'You can have a tiny drop, as long as it doesn't make you bubbly too,' her father says, pouring her a thimbleful.

Teresa has thrown together a wonderful feast with what she had in her larder. Free-range eggs made into a huge *frittata* containing *zucchini* flowers and red Tropea onions, sprinkled with shavings of *parmigiano*, browned under the grill until bubbling and golden; stuffed tomatoes and aubergines roasted in the oven and portions of rabbit and chicken seasoned with garlic and rosemary with tiny crisp potatoes. They finish off with bowls of *ricotta* topped with the first wild strawberries, picked from the slopes above the *agriturismo*.

'I shall be getting so fat if my leg doesn't heal quickly,' Anna says, leaning back against the pillows, feeling full and relaxed.

'Don't worry,' Alba pipes up, 'Babbo has found you a job. So, when you are better there will be no time for getting fat.'

'What job?' Anna looks at him questioningly.

'I was going to discuss that with you. Maybe later, when I've put this chatterbox monkey to bed.'

He picks Alba up and holds her upside down, much to the little girl's delight. She squeals and shouts, '*Ancora, ancora*. Do it again!'

Teresa, who is clearing away the dishes into the big basket to carry back to the *agriturismo*, tells him off for making her overexcited.

Anna suggests a story to calm her down.

'Come and sit next to me and I'll tell you about my friends who used to live at the bottom of my garden in England, when I was little.'

Francesco plonks her down onto the bed next to Anna, who proceeds to tell her about the characters she invented to fill her lonely English childhood. It's the first time she's ever told anybody these stories.

Just after eleven, Francesco returns from putting Alba to bed. 'I hope it's not too late. Teresa was right, it took me longer to settle Alba tonight.'

'Don't worry, I'm not tired at all. I've been asleep most of today.'

She watches as he pulls up one of the leather armchairs and then says, 'You must be so happy to have her back to normal.'

'I can't describe it.' He stops, the joy in his eyes speaking more than words.

'Tell me about this work idea,' she says, to break the silence.

'It was really Teresa's idea, not mine. But of course, it depends on your plans. I've told her it won't work.'

'Why not?'

'Well, you won't be staying, will you? Not after meeting up with your partner again,' he says, tapping his foot on the tiled floor.

'You mean Will?' She feels the need to name him, to stop skirting around the issue, and remembers Teresa's advice. It is now or never. 'Will and I have no future. It's over.'

'It didn't look like that to me.' He looks at her, daring her to contradict him.

'What are you talking about?'

'Don't lie to me, Anna. I saw you in the piazza down in Sansepolcro. You looked very much together.' He rises from the armchair. 'I knew it was a mistake to come and talk to you.'

'Have you been spying on me?' It's her turn now to raise her voice. 'That's unforgivable. I didn't have you down as a typical jealous Latin lover.'

'And I didn't think you were like all the other English women who come over here to have a romantic fling. To see if we Italian men are as good as they say.'

He is about to leave when she bursts out laughing. 'Just listen to us, Francesco. We are ridiculous.'

He looks at her, then, raising both hands in exasperation, sits down again.

'Can we start again, do you think?' she asks.

When he doesn't object, she tells him everything about her meeting with Will. 'But we parted friends,' she ends her explanation. 'Even if we never see each other again, we'll always be friends. That's just the way it is.'

'So I got the wrong end of the stick. I do have a tendency to speak sometimes before I think.'

'Well, now you know. And for the record, I'm *not* doing a piece of research into the romantic habits of the Italian male species.'

He looks sheepish. 'We've both come out with huge generalisations this evening! I don't know why I said that.'

'Because those sorts of things have always been said about our two cultures.'

'We have a saying, "*Tutto il mondo è paese*". You should think more along those lines, instead of focusing on the differences.'

She doesn't understand, and he tries to explain. 'I think there is a saying in English, "It's a small world", but that doesn't quite express the same notion.' He searches for the words. 'Or… the same observation about life.'

He pauses before continuing. 'In the end, people are not so very different from each other, you know.'

She is quick to disagree. 'But there are *huge* differences. You Italians are more gregarious. We English will go to great lengths to find places where we can be on our own.'

'I have a few Italian friends who like peace and quiet too. What else can you come up with?'

'*La bella figura?* Keeping up with the Italian Joneses, strutting the fashion stuff, giving a good impression and all that jazz.'

'Oh, that old cliché.'

'Is it? The *passeggiata* in the evening, showing off how beautiful you are, worrying what people will say about you.'

'I think you've been watching too many old black and white films, like *La Dolce Vita*. And what's so wrong with fashion, anyway? It's one of our main exports. Go on, you'll have to do better than that. Admit it – you English care about what people think, too. Keeping up with the English Joneses?'

'I once read that Italians live to eat, not eat to live.'

'Well, thank God for that. I have to say the food my American friends ate was not good. Fries and burgers with ketchup, and hot dogs… I think I prefer Italian food to fast food any day, thank you.'

'I have to agree with you on that one.'

'In any case, Anna' – he waves his hands about enthusiastically as he comes up with another point – 'what is so wrong with differences? What is wrong with the idea of mixing up the differences that you seem to worry about, and creating a wonderful new recipe?'

She laughs. 'Actually, I've thought of another. I remember when I sat in a café and did my first serious bit of people watching in Italy…'

'People watching?'

'Oh yes, people watching. It's a very serious pastime, you know.' She laughs. 'I thought everybody was arguing. People all around me were talking with raised voices, waving their arms about, prodding each other when they wanted to reinforce a point. I thought a riot was going to break out at any minute. I was quite worried. But I know now it's your way of having a conversation.'

He laughs at her description. 'But it's *good* to talk!'

She smiles at him. 'Yes, it is! It's *really* good to talk.'

They sit for a while and then she asks him to tell her about his work idea.

'Teresa and I think you could develop your teaching. We've seen how good you are with Alba. The long summer break is nearly here, and there must be other parents who would welcome a chance for their children to learn English. You could create a *Scuolaclub*.'

'But I'm not qualified.'

'Who cares? You are wonderful with Alba. A natural teacher.'

'You're very kind, but I'm not the best person for your idea. I didn't even finish my studies.'

'And so? What does that matter? What did you study, anyway?'

'Don't laugh, but…' Anna trails off, wondering if she dare admit what she was going to say.

'You need to have more confidence in yourself,' he chides. 'I think you have very low self-esteem, and you don't deserve to think that way.'

His encouragement spurs her on to explain. 'I started a degree in Italian when I was eighteen. I suppose, deep down, I always wanted to find out more about my Italian side. But the course wasn't right. There was too much Renaissance literature and not enough everyday stuff. It didn't seem relevant to me at the time, and so I dropped out. Then I tried a teaching course and dropped out of that, too, and finally I did a secretarial course – a means to an end, really. I drifted from job to job and ended up working for an estate agency. Then I met Will when he came in to look for a house. End of story.'

'Why do you say "end of story"? It makes you sound old and defeated. *Su – coraggio*, Anna! You're not that old. Actually, how old are you?'

She laughs. 'That's not the sort of question a gentleman asks a lady!'

'*Coglioni* – there you are, a new word for your vocabulary list.'

She laughs. 'I already know the word for bollocks. It's one of the first things I learned. And I'm thirty-three – but don't tell everybody.'

'Wonderful! Three is a special number. Your life is just beginning. I'm forty soon, so I know what I'm talking about. And
late development runs in my family. My father was in his late
forties when Teresa and I were born. Have a good think about
the teaching idea. Sleep on it, and let me know.'

He gets up to leave, but stops just before he reaches the door.
'Before I forget, I've translated another section of the diary. I
don't know who's more interested – you or I.'

He hands her a folder containing a few typed pages and her
face lights up.

She grins at him. '*Grazie mille*, Francesco. Has Teresa been
talking to you?' She hugs them to her heart. 'I'm so grateful. I
can't wait to read on. Thanks so much.'

'*Buona notte*, Anna!' he says as he shuts the door behind him.

Before continuing with her mother's story, she thinks over the
idea of teaching English to local children. She needs a job. Setting
up a *Scuolaclub* won't bring in bundles of lire, but it will be a
start. And if she is careful, her earnings will allow her to save the
money Mamma left her, and buy extra time to stay and complete
her research into her mother's diaries. She can't possibly shelve it
now. She decides too to ask Teresa if she can take over Francesco's
jobs round the *agriturismo* once he returns to Bologna at the end
of the summer. If she agrees, it will make her feel better about
staying on in Tuscany.

Snuggling down in her improvised bed, she opens Francesco's
envelope and pulls out the typed sheets.

CHAPTER NINETEEN

Sunday, 18 November 1944

It has done nothing but rain and rain this autumn. As if the gods are crying in despair over man's stupidity. Missing Jim is a physical ache. I lie next to Nonna, her snoring and my worrying keeping me awake, so that each morning I leave my bed unrefreshed. And Davide is still missing. It is almost two months since we last saw him. Capriolo told us he would be back soon, that he has probably joined up with another group of *partigiani*. It happens all the time. I want to believe him, and I repeat this theory to Mamma over and over when she stands there, wringing her hands and calling on the Virgin and all the saints to look after her son, but I'm not sure any of us believe Capriolo. Davide's girlfriend, Carla, pesters us for news and visits us most evenings, sitting by the fire, helping my mother wind wool and joining in with rosary prayers. It's a miserable time, and the weather does nothing to lift our spirits.

Capriolo tells us the war should have been over months ago if it wasn't for the rain. Soldiers on both sides are holed up in the mountains like rats in drains and tanks can't operate properly, slithering and sliding down the mountain. No progress has been made by either side. Mud and the cold add to everybody's misery. Crops are ruined and work at the mill has stopped. The river is fuller than we ever remember and rushes past the mill like an angry beast. We have to shout to make ourselves heard above the roar of the water.

Then, a couple of days ago, the land warmed up with unexpected sunshine, causing fantastical mists. Montebotolino floated on clouds, its roofs ghostly cut-outs against the sky.

'It will hold tomorrow,' said Papà, who could read the weather perfectly. 'We'll start grinding at dawn.'

In the early morning, he lifted the planks to the mill race and I watched the water gurgle and rush with a whoosh down the channel at the side of the meadow. I ran inside to the room next to the chamber where the millstones were already turning.

'Help me load the meal into the hoppers.' My mother was forced to shout to be heard above the storm of water below us and the grating of huge stones grinding over stone. Beneath us water was funnelled through two narrow channels, revolving the paddles which turned the stones.

'These sacks over here are full of maize,' she hollered. 'We'll do these first and then the corn.'

There was much less work for us at this stage of the war. The *tedeschi* have been quick to take hay for their horses, and much of the grain has been left to rot in the fields as there are no men to bring it in.

'Mamma,' I yelled above the clatter, 'one of the stones isn't grinding properly. I'll go and tell Papà.'

It is a nuisance when this happens. Sometimes a block of wood or a knot of brambles clogs the paddles.

'Let's hope it's a baby boar like last time,' my mother shouted. 'We could do with meat in the larder.'

I ran to tell Papà, who was unloading sacks from a customer's donkey. He shouted at me over the noise of the water. 'Go below and see what's happening.'

I sped down the slope at the side of the mill to the archway where the water should have been gushing out, turning the paddles on the shaft which drove the millstones. It reminded me of games I used to play with Davide, when he would snatch my headscarf from my head and toss it into the mill race.

'Run, run, Ines – before it's too late,' he'd shout, laughing at my dismay. Off I would scamper, as fast as my little legs could carry me, trying to retrieve my scarf before it was swallowed up by the paddles under the mill. Once, I'd tripped before I could catch it and Mamma had scolded me for being careless and losing my only scarf. She made me wear a rag on my head until she had time to sew me another one.

'The water's not flowing properly from the funnel on the left, Papà,' I shouted.

He fetched his long pole from the storeroom and stood on the wall of the millpond, prodding the mud.

'There's something stuck fast in one of the funnels,' he yelled. 'I can't move it. There's nothing for it – we'll have to drain the pond.'

He swore. The extra work meant losing a whole day's grinding. I hate it too when we have to drain the pond because of the stinking, rancid mud and the smell that lingers in the mill for days afterwards.

Slowly the water drained away through the funnel on the right and we stood together on the mill steps, waiting to see the cause of the blockage.

Even before Papà jumped down into the sticky mud and turned the body over, I knew it was him.

Davide's poor face was barely recognisable. Fish had nibbled at his eyes and the hollows stared blindly up at us. Mamma screamed and howled like a dog in agony, a sound I shall never forget. Papà had to pull her away from Davide's body in the mud as she keened over and over, 'My son, my only son! What have they done to you?'

I stood there, numb. My tears couldn't fall, for in my heart I'd sensed he wasn't returning to us. I'd been crying inside for weeks. I concentrated on my mother instead.

News spreads fast among mountain people, and friends and neighbours started to appear down the mill track that day offering condolences. There is practical help, too. Davide's body was lifted gently out of the mud and kind souls washed him, arranging him on our kitchen table so we could lay him out. The men helped fill the millpond again and finished the jobs that we had set out to do that day.

I cannot recall exactly who came that afternoon. Those hours are a blur of misery, with my poor parents inconsolable. My feelings are frozen but I do remember Capriolo staying the whole day. He sat there, tears coursing down his face unchecked. Later on, he helped, as best he could manage with his injured hand, as my mother and I prepared poor Davide's body for burial. We covered the bullet hole which had taken away half of the back of his head with one of Papà's caps and we dressed him in Papà's Sunday suit.

'I shan't need it any more,' he said. 'I shan't be going to Mass again.'

We removed his river-soiled trousers, and in the pocket I found the rosary beads I'd pressed into his hands to keep him safe. I flung them on the fire. Then I fetched the letter he gave me before he left from the trunk at the foot of my bed.

'Read it to me, Ines,' Mamma whispered.

We sat in the dark and I leant into the dying glow of the fire to read aloud his words. His letter had been written in neat script on a page torn from his old schoolbook. It was brief, and a couple of words were blotted with smudged ink. Davide was never a good scholar. He preferred to be outside, helping tend livestock and driving the oxen to plough our field. I pictured how he must have struggled to guide his pen across the paper, tongue at the corner of his mouth, and that is when I started to weep.

My dear parents,

I am sorry I will not see you again.

I am sorry I will not be there to help you with the grinding.

I am sorry I will not bring grandchildren to your fireside.

But I am not sorry that I die for the freedom of Italy.

Your loving son, Davide

With a strangled cry, Capriolo strode out of the kitchen, leaving the door open to the darkness outside.

CHAPTER TWENTY

November 1944

Capriolo found me in the cemetery. I'd picked a bunch of white *vitalba* seed heads for Davide's grave. It was all I could find in the November landscape. With my brother's old jacket round my shoulders, I sat listening to the wind moaning through the coppice of firs planted along the cemetery walls. I stared at the photo of him we had found to place on his stone. I wanted to talk to him, but I couldn't equate his handsome, cheeky young face beaming at me from this picture with the rotting corpse half buried in mire at the bottom of our millpond.

The cemetery gate was rusty and it creaked as Capriolo let himself in. He sat beside me on the ground. Neither of us said anything for a while, and I was pleased he didn't try to fill the silence with empty words. Eventually he took my hand, and then the tears that I had held back in front of my parents spilled down.

'He was a brave young man, Ines.' He spoke softly. 'You must remember him with pride. Before he died, he saved many lives through the documents he found.'

Wiping the tears angrily from my cheeks, I withdrew my hand from his. 'Does it really matter?' I said dully. 'Does any of this stupid, stupid war matter? I can't bear it. I can't bear all this pain and hatred. And I can't bear to be here any more.'

'Yes, there's hatred and there's certainly pain. But there's good, too. You have to remember why we're fighting.'

'I've forgotten why. It seems pointless.'

'Then Davide's death will have been pointless too.'

'He was too young to die.'

'I know,' he said, looking away from me. 'And I feel I am to blame.' He picked a pine cone from the grass and crushed it in his good hand, before saying, 'We will remember him always young.'

'Who did this to him, Capriolo? Who? Find out who it was and do the same to him,' I cried.

He put his finger under my chin and lifted my face, wiping a tear away. 'Come on, Ines. *Su!* Talking like that won't bring him back. Talk about him. Talk to me about your brother. Don Luca performed his funeral Mass, but we shall perform our own service for him up here where he loved to be.'

He gestured to the mountains behind us. 'You start. Tell me the first thing that comes into your mind. Talk, little one.'

I looked at him, frowning, thinking his idea was a little crazy, but then pictures came to me. I started, hesitant at first. 'I remember when the three of us were in trouble with Don Luca.'

Capriolo took up the story. 'We were conducting our own flying experiment after school.'

'We'd been learning about Leonardo da Vinci and his marvellous inventions, and Professor Gerico had shown us a huge book with pictures of his flying machines, wheels and other contraptions. The three of us spent ages trying to design our own aeroplane.'

'*Dio mio!* I remember when we tied home-made wings to your arms and made you stand on the edge of the ridge behind the church in Rofelle.'

'We'd collected feathers for weeks from Giorgio's chicken run to make them and we'd got Davide to sneak in under the wire because he was the smallest. I was so scared, you know. As I stood there on the edge of the meadow staring down at the river and rocks below, with those ridiculous wings on me which I knew would never work, I thought I'd wet my drawers.'

'Thank God Don Luca turned up when he did. He was furious! I can remember his words like yesterday: "What in the name of Jesus, Mary, Joseph and all the holy saints are you three doing out here?" Do you remember, Ines?'

'But of course! Davide ran off and hid behind the church, but you and I had to spend the rest of the afternoon polishing candlesticks in the sacristy.'

Then we were laughing. In between our laughter, Capriolo said, 'He had an appalling sense of humour, too, your brother. He always laughed at his own jokes and they were crap.'

'And when he laughed,' I continued, 'he would throw back his head and open his mouth wide, roll about on the floor sometimes. It was infectious. Nonna actually did wet herself once. She laughed so much watching him laugh, she couldn't help it.'

We smiled at each other and then I said, 'Now you tell me something about him.'

His head down, he thought for a moment, then he began, his voice barely audible.

'He was the younger brother I never had. I used to think he was a pain, always tagging along, asking annoying questions about how to shave, how to make smoke rings. And then later...' He looked at me when he said this, pausing, 'questions about what women liked. He spoke to me about his first girlfriend, Carla. I tried to advise him on a few things. But after a while, the difference in our ages didn't matter. War is a leveller, if nothing else.'

'Carla is a lost soul. She comes to our house most evenings. She says she feels his presence by the hearth. I can't bear it,' I said.

'She's young. Time will heal.'

'Will it, Capriolo? Do you really believe that?'

There was silence for a few seconds, almost as if Capriolo was considering whether to share a detail. We'd spent so many hours of our childhood together that sometimes I feel I know what he is thinking. He took his cap off and his hair flopped down over his face as his fingers plucked at tufts of grass at the edge of the grave. His right hand was still bound in a piece of rag.

'Your wound is taking a long time to heal,' I said. 'If you take off that filthy binding, I could have a look. It probably needs bathing in salt water, and I could prepare you a salve of garlic and honey.'

He looked up, pushed his hair back from his face.

'There's no need, Ines. It will heal by itself.' He shoved his hand in his pocket and I saw sadness cloud his eyes as he continued to speak.

'Your brother was very brave. Back in August, we were fighting side by side. It was blazing hot. We were down near Coriano, on the road to Bologna, sheltering in a bombed-out farm. Davide needed a smoke. I remember him saying he'd give anything right then to jump in the sea, that he'd never been down to the coast and that he'd made himself a promise to go down to Rimini when the war was over. He'd take the mill cart, he said, and spend a day down there with you and Carla and your folks. We talked about all kinds of things that afternoon – our plans, our dreams. My guard was down, I suppose. We left the farmhouse, and the next thing I knew I was in the dirt, Davide on top of me, the rat-a-tat-tat of tracer bullets from a *tedeschi* machine gun bouncing dust up all around us. Then, in the few seconds when the machine gun crew were blinded by their own fire, he hauled me to my feet and we were up, stumbling away and into another doorway. He saved my life that day, covering me with his body without thinking of his own safety.'

Both of us went quiet then, and I saw tears running down his face again. 'He was too young, yes, and at times I think he saw war as a kind of game, but his death wasn't pointless, Ines. You must never think that.'

The November air is chilly. I shivered and he started to take off his scarf. He would have wound it round my neck, but I stopped him.

'I have to get back,' I said. 'Mamma's in a state at the moment, so I have to cook supper and take care of all the household chores. All she does is sit in her chair by the fire. It's my job to light it now, when it was always her first task each morning. She doesn't even acknowledge Carla when she visits. The pair of them sit there, like ghosts.'

'Before you go...' He took hold of my arm. I wondered what he was going to do. He moved closer.

'Davide asked me to look out for you, to check on you and the *inglese*,' he said.

'You mean Jim? He does have a name, you know.' I moved away from him so we were no longer touching.

'It was something you said earlier,' he persisted. 'You said you couldn't bear to be here any more. Is that why you're marrying him? So you can escape all this? Your memories will chase you wherever you go, you know. Are you sure you know what you're doing?'

He raised his voice when he said this, but I was angry too and I shouted back, 'What are you talking about? I am marrying him because I love him.'

'And how will your parents manage now that Davide lies here?'

He pointed at the freshly dug grave. 'Don't you think you should be staying with them? I didn't expect you to go to *Inghilterra* with him after this. I thought I knew you better.'

'You don't know me at all. Just because we've lived near each other all our lives and gone to school together, it doesn't mean to say you know me and what goes on inside my head, inside my heart. And anyway, what do you know about love?'

I was in full flow by then, anger and guilt making for potent ammunition. 'You're just in love with the war and your beloved communist ideals. That's all you know about. You don't know the first thing about love.' I was crying noisily, great sobs welling up from deep within me.

He didn't attempt to console me. He pulled his cap firmly down on his head and left the cemetery, muttering, 'I know all about love, Ines.'

I listened to the gate clang against its metal post, the harsh sound echoing into the soughing of the pines, and the sound of his feet trudging down the path back to the village.

CHAPTER TWENTY-ONE

Anna sits on the step outside her mini-apartment with her morning mug of tea, feeling unbearably sad about Davide. How did he end up in the millpond? Who placed his body there so cruelly for the family to find? That can't have been an accident. How can a parent ever recuperate from the death of a child? And a death so terrible. Perhaps Mamma never talked to her about the war because some things were too painful to recall. Now Anna can hear her voice speaking through her diaries.

Billi has found her and seems to sense her mood, and tries to coax her into playing, biting her bare toes with his sharp little teeth. She tickles his tummy and says aloud, 'Careful of my sore leg, little fellow. It's all right for you, with nothing to worry about except when your next meal's coming.'

Deciding she needs human company, she hobbles round to Teresa's.

'*Permesso?*' she calls, pushing open the door to the *agriturismo*.

Francesco is reading a newspaper in the dining room. He looks up as she comes in. 'Hey! What are you doing up and about? *Buongiorno. Che muso lungo stamattina.*'

When she looks puzzled, he translates. 'You have a very long face this morning. What's up?'

She sits down opposite him, leaning her elbows on the table, her head in her hands. 'I finished reading what you translated,' she sighs. 'About Davide. I want to weep.'

Folding up his paper, he reaches across and touches her hands. 'So cruel,' he says, and she nods in agreement.

'Man's inhumanity to man. I doubt animals are so heart-less… Sorry, I'm not good company today, Francesco.'

'Well, we need a remedy. How about a change of scenery? It's a lovely day. Alba's playing with friends, and there are no jobs to be done for Teresa with the *agriturismo* empty of guests. You need a good dose of distraction.'

'That would be lovely.'

'How about I take you to see the watermill where your mother lived? Do you think you can manage?'

'It depends how much walking is involved. But I thought you said it was a pile of stones? I'd love to see Mamma's place, but the grouchy old honey seller warned me not to go near it. Isn't it dangerous?'

'It's uninhabited, run-down and covered in brambles, but most of it is still standing.'

Teresa interrupts them, hands on hips. 'What a ridiculous plan, Francesco. There's no way Anna can manage to walk along the river with her leg like that. Give it a week, at least. What are you thinking of, the pair of you?'

Anna is disappointed, but she knows Teresa is right. She spends the following days doing strengthening exercises for her leg and reading back through the diaries. Teresa gives her little jobs to do now and again, and the two women often find themselves sitting at the kitchen table, preparing vegetables, chatting while they work.

'Do your parents ever mention the war years?' Anna asks one day.

'Only to say it was a bad time. My mother talks about her grandparents sometimes, especially around November, when we remember our dead at the *Festa dei Morti*. We visit the cemetery and place fresh flowers by our dead relatives' tombs. Her grand-parents were shot by German soldiers for refusing to give up their cow for provisions. Bisnonno told them they couldn't manage without her, that they were nothing but thieves and to get out of his stable. And they shot them where they stood. Poor things.'

'I can't imagine how terrible the Occupation was.'

'Our older people have internalised those times. Up at the day centre, where my friend Patrizia works, the elderly with dementia talk about the past and their memories trickle out. We should really record what they say.'

'I'll think about that,' Anna says. 'And maybe I'll donate my mother's diary to Egidio's museum,' she adds, not sure whether her mother would want her to do that.

One week later, she is down at the river near the start of the path leading to the mill, where a few sunbathers are relaxing: families up from the sweltering, congested coast enjoying picnics in the mountain air. Francesco and Anna soon lose them as they make their way slowly downstream to where the river forks.

'The river has changed over the years,' he explains. 'It used to run in one continuous flow at this point, but nature does what it wants. We'll take the right fork. I hope it's not too overgrown, I haven't been down here for a while. Let me check the path first. Wait here.'

She watches him as he steps over large boulders and wades through the water in his river shoes. Willow branches, olive green and silver in the breeze, stroke the surface of the stream and the cicadas keep up their noisy, sawing racket. He turns back and comes to sit next to her on a large boulder. 'Careful how you go, Anna. I don't want Teresa on my case. Can you manage…?'

He stops, turning slowly to her, a finger to his lips. Upstream a mother deer is drinking at the water's edge, her fawn close behind. When she catches their scent, she lifts her head and then she is off, scrambling up the bank and into the dense oak woods, her fawn not far behind.

'How sweet they are!' whispers Anna. 'It's the closest I've been to deer so far. My next ambition is to see a porcupine.'

'They're nocturnal, so we won't see one today. But we can keep a lookout for their quills another time. Alba collects those.'

He points to a hollow in the mud, bending down to examine marks left at the river's edge. 'What do you think these are?'

'Maybe holes from somebody removing the stones?' she suggests. 'They're so beautiful. In England they're sold for exorbitant prices at garden centres. Somebody with the right machinery could make a fortune here.'

'Fortunately it's forbidden to take stones from the river without a special permit. No, this hole has been made by a wild boar, cooling down in the mud.'

She finds being in his company so interesting. 'You know so much about the wildlife around here. You'd make a great guide,' she tells him, hunkering down to examine the muddy hole. It smells strongly of animal, and she wonders if a boar might be watching them from within the bushes lining the riverbank.

'My father often took me on walks when I was very little. That is, when he was feeling well enough. He was injured in the war and suffered with poor health afterwards. He knew this place inside out. As a boy he explored every nook and cranny, gathered chestnuts, hunted boar, played and hid in the caves.'

He picks up a stone, throwing it into a deep pool. 'I miss him, he was special.'

'You're lucky to have a father you loved. I never felt close to mine.'

They continue their walk, the vegetation so thick in places Francesco has to cut brambles and branches with his knife to clear a route. He is solicitous, asking at regular intervals if her leg is all right, urging her to be careful as they step from stone to stone. Round the next bend of the river, where the current is stronger, they come upon a ruined mill, little more in parts than a pile of stones tumbling into the water. She follows Francesco to a flight of stone steps, each tread almost concealed by ferns and moss.

'Be very careful,' he turns to warn her, 'this staircase is leaning away from the side of the building.'

She doesn't want to injure her ankle again but at the same time she's eager to explore where her mother spent the first eighteen years of her life. The paint on the front door has almost peeled away and the knocker, in the form of a lion's head, is rusting and about to fall off. She prises it away and puts it in her pocket. 'I don't care if it's stealing,' she says, rubbing the lion's head, knowing her mother has probably touched it.

'Do you know who owns the mill now?' she asks. 'So far Mamma makes no mention of any other relatives in her diary, other than my grandparents and of course poor Davide. And they've all passed away now.'

'No, but it's bound to belong to somebody, even if it's been divided up and different people own different rooms in the place. That's often the way with property here. We could find out for you at the *Comune*.'

Next to the door, tangled in ivy, are traces of an old bread oven, its door rusting and full of holes. A long-handled shovel propped against the wall is speckled with woodworm. She wonders who last used it to push *focaccia* onto the hot ashes.

'Once the oven was lit,' Francesco tells her, 'they used the dying embers to bake other dishes. And people nearby who didn't have ovens would bring along their bread or vegetables for roasting on allotted days.'

Francesco picks up the shovel, examining it carefully. 'I think you should take this back and clean it up. I'm surprised it hasn't already been stolen. You see these old tools for sale in antiques markets nowadays. I saw some at the Sunday market in Arezzo recently, and they weren't cheap.'

She fingers the hand-beaten metal rings fixed into the cracked mill wall, and he tells her how mules were once the main means of transport and were tied up to the rings while their owners waited for their grain to be milled. He bends down, worrying at a piece of iron dug into the earth near the door and pulls up a mule shoe.

'We hang those up in England and they are supposed to bring good luck,' she tells him.

'Take this as a souvenir, too. We say to go "in the mouth of the wolf" when we wish somebody good luck and the reply is, "may the wolf die first".

'We say "break a leg",' she laughs. 'But I definitely don't want to do that – a twisted ankle is bad enough.'

She rummages for her camera in her backpack to photograph the mill and thinks about sending some pictures to Jane and Harry, wondering if it will pique their interest. Climbing gingerly down to the river and the arched space under the mill, she finds the remnants of a huge shaft that once turned the millstones. Francesco ventures further into the hollow and shouts above the noise of the river from within the dark space. '*Accidenti!* Somebody has sawn the paddles off and stolen them. *Peccato!* A pity!'

He jumps down to where she stands and brushes dust from his knees after his inspection of the mill workings. Anna is angry at the thought of strangers plundering souvenirs from her ancestors. She knows her feelings are irrational. After all, until this morning she hadn't even known there was anything left of her grandparents' mill. Her past feels so fragile. Without her diaries, it would be almost lost.

'I'd like to go inside, see where my mother lived. You've no idea how churned up I feel.'

She lets him take her hand as he pushes open the door, telling her to tread carefully on the rotten floorboards. When her eyes adapt to the gloom, she makes out a cracked stone sink under the window. Walking over to it, she tries to imagine her grandmother washing pots while looking out at the forest opposite the mill. It is very low, level with her thighs, making her think Nonna must have been short. A hole beneath the window shows how the sink drained primitively into the river below. Discarded on the floor are a broken colander with one leg missing and a ladle without a handle. On a shelf in a built-in corner cupboard with one door hanging aslant is a rusting tin of Lavazza coffee. She picks it up as another souvenir. In a magazine she's seen herbs planted in these vintage tins; she'll copy the idea and it can sit on her sill as another memento of her mother's story.

'I want to go upstairs to see where they slept – Nonna, Nonno, Mamma and Davide.' The names trip off her tongue as if she's been saying them every day of her life.

Very carefully, she climbs the ladder which serves as stairs to the bedrooms. It leans precariously against an opening to the upper storey. Plaster crumbles from the walls. There's a hole in the roof through which she sees picture-book clouds drifting across an azure sky. A crucifix hangs above an old metal bed frame holding a mouse-nibbled mattress. She imagines her grandparents falling into bed soon after dark and rising at sunrise, anxious to be at their tasks before the hottest part of the day. Stepping over to a window, with no glass or shutters to protect it from the elements, she gazes at the indigo-blue mountains. Wisps of sugar-spun cloud are caught in the trees on the summit. She places her hands on the stone sill and leans out to stare at the silver ribbon of water below as it dances its way down to the sea at Rimini. Sadness fills her and she shakes her head. Francesco comes over and takes her in his arms, not saying anything, just holding her. After a while he releases her, suggesting they go out into the sunshine.

They find a flat rock to sit on. She doesn't feel like talking, and he seems to understand her need to stay quiet. She watches him unpack their picnic. Francesco arranges a bottle of wine in the shallows, wedging it firm with a stone. Next, he spreads a cloth on the grass and lays out a half-loaf of *toscano*, a hunk of pecorino cheese, a jar of peppers in oil and a bunch of grapes. They eat in silence. The only sounds are the river and distant sheep bells. Slowly she grows calm, restored by the delicious lunch and grateful for his tactful presence.

'*Grazie*,' she says, draining the last drops of wine from her beaker. 'Having read about my mother enduring the brutalities of war, trying to be brave when my father disappeared to who knows where, it all suddenly overwhelmed me. The poor woman had gone through the war here, and then I know she had another type of personal war to deal with in England. She wasn't a happy woman. It's so, so sad, this old building in ruins, crumbling into nothing. It seems to mirror what I'm learning of Mamma's past.'

'It didn't crumble into nothing, as you put it. There's you, and your brother and sister. Your mother lives on through you all.'

'I wish she'd been able to talk to me properly about her life.'

'She's doing it now, Anna, through her story. Listen to her. If you need more help, I'm here too. Maybe we can find other people who knew your family. In those times, people came to sit in each other's houses in the evening, to keep company. It was called "*la veglia*". Theirs was a very close-knit community. And there was a lot of intermarrying between the families too.'

'Yes, I'd like to talk to more people about her. Thanks, Francesco. You're a very kind man.'

'You're a kind woman, who's been very good with my daughter, so we're all square. Come on, *andiamo*. The clouds are warning me there's another storm brewing. Best to get back before the river plays its tricks on you again.'

She helps him pack up the remains of their lunch, being careful not to leave any rubbish behind. They set off for the village without dawdling on their return journey.

Kissing him on the cheek when they arrive back at her house in the piazza, she says, 'Thank you for an amazing afternoon.'

'You're welcome. We must do it again. Good night, Anna.'

He cups her cheek briefly in his hand and leaves her standing at the door, and she watches him walk over to the *agriturismo*.

Removing the lid from the old coffee tin to wash it out, Anna finds a roll of paper inside, which she carefully withdraws. It looks like an official document, stamped and dated 1947, with a couple of signatures at the bottom. And wrapped in a piece of cloth is a medal, similar to those she saw displayed in Egidio's museum. Francesco will know the significance, she's certain. Yet another favour to ask of him. But she's sure he won't mind. Today, he showed such warmth and understanding. She enjoyed being with him.

Humming to herself, she slips a pot of basil into the beige-and-red-patterned tin and arranges it on her sunny windowsill.

Lessons at her *Scuolaclub Inglese* continue the following afternoon in the fresh air. Word has spread and she now has a regular group of six youngsters.

After quizzing them on their English words, she watches them play in the water. Teresa has told her the locals call the pool *la spiaggia*, the beach. During the war, German soldiers used to come to this spot on the river under the baking August sun and strip off their uniforms to cool down in the mountain water. She's sure this river could tell a tale or two. In the evenings she's taken to walking along the banks before sunset, relishing the cooler air, looking for fossils, watching dragonflies skim across the dancing water. At times she fancies she can hear voices murmuring, but when she turns to look, nobody's there; only the gurgle of water as it trips over the stones. Her head is full of the past and playing tricks on her, she concludes.

When the children have been collected from *Scuolaclub* by their parents, she helps Teresa in the kitchen for an hour or so, preparing the evening meal. A party of twenty is booked in for supper that evening, and she's pleased to offer an extra pair of hands.

'Can you slice those courgettes very finely for me, Anna? We'll make *carpaccio* of *zucchini*. Then pick a handful of borage flowers to sprinkle on top. And remind me to give you the rest of the translation before you go. Francesco's done some more.'

The vegetable garden is on a slope with a view of Montebotolino. As she fills a basket with purple borage flowers and gathers windfall cherry tomatoes, she glances up at the lonely village on the crags and decides she must brave another visit to the old honey seller. She's determined he will not get the better of her. It's frustrating knowing he was alive when her mother lived here and she still hasn't managed to talk to him properly. He might even have been around when her uncle was tragically killed and be able to fill her in on more details. But he's so difficult to approach, so stubborn in his refusal to talk about the war. She wonders if there is a saying in Italian for taking a horse to water but not being able to make it drink. She decides to ask Francesco the next time they talk, when she shows him the contents of her tin.

CHAPTER TWENTY-TWO

May 1945

On 2 May, the *tedeschi* surrendered. The war is over. People swarmed out of their houses as the news was relayed. They banged tin lids, struck metal ladles on buckets, swung cow bells to and fro, grabbed anything they could lay their hands on to create a din that spread across the valleys from hamlet to hamlet. Church bells pealed and people hugged, laughed, danced and cried.

We joined in with heavy hearts, for the loss of Davide is an open wound. Neither has there been any word from Jim since I kissed him goodbye seven long months ago. Capriolo visits whenever he can to keep us company. He understands the hole Davide's death has left in our lives. Over the hard winter of 1944, he'd knocked on our door as often as he could in the evenings and tried to fill Davide's space round the hearth. Nobody can explain his death to us, but war creates beasts of men and there are too many other accounts of cruelty to fathom – Davide is just one more number in a list of thousands. Only two days before the end of the war, we heard reports of the killing of another elderly couple in Rofelle who refused to move from their home along the Gothic Line. 'We are too old to move now,' they'd protested, 'and we've paid our rates. You've no right to do this to us. This is our home.' The *tedeschi* shot them as they begged to stay, two frail people who were no threat to anyone.

I continue to press Capriolo to pursue Davide's murderers whenever I see him. 'You must know something,' I insist, clenching my fists in anger. 'When you find who did it, let me know and I will be the first to take my revenge.' He listens, but he has no answers.

Farmers have started to bring grain to the mill again, gleaned later than usual from the meadows. Some of it is bad, the result of last year's meagre harvest, and has to be discarded. Despite it being the end of the war, nothing much has changed in the way of food supply. We are still short of too many things.

'Ines, spread all this grain onto sacking and pick out the bad. Save everything you can. Waste nothing.'

My father shouted instructions above the noise of rushing water. I was in the room leading to the machinery, collecting sacks of grain from our customers. He had made sure the millpond was filled, and we were to start grinding that afternoon. I welcomed the hard work, for it served to pass the time, which dragged.

Capriolo has disbanded his *partigiani* and started to visit us again more frequently. 'He won't come back, Ines, your fine Englishman,' he said to me. 'You'd best forget about him. He's gone back to his English women with their blonde hair and blue eyes. Not to mention their long legs. You're better off with one of us.'

I'm not sure if he is teasing. But over the past few months I've started to think there might be truth in his words. Last winter seemed to go on forever. It was wet and miserable and there was too much time spent cooped up indoors, too much time to think. Even now, when I try to visualise Jim's face, or the way he used to pronounce his Italian words in that funny way that made me smile, I find it difficult to remember him.

This May sunshine is more like August, and I took our couple of remaining sheep up to the pastures above the river. I rolled up my sleeves and undid the top buttons of my blouse, feeling like a lizard savouring the first sun after months of hiding away in the boulders. The grass was perfumed, the rock behind my back comfortingly warm and the first spring flowers nodded their heads in the breeze. Life would have been almost perfect if Jim were sitting beside me.

I jumped as a stone slithered down the bank. Maybe it was a viper also coming out of hibernation; they were at their most poisonous at this time of year. But it was only Capriolo. He jumped down and came to sit near me.

'You need to stock up now with more sheep,' he said. 'Tell your father I could take him down to market at Pieve next Monday and help him load a decent number onto the cart. Business is slowly starting up again.'

'I thought you were needed again down in the city? What about your office job?'

He picked a stalk of grass and chewed on it. 'They gave it to somebody else. But I don't mind. How could I stay holed up in an office after all these years on the mountains?'

'But those were years of fighting. There's no fighting any more, no battles to be won.'

'You're wrong there. There are plenty of battles to be fought. If we want the Italy we fought for, we have to keep up the political fight. I've been asked to stand as the local party representative. I can't do that from the city.'

'Won't you miss it? There's not much to do here.'

'I could never go back to the city. You'll miss this place too if you go to England, believe me. I've been to more places than you and there's nowhere that compares. The war has taught me a lot, not just about fighting. It's taught me more about life than I would have learned in peacetime.'

'I can't wait for Jim to come back and take me away.'

'Do you really think he's going to come back?'

'Of course! Why do you say such stupid things to me?'

'Because I'm a man and I know what men are like.'

'He's different.'

'Yes, he's different. That's what worries me.'

He got up and walked to the edge of the hillside. 'You think you want to escape from all this,' he said, gesturing to the horizon edged with the Apennines, blue in the afternoon sun. 'But you won't realise how much a part of this place you are until you've lost it. You'll be nothing when you leave here.'

'You talk such rubbish. I shall be Jim's wife. I'll be more than the miller's daughter who sometimes takes sheep and cows up onto the hillside.'

'You're so naive. You don't understand what I'm trying to tell you.'

He came close to me; I could feel his breath on my face and, embarrassed, I moved away.

'And you sound like a boring old man. You can stay here and fester and drink away the hours in the *osteria*, but I'm leaving for good. You're welcome to this place.'

I smacked the sheep into moving down the path, leaving him to think his lofty thoughts on the hillside.

Approaching the mill, I noticed a man waiting on the bridge. A tall stranger with short, blond hair, dressed in a British uniform. It looked like Jim and when he shouted my name, I dropped my stick and ran as fast as I could. He swept me into his arms. I could feel his bones through his shirt; he was gaunter than when he had left us in October, paler and more smoothly shaven. He looked very English in his neatly pressed uniform. Suddenly I felt shy.

'You're back,' I said, for loss of anything better to say.

'Did you ever doubt me, Ines?'

'It's been such a long time. Where have you been? I was worried you would want to return to England – to women with blue eyes and blonde hair, and—'

He interrupted. 'Ines, I've been – I've been to some dreadful places. I was so happy with you here in the mountains… the happiest I've ever been. Of course I came back to you. I've waited for this moment…' His eyes were wet with tears when he took me in his arms, and he held me so tight I could hardly breathe.

Then a crowd started to gather. My parents, people from the village who'd seen the British jeep arrive in the piazza and drive down to the river. Everybody wanted to shake his hand.

'We always thought you were an *inglese*, one of them said. 'But we couldn't be sure. *Bravo, bravo.*'

His hand was pumped up and down in grateful thanks so much that he told me later on he thought it was going to be pulled off. Everybody wanted to touch him, to thank the *inglese* for helping to bring about the end of the dreadful war – as if he had been the sole soldier in the whole of the British Army. But he was the only one to make it back to our village so soon after the end of the war.

5 June 1945

'Keep still, Ines… if you wriggle I shall be sticking pins in you instead of in the material.'

'Nobody will ever know it was a nightdress, Mamma, it's perfect. You're so clever, and the material is so fine.'

I ran my fingers along the lace-edged hem, the silk soft and cool against my skin. I had never worn anything made of such material. I'd grown used to wartime 'make do and mend' work clothes, hand-me-downs from my brother. I felt beautiful. I turned to look at myself in my mother's cracked mirror.

'If you bend like that again, the hem will be up in front and down at the back. You're worse than a fidgeting child today.' My mother had pins in her mouth, making it difficult for her to talk. 'I can't spend too long on this, so hold still. We still have so much to do before tomorrow.'

Tomorrow is my wedding day. There have been very few occasions in the last years for celebration and, with the relief of the war coming to an end and the announcement of our marriage, everybody has rallied to help us prepare a special feast. Neighbours have been leaving anything they can spare on the steps to our mill for days since Jim's return: baskets of vegetables, jars of preserves, wine and bundles of herbs.

'I can help you make *cappelletti* afterwards, Mamma.' We were given a basket of fresh eggs yesterday to prepare the traditional hat-shaped *ravioli* for our wedding breakfast.

'Why do you think I got up this morning at five o'clock? While you were sleeping, I was busy rolling the pasta. But we still have to decorate the stable for the party afterwards. I can't believe it's twenty years since your Papà and I danced in there for our wedding.'

She removed the pins from her mouth and rummaged in the trunk at the end of the cherry wood double bed where she and Papà slept after Nonno passed away. 'Come here, child. Let me fix this on you.'

She held up the veil she'd worn on her own wedding day. It was yellowed with age, hand-embroidered by my great-grandmother, who had been the first woman in our family to wear it on her special day.

'I'll wash it carefully and soak it in lavender water and it'll come up fine. Today is sunny, and we'll dry it in no time on the bushes.'

My father shouted up the stairs, 'Assunta, there's nothing left. Somebody stole our things.' Mamma went to the top of the ladder leading to the floor below and shouted down, 'You're searching by the wrong tree, Aldo. Look for the oak tree with the arrow carved in the bark.'

A few months after the start of the war, when the Germans rolled into town with their half-tracks to occupy Badia, many villagers buried possessions in boxes in the woods to stop them from being looted. As it was, houses were ransacked, and our hay was stolen for the troops' horses. Now it was time to retrieve the bottled vegetables, wine, linen and whatever else went into these secret stores. I think even Mamma forgot what she had put in there over two years ago.

'Come and help me yourself if you're so sure,' my father shouted again, 'but I think a bloody thief has taken our stuff.'

My mother hurried outside, muttering as she went, 'I really don't know how you would survive without me, Aldo. I have to do everything round here, and more besides.'

She took the spade roughly from his hands and started to dig a few metres away from where Papà was standing. The sound of metal striking metal proved she was correct. It is often the way with my parents. My mother has a great deal of common sense. Some of the linen was spotted with mildew, a jar of *zucchini* had spilled and we hoped the wine hadn't turned sour.

I shall always treasure my last afternoon spent with my parents as a signorina. We walked through the meadows together, gathering wild flowers that bloomed where crops grew in peacetime: vetch, harebells, purple orchids, dog daisies, sweet-scented yellow *ginestra* and garlands of old man's beard to wind around the beams on the stable rafters. We swept the stable floor clean and arranged wide planks on blocks of wood. My mother, hands on hips, looked satisfied as she inspected our afternoon's work.

'Tomorrow morning we'll arrange Nonna's sheets over the planks as tablecloths and scatter petals of briar roses round the plates, and our celebration will be one never to be forgotten. Aldo, go and chop wood for the oven. Ines and I must talk.'

We walked together in awkward silence along the mule track by the river. I had an inkling of what was coming.

'Tomorrow,' my mother began, 'you might not like what will happen when you and Jim are alone. When you're in bed together, tomorrow night after the *festa*, don't be frightened at what he'll do to you. It may be painful down below at first, but you'll get used to it. A wife has to do it for her husband, and if you're lucky, you'll make a baby and your family will start.'

All this was said in a rush, with Mamma never once looking at me, just staring straight ahead, her cheeks very pink.

I picked a pebble from the bank and skimmed it across the water as I'd often done in childish games with Davide. I didn't know what to say. Presumably what was going to happen tomorrow wouldn't be too bad, because she and Papà still slept together in the same high bed. Tomorrow Jim and I would sleep there, and a few days previously my mother washed and pressed a pair of old linen sheets for us.

'I've had to patch them,' she said, showing me her perfect, tiny stitches as I helped her fold the sheets after they'd dried on the bushes, 'but they're still fine quality and they'll do.

'They belonged to Nonna, God bless her. Such a pity she's not here for your wedding feast. She'd have loved it, Ines, but losing Davide was the death of her...'

My mother broke off and sighed. 'But, let's not be sad today. Just think of her tomorrow. She made the beautiful lace on all these pillowcases. If the war hadn't come along I could have taught you how to sew like this too.'

Mamma paused in our walk along the riverbank. 'Jim seems a kind man, but he's not one of us. My heart is breaking at the thought of losing another child.'

She cupped my face with her hands, a rare gesture of affection, and then her tears began to fall, despite her best attempts.

'First I lose Davide, and now you. England is too far away. How can I help you be a wife? Who will you talk to when you need advice? Are you sure you know what you're doing, child? The thought of you travelling all that way by yourself to England fills me with worry. How will you manage?'

'Mamma, we've talked and talked about this.' I tried not to show my impatience. 'Jim has to finish serving his time with the British Army. I've explained this so many times. He'll join me after three weeks. It won't be too long. He's managed to buy me a special train ticket, and his parents will fetch me from the station. They'll look after me as if I were their own daughter, and Jim has told you he'll bring me back often – every summer. Don't you believe him?'

'Saying and doing are two different things altogether. What if he can't find work? Or if the fare is too expensive? I know I'm being a selfish mother. I should be pleased you're so happy, but I only have you now.'

I folded my mother in my arms. Up until now it was always the other way round. She was the one to comfort and guide me. 'Mamma, I'll write to you often and tell you all about my new life in England.'

'What good are letters to me?' she whispered. 'I can't read or write. You know that.'

'You can ask Father Luca or even Capriolo to read the letters out to you. Please don't tell me not to go, Mamma. I love Jim, and he loves me. I can't stay here without him.'

This evening, my mother bravely stopped her tears. I am still none the wiser about the dreadful things which might take place in bed with Jim, but I'm not worried. Every time he takes me in his arms, kisses me, fondles me, I don't want him to stop. But I keep those thoughts to myself.

'Remember, Ines, you can always come back to us,' Mamma said as she straightened the ribbons on my wedding dress hanging from the wardrobe in her bedroom. 'You'll always have a home here.'

I couldn't imagine why she needed to say such things. I am happier than I've ever been and can't wait for my new life to begin.

7 June 1945

Everybody from near and far came to celebrate, even though the rain poured down on us on our special day.

'*Sposa bagnata, sposa fortunata,*' Mamma kept saying as she brushed my hair, consoling herself with the old belief that rain fell on a lucky bride.

Father Luca arrived late because the track was a quagmire, and he had to rush through our Mass because he was needed elsewhere to administer Last Rites to an old woman in Fresciano. We'd planned to walk from the church to the stable in a procession, carrying candles in jam jars to guide the way, but the rain put paid to that too. My silk dress was spattered with mud and the flowers drooped in my hair, but I hung onto my handsome English husband's arm and felt I was the most beautiful bride that had ever existed.

People came to the stable not only to celebrate our marriage, but the end of the terrible years of war. In my excitement I wasn't hungry enough to do the meal justice, but my eyes feasted on the spread. I couldn't remember when I had last seen such an amount of dishes: plates of ham, preserves of walnuts, *zucchini*, aubergines and mushrooms, wild salad leaves from the meadows sprinkled with grated truffles, roasted pigeons, pork, chickens and a whole young boar. The wine flowed, faces grew redder and jokes became bawdier. Then the music started. My father lifted his accordion onto his shoulder and after a rusty start, the music sang into the air. The planks that had served as tables were cleared from their supports, the leftovers tidied away into baskets to be carried home by our guests and the dancing started.

'You'll have to show me the steps,' my husband whispered as we moved into the empty circle of smiling faces. 'The dances are different from the ones I know.'

'Just listen to the music, we'll be fine.'

He clutched onto me as if he was about to fall, and our first waltz wasn't as smooth as it could have been, but it didn't matter as the floor soon filled with other dancers and we were swept round in the throng.

'Thirsty work, this dancing!' Jim stopped and a couple bumped into us. 'And my leg is hurting.' He led me from the dance floor to the corner of the stable where most of the men were congregated round barrels of wine. Some of them were already unsteady on their feet and they clapped him on the shoulders, congratulating him and pumping his hand up and down again. I watched him knock back a couple of beakers and then I joined Mamma. Just for today she'd changed from her black mourning clothes, worn since Davide's death. But her best Sunday frock of blue polka dot fabric hung off her and her face was sad. As I went over, she patted the empty chair beside her and I took her hand in mine. The music was too loud for talk, but we both understood what lay in our hearts.

At the edge of the dance floor, a crowd of men suddenly surged forward in an angry cloud. Papà stopped playing mid-tune, the notes from his accordion sighing into a discordant gasp as two men fell to the floor in a whirl of fists and curses. Capriolo pushed Ezio through the dancers, knocking a woman to the floor as he moved. Her partner, shouting in fury, tried to force the two men apart and was rewarded with a fist in his face, blood gushing onto his white shirt from a broken nose. I looked on in horror as Capriolo, his face dark with emotion, continued to manhandle Ezio, prodding him in the chest as he shouted, 'How could you dare turn up here today, *bastardo!* What did you do to him?'

He punched his victim to the floor and sat astride him. The sound of his fist banging into Ezio's skull was like an axe hewing a log. Ezio whimpered, 'Get off me, leave me alone,' and tried to wriggle free from Capriolo's thighs, but he was no match for the stronger man, and while his prisoner was pinned down, Capriolo continued to rant, slurring his words from the drink he'd consumed. 'It was your fault he died, you fucking weasel bastard. Prying into our lives like the rat you are. You don't deserve to live!'

Ezio's whining answer was almost unintelligible, but with my mouth wide open in shock, I heard him stammer, 'If you hadn't interfered that night, he'd still be alive. It's your fault, not mine…'

Capriolo let out an ear-piercing howl as he started again to pummel Ezio with his fists.

It was too much for me to bear. I pushed my way through the ogling guests and, grabbing a chair, I smashed it over the fighting pair.

'Stop it, the pair of you. This is my wedding day!'

Capriolo, about to deliver another blow, stopped mid-action, his ribcage heaving as he breathed in and out. He looked up at me and released his grip on Ezio, who lay whimpering and defeated in the dirt.

'I hope you're ashamed of yourself,' I said quietly, staring down at Capriolo. 'Haven't you had enough of fighting? The war is over now.'

'Some wars will never be over,' he replied, rising slowly. As he moved away, the crowd of guests parted to let him through. Ezio was left to stagger painfully to his feet. His front teeth were missing, his face was a mess, but nobody came to his aid as he limped away into the darkness. The party was over. As they wandered away, our guests mumbled their apologies, casting pitying looks at me, and I wondered what had caused Capriolo to be so full of venom. I searched for him in the crowd, but he was gone.

*

Usually the happy couple are escorted to the bedroom with songs and laughter and guests shout to the groom, 'Carry her in to bed, carry her in.' But there were no revellers left on our night. The bed was already strewn with flowers, and my mother had arranged her best nightdress for me on the pillow. Standing in the shadows, I was suddenly afraid, remembering my mother's words by the river.

'I'll leave you for a few minutes, Ines,' my husband said.

He closed the door and I undressed, shivering a little in the cooler night air. I lowered the flame on the lamp and caught a glimpse of myself in the mirror. There is no mirror in the bedroom I used to share with Nonna, and I've never seen my naked reflection. My breasts are full and the triangle of hair between my legs was obvious in the gloom.

Jim returned to me before I had time to put on my nightdress and I hurried over to the bed where it lay folded. He looked at me, and after a sharp intake of breath, he whispered, 'Don't put it on. Stay how you are.'

I covered myself with my hands but he pulled them away and bent to kiss my breasts and then he knelt, his tongue licking my belly, his fingers feeling inside me, making me tremble. He moaned and stood up, pulling off his clothes, swearing as he fumbled with the buttons on his trousers, and sat on the edge of the bed to remove them. I couldn't take my eyes off his nakedness. He picked me up and carried me to the bed. It creaked as he climbed on top of me and then creaked some more as he thrust himself inside me, a strange look on his face as he moved up and down, and then he cried out and lay heavy on my body. Grunting, he rolled away, blew out the light and within seconds he was asleep. I lay motionless in the dark, remembering what my mother told me about the duties of a wife. I throbbed. I was sticky and sore. I wanted Jim to talk to me and tell me everything was all right, that what I'd had to do I'd done well. I wanted to talk to him about the way our party ended, ask him if he had any idea why Capriolo had beaten Ezio up. Turning towards him, I gently prodded his side. 'Go to sleep,' he mumbled.

But I didn't feel sleepy. In the darkness, I listened to the water rushing past the mill, wondering if the same thing would happen again the following night.

And as Anna lies in her bed in San Patrignano, reading her mother's account of her wedding night, she feels a closeness that is almost unbearable, as if her mother is reaching out her hand for Anna to hold. The picture of her parents' first night is uncomfortable. When had their promise of romance started to turn sour? Presumably, married life had improved as time went on; Ines had given birth to three babies, after all.

How many daughters ever learn the intimate details of their parents' love life? How many women of her mother's generation were as innocent and ignorant about what went on between the sheets as Ines had been? Anna feels like a voyeur reading about these private moments, and yet, she reminds herself, her mother intended for her to read her diaries.

CHAPTER TWENTY-THREE

August 1999

The best kind of early alarm in the world, an August sun streaming through the window, wakes Anna. It's seven o'clock, and still cool enough to need a light fleece on top of her standard summer outfit of shorts and T-shirt. Breakfast on her front doorstep has become a routine, and she decides to look out for a little garden table and chairs when she is next down at the market in Sansepolcro. She sets about boiling water for her cup of tea. Some habits die hard.

Sitting on the step, mug in one hand and bread liberally smeared with home-made plum jam in the other, her head filled with thoughts of what she read last night, she observes a lizard peeping from behind a pot of white geraniums, waiting for a stray crumb or insect. Teresa is already up. A counterpane and pillow are airing on the windowsill of her bedroom and the flick of a duster from another window gives away her morning cleaning.

Francesco is up, too. Coming round the corner into the square with a basket of salad from the vegetable garden, he waves and she invites him over for a cup of tea.

'I'll bring my coffee instead, if you don't mind.'

She'd tried a mug of English tea on him once before and he'd hated it, preferring his tea weak with a slice of lemon.

A little while later they clink cups, one enormous, one tiny.

'Cheers! Thanks once again for what you've done, Franceso, but...'

'... it's strange to read about your parents in bed.'

'Exactly! We never imagine them like that, do we?'

'And yet, here we are,' he laughs, 'proof that they did it.'

'Poor Mamma, it wasn't exactly the best night of her life, and they certainly didn't live happily ever after.'

'Not many couples do. Anyway, what plans do you have for today?'

'I want to go up to Montebotolino again to try and get through to Danilo. The plot thickens, as we say, and I absolutely need to talk to him. There are so many threads I need to tie up. What was that fight all about? If everybody was at that wedding, it's likely Danilo was there too. I need to pick his brains.' She sips her tea.

'You won't find him there today. He has a market stall down in Pieve on a Thursday.'

'Oh, that's so annoying he won't be home! How frustrating. I'm not giving up on him, you know.'

'There are other places I can take you that feature in the diary, Anna. Fancy another trip with me?'

'Can you spare the time?'

'It's August. University is closed. I'm at your disposal, signorina,' he says, rising to perform a mock bow. 'Give me ten minutes to sort Alba out and I'm all yours.'

'*Troppo gentile, signore!* But before you dash off, kind sir, I've something to show you.' She fetches the medal from inside. 'What do you make of this?'

Francesco pulls on his glasses and whistles as he examines the white and gold medal. 'Wow! This was given for exceptional services to Italy. See the crown set in the middle?' he says, pointing the detail out to Anna. 'Where did you find it?'

'In that old tin I picked up inside the mill. I cleaned it out and found it. Oh – and this piece of paper was rolled up with it.' She hands the flimsy document to Francesco, who peers at it, removing his glasses and bringing it close to his eyes.

'I wonder why it was in my mother's mill?' she says.

'No idea. What a shame! The writing is illegible in parts. Can I borrow this? There's a friend in my department who might be able to help decipher it.'

Anna wraps the medal with its red and white ribbon into a piece of kitchen towel. 'See you this afternoon,' she says as he leaves.

In his car, he turns to her before they set off.

'Right! You were upset when we were at the mill, and I'm in two minds about our itinerary this afternoon. I'll let you decide, Anna. We could go to Caprese Michelangelo, the supposed birthplace of Michelangelo, or we could follow up another village described in your father's account – Fragheto. It's a sad place, but the countryside round there is stunning and not touristy at all.'

'Remind me why that name is familiar.'

'It was the site of a massacre.'

She pauses as the memory of her mother's diary comes to her. 'Oh yes, that was near the beginning, wasn't it? I think it was Toni who told that awful story. Goodness, please let's go. I want to do anything to help me follow up my parents' early years. *Andiamo!*'

'If you're really sure… *Andiamo a Fragheto.*'

They drive for a good ten minutes, neither of them speaking, comfortable in each other's company, Anna enjoying the scenery along the way.

The sun burns down but the countryside is still green and lush. They pass through hamlets with old houses brightened by geraniums and summer flowers planted in all kinds of containers – olive oil tins, wooden troughs, old tyres painted in cheerful colours. There are neat vegetable plots wherever there are gaps, even in the tiniest of spaces at the foot of steep crags along the road. It's too high for vines and olive trees to survive the winter, and the scenery is different from the typical Tuscan postcard views displaying cypress trees and elaborate villas. But this landscape feels more lived-in to Anna, a place where people have to respect nature in order to graft a living. Francesco pulls out to overtake a tractor laden with hay. The road is narrow but she feels safe. He doesn't take risks, which is understandable in view of how his wife died.

'I calculate you're more than halfway through your mother's diaries by now,' he says, pulling back onto the right-hand side of the road.

'I was flicking through what's left. I've read more than three quarters of them. Mamma seems to have written less as the years went by. And I think most of the remaining pages are in English, so you're off the hook there.'

'Well, if you think about it, she lived more years in England than in Italy, so English had become her day-to-day language.'

'You're right. More than fifty years in England compared with eighteen here. She never lost her lovely Italian accent, though. God knows why they chose the name Harry for my brother – she never could pronounce "h" properly.'

'Maybe it was your father's choice – 'Arry.' Francesco tries to pronounce Harry and she laughs.

'We have "h" in our alphabet but we don't ever pronounce it, so what do you expect?' he retaliates. 'Have a go at saying Roma the way I do.' He rolls his 'r' and Anna fails to copy him, and she giggles at her failure.

'*Ecco!* Same difficulty for you,' he chuckles.

After another couple of bends, he stops the car before a bridge spanning the River Marecchia.

'I think we should get out here so you can introduce yourself to the history of this particular area, Anna.'

Francesco takes her arm and they walk across the narrow stone bridge. The valley is wide at this point, and a fresh breeze funnels through, even though it's the height of summer. San Marino is perched on her steep crag in the distance, the Apennines falling away on all sides. Anna thinks it would have made a perfect vantage point for snipers on the lookout for the enemy. Young cyclists in bright yellow sportswear race past them in a group, strong legs pumping, cheery voices urging each other on. A tourist notice displaying a map and a grainy photo of eight dead men is posted by the bridge. She reads that some of them were aged only nineteen and twenty, probably the same age as the youngsters who have sped by her.

'This is called *Il Ponte degli Otto Martiri* – The Bridge of the Eight Martyrs,' Francesco explains. 'Eight young partisans were shot by the Italian militia here. The Germans ordered the shooting.' He points to one of the names. 'This boy was dragged from his hospital bed.'

She looks down the list of names. Standing in the crisp sunshine, mountains soaring into a perfect sky, it is impossible to imagine such an appalling event.

Francesco runs his fingers over the letters on the board and reads out: '*Il viaggio della memoria. Imparino i vivi dal destino dei morti.*'

She translates slowly: 'The journey into memory. May the living learn from the fate of those who died.'

'It could have been written for you, and the journey you're making through your mother's diaries. I've no doubt your father and uncle would have been involved in some way or other in the attacks leading to this reprisal. I know it's an event my father talked to me about.'

'My mother often writes about a young man who calls himself Capriolo, an important partisan leader, but she never writes his real name.'

'She was correct not to identify him. It wasn't only Germans they were up against. On this notice here we've read it was the Italian militia who shot those boys. The local Italian fascists were more dangerous in many ways because they knew the routines of their neighbours, people they grew up with. They knew the tracks criss-crossing the mountains and they spied on their compatriots. It was best his name remained a mystery.'

She shivers and he again asks her if she is sure she wants to continue.

'I think so.'

The road to Fragheto is narrow and eroded by landslides. They pass through a pretty, wooded approach of mushroom and truffle reserves. Two kilometres after a tiny hamlet called Ville Fragheto, they reach Fragheto itself. The place is deserted. Several of the houses look as if they haven't been lived in for a long time, and the ones that are inhabited are unwelcoming and dilapidated.

Outside a locked church, wind chimes welcome them with hollow notes and a notice bears a simple message:

THIS SITE HAS BEEN DEDICATED
AS A PLACE OF PEACE

On the wall of a run-down house hangs a rusting blue sign barely showing the letter 'T', indicating it was once a tobacconist's. Next to it is a plaque with faded writing, and Francesco explains this is the spot where the dreadful massacre of innocent civilians took place. It's almost impossible to decipher the engraved names, but it seems to Anna that most of the surnames are the same: Gabrielli.

Francesco takes her arm again as they climb the short slope to a gaudy shrine near the cemetery. A ripped Italian flag flutters in the breeze and plastic flowers are haphazardly arranged in vases. Like a cliché, a buzzard chooses that moment to mew its plaintive call high on the warm currents of air.

Her eyes scan the list of the massacred while, in a sombre voice, Francesco explains that on 7 April 1944, thirty civilians were shot in reprisal by the Germans under the command of Hermann Göring and members of the Italian Republican Guard. There had been heavy partisan activity in the hills around, but no partisans were caught. The reprisal against innocent citizens was carried out in anger, with the youngest victim a little girl of two called Giuditta, along with her mother, twenty-six, Maria Gabrielli. The oldest to be massacred was a man of seventy-three.

'No wonder we never heard all these stories – they're too heartbreaking,' Anna says, a huge lump in her throat. 'I am determined not to cry.'

He pulls Anna to him, rubbing her back with his hands as if to try and warm her. She would like him to kiss her, too, to numb her against the horrors conjured by this place. Eventually he steps back, but takes her hand firmly in his as if not wanting to break the closeness of the moment. 'Come on, let's go and find a bar.'

They stop at the first place they come to in Casteldelci and, sitting at an outside table, order two large glasses of local red wine.

Taking one look at Anna's face, the bartender asks if they have come from the shrine.

'Do you know,' he continues, 'my mother was only seven at the time of the war, and she tells me she could write nothing about the present, but a whole book about those terrible days.'

He wipes the bar top vigorously with a damp cloth. 'Our people really suffered. I know the war is long over, but we should never forget.'

'This lady is here to see places where her English father fought and where her Italian mother lived,' Francesco explains.

'You don't sound Italian, signorina, although you have dark hair. We are grateful to the *inglesi* and all the others – *canadesi, polacchi, americani.* At long last the authorities are putting up monuments in preparation for the millennium. Anyway, signori, the drinks are on me.'

He pours them two generous glasses of red. 'Try this, from my family's vineyard on the coast.'

The wine is good. Tipsy from strong wine in the afternoon, Anna leans over and kisses Francesco on the lips.

'What was that for?' He laughs, catching hold of her hands, not letting them go.

'For being you. For today. For helping me feel relaxed whenever we're together. I've never felt like that with anybody before.'

'Not with *any*body?' he teases her, still clasping her hands.

'Well, all right – I've never truly felt like this with any other *man* before.'

'*In vino veritas*, as they say. I'll take it as the truth, then. I'm very flattered…' He squeezes her hands tighter. '… And very happy.' They look into each other's eyes, Anna's stomach flipping over at his intense gaze, and then he releases his grip. 'I suggest a walk around the town and something to eat back here afterwards. We need to soak up this alcohol before returning up the Rimini road.'

They wander arm in arm around the hilltop town, along alleys where the shutters of tall, narrow houses are closed against the heat of the afternoon. Trailing geraniums splash primary colours against ancient stone, and she keeps extricating her arm from Francesco's to use her camera.

'I'm collecting pictures of doors to make a collage, maybe frame it as a poster for the wall. You probably think I'm mad taking snaps of ancient doors and handles, but I find them beautiful.'

She steps back to fit a particularly fine carved hinge into the frame.

'And I take pictures of water and stones in the river,' he says. 'There are blocks of river photos all around my living room walls, which I'll show you when you come to Bologna.'

'*When* I come?' she says, raising her eyebrows.

'You will come, Anna, won't you?'

'Yes, I will.'

He turns to kiss her on the lips. She feels as giddy as a seventeen-year-old as he tucks her hand in his and they continue their amble through the town. They stop at a fountain and sit on its steps and she leans against him. They are quiet for a few minutes and then he pulls her closer, hinting that maybe Teresa might look after Alba the following weekend to give them time together.

'*Buon' idea!*' she says, pulling him to his feet. They walk towards the centre of the town, swinging hands like children. 'Do you know what I'd love to do, Francesco?'

'Surprise me.'

'I'd like to take Alba to the sea tomorrow and switch off from the diaries and the war in the mountains. Just for a day. And I think Alba would love it.'

He groans. 'Alba would love it. I *hate* the seaside in summer. But if it's just for one day, then maybe I could put up with it. That is, if I'm invited too, of course.'

They watch the town come back to life after the siesta. Shutters are flung open to let in the cooler air, and people dribble out into the streets to make purchases for supper. Outside a bar, old men slap down playing cards on a metal table, cursing good-naturedly, laughing at each other. Mopeds rev up as youngsters set off down the hill to the sea. People are living their lives. Everything is more vivid to Anna as she shares the early evening with Francesco.

Back at the restaurant, a table is reserved for them in a corner. The proprietor comes over. 'If you leave the choices to me,' he says, 'I'll bring you the specialities of the house, the best my wife can prepare. I can tell it's an important evening for you.' He winks and hurries back through the swing doors into the kitchen.

She bursts out laughing. 'He's cheeky. Did you see that wink?'

'Maybe he thinks we're having a clandestine affair, and we're cheating on our partners.' He takes her hand and kisses her palm. It tickles and she giggles. He continues to cover her wrist with tiny kisses and then pushes up her sleeve, murmuring as he does so. 'And he thinks I'm going to take you back to a hotel room and have my evil way with you all night long, like a real Latin lover.'

He finishes off in mock-dramatic form, his lips kissing their way up her arm to her shoulder and then her lips.

She pushes him away, laughing. 'Move over, idiot, there's a huge plate of *crostini* about to fall into your lap.'

The owner is back with two laden plates, a broad smile on his face.

She can't remember much about the meal. She only remembers thinking that if this is falling in love, she's never been in love before.

They don't go to a hotel. They creep into her house in the piazza like adolescents playing truant, and as soon as they are inside, he pushes the door shut with his back and drags her into his arms. They kiss passionately. She can feel him hard against her straight away and they pull at each other's clothes. They don't make it to the bedroom. He pulls down her panties and lifts her, leaning against the door for support, and enters her as she straddles him, her legs round his waist. They come together. Afterwards, he gently drops her back to the floor, tidying a strand of hair from her face and she whispers, 'Let's go upstairs.'

A soft glow warms the whitewashed walls when she switches on the bedside light. They lie down on top of the covers, removing the rest of each other's clothes. She traces her fingers through the hair on his chest, which is greying like his salt-and-pepper sideburns. His body is trim and she kisses his flat stomach, butterfly-kissing his groin, then licking him until he groans. She pulls away, not wanting him to climax too soon, and lying on her side, he draws her close, cupping her breasts from behind, his fingers tracing circles round her erect nipples. She moves her pelvis to rub him. Then he turns her over, kissing her long and deep, his tongue playing with her tongue, tracing a slow, wet line with his lips between her breasts, down her tummy and then, when she can't wait any longer, she parts her legs to receive him again.

In the morning she wakes alone. On the bed is a note.

Anna, carissima. Grazie! *You are beautiful. I hope I can stay all night with you soon but I had to be back for Alba. We'll pick you up at ten for the seaside.*

The day is a blur of heat and confusion. She remembers people crammed on a beach, the golden sand raked and manicured to perfection by a toned, sun-bronzed *bagnino* who ensures the stretch near a group of topless young girls is cleaner than the rest. He moves his rake like a dancer, bending down to pick up a stray cigarette end, lingering to chat, chancing his luck with an invitation for a dance later on at the *discoteca* on the seafront. And she remembers beautiful youths cavorting where the waves lap at the toes of girls, throwing themselves acrobatically at a beach ball, splashing the girls so they squeal and scream. And illegal African immigrants, *clandestini*, touting armfuls of gaudy beads and slices of coconut. Anxious mothers shout at toddlers not to stray too near the water's edge. Shamelessly fat ladies with red-polished toenails wearing leopard-print thongs. The smell of fried fish and suntan oil and Italian ballads on a radio on the beach, crooned by Zucchero. They paddle with Alba and buy ice creams from the bar; they even hire a *pedalo* to view the packed beach from a few metres offshore.

But all the time her mind is on Francesco and their lovemaking. Catching the longing gaze in his brown eyes, she knows he's thinking the same.

CHAPTER TWENTY-FOUR

They are all tired from the sun and the beach when they return from the coast that evening. Francesco takes Alba back to Teresa's. 'See you very soon,' he murmurs to Anna, the pressure of his hand on her arm making her yearn for soon to be *now*.

She wonders if he'll manage to sneak away later to her bed. As she washes sand from her body in the steamy spray of the shower, she remembers the touch of his kisses, his hands loving her. The memory makes her languid and lazy, like a cat. Wrapping herself in a bath towel, she stretches out on her bed and, in an effort to stay awake, in case he comes to her, she reaches for her mother's diary.

A note written in English in her mother's scrawl is pinned to the remaining pages, the paper clip beginning to rust.

> *I was too busy in the early months of arriving in England to keep a regular diary, Anna. Everything was so strange, and my brain was tired from learning all the time. My new life was totally different from anything before. The rest of these pages are a mixture of diaries I kept at the time as well as memories I wrote long after the events. Everything poured back to me as soon as I put pen to paper.*

Memories of September 1946

The train seemed to chant '*arrivederci, arrivederci*' as it chugged its load of war victims across Europe. I stared out of the window at the scarred landscape, the stumps of houses like necks with their heads blown off. I remember how I shuddered at the devastation, and forced my gaze back inside the carriage.

Opposite me, a pair of weary soldiers slept, their heads thrown back against the seat – one was blond and his mouth gaped open, dribbling like a baby. His older companion had looked me up and down earlier and I'd cast my eyes down modestly, thrusting my left hand further forward on my lap to make the shining gold band on my finger more obvious. An old lady was huddled in the corner seat, a basket of vegetables held fast to her breast. My belongings were on the shelf above me in a battered suitcase which Mamma had insisted on tying up with thick rope before I left.

'You can never be too sure,' she'd said, as if she were a seasoned traveller. 'We'll do this in case anybody thinks they can put their thieving hands into your bag.'

The woman opposite seemed to me to be a country person too, and I kept glancing at her to reassure myself. She made me feel less shabby, less strange. She'd only left her seat once in the whole twenty-four hours, asking me to keep an eye on her belongings while she excused herself. The rest of the time she'd spent crying quietly into a large handkerchief, her age-blotched hands twisting and kneading the cloth. I watched her bony fingers in fascination. They reminded me of Nonna's. Before she died she used to sit all day in the kitchen, rocking back and forth, lost somewhere in the past. If my own heart had not been so full, I would have offered comfort to the old lady, but I too was on a difficult journey.

'So near, so far, so near, so far...'

The train continued to taunt me with its rhythm until we screeched to a halt on the edge of a town somewhere in the middle of France. Such vast stretches of countryside we'd crossed, broken now and again by hamlets, bullet holes polka-dotting abandoned houses. Hands reached up to our open windows, hands offering bread and produce, voices beseeching.

'*S'il vous plait, s'il vous plait, mesdames, messieurs.*'

At home, Mamma always cut the bread in the same way for every meal. She cradled the big, round *pagnotta* in her left arm next to her heart, while with her right hand she held the knife and cut towards her body.

'I won't harm myself,' she would say to Davide and me when we warned her to be careful. 'This bread is a gift from God, precious. The good Lord won't let me come to harm.'

This French bread being waved to us through the train window was long and thin. How could a French mother hold that to her heart?

As the train carried me further and further away from my Italy, it was one of the first differences I encountered between our two countries.

When we crossed the soupy-grey stretch of water between France and England, I could no longer hold back my tears. On that crossing, the umbilical cord connecting me to my homeland was well and truly severed and I began to understand a little of what Capriolo and Mamma had warned me of. This was the hardest thing I had done in all of my nineteen years so far. I was terrified and excited at the same time.

Later on, from another train window, I stared out at the green English countryside. I looked but I didn't

really see. I was listening to the train as it rocked me
with its clattering rhythm, echoing my thoughts: '*Please
be kind, please be kind, please be kind.*'

The train pulled into Victoria station with a screech and
a jolt. Jim had taught me a few basic phrases: 'Good
morning', 'How are you?', 'My name is Ines Swilland.'

Try as I could, my tongue couldn't manage my new
surname and I was anxious I might not be able to tell
anybody who I was. Jim had written a letter to his
parents with the time of arrival of the Dover train. He
had managed to buy me a second-class ticket on the
Golden Arrow, a smart train put into storage during
the war. He described me to his parents in a letter he
had sent earlier. I would be wearing a grey skirt and
jacket with a white blouse, I was just over five foot
and my hair was dark brown and curly. He told them
I would most likely be wearing it up, but a few of my
hairpins had fallen out during the journey and now it
was half up, half down. I hoped they wouldn't think
I was untidy.

The chill air made me shiver. In my geography
textbook at school, England was described as a country
of rain and pea-souper fogs, but that afternoon the
sky was crisp and clear. The sun shone but it was
biting cold, and I was afraid my light clothing was not
going to be adequate for the climate. Back home the
September sunshine could sometimes be as warm as it
was in August. But I had to stop thinking of Rofelle as
home. England was to be my new home. Taking a deep
breath to calm my nerves, I gathered my belongings.

Doors slammed, a whistle blew and on the platform people scurried past purposefully, greeting each other with words I didn't understand. Suddenly I wanted to turn round, stay on the train and go back to my family in Italy.

And then an elderly couple approached me.

'Ines?' the woman asked, inclining her head towards me, wispy grey hair escaping from an untidy bun. When I nodded, she stepped forward to kiss my cheek. Her skin was dry and smelt of soap. I recognised Jim in his mother with her blue eyes and long nose. And when she smiled at me, I saw that she had the same gap between her front teeth. She spoke slowly at first, and I could follow most of her words.

'Welcome to England, my dear new daughter. Let me take a good look at you!'

She stepped back an arm's length and peered into my face. We were about the same height and I was surprised, presuming all English women were tall and slender, but she was short, like me, and quite plump.

'You are far prettier than Jim described,' she said, grasping my hands in hers. 'My name is Freda and this is John, but you can call us Mum and Dad. It will be much easier for you, and you are family now. Do you understand me when I talk, Ines?'

I nodded again, although I couldn't understand everything and I didn't feel ready to reply or utter any words in English myself.

Then 'Dad' kissed me too, his whiskery sideboards brushing my cheek. He smiled shyly. 'Welcome, Ines. Let's be getting you back home. We have to catch another train. It will take an hour.'

I only caught a few of his words because he spoke much faster than my mother-in-law, and I understood how much I needed to improve my very slender grasp of English. I was beginning to feel more sympathy for the struggle Jim had in trying to learn basic Italian, and I wished now I hadn't teased him so much.

Jim's parents must have seen how exhausted I was, and I was relieved I didn't have to keep up polite conversation with them on the final train journey. Before dusk fell, I looked out of the window at the neat rectangles of gardens lined up alongside the track. Most of them had been converted to vegetable beds, though some had swings; I saw cats sitting on window ledges, washing flapping on lines. There were gaps where houses had most likely stood. Bombs had fallen in England, too. Looking at these everyday scenes unfolding outside the train comforted me. I dozed off with the thought that although I'd travelled hundreds of miles, people here had ordinary lives like ours back in Italy. They grew vegetables, hung out washing and kept animals. Everything was going to be fine.

Mum and Dad, as I had to call them, lived in West Croydon, in a street full of houses that looked identical. Number 20 East Park Road was the same as numbers 22 and 24, and I made a mental note to memorise their house number. I didn't want to lose my way back if I ever went out on my own.

'Well, here we are, dear. This is our palace,' said Freda, guiding me down a short front path to a bottle-green door. John carried my old suitcase while Freda stopped to search for the key. She rummaged in her handbag, then in her pockets and eventually found it where she had looked first of all, in her handbag. She chattered all the while but most of it washed over me. A couple of words like 'garden' and 'Mussolini' I understood. John stood patiently behind us, waiting for Freda to find the key, and I couldn't help thinking how much more shouting and waving of hands would have gone on back home, if Mamma had lost the key to our front door.

'Freda,' said John, '*shhh*! Remember, no talk of the war.'

The last words were said in a whisper and Freda covered her mouth with her hand. I think she went on to say sorry, but I didn't really understand. A loud cough from John stopped her in mid-flow and she caught hold of my hand, looking very embarrassed and telling me she would make us all a cup of tea.

Before I left, Jim had talked to me about the difficulty some English people would have with me being Italian. First of all we had been enemies, and then we had switched sides. It would be hard at times, he'd warned, and maybe this was what he had meant. I wished I knew enough words to tell them none of it mattered, that the war was over and this was the start of new beginnings.

I wished Jim was standing next to me, but it would be another two months before he was to join me. He'd explained how he had to be decommissioned from the British Army and that there was nowhere for me to live with him during that time. I'd been anxious to escape from Rofelle and start my new life, so I didn't mind, but I was already beginning to regret my adventurous spirit. It was too late now, and I had to get on with it.

My in-laws' house was like a doll's house, with two rooms and a small kitchen and bathroom downstairs and two bedrooms upstairs. The ceilings were higher than in our mill and the walls were covered in coloured paper, unlike our whitewashed walls. There were carpets on the floor and the little house was bursting at the seams with ornaments and plants.

Freda took me upstairs to the back of the house. She drew the curtains.

'This is your room until Jim gets home,' she said, 'where he's slept since he was a little boy. But you shall have our room with the big bed once he comes back, and until you can get sorted and find a house of your own, although that might be difficult with the housing shortage.'

It took her a while to explain all this to me. She was very patient, and at one stage she found a notebook and pencil in Jim's desk and drew a picture of houses and bombs to help me understand. She showed me where to hang my clothes in a narrow wardrobe that stood in an alcove next to the fireplace, gave me a clean towel and then left me alone while she went downstairs to prepare a meal.

I sat on Jim's narrow bed looking at the relics of his boyhood. A teddy bear was perched lopsided on a shelf next to a row of well-thumbed books. A rusting model of a steam train and a box of metal soldiers completed the shelf's contents. Davide and I had no toys like this when we were children. My father had once carved me a tiny wooden doll for Epiphany, the feast of La Befana, when I was about six years old, and Davide had managed to get hold of a pig's bladder before the war, when the January slaughter of the pig took place. He and his friends kicked it around the yard below the mill, laughing and jostling each other for their makeshift ball until eventually it burst. There had never been spare money for toys or spare time for playing, either, because we were always too busy with chores.

It felt uncomfortable to be sitting in Jim's room, spying on a part of his life that I knew nothing about. I suddenly felt he was a stranger, despite the new gold band on my finger, and I rubbed it to prove to myself that what was happening was real. A wave of homesickness came over me as I imagined Mamma and Papà sitting on their stone bench outside the mill, watching the sun fall behind the mountains. I wondered if they were thinking about me, and felt tears prick my eyes. Then I shook myself and decided that in the morning I would write a letter for Capriolo to read out to them, if Freda could show me where to buy a stamp and post it.

'Tea's ready, Ines,' Mum called up to me from the kitchen, just in time to stop my tears.

'Just you wait and see what I've got ready for you, my dear,' she said as I came into the tiny kitchen. She was stirring something in a pan on a modern gas cooker. Mamma always cooked over the open fire in our huge fireplace. This looked easier. I hoped Jim would buy a cooker for me too and maybe, if I was lucky, a refrigerator like the ones I'd seen in American kitchens in the movies.

'There you are, dear. Something Italian!'

Jim's parents watched over me as I stared at the plate of bread and what looked like a heap of maggots in red sauce. I had no idea what Mum had prepared, but I didn't want to seem ungrateful. She was so very kind to me. Calling her Mum had begun to feel natural.

'Go on then… don't hold back! We thought you'd feel at home if we cooked you one of your dishes. We know you Italians eat it all the time.'

My special surprise was Heinz tinned spaghetti on toast, which I later realised had been acquired by exchanging coupons, saved carefully for my arrival, to make me feel welcome. Each mouthful made me want to heave. It was sugary, and like no pasta I had ever eaten in my life. But I appreciated their kindness and struggled through as much as I could.

'Thank you,' I said, trying to hide half of the soggy mess beneath my knife and fork.

'Would you like anything else?'

Freda went to her larder and returned to the table with an apple pie. The pie looked mouth-wateringly good, but from early childhood we had been taught it was impolite to accept any offering straight away. Only when the host or hostess insisted were we to say 'Yes, please'. So, being the polite girl I had been brought up to be, I said, 'No, thank you.' I waited for my mother-in-law to offer again, only to see the pie whisked away and stored in the larder at the side of the kitchen.

The same thing happened over the next few days with food, cups of tea, coffee. They would offer and I would decline, expecting them to insist and ask me again. But a second offer never came. After a week, I grew very hungry. One night, when I was sure Mum and Dad were fast asleep – their snores coming loud and clear through the thin walls – I crept downstairs, avoiding the last-but-one creaky step and, opening the larder door, I gorged myself on bread, jam and a hunk of cheese. Only when Jim came home to England, after being decommissioned, did I learn that it wasn't impolite to say yes the first time. He laughed at me and called me a silly goose.

*

As I said, Mum was a kind woman. It must have been equally difficult for her to have a stranger in her home. One Wednesday morning we went to market together, and when we'd finished buying fish and a new saucepan, we went for a cup of coffee. That was another thing I found strange at first. English coffee was too milky and weak, but I found that if I added three or four spoons of sugar, it was more drinkable. After a few occasions watching me do this, Freda had to explain gently that sugar was still rationed, showing me her ration book, and told me about the system of coupons everybody was expected to follow. John kept bees, and she didn't mind how much honey I used in my drinks at home but sugar was another matter. There were so many new things to learn. Anyway, two women sitting at the next table in the tea room overheard my stumbling efforts at conversation with Freda and must have made some comment to which Freda took exception. She got up, shoulders squared, chin held high and even though we hadn't finished our coffee, she pulled me up and said something to the women as we left. On the bus home she warned me this kind of thing would probably happen again, but that I shouldn't worry about it.

'Ignorant women like those have got nothing better to do with themselves. The war's over, and it's not your fault you're Italian.'

And then she changed the subject, telling me how busy we were going to be that afternoon. As it was a sunny day, we would clean the windows with vinegar and newspaper.

I hadn't thought being Italian could be a problem, and it made me self-conscious whenever we went out. I never ventured out alone again until long after Jim returned.

Freda taught me English recipes so I could impress Jim on his return. One morning she explained that we were going to bake toad-in-the-hole. When I looked up 'toad' in my dictionary, I was horrified. I couldn't stomach the thought of eating frogs, let alone a toad, and I wasn't looking forward to this new dish one little bit.

'But when do you add the toads?' I asked Freda after she had put the dish of batter and sausages in the oven. She laughed so much, and so did John that evening when she served it up. Freda had me stand next to her on other days when she cooked hotpot, Yorkshire pudding, Victoria sponge cake and custard. I loved the puddings she made, but I yearned to flavour the bland savoury dishes with herbs and full-bodied wine. But at the same time I wanted to learn to be a good English wife.

'Oh, we don't drink wine very often in England,' Freda said, shocked when I suggested adding wine to her gravy. 'Only on high days and holidays – you know, Christmas and New Year, special occasions. You are a funny little goose, Ines.'

I wondered why the English found geese so amusing. Some of their expressions were hard to understand. Freda told me Jim said I was the apple of his eye, that I warmed the cockles of his heart, and the local butcher was as sly as a fox. I was to find out that there was a lot to learn, even though my English was slowly improving.

*

September turned to October. The days grew colder and the house more freezing. The only warm place was in the kitchen by the boiler, and at night I wore all my clothes in bed. I put my coat on top of the bedcovers and still I shivered myself to sleep. Freda came to find me one morning when I had overslept and was late coming down for breakfast.

'Well, bless my soul. Look at you, as snug as a bug in a rug.' She laughed at me hidden under my mound of bedding. 'Are you cold, my duck? You should have said. We can't have you freezing to death. We'll sort you out tonight.'

From then onward, every night until Jim came back, she filled a stone bottle with boiling water from the kettle to warm up my bed. She knitted me a hideous pair of pink bedsocks with wool unravelled from an old cardigan and finally I felt warm. I wondered whether Jim would be able to find me in bed in my bundles. I missed him, and couldn't wait for him to join me. Once we were together again I felt sure he would banish my homesickness and make love to me the way he had tried in the mountains. I blushed when I thought about it. Freda and John were kind, but they weren't my mother and father and I hated the food and the dreary weather. I was much thinner, too, and I worried Jim would no longer find me attractive.

On a drizzly Tuesday afternoon in November, I waited at West Croydon railway station dressed up in my best suit, hair newly washed and curled, wearing a pair of gloves and a scarf that my mother-in-law had knitted me from scarlet wool put by for a special occasion.

'I reckon meeting your husband again after so many months counts as a special occasion. You want to look pretty for him, don't you?' she said. 'We need something to brighten up that grey suit of yours. It's well cut but drab. You could do with a bit of colour – you're looking peaky lately. Don't want Jim to think we're not looking after you properly.'

I was growing used to mother-in-law's plain speaking.

'And he'll love that fruit cake. He always did love a fruit cake.'

I was confused when I'd helped her bake the cake. She told me we needed flour and I'd gone out to the garden, returning empty-handed.

'No flower,' I'd said, 'too cold, winter. No flower.'

And then she'd got out the packet of self-raising flour from the larder and pointed at the spelling. So many words sounded the same. Later on, I understood she'd swapped cheese coupons with Mrs Hawthorne next door for half a pound of raisins. That was the way it was in the years after the war. People had to improvise. Freda made a new set of curtains for the bedroom for Jim's return, too. She'd dyed plain cotton sheets a pretty apple green. As it turned out, I'm sure Jim didn't notice. But it made Freda feel better.

My tummy was bubbly, full of butterflies. Jim was due back in England. On the station platform I hopped from foot to foot. I didn't know what to do with myself and I couldn't settle to anything.

The train drew in and Freda and John stood discreetly in the waiting room to give us privacy. I recognised him straight away among all the other men. He was thinner and his hair was shorter but it was definitely my Jim.

'*Tesoro, tesoro*, my darling,' I shrieked, racing up the platform, calling him at the top of my voice, flinging myself into his arms.

He frowned down at me, unwrapped my arms from around his neck and told me everyone was looking and not to make a show of myself. As far as the eye could see there were couples all around us locked in embraces and I couldn't understand why he was so cold.

From that moment on my heart began to shrivel a little more each day, like the sweet grapes that turned to dried fruit on Papà's vines. That night when we went upstairs to Freda and John's bed, he undressed quickly, slung his trousers and shirt over the chair, switched off the light and turned over on his side. I moved closer to him, moulding my body into his, like in the nights after our wedding.

'Not tonight, Ines,' he muttered. 'It's been a hell of a day. In fact, these last months have been worse than hell. I'm tired. Go to sleep.' And he moved further away.

I wondered what I'd done wrong.

I lay in the dark, feeling colder and lonelier than I'd ever felt in my life, and I turned away from my husband so he wouldn't hear me crying. Why didn't he want me any more? What could I do? I needed my mother. I wanted her advice. And then it was as if she was beside me in my cold English bedroom. The curtains stirred in the night breeze and she was talking to me. I could hear my practical, wise mother telling me to snap out of it and get on with the new life I had wanted so much. I felt ashamed to be crying in bed, and so I lay still and planned what I could do.

Freda had said I looked thin. Maybe Jim would love me more if I put on weight. I didn't like most of the food but I loved Freda's home-made cakes and biscuits. I decided I would eat more of those to help my curves return. I'd buy scarlet lipstick at Woolworth's to make myself desirable. I would make him love me again.

CHAPTER TWENTY-FIVE

5 December 1946

Dear Diary,

I hate it here.

I hate the cold, the food, the unsmiling, sunless people with their pale faces.

I hate my cruel husband, who is so different from my Jim whom I loved to distraction in beautiful Tuscany.

I miss our *mulino*, hidden in the folds near the Mountain of the Moon, where the sun sets from jewel-red skies behind misted blue peaks.

Why didn't Mamma prepare me better, and talk to me more about my duties in bed? I try to please my husband. But I hate sleeping with him. I hate him when he forces himself on me with his heavy, beer-smelling body, even when I have my monthly bleeds. And if I tell him I'm tired, he shouts. Sometimes he lashes out and hits me. I never know when it will happen.

We've moved out of Freda and John's house and, away from his parents, the beatings have increased. I longed for us to have a house of our own, but when Jim is cruel to me, I wish we had not been so lucky. There are long waiting lists, as so many lost their homes to German bombs. The English suffered too; we were not alone. Jim had enough cash to buy our new house, otherwise we'd have been in a queue for months, maybe years.

I'd hoped having our own place would relax Jim more, but if anything he is worse.

The English queue for everything. Even if there are two people waiting for something, they queue one behind the other. It makes me want to laugh sometimes, but I suppose people laugh at our ways, too. Jim is always scoffing when I worry about being in a draught. He tells me nobody died from fresh air, and he opens the window even wider to tease me.

We have a coal fire in our living room and I light it as soon as I get up. It feels strange not to collect wood from the riverbank or from Papà's neat log pile. Coal is delivered by a man with a horse and cart and I rush into the street to collect the droppings and put them on our vegetable garden. When the fire burns, it smells different from woodsmoke but it stays alight longer. I don't like the smell, and when you walk in the street some days, you can't see your way easily because of the fog and Jim says it is because of the coal smoke.

Jim never strikes me where it will show. There are bruises on my ribs and thighs that some days are so sore I cannot bear to feel the weight of clothes against my skin.

I want to run away. I put some housekeeping money by for a train ticket. I hid it on a shelf in a cocoa tin at the back of the larder. But he found it. And that gave him another excuse to give me a beating, accusing me of stealing money instead of buying food.

And when the beatings are over, he cries. He holds me tight and his tears soak into my nightdress. He promises he never meant it, that he loves me, tells me he will never lay a finger on me again. He begs me not to leave him, and I know I can't. It's my duty now in life, to honour and obey him, as Padre Luca told me on our wedding day. But I can't love him. I feel so ashamed at how my life has turned out. I long to be back with Mamma and Papà again, back in the mill where the hearth is warm with real love.

Each morning when he leaves for work I tell myself, *Coraggio! Things will improve. If I become more English, then he will love me once again.*

But I shall never love him back, not in the way I once hoped. And I can't believe how much he's changed.

Anna is horrified. She can't bear to read about her mother's unhappiness, that started so very early on in the marriage. But she reads on, in the hope things will improve. Her parents stayed together until her father's death; surely Ines would have left him if life had grown too unbearable…

Glancing at her watch, she sees it's gone midnight. Francesco won't come now, so she changes into her nightdress and slips under the cotton sheets, tiredness banished.

6 January 1947

Today is not a feast day in England, but I picture Mamma preparing chicken and polenta on the hearth for this special Italian celebration. Maybe Papà is setting off to the *osteria*, to drink a glass or two of wine with Giacomo and Giorgio. I went to Mass today, the Feast of the Epiphany, La Befana. Only Catholics do that here. English children don't leave their shoes out the night before to be filled with coal or sweets by Befana, the little old witch that followed the Kings. Here, they receive gifts on Christmas Day instead.

Freda calls me a Papist, but says she doesn't mind one way or the other. She's taught me how to make English cakes and I am getting fatter by the week.

She asked me if I was expecting, because she noticed my skirt was tight. But although I would love a baby, I'm not pregnant yet.

Jim has left me alone recently. I'm still wary of his moods because there seems to be no pattern to his beatings. Maybe it's because he's tired. He's been promoted in the sales department at the airport and that brings extra responsibilities. It also means we can buy airline tickets at a special price. I'm frightened at the idea of travelling so high in the sky, but if it means I don't have to make the long train journey again, that will be wonderful.

At the Epiphany Mass this morning there was a woman two rows in front of me who I was sure wasn't English. There was something about her. She had dark hair like mine and she was about my height. I plucked up courage at the end of the service and tapped her on the shoulder and asked outright, 'Are you perhaps Italian?'

It was as if we had known each other all our lives. She shouted '*Sì*' at the top of her voice and we wrapped our arms around each other, although we'd never met before. Although Tiziana is from Rome and nowhere near our Tuscany, we had so much to talk about and we arranged to meet next week for a cup of tea. Not for a coffee, because English coffee is quite awful. I drink tea now, like an English milady.

Last week I had a cold and I've been off my food ever since, but I'm still putting on weight and Jim says I look better than when he first came back from Italy. I've learned to make rock cakes and sponge cakes. Freda gave me a recipe for a fruit cake, rich and heavy, and Jim loves it. Mamma used to say I was capable of burning water. But I've changed, and she would hardly recognise me.

How I wish my parents could come and visit us some day. I worry they are lonely and still mourning the loss of Davide. I weep when I think about him. Sometimes he appears to me in dreams; we're children, playing hide-and-seek in the trees behind the millpond. It's my turn to hunt for him and when I call 'Ready or not, I'm coming', I hear him scream. I run to help and he jumps out in front of me, his hands covering his face. And his face is a gaping wound, his eyes hollow sockets. At first, Jim comforted me after these nightmares, but now he grumbles that I keep him awake and tells me to go back to sleep, he has work in the morning. What must it be like for poor Mamma? It must be a thousand times worse.

But it's pointless to wonder why he died the way he did. My life is now. I have to keep positive and move forward.

We have a small garden at the front of our house, filled with perfumed roses. Mamma would love them. At the back, there is a line for me to hang clothes on to dry (that is, when the weather is good enough). Some days I long for the breeze that dances up from the river to dry the clothes on bushes, like at the mill. Jim has his vegetable garden at the far end, by the railway line. The trains disturbed me at first with their clattering but now

I like them. Sometimes children wave at me when I'm in the garden and I wave back. Jim tells me most of the passengers are travelling to London for work. The train brought me here to England and I wonder if there are any other women like me, arriving to start new lives. After Jim has left and I've finished my household chores, I write in my journal and sometimes I jot down lines of poetry.

10 February 1947

I've been terribly sick in the mornings. I thought I had an awful disease because it went on for days and days, and eventually I went to the doctor.

I'm going to have a baby.

It's due at the end of August.

How I long for my mother to be with me for my confinement! We won't be able to visit Rofelle this summer, as hoped, as Jim doesn't want me to travel in my condition.

I feel so sick, and I've lost a lot of weight, but Freda is taking great care of me. She makes me chicken soup and toast. I haven't the heart to tell her I can't abide her chicken soup. What would I give for some of Mamma's *cappelletti* in broth.

I tried to knit a cardigan for the baby but there are so many holes in it where I dropped the stitches, it looks more like a string shopping bag. Freda laughed when I showed her, but she loves knitting and said she'll make the baby's wardrobe. I pity the baby when he or she arrives, as Freda's wool mostly comes from clothes she unpicks. Maybe our child will be the first one to be dressed in mourning…

She presented me with a pair of black bootees last week made from an old shawl. The wool is lovely and soft. I don't know if I shall ever use them but I don't want to hurt her feelings.

I've been in tears a lot recently, and she managed to find out where Tiziana lived by going to speak to the Papist priest, as she calls him, and I had a wonderful surprise when she knocked on my door last week.

At first, I wasn't going to open the door. It was ten o'clock, the grate needed emptying, last night's supper dishes were still in the sink and I was in bed. Jim was away for a couple of days for work and, sick and unhappy, I couldn't see the point of getting up. I ignored the knocking and turned over again under the snug blankets and eiderdown.

Knock, knock, knock.

Whoever it was, they were insistent. And then I heard the flap on the letter box clatter open and Tiziana's voice calling to me.

'*Puttana Eva!* Ines, you lazybones – open up! It's only me. I know you're in there. Come and open the bloody door.'

It was good to hear Italian spoken, albeit scattered with ripe swear words. There stood Tiziana on the doorstep, wearing her new mink coat, stamping her fashionably clad feet in the cold.

She once confided in me how she'd met her husband in a brothel along the banks of the River Tiber in Rome.

'It was only temporary,' she told me when she saw my mouth drop open in shock. 'You'd have done the same, *cara mia*, if you'd been stuck in Rome with nothing to eat and brothers and sisters starving at home. It was all right for you jammy lot in the country with your nice fat pigs and hens.'

It was pointless arguing with her once she was in full swing. She was quite unashamed of the way she'd snared her husband Denis.

'He has something missing up there,' she said, drumming the side of her head with her finger, adding with a cackle, 'but not down below.'

As far as she was concerned, her slow English husband had been her passport out of poverty. We were very different, Tiziana and I, but I was fond of her nevertheless, mainly because she was Italian.

'*Brrr*! It's freezing out there,' she said, sweeping into the hallway. 'I wouldn't let a dog go out in this shitty weather. Make me a coffee, there's a darling.'

She enveloped me in a hug. My tears welled up and wouldn't stop.

'Hey, Ines. Come on, my love. *I'll* make us a coffee. Look what my folks managed to send me.' She pulled a brown package from her handbag and dangled it under my nose.

I gagged. Coffee was one of the many things I couldn't stomach at that moment and its rich aroma made me heave.

'Whoops, sorry, I forgot about your condition. Well, tea it will have to be then. I'll keep the coffee for when your taste buds start behaving again, 'cos they will, Ines, I promise you. You won't go on feeling like shit forever. And just for you, I won't light up. How's that for friendship? I remember when my sis was in the family way. She couldn't stand the smell of fags. You're probably the same.'

She bustled about, making tea, finding cups. 'You go and get yourself dressed, there's a good girl, and I'll see to the fire and then we'll have a natter when you've decided to turn off those waterworks. You're only pregnant, *cara*. You're not going to pass away just yet. Come on, hurry up! I've got to be back to cook Denis's dinner for one o'clock. I can't stay long.'

Half an hour later, sitting next to a glowing fire, I began to feel better. 'I don't know what I'd do without you, Tiziana.'

'Don't talk rubbish. The feeling's mutual, *carissima*. England's all very well, but an Italian girl needs a pinch of Italy now and again, and that's what we can do for each other. By the way, my folks are coming over for Easter. They're driving. My uncle's bringing them in his taxi. Don't ask me how he's managing to get petrol – I never ask him any questions. He's got his connections, and he manages to find us loads of goodies. So, if you want anything, have a think and let me know. Pasta, olive oil, *parmigiano*. The food situation's better than over here but it's not always easy to get hold of things, even though the bloody war's well and truly over. They go into the countryside to see what they can find, speak to people they know. You know what I mean.'

She touched the side of her nose and winked at me.

I began to cry again.

'God, you're all over the place, aren't you?' she said, crouching down in front of me, taking hold of one of my hands, a frown on her powdered forehead.

'What's the matter really, Ines? It's not just being pregnant, is it? Tell Aunty Tiziana.'

I didn't know how far I wanted to confide in her, but I needed somebody to talk to. I blew my nose on the handkerchief she thrust at me, tried a smile and mumbled, 'I feel too embarrassed to talk about it.'

'There's nothing will embarrass *me*, you know that. Good God, Ines, when you've been brought up in a family like mine, all squashed into the tiniest of flats in Trastevere, then you'll know nothing could make me blush. My parents slept in the same room, just a curtain hanging between our beds to give them a bit of privacy. Well, I learned all about the facts of life from a very early age, I can tell you.'

'I don't think Jim loves me any more.'

I dissolved into tears again.

Tiziana laughed. 'You great lump. You're pregnant, aren't you? Your hormones are making you mixed up and peculiar. My mamma even took to eating bits of furniture whenever she was expecting. We had teeth marks in the kitchen chairs.'

She produced a comb from her handbag. 'Just look at the state of this haystack, *caruccia*. When was the last time you looked at yourself in the mirror?'

And she started to tease out my tangles. It was soothing, relaxing. After a while she began to talk to me again.

'Look, Ines, of course Jim loves you. If he didn't touch you, or neglected you, never came home to you at night, then maybe I'd start believing he didn't love you. But you're pregnant, girl. That isn't an immaculate conception like with the Madonna, I'm sure.'

'Don't laugh at me, Tizi.'

'*Porca miseria*. You've got it bad.'

'Yes, I'm pregnant. But I didn't enjoy getting pregnant. I don't like it when we're in bed. It hurts, and I always want it to be over and finished.' I said all this in a rush, my cheeks turning redder than sun-blushed Marzano tomatoes, but relieved at last to put my feelings into words.

Tiziana sat on one of Freda's hard chairs and crossed her legs, pulling her skirt down. Her legs were solid and encased in silk stockings. It was hard to gauge her age under the heavy layer of make-up, but she had let drop into conversation she was ten years older than me. She seemed very worldly-wise.

'Well, darling, all men can be rough at times. Take it from me, it's quite normal when they get excited. But if you're not enjoying sex at all, then that's not your fault. As far as I'm concerned, if he can't make you feel good, then it's his fault.'

Maybe I should have opened up to her completely, showed her my bruises, asked her if *they* were normal. But I'm so ashamed and worry it's something I bring upon myself. But still I needed her reassurance.

'But at home...' I quickly corrected myself. 'In Italy, before we married, it always felt so good when we were together. I mean, we didn't go all the way or anything... I made him wait until we were married. But then, when he came back at the end of the war, he'd changed. He was colder, as if he didn't care any more. Or maybe I've changed.'

I wiped my eyes with her sodden handkerchief and looked at her. She sighed and raised her hands as if to say, what do you expect?

'It's never going to be like it was at the beginning, Ines. Marriage isn't a fairy story. And you have to understand about men. Once they've got what they want, they're lazy, believe you me. You have to be a bit more cunning, *bella*, tease them.'

I looked at her, with her pretty face and matronly figure. Her tight mohair jumper looked as if it had been painted on her bosom, leaving little to the imagination. We weren't the same type of girl at all, but she was my only friend in England and I'd never talked to anybody in my life as openly about these things. If we had met in Italy, I doubt we would even have said *buongiorno* to each other. And yet, alone as I feel in Croydon, I trust her advice.

'Thank you, Tizi. I've got a lot to learn, I can see. I've begun to think I made a mistake marrying Jim and coming here. I should have stayed to look after my parents and...'

'... and lived a life of misery in a dead-end village in the mountains, having to piss in a hole in the ground and working from morning to night to die an early death. No thank you very much. I'm much happier here in *Inghilterra* and soon you will be, Ines. You're just feeling like this because you're pregnant. It affects women in different ways. My nonna talked to me a lot, and so I know about these things. She was an expert on everything to do with childbirth. She used to deliver all the babies in our block of flats and if she'd known how to write, then she would have been able to produce a manual about it. Now wash your face and take this lipstick.'

She rummaged in her crocodile-effect handbag and produced a stick of Woolworth's Ruby Lustre. 'It's nearly finished, but put some on tonight when Jim gets home. Undo some of those buttons on your starchy old blouse and cook him a delicious meal. The way to a man's heart is through his stomach as well as his cock. Let me know how you get on, darling – I have to dash now, but I'll come and see you again next week.'

And bestowing a hearty kiss on each of my cheeks, she let herself out into the cold morning air, tottering down the front path on her high heels.

When Jim's key turned in the latch at six o'clock that evening, I rushed to take up position in the kitchen. With Tizi's lipstick applied as thickly as I thought acceptable without ending up looking like a clown, I'd been practising pouting at myself in the mirror. She'd suggested leaving a few buttons open on my blouse, but I'd decided to go further. It was a huge extravagance but I'd lit the boiler that afternoon and dragged the tin bath into the kitchen for a long, bubbly soak. With a generous splash of Gala Affair that Jim had bought me for Christmas, and dressed in my flimsiest nightdress, I was ready for him. It was freezing, but I'd been warned about working hard to keep my man, so feeling cold was something I had to put up with.

'What's burning?' Jim rushed into the kitchen. The gas was too high and the soup had boiled over. I still hadn't got the hang of my modern cooker.

'Are you feeling sick again?' Jim threw down his newspaper on the table I had carefully laid, squashing a napkin that had taken ages to fold into a lily shape, just like in the *trattoria* in Badia.

'Why aren't you dressed, Ines? Have you been like this all day?'

My seduction plan didn't seem to be working. I wasn't going to give up, though. Letting my dressing gown drop to the floor, I revealed my see-through nylon nightdress.

'Ines. You'll catch your death like that.' He picked up my dressing gown and held it up for me to feed my arms into.

'Why don't you love me any more?' I flung myself at him, pummelling his chest in despair. 'What have I done wrong?'

He looked totally perplexed, his mouth half open as he stepped back from me.

'Ines, what on earth's got into you?'

'*Sono stufa…* I'm fed up, that's what – fed up, fed up, fed up, and I want to go back to Italy.'

He came over to me and started to rub my back. 'It's your condition, that's what it is,' he said in a calm voice that did nothing whatsoever to soothe me. 'It's making you talk nonsense. Come and sit down and I'll serve up the soup.'

'It's burnt. I don't want any *stupida* soup. Let go of me, *cretino*.'

I pushed him away. Despite vowing not to cry, my tears started to flow again. I was embarrassed at my attempt to seduce him, and frustrated. I didn't know what to do any more. From one day to the next I never knew what sort of mood he would be in. Wiping my tears away with the backs of my hands, I tried another tack. I would be firm and reasonable with him. Taking a deep breath, I looked him in the face. 'Do you still love me?' I asked. 'You *must* be honest with me.'

He was embarrassed now. He sat down at the table, avoiding my gaze. I repeated my question, this time louder.

'Keep your voice down,' he hissed. 'You're giving the neighbours a real treat tonight, and you're talking daft nonsense.'

'I don't care about the bloody neighbours. Answer me!' I shouted.

'Don't swear! You've been with that girl from Rome again, haven't you? She's got a mouth like a sewer. I can always tell when you two have been keeping company. She's a common—'

'She's my friend, and stop changing the subject. I asked you a question. Do you still love me? Like you did in Italy?'

He fiddled with the knife and fork on the table I'd laid so carefully for our special supper. His hands were shaking, and I felt he was likely to lash out at any moment. But when Tiziana told me that Jim was at fault with our lovemaking, it had given me the strength to face up to him. There were to be no beatings that evening, just a sad, thin smile when he eventually returned my gaze. 'It was never going to be the same as it was in Italy,' he mumbled. 'We're here now, and life is different.'

'But you're still Jim and I'm still Ines. That shouldn't be any different. If you tell me you don't love me any more, then I think I shall kill myself.'

'Now you're being overdramatic, like a typical Eyetie. Calm down. Think of the baby.'

'*Uffa!* I can think of nothing else! And you married an Eyetie, as you so kindly call me, so what did you expect? *Madonna buona!* I don't want this baby to be born into a family where there is no love.'

'I've never said I don't love you, Ines.' He sounded tired, defeated. Coming over to the chair where I was slumped, he pulled me into his arms. 'I can't always show you in the way you want. Now dry those eyes and let's eat.'

I wanted him to undress me, tear off my nightie and make love, to cover my body with tender but passionate kisses, make me feel how I'd felt that afternoon in the river. I had begun to wonder if I'd imagined the whole scene and turned it into a romantic fantasy.

Instead of making wild, urgent love, we finished our burnt soup and the stodgy apple pie and lumpy custard he'd insisted Freda teach me how to make.

Afterwards he switched on the wireless to listen to the evening news, and after giving me a good night peck on the top of my head, he went upstairs. When I came up ten minutes later, he was fast asleep, on his back, snoring. I pulled off my nightdress, rummaged in the drawer for a pair of his warm pyjamas and slid into our icy bed.

CHAPTER TWENTY-SIX

August 1999

It's gone one in the morning when Anna finishes reading, tears streaming down her face, soaking her pillow as she falls into a restless sleep.

Next morning, she wakes early, her mother's papers strewn about the floor beside her bed. Dragging herself downstairs, she prepares a strong coffee instead of her usual tea. The bitter taste matches her mood, as she reflects on how much unhappiness her mother kept to herself, how lonely she'd been, thrown into a strange culture, desperately clinging to Tiziana, a fragile link with Italy.

Francesco calls round at seven o'clock and Anna is still not dressed. Puffy-eyed, hair tousled, she opens her front door.

'What have I done to you?' he says. 'Couldn't you sleep?'

'It's not you,' she says, stepping into his arms, 'it's my mother. Her life went from bad to worse.'

'She didn't have an easy time, did she?'

'If it had been me, I wouldn't have put up with him. If a man lifted one little finger in anger to me, he would be out immediately.'

'Things were different back then.'

'No excuse. Poor woman.'

He kisses her, pulls her closer, and if it weren't for Alba appearing to tell him that Teresa has put his coffee and breakfast biscuits on the table, he would stay longer.

'I wish I could cancel it,' he says, 'but I've been summoned to Bologna for a two-day staff meeting – there are problems with timetables and all the usual stuff to prepare for a new university year.'

Alba tugs at his arm to drag him away and he kisses Anna again, lightly this time because Alba is standing there like a school monitor, hands on hips, glaring at the pair of them.

'I've left the rest of the papers with Teresa,' he adds. 'They're in English, so you won't need my help any more. But I'd love to read them properly to the end, if you'll lend them to me afterwards. I feel personally involved. Oh, and I haven't forgotten the medal. I'll let you know how I get on.'

Blowing him a kiss as he leaves, making Alba giggle, Anna goes upstairs to pull on some clothes, remembering how Francesco undressed her less than twenty-four hours ago and wanting him to return from Bologna soon to do it again.

Her mother has attached another note to the next few pages.

In 1984, when you were eighteen, off you went to university and the house was empty and echoing. Harry and Jane were busy with their own young families and I had no one but myself for company, with too much time to think.

One afternoon I saw a notice about creative writing at the library, which appealed to me. The course was entitled, 'Want to Write Your Story?'

I took courage in my hands and enrolled. The teacher was encouraging. It was therapy. She helped me gather the threads of my life together – she called them my 'memory pearls' – and one of the first tasks she set was to write about the arrival of a stranger in our lives.

I found myself describing the birth of your brother. We had to start with 'I remember…' She asked me to read

mine aloud and because I didn't know anybody there, I
didn't mind telling them it was my own story.

I remember the first words my husband uttered about
our new baby, who was born on 10 August 1947.

'He looks like a monkey on a barrel organ,' said Jim,
holding our son away from his body. 'Here, have him
back, Ines. He might be sick on my work suit.'

Freda, my mother-in-law, took the baby instead,
expertly wrapping the shawl tighter round her first
grandson.

'Shame on you, son! Hand him to me,' she scolded.
'Honestly, what a thing for a new father to say.'

I watched my mother-in-law, marvelling at her confidence, thinking I would never get the hang of looking
after this new baby. I was scared of dropping him, and
I couldn't seem to satisfy his hunger. Hardly had I fed
and changed him, when his little mouth opened like
a beak and he cried for more. He cried all the time.

'He's going to be a big lad, that's for sure,' the midwife
had said to me after the birth. 'You might have trouble
feeding this one. A bottle before too long, I think.'

Freda was in her element. 'I've knitted something
for him,' she said, proudly presenting me with a heavy
green and orange shawl with pink and turquoise tassels.

'It's wonderful. Thank you so much,' I said, grateful
that she could not hear my inner voice thinking what a
fine dog blanket it would have made… if we had a dog.

I missed my mother. The birth was long and painful,
a pain like I'd never imagined. I'd thought I was going
to die, and apparently I'd screamed for Mamma over
and over again. And when I looked down at my son for

the first time, covered in mucus and blood, I felt a wave of sadness. I understood only then the tie a mother has to her child; a tie which I had severed from my own mother by coming to live so far away. I wept for what I'd denied her.

Afterwards, I was very sick. I feel so ashamed now as I write this, but there were nights when Harry cried to be fed yet again and I wanted him to fall asleep forever, never to wake up. Freda was wonderful to me, where Jim was bewildered and useless. I hardly saw him in those early days of our son's life. He stayed late at work and left the house just after dawn and he was often away overnight.

Freda moved into our spare room and took over the cooking and cleaning while I recuperated from the birth. In the middle of September she brought me my usual cup of milky coffee for elevenses and then, instead of hurrying back into the kitchen, she sat with me for a while.

'Now then, Ines my dear, it's been nearly a month since the baby was born and I think it's time I went back to my John. I can call in from time to time, but you have to make an effort now. The baby needs you and Jim needs you, and so here's a duster. You set to and I'll finish off washing his lordship's nappies while he has his morning nap, and this afternoon I've arranged for you to meet your friend in the park. You can push your prams together and get some fresh air into your pale cheeks.'

Tiziana, my Italian friend, had discovered she was pregnant not long after I did and we spent as much time together as we could. Where I'd felt very nauseous, she had sailed through eight months until she was confined to hospital with pre-eclampsia for the last weeks. She was lucky to survive. Our friendship became dearer to me when I realised I could have lost her.

Feeding the ducks on the pond in the park became our afternoon routine. Tiziana had twin boys, born a few weeks after Harry, and she too was finding motherhood difficult. We made a pact to try and stick to speaking English, but it was very tempting to resort to Italian.

'This bread is only fit for ducks anyway,' she grumbled, tossing half a loaf into the green water and setting off a squawking and fluttering of feathers from the geese and mallards as well as a stray gull. 'What I wouldn't give for a *pagnotta* fresh from the *panificio* back home. This stuff is like cotton wool, and it's too salty. Yuck! *Schifo!*'

She brushed crumbs from her dress and rocked her pram to settle Luca and Giuseppe.

'Listen to you,' I said. 'Who's longing for Italy now?'

She had told me off in the past for constantly harking back to our beautiful country that we always referred to as *il bel paese*.

'You try looking after these two on your own,' she retorted. 'If I were back home, there'd be Mamma to help, or Aunty, or my sister, or the woman in the flat next door – the road sweeper, even. Here it's all down to me. *Dio buono*, I swear I'm going to tie a knot in Denis's willy. I'm not having any more babies, and I've told him he's not coming anywhere near me unless he dangles a condom in front of me. I've done my bit now. Jesus, two's more than enough.'

'Freda's really good, and now I'm giving the bottle to Harry, he sleeps through the night.'

'Are you only just using the bottle now? *Madonna buona*, mine had to get stuck into bottles straight away. No way was I going to let them chew on me. It's enough having my old man interfering with them.'

She stuck out her breasts and patted them as if to reassure herself they were still there. 'I'm proud of these – they're my two main assets.'

I laughed. 'What are you talking about, Tizi? You're a married woman.'

'So? You never know what might happen, *amica mia.*' She wiggled her finger at me. 'He might leave me, I might leave him, you never know.'

Tizi was a one-off, and although she shocked me with her pronouncements, I always felt better when I'd been in her company.

'Right then, Ines, seeing as the subject's come up, I've got to tell you. I wasn't going to, but maybe you ought to know.'

She lowered her voice as if she was about to impart gossip she didn't want anybody else to hear.

'Know what?' I was only half listening. Harry was crying, so I'd lifted him out of his pram to wind him and was pacing around our usual park bench.

'Denis thinks your Jim is chasing skirt.'

'Chasing skirt? What do you mean?'

'Haven't you ever heard that expression? *Dio*, where were you born? Oh yes, in the country, I forgot. Cows and sheep don't wear skirts, do they?'

She laughed, and then, seeing the puzzled look on my face, she sighed and stood up to arrange the twins' blankets, muttering so I couldn't hear what she was saying.

'What were you saying about Jim and skirts?' I asked when she came back to the bench.

Tiziana took a deep breath and then, in her blunt way, hit me with her news.

'There's no easy way to tell you this, *cara*, but... Denis says your Jim is having an affair with Phyllis, who works in Boots. That blonde girl, you must know the one I'm talking about. Tall, with a face like a donkey and enormous breasts.'

Harry was still grizzling and I picked him up and jiggled him in my arms, trying to pacify him. My head was reeling at what I'd just heard. He was crying properly now, and I could hardly hear what Tiziana was saying as she prattled on.

'I really didn't know whether to tell you or not but we're friends, aren't we? And do you remember when you talked to me before Harry was born, how you were so worried about Jim not paying you enough attention? Well, doesn't that explain it? He's got another woman. A fancy woman, they call them over here. And by the sound of things, it's been going on for some time.'

I still hadn't said anything. I didn't know what to say. Eventually, despite Harry's loud complaining, I dumped him back in his pram and started off for home, Tiziana shouting at me to come back and talk. I ignored her.

I strode through the park, pram wheels stirring up fallen leaves on the path. I ignored the curious looks from people strolling leisurely and hurried past them like a madwoman, ignoring my baby's hungry screams. I pushed the pram out of the park gates and bumped it down the narrow pavement, past houses and front gardens that all looked the same.

Leaving the pram by our doorstep and hoisting my son on my hip, I flung the front door open so hard it chipped green paint off the wall. Jim kept a bottle of brandy in the sideboard in the front room and, still carrying Harry, I poured myself a generous measure. I coughed and spluttered; it was strong and unpleasant but it helped calm me.

'Come on, Harry. We'll be all right. Don't cry, little one.'

The baby sensed my anxiety. He was still grizzling as I prepared a bottle of milk for him, my fingers clumsy as I measured out formula in a daze, not completely aware of what I was doing.

Half an hour later, with Harry asleep on the sofa beside me and having drunk the best part of half a bottle of brandy, I resolved to confront my husband when he returned from the business trip he'd pencilled in on our kitchen calendar. Now I wondered if he truly was away for work, or if he was in the arms of that Phyllis woman, and I bit back my anger. And I was sick of tears; so far, they had done me no good. Jim didn't want me but I wasn't ready to give him up yet, and I wasn't going to let him get away with having dragged me all the way to England only to dump me. Deep down, and as strange as it seemed, given the way he treated me, I still thought I loved him. What's more, I had meant those marriage vows I uttered in the little chapel in Rofelle – that we would love each other for better, for worse. I couldn't accept that the man I'd fallen in love with in Italy had turned into such a monster. I had to fight for him, and there was Harry to think of now as well.

In the morning my head was thumping but the baby had miraculously slept through the night. I packed extra nappies and bottles of milk into his pram and hurried round to my parents-in-law's house. Freda and John were in the middle of breakfast, surprised to see me so early.

'Please, Mum, could you look after Harry for me today? I forgot about my postnatal check at the hospital, and with Jim away, it would be so much easier for me to leave him with you, what with the bus journey and all.'

All this was said without looking her in the face in case she could detect I was telling lies, while I busied myself tidying spare nappies in the wire basket below the pram.

Freda bent to pick Harry up, all fists and grumbling for his bottle.

'Of course we'll look after the little man. You won't mind being with Nanny and Grandad, will you? We'll wheel you out in the sunshine and you can watch us gather the early windfalls. Remind me to give you a bagful for your pies, Ines. Now off you go. You don't want to miss that bus.'

I marched down the road to the bus stop, but my destination was not the hospital.

By the time I had made my way to the centre of West Croydon and found Boots the chemist, it was nearly midday. I wandered around the store, pretending to look at cosmetics, spraying samples of perfume on my wrists and looking at packets of nylon stockings until a sales assistant asked me, 'Can I help you, madam?' She was in her fifties, grey-haired, short and stout.

'I'm looking for a present for... for my mother.'

'How about a lovely new lipstick? You're never too old for lipstick.'

She rummaged in a drawer below the counter for a sample and then tried the colour on the back of my hand.

'If your mother looks anything like you, I think she could do with a darker shade.'

All the while she rattled on about make-up that my mother would never dream of applying, while I kept looking around to see if I could identify Phyllis.

'Are you French, my dear?' she asked. 'Only you've got that continental look about you.'

'Italian,' I replied.

I took the mirror she handed me so I could smear the sample on my lips. My angry reflection glowered back at me. Behind me, in the mirror, I caught sight of another woman in a Boots uniform. She wasn't a true blonde; her dark roots were beginning to show. She looked older than me and her blouse was straining at the seams, the buttons in danger of popping open at any moment. She wasn't pretty, but she was sexy. I was certain she was Phyllis, the woman Tizi had talked about. I dropped the mirror on the floor and it smashed.

'Oh dear,' the grey-haired woman said to me, bending down to rescue the pieces. 'You haven't hurt yourself, have you? Are you all right, madam? You've turned quite pale.'

'Sorry,' I said as I pushed past her. 'I've changed my mind.'

I needed fresh air and time to think.

It was drizzling. People scurried past, heads hunched in like tortoises, trying to escape the raindrops. The downpour increased and I stood back in a doorway, watching people splash by in the puddles, wondering what I should do. In the shop it had taken all my self-control not to march up and slap Phyllis's stupid face. But that wouldn't solve anything, and anyway, I had to be sure she was the right woman.

As I dawdled outside a shop window, trying to sort out my thoughts, I saw Jim approaching on the other side of the high street, his trench coat collar turned up against the damp. I watched him enter Boots, but even then I crossed my fingers inside my coat pocket, willing Tizi's bombshell not to be true.

A few minutes later and my hopes were dashed when the pair came out of the shop arm in arm. I followed them to The Wheatsheaf, a pub where Jim had taken me for dinner one Saturday evening before I was pregnant. I waited until I thought they were settled and then I made my entrance. They were seated at a corner table and he was holding her hands. Outwardly I was calm, but inwardly I was boiling like a huge pan of pasta. I made my way over to them and sat myself down.

'I'll have a double brandy and a roast beef sandwich please, Jim,' I said.

Jim's mouth fell open in astonishment.

'Are you going to introduce me to this – person?'

I looked her up and down, taking in her cheap clothes and shoes with heels too high for her fat legs, and I wrinkled up my nose as if I were breathing in the odour of sheep manure. I stared her out.

She looked away in embarrassment, picked up her handbag from the floor and rose from her seat.

'I'll be off then, Jim,' she said, almost falling over in her haste to get away. She threw a worried look over her shoulder at us as she tottered out.

'Yes, I think you had better leave… I need to talk with MY *HUSBAND*.'

I yelled the last two words, so that the men on the table next to us grinned at each other. I turned on them and in the same loud voice I said, 'Yes, it's *very* funny, isn't it? Funny for you and funny for my husband! But not so funny for me and our son.'

'Ines, people are staring at us,' Jim muttered, looking round at the audience in the pub, agog at the free entertainment I was laying on for them.

The publican came over from behind the bar and bent down to Jim. 'Sir, you'd best take your troubles outside. You're disturbing my customers.'

As Jim and I moved towards the door, he tried to take my arm but I shook him off. The men at the table cheered and I turned round, retracing my steps, and picked up a glass of beer and threw it over them.

'If it's a circus you want, then I can perform too.'

Once out in the street, I marched away from the pub, Jim following behind as I shouted, 'I'm going home now, and I'll expect to see you for tea. If you don't come home and explain who that woman is, then I shall pack my bags and take Harry back to Italy with me.'

'Ines, please, let's talk…'

'Not here in the street.'

I turned to a couple of bystanders gawping at us and shouted at them too. 'Mind your own bloody business! Haven't you got anything better to do?'

The man had the grace to turn away but I heard the woman tut and mutter, 'Bloody foreigners.'

'It's up to you, Jim. That's all I've got to say for now. I'll either see you later or I'll be at your parents', explaining to them why I'm leaving for Italy. I wonder what they will have to say then about their *darling* son.'

I hailed a taxi, not caring tuppence about the expense. He had obviously been spending our money on his fancy woman, while I carefully saved for our trip to Italy next summer. I sat in the back of the taxi staring at the streets lined with monotonous houses and drab people walking along with solemn faces. I bit hard on my lip to stop myself from breaking down in front of the driver but once I was inside our house, the tears returned.

Pouring myself more brandy, I was shocked to see I'd finished almost a whole bottle, but it calmed me, dulled my anger and sadness, so that when I heard Jim's key in the latch, I was still sitting in the front room, nursing an empty glass. I was exhausted.

'Ines, I'm sorry.' He came to sit beside me, and I didn't have the energy to push him away.

'You are a bastard, Jim. You told me you were away on business but all the time you were with that...' I hardly knew any bad words in English, despite Tiziana's introducing me to a few ripe expressions. I finished my sentence lamely. '... With that *puttana*.'

'I really did have to go away on business for the airport. This was the first time I lied to you, Ines. I swear.'

'So that makes it all right, does it? How can I believe one word you tell me? Why did you bring me to England? You promised to look after me. In front of a priest you promised to look after me. What have I ever done wrong?'

I stood up to leave the room and he caught hold of my arm.

'Ines, please let's talk about this calmly.'

'If you had wanted someone who was *calma e tran-quilla* like your English women, you shouldn't have married *un' italiana*. Why didn't you just marry that *puttana* whore?'

I slapped his hand from my arm and threw the empty glass at the fireplace, where it smashed into pieces.

'You've not been the same since the day we married. Why did you bother to come back to Rofelle? My family were right. They warned me I didn't know you well enough, that none of us really knew you.'

At that moment, Freda rushed into the room. 'What on earth is going on? I've been knocking on your door these past five minutes…' And then, realising she had walked in on an argument she asked, 'Shall I make us all a nice cup of tea?'

'Oh tea, tea, tea,' I yelled, 'the answer to all English problems. No, I don't want a nice cup of tea, Freda. I hate your tea. I hate England. And most of all, I hate your son!'

I pushed past her and in my haste to get away collided with the pram Freda had left in the hall. Without thinking twice, I pushed it away from the house. Harry was still asleep. I could hear Jim shouting for me to come back, but I ignored him. The park gates were still open. They would shut at dusk. Other mothers and children I usually saw in there would be at home now, busy with bath time and peeling potatoes for supper. I made my way to the duck pond and sat down. In my rush to escape, I had forgotten my coat and so I draped a spare baby blanket round my shoulders. Sitting there on the bench, staring into the muddy green water, I thought of the Marecchia flowing cold and clear beneath our watermill and tears flowed down my cheeks unchecked.

After about half an hour, Harry stirred. It would soon be time for his evening feed. My route home took me past the church of Saint Mary Magdalene where I sometimes attended Sunday Mass. Leaving Harry in his pram in the porch, I slipped inside and pushed a penny into the box and lit a candle. The flickering lights cast a gentle glow, and kneeling down in front of the statue of Our Lady, I bent my head to pray.

Ave Maria, please help me, I feel so lost. Guide me on the right way to continue. We cannot go on like this. Bless my family back in Italy, and bless my little family here. Amen.

Harry started to whimper for his milk. I genuflected before the altar, and after making the sign of the cross I left, pushing the pram as fast as I could through the twilight.

*

The people in my writing class applauded when I finished reading and asked me if I would write a sequel because they wanted to know what happened next.

I did continue to write from time to time, but it was just for me, whenever I needed to disengage from pain, and I never shared my words again.

CHAPTER TWENTY-SEVEN

Memories of autumn 1947

Jim came with me to town the next market day. I suppose he felt guilty and was trying to make amends. He told me he wasn't needed at work. He was unusually playful with Harry and attentive to me, offering to carry my shopping basket.

'Don't know how you do it all on your own,' he'd said, lifting the pram onto the bus.

That day, for a little while, we looked like an ordinary family: an ordinary family unit off to the shops together. But we weren't ordinary at all. I couldn't bear the thought of Jim touching me any more, knowing he'd been with another woman. And recently he hadn't wanted to make love to me anyway. I was pleased, but I knew in my heart it wasn't right. We lived in the same house, but we weren't living together as I'd imagined being married to him would be. Was I simply a naive Italian country girl; were all marriages like this in England? I'd never heard about unhappy wives in all the talk around the fireside back home in Italy. Yes, back home. This place didn't feel like home to me. Would it ever? I didn't want to turn to my friend Tiziana every time Jim and I clashed, so, to keep sane, I reasoned with myself in my head. Round and round went my crazy arguments.

He beats you, Ines, and sleeps with other women. Leave him.

But how can I, the other voice said, *how can I possibly leave him? I made my vows before God.*

God wouldn't want you to be unhappy. Pack a bag and take your baby and return to Italy. It's simple.

They would be ashamed of me. I made my bed, now I have to lie on it.

It's a bed of thorns, not roses. You deserve better.

On and on went the mental tussle. In the end, I decided to accept the situation for what it was; I would have to prove to him that I was a better woman than Phyllis. 'For better, for worse' was the vow I'd made at my wedding. It was my duty.

We sat on the top deck at the front. He remembered I liked to see the view. There were no double-decker buses in Italy. Even though the war had been over for a couple of years, there were still potholes in the road and it was a very bumpy ride.

'Teach me that rhyme again, Jim,' I said, 'the one about the farmer, so I can do it with Harry.'

I was keen to learn and fit in with the English way of life. If I couldn't be a good wife, then I would be a good mother and bring up my children perfectly.

'This is the way the farmers ride,' he started to sing, pulling Harry onto his knee, pretending it was a saddle. He squealed with laughter as Jim danced him up and down in time with the words. But after a while Jim's mind seemed to be elsewhere as he continued to jog Harry higher and higher, not understanding that he was hurting his son.

'This is the way the soldiers die, the soldiers die, the soldiers die, this is the way the soldiers die on a crisp Italian morning,' he sang tunelessly.

When he stopped, Harry held his arms out to me, his little face balled up with crying. I took him and he buried his head in my coat.

Jim stared into the distance. 'All those scrawny mules,' he said, 'trotting up and down those rutted tracks, laden with sticks and guns.'

Trying to change the subject, I cleaned the mist off the window with my gloved hand.

'Ooh look, everybody! It's snowing. How do you say *nevischio* in English, Jim?'

'Sleet.'

'Slit,' I pronounced.

'No, *sleet*, Ines. Like the bloody sleet that stopped the tanks. Muddy ruts. Digging them out in the perishing cold. Bloody weather!'

I looked behind at the other passengers. The bus was quite full now, as we approached the centre of Croydon and Surrey Street with its market stalls.

'Don't swear, Jim,' I scolded. 'You need to set an example right from the start for 'Arry.'

'Why can't you say *Harry*? *Harry*'s too young to understand anyway, lucky bugger,' he rebuked. 'You can say "h", I know you can. You say *hoak* trees, *hold* man... his name is *Harry*.' He emphasised the 'h' petulantly.

'It's 'ard,' I replied, trying to make him laugh, to distract him, but he was off again, his legs still jiggling up and down although he was no longer playing the game with Harry.

'It's *hard*,' he repeated, 'bloody hard with sleet on the hills, waking in the morning, cracking ice off sacking covers, blowing on fingers, bone cold. Bones! Bob's old bones sticking out of his trousers, stick-thin scarecrow limbs.'

Suddenly the bus braked hard, throwing us all forward in our seats. I cracked my head against the window. Harry burst out crying. I screamed as Jim dived down, shouting at the top of his voice, 'Get down, everyone! Get down for cover!'

'Get up, Jim!' I pleaded. 'Baby's hurt.'

Harry was screaming now. A middle-aged woman came over, staring at Jim cowering on the floor. He was shouting at us to get behind the rocks and to duck down from the bullets.

'Are you all right, lady?' she said to me. 'I don't want to interfere, but my son was like that. It's the war, isn't it?'

I nodded and she took my place, taking Harry from me and speaking in a gentle voice to Jim, 'You're all right, son. We'll all get off at the next stop and have a cuppa together. All right? Them soldiers have disappeared over the horizon. We're safe now, son.'

Jim seemed to calm down and I whispered a thank you.

Two women sitting behind us muttered behind their hands and my new friend leant towards me and said, 'Take no notice of them, pet, concentrate on yourself and your family.'

Our little group left the bus at the next stop, the woman lifting down Harry's pram so I could keep hold of Jim. There was a Lyons Corner House opposite, but the woman guided us instead to a greasy spoon café.

'Less fuss in here, dearie. And there's a table free near the window. Your hubby will feel less hemmed in.'

Elsie introduced herself after I'd ordered the drinks. Our guardian angel. She shared a pot of tea with Jim. I tried a coffee, but it was nothing like as strong as I needed.

She took us under her wing. 'We can't talk much in here, my ducks,' she said, commandeering us and the teapot, 'but take it from me, that's what you two need to do, in the quiet of your own home. Talk. I had nobody to tell me anything, and now I like to help when I can.'

Jim was very quiet, a haunted look in his eyes, and I watched as Elsie grasped hold of both his hands. 'You've no doubt seen and done far too much in that awful war, haven't you, my love?'

He looked at her, and with the slightest of nods, mumbled, 'Yes.'

Then she turned to me. 'And you, my girl, need to get this one to open up. That's the only thing that worked for my Norman.'

I started to say something and she interrupted, 'He hasn't got a label hanging round his neck telling you what's the matter – you've got to winkle it out of him, see. It's not going to be easy. God help us, marriage isn't ever, but this blinking war has stirred us all up. You need to be patient.'

I wanted to tell her I'd tried to be patient, that he hit me for my patience, but how could I? With our child in front of us, people eating their egg and bacon breakfasts at the next table... It would be too shocking.

She turned her attention to Harry, cooing and gurgling along with him, and I covered Jim's hand with my own, telling myself I would make this work and help my husband return to the man I'd fallen in love with in Italy.

Elsie wrote her address on a scrap of napkin and handed it to me. 'If you ever need me, here I am,' she said and I folded the paper into my purse, hoping I wouldn't need to call on her, as kind as she was. 'My Norman's fine now,' she said, doing up the buttons on her raincoat. 'Got a job in a garage polishing up cars. It took time, but he got there in the end.'

Back home, I sat Jim in the lounge and asked him to look after Harry while I prepared supper.

'We'll get baby settled and then eat together,' I said. 'I think your mum's left another of her famous casseroles for me to pop in the oven. We'll have a nice, quiet evening.'

He looked at me anxiously and lifted Harry out of the pram.

Although I'd told myself to try and stay calm and be understanding, the task before me seemed colossal. Kicking off my shoes, I bent down wearily to rub my sore toes. I felt like running away, but Elsie's words were ringing in my ears, so I simply took the baby upstairs to change his nappy and asked Jim to light the gas stove to heat up his mother's stew.

During supper, we hardly spoke. I kept stealing glances at him, telling myself he was the same man who had loved me in Italy and that I should give him another chance. Although I wanted him to be the one to take the lead and start the talking, I knew he wouldn't. Maybe he couldn't – just as Elsie had suggested. It was up to me. Pushing our plates to one side instead of getting up to clear them into the sink, I took his hand.

'Look at me,' I said, without raising my voice. 'Look at me and tell me about that woman, and what you think has gone wrong with us.'

His eyes met my steady gaze. He frowned, bit his lip. It was obvious he didn't want to talk but I never let go of his hand. I waited.

'I knew her before the war,' he said eventually, 'she and I used to walk out together. Mother and Father never approved.'

'She's called Phyllis, isn't she?'

'Oh, Ines – what's the point?'

He pulled his hand from mine, leaning back from me in his chair.

'The point is, we *must* talk. We are both very unhappy.'

'I swear she doesn't mean a thing to me.'

'Well, why?' I asked. 'Why have you been with her? And why are you so cruel to me? Do you beat her as well? Do you think that's what women like?'

I didn't shout, willing myself to remain calm. Deep down, I knew that if I couldn't get through to my husband this evening, I never would.

'Elsie told us we should talk,' I continued. 'The way you were on the bus... it frightened me.'

He thumped his fist on the table. 'She was a busybody.'

'She was kind. I think she's right. You need to talk to me, Jim.'

I waited a little and then I asked him again why he felt he needed to be with another woman.

'I want to know what I have done wrong. Tell me why I'm not enough for you any more.'

He ran his hands through his hair. It was thinning at the top. I remembered how thick it used to be, what a problem it had been when we were trying to disguise him in the mountains.

'When I'm with Phyllis, everything seems less complicated somehow,' he said. 'As if the war hadn't happened. Like life was before.'

Hearing that was like a stab to my heart. He was more or less saying he wished he had never met me.

'So you don't love me any more,' I whispered.

'I do love you. Of course I love you.'

'It doesn't seem like that to me.'

I couldn't help it. I started to cry, silently.

'Please don't,' he said, getting up and coming over to me.

He pulled me into his arms and as he rocked me, I sobbed. 'I don't understand. You say you love me, but you seem to say you were happier before the war. It doesn't make sense.'

'I love you,' he repeated, 'but it's not been easy, with the baby and starting a new job. And my mind…' He held his head in his hands. He looked so pitiful. I told myself to be patient.

'Maybe we could go back to Rofelle and start again,' I suggested. 'Maybe you could get a job there. We were happy in Italy.'

'I wondered about that too. The time we had together there was the best part of my life – that's why I came back to you in Rofelle. But what could I do there? There aren't enough jobs even for Italians. I thought that once I came back to England then I could leave the war behind, but…' He stopped.

I lifted my hands to his face and told him to keep talking.

'I can't empty my mind of what I saw.'

His voice was barely a whisper.

'Talk to me, Jim. Tell me.'

I took his hand and led him upstairs to our bedroom. We lay down on top of the eiderdown and I settled into his arms. At first he was very hesitant but once he started talking, he couldn't stop. I listened to the horror of what he had seen and had had to do in the time we had been apart. It was like lancing an abscess and releasing its poison.

Because he knew a little Italian, he had been sent with other 'D-Day dodgers', as they were described, to help with the evacuation of Italian prisoners held in a camp called Bergen Belsen, after the Armistice. Thousands and thousands of men, women and children of different nationalities were in the camp, most of them Jews.

'None of us could believe our eyes when we walked into that place,' he whispered. 'We'd never seen anything like it. There were bodies piled everywhere, stick-thin bodies. Naked men and women, little children… We had to shoot the dogs to stop them eating the bodies that were left unburied for weeks. And the smell… even if you lit a cigarette you couldn't avoid the stench. There were creatures stumbling about – you could only describe them in that way – they didn't look like human beings any more, they were living skeletons… We gave them our rations. We didn't understand that it would kill them. They hadn't eaten properly for months, and the food we gave them was too rich. And the hardest thing was not showing them our horror, our disgust at their smell, the lice, their staring eyes in their hollow skulls, trying to treat them with dignity when we just wanted to turn away and vomit...'

After a while, he stopped talking and his body started shaking. I took him in my arms and soothed him like our baby, patting his back.

'There, there.' I spoke softly to him while we clung together.

After a long while he raised his head and looked at me. 'Don't leave me, Ines. I couldn't bear it.'

And I understood then that I couldn't. The way he acted wasn't his fault. How could I leave him?

That was the night I started to feel old.

CHAPTER TWENTY-EIGHT

In the meantime, Tiziana and I met occasionally. I couldn't burden Freda and John with my worries: I was fond of them and didn't want them to know how their precious son was behaving. Maybe I was naive; I should have taken him to the doctor and sought help. But in those days, nobody talked openly about these things. One day, at the end of my tether, I blurted out my worries to my friend.

'What am I going to do, Tizi?'

We were sitting in her untidy living room, the children playing on a colourful, home-made, tatted rug by the fire. She'd received another parcel from Rome containing Italian biscuits and coffee, and she'd added a splash of *anice* liqueur to her espresso.

'I've told you often enough, *cara*, be firmer with him.'

'But how can I when he's like that? You've never seen it – he's like a child when it happens. I feel as if I've two children to look after.'

Tiziana shrugged her shoulders, pouring another tot of *anice* into her cup. 'I would have left him long ago. I haven't got your patience.'

I knew what her answers would be, but it helped to confide.

'What you need to do is to forget about him for a while,' she said, kneeling down to separate her boys, who were squabbling over a toy tractor. She smacked them hard on their behinds.

'*Basta così*, you two, that's quite enough, and if I have to tell you off again, there'll be more where that came from.'

Hoisting herself back onto the settee, she poured herself another coffee.

'This will make me even more *nervosa*, but who cares? You only live once.'

She stirred three heaped spoons of precious sugar and another generous measure of liqueur into her cup.

'Tell you what, Ines, we'll go out next week to the flicks or something. Bring the *bambini* over here, and Denis's kid sister will look after them. She's always keen to spend time alone with that boyfriend of hers. You can save a couple of bob out of your housekeeping to pay her.'

So I did what she suggested. I sat through *Brief Encounter*, bawling my eyes out and imagining Jim was Trevor Howard. It was so romantic and sad. I wasn't really crying about their doomed love affair; I was crying about mine. Tizi apologised afterwards, saying that we should have seen something funny, like *Dreaming* starring Bud Flanagan, but I don't think anything would have helped me at that time.

Jim had been told to take leave from work to 'rest', as his employer put it, and he was under my feet all day long. He had never liked Tiziana, and he was convinced we had both gone out that evening to meet men. No matter how many times I promised him we had only gone to the cinema, he didn't believe me. The beatings started again. Rofelle and our courtship in the mountains seemed a lifetime away.

*

When everything wore me down, I wrote out my thoughts or composed snippets of poems. I remembered a history lesson at school when we learned about Etruscan women storing away their wedding sheets after their husbands died. They no longer needed them for the marital bed, so they saved them to use as shrouds when they died. To me, it was as if the Jim I had known in Italy had died and I was now a widow. So I found a beautiful pillowcase that Mamma had given me to bring to England and I wrote on that. I wrote what was in my heart, the ink blotting with my tears. Jim discovered it and we had a huge row. The beatings continued.

'Who is he? Who is this man you are writing to?' he shouted, hitting me about my face this time, so I couldn't leave the house for a week.

'Tell me, you barmy bitch,' he shouted. 'Tell me or I'll hit you again. I always thought you were a loony and now I know for sure.'

I couldn't give him an answer. I didn't know myself who this man was I had begun to dream about. I only knew it wasn't Jim, and I asked myself if this was all there was to life.

Jim yanked me by the hair and I saw a fistful of curls clasped tight through his knuckles. Next morning I combed my hair in a different style to cover the bald patch.

Anna pulls out the yellowing pillowcase from its brown paper wrapping, unfolding the material to read her mother's words, the letters faded in places.

Your hands are gentle hands, touching my body, silk on silk.
They are not the claws of a hawk, tearing the innards
from its prey.
Your eyes are full of the light of a sun slipping down
folds of mountains
Bathing me with warmth and promise.
Your eyes are not sparks, singeing with acrid stench, jumping from
spitting fire, burning holes in my Sunday dress.
My petticoat hangs on branches of willow,
I lie down with you under the hot August midday sun
in the shallows,
Your mouth is soft, your tongue like the smooth underbelly of a
tickled trout as you caress my breasts.
You are not the frost, not jagged spikes of wild rose or bramble
Nor splinters from the handle of my hoe,
Nor the viper coiled near the washing line. Your hands are gentle
hands, touching my body, silk on silk.

'Why, oh why didn't she get out while she could?' Anna is on her mobile, needing to talk about the latest entry in the diary with Francesco, who is shopping in Arezzo with Alba in preparation for the new school year.

His reply is immediate. 'Easy to say that from where you're standing now, but try to imagine yourself in those times. There wasn't the same freedom.'

'I know you're right, but I still feel like shouting at her to leave him.'

'Hey, you've just told me about what he had to do in Belsen. You said you felt sorry for him. Nowadays people receive therapy for far less. He was obviously suffering from post-traumatic stress disorder. If *you* are confused, Anna, then think how it must have been for her.'

'I know, I know. But it's so heart-rending reading about it.'

'It must be. Poor you and poor her. Anna, before I forget again. About the medal. Sorry! I meant to tell you. It's Danilo's, awarded for exceptional services. Goodness knows why it was in the mill. We'll have to return it to him. Maybe he lost it.'

'That's so strange. You'd think he'd be proud of it, and would keep it in a special place. Maybe it was stolen. He told me about thieves who stole antiques from his neighbours.'

'Well, when we return it to him, we can ask.'

'Will you come with me next time? He can't bear the sight of me, and… I'm not sure how to approach him, to be honest.'

'Of course I will…' He breaks off and she hears him say to Alba, 'Absolutely no way… they're ghastly.'

'How's the shopping going?' Anna asks.

He lowers his voice. 'I could do with you here right now. The little monkey keeps picking out the most hideous stuff and convincing me it's what she has to have for school. What do you think about pink sneakers?'

'Do they fit her? Are they sensible pink sneakers? There's nothing wrong with pink. They sound better than the brown lace-ups I was made to wear for school.'

'*Aagh*! It's a conspiracy. You women are ganging up on me.'

'Just enjoy your day together. Go with the flow. See you later. Ciao for now!'

She switches off her mobile and thinks of Francesco trawling the shops with his daughter, feeling guilty for not being there to help him. But it's not her place, and Francesco needs time with Alba. Last night she threw a wobbly when Francesco cut short her bedtime story. She'd worked out her daddy was planning to spend time afterwards with Anna and clung to him, making him stay to read two more stories. They talked about how to deal with Alba's tantrums when he knocked on her door nearly two hours later, and decided a shopping trip seemed a good option for some one-to-one time together.

Tidying away her mother's papers, Anna thinks about Francesco's comments. He's right. It's all too easy to judge from afar, and her own love life, although nothing like her mother's, hasn't exactly been smooth.

As Anna has the day to herself, she decides to track down Danilo again. She can't put it off any longer. She feels bad about taking the tin with the medal, now she knows who it belongs to. It's strange he hasn't kept it somewhere more secure. War veterans are usually proud of their honours. Maybe Danilo is modest about his commendation and doesn't like to flaunt it. But to Anna, he seems more arrogant than modest. More and more she yearns to learn about her parents' young lives, and to understand what happened to unravel their romance. She hopes Danilo will be more forthcoming this time.

As she walks up to Danilo's hamlet, she thinks back over her stay, to when Francesco showed her around a simple folk museum in the tiny village of Casteldelci. There she learned how people managed from day to day: how they used ashes from the fire to wash their clothes using wood ash soap; how they slept on the first floor of their houses with the animals on the ground floor providing heat that would percolate up through wide gaps in the floorboards. She's read in her mother's diary about how heavily the war impacted these ordinary people's lives. The museum displayed gruesome photos of dead partisans arranged on the bridge beneath the village as a warning by the Germans not to support them.

She'd been struck by the wording on a simple banner hanging in the main exhibition room: OUR PAST IS THE COUNTER-WEIGHT TO OUR FUTURE. These words touched a chord and gave relevance to her reading of Ines' secrets. As she learns more about her mother and father, she hopes she'll come to know herself better, too.

The weather is still warm, but not the baking heat of July and early August. From the woods the noisy whirring of chainsaws is a reminder that winter is just around the corner. Woodcutters are busy at work chopping and piling up logs, as fuel for storage. On the slopes above her, the clanging of heavy bells round the necks of Chianina cattle is like a kind of music as they munch on the last of the summer pasture. On her walk up here in July, she'd stopped to admire orchids and helleborines, but now they're withered. Chicory and field scabious nod blue and purple in the breeze, and as she brushes past juniper bushes, she squeezes a berry and inhales the scent of gin.

She picks her way over stones left by the latest landslide, and as she arrives at the edge of the tiny village square, she is surprised to see women washing fruit and salad leaves in the village fountain. Last time she was there, the place had been deserted except for a solitary stray cat. They wave and ask if she would like to join them for a picnic, but she declines and continues on up the path alongside the church to the old man's house. The door is shut but she can hear a radio playing inside, so she knocks. There is no answer. She knocks again.

Grumpy old sod, she thinks, *he's probably hiding from me.*

Taking a notebook from her rucksack, and a photo of her mother she has purposely brought with her, she scribbles a note, hoping this will not turn out to be yet another wasted journey.

Dear Signor Danilo,
    I don't know your surname, so excuse me and excuse my poor Italian. I came to see you before, but you were too busy to talk.

I would like to ask you about the war and especially about my mother. This is a photo of her. You may remember her. She was Ines Santini before she married my father, Jim Swilland. I am their daughter.

You can contact me at Teresa Starnucci's holiday house in San Patrignano.

Thank you and best wishes,
Anna Swilland

PS Please return the photo as it is an original and very special to me. Thank you!

Just as she guides the note and photo carefully through the slight gap under the door, the door bursts open.

'You again! I told you to keep away,' Danilo shouts.

'I only want to ask you some questions about the war.'

'And what if I don't want to answer? War, war, war... we don't need to be reminded of that time. I told you before. You have no right to come here, stirring things up.'

He pushes his way past her, almost knocking her over and she staggers back, but he offers no apology.

'I saw you down at the mill,' he says, pulling a shirt off the line. 'I told you not to go there either. It's private... and dangerous. The roof could cave in at any time.'

'I didn't see you.'

'I was fishing. I heard voices. You were with young Starnucci.'

'Francesco?'

He nods. 'Now clear off. I have to go down to Badia, and I don't want you snooping around my house.'

'I've left you a note...' she starts.

'I'm not interested.'

He slams the door on her, and she wonders what could have happened in his life to cause such bitterness.

Concerned he might destroy the precious photo of her mother, she knocks on his door again. Depending on his reaction, she'll own up to finding the medal, offer to return it. She's half relieved when there's no response, but, like a dog with a bone, she can't let go of wanting to talk to this old man about his war. She's sure he's hiding something from her. Maybe he would be more open if she got Francesco to come with her next time.

Determined not to let angry thoughts ruin her afternoon, she diverts from her usual route back to San Patrignano and follows a sign indicating the way to the remains of the Gothic Line. The path is steep, strewn with slippery dried pine needles, and she picks up a stick to help her balance.

At the top, somebody has erected a crude wind structure made from rusting metal pieces; the sounds in the gentle breeze as the pieces knock together are mournful. She reads a sign about the Gothic Line, nailed to an oak tree. All that is left of this German machine gun position is the main trench, now almost clogged with dead leaves and fallen stones, and a hollow in the rocks further back that served as a store. A pear tree, withered and gnarled, leans almost horizontally from the incline below, and she wonders if it was there when soldiers guarded this spot.

Her phone rings, interrupting her daydream. 'Where are you?' Francesco asks. 'We've finished our shopping, thank God. We were wondering about going to the pizzeria for supper. Do you want to join us?'

She laughs. 'I'd love to. At the moment, I'm above Monte-botolino, admiring the most amazing view in the world. No luck with that cantankerous old man, though. Maybe I need to take you along next time.'

'Join us for pizza and forget about him for now, Anna.'

'Brilliant. See you later.' She wants to add 'Love you', but it's too soon and she knows Alba might overhear. She doesn't want to upset the little girl, but sooner or later she'll have to accept that she and her daddy want to spend time together.

Francesco drops her home after their evening at the pizzeria, kissing her on the lips as he says goodbye.

'That's so yucky,' Alba says from the back of the car, and Anna has a sinking feeling of complications to come.

Climbing the stairs, she feels lonely. She wishes she could share her bed with Francesco and have Alba sleep in her spare room, like a family. Not tired at all, she pulls the final pages of her mother's writing from the folder on her bedside table and, flopping down on top of her bedcover, she starts to read again.

CHAPTER TWENTY-NINE

June 1949

In June 1949 we finally returned to Rofelle. It had taken longer to save up for the fares than Jim had calculated, and both our babies had been born in the meantime. Baby Jane was placid and bonny, feeding well and sleeping through the night at three months. She was a far easier baby than Harry, and her arrival into our troubled family was a comfort for me.

We were juddered and jolted about on the train, with Harry crying at the top of his little voice because he'd dropped his dinky car at Victoria station. Being so preoccupied with baby Jane, I hadn't noticed. She was teething, poor little scrap, and during the train journey she grizzled nearly all the time she was awake. I had wanted her to be christened Assunta after my mother, but Jim had insisted on English Jane and I didn't have the strength to fight. But when he wasn't around I would call her Assunta and I would speak to her in Italian. And I sang to her of the mountains, deer, spindle berries in the forest and mushrooms in the meadows. I made the songs up. The words came out of my lips like birds set free.

'*Shhh*, baby Assunta! Mamma's here,' I whispered, rocking her back and forth, holding her soft cheek next to mine to still her crying.

And little Harry would shout, 'Why are you calling her Assunta, Mummy? She's Jane, Jane, Jane,' and he stamped his little feet as he shrieked her name.

Harry was too clever for his age. He was a miniature Jim. When I told him off, away he would scamper, sticking out his tongue at me from a safe distance. Or he'd kick my legs, the way he'd seen it done.

We travelled for two and a half tiring days in dirty carriages, with the smell of urine rising from nappies and soiled clothes. It was stuffy in the carriage, but I hadn't wanted to open the window because Harry was up and into everything and Jim kept disappearing down the corridor for a smoke. It would have helped if he'd offered to keep an eye on his son. But by now I was accustomed to doing everything by myself, and nothing really mattered, for I was going home to Tuscany. The children had been seasick on the Channel crossing and I'd tried my best to clean them up, but we all looked dishevelled.

The train chugged its way through France and Switzerland and we stopped for border control before entering Italy. Up to this point in the journey, the French and Swiss guards, the vendors on the platforms, had all seemed half-dead, going about their business so seriously, so quietly. Once we were over the border, however, I was struck immediately by the noise of shouting and friendly chatter outside the train. Pushing open the window, I sniffed the air like an animal scenting home territory. The name on the platform, CHIASSO, which means 'din' in Italian, made me laugh out loud. I thought the name so appropriate – that the first city to pass through in Italy had such an honest name.

The couple of hours before Milan, where we had to change trains once again, seemed to drag into ten hours. We snatched a drink at a bar on Milan station and I felt embarrassed as I stood and watched my elegant countrymen pass by. Even though the war had only been over for five years, there was a beauty and a pride to these Italians. They were stylish, in well-cut clothes and fashionable hairstyles I hadn't seen in post-war England. I felt like the mother of a gypsy family. We had set out on this journey clean, but now we looked like chimney sweeps, the soot from the steam train leaving smutty smears on our faces. Even our sandwiches tasted of coal, and the toilet facilities were totally inadequate for washing a baby and a toddler.

On the next and final leg of our long journey, I fumbled in our suitcase to find the new summer clothes I had bought for Harry and Jane. I was so proud of my babies. I wanted to show them off to everybody in the village once we arrived. Just before the train at long last drew into Rimini station, I pointed out the sea to Harry. The water glinted invitingly, lapping gently at the sand, a few people already stretched out on the beach, taking the sun. How different from the pebbly shore and grey swirl of water on Hastings beach, where Jim had taken us one drizzly Sunday last spring.

Papà was waiting on the platform. Shyness suddenly came over me, but as soon as he saw us climb down the steps, he pulled off his cap, waving it to attract our attention. He ran towards us with arms outstretched, and I was his little girl again. He lifted Harry into the air, threw him up, kissed him with so much fervour that he started to cry, which then set Jane off. I was crying too by now, but mine were tears of joy.

'Where is Mamma?' I asked, looking along the platform for her. He told me she was waiting at home, that the taxi was too small to carry us all up the Marecchia road with our luggage, and so she had stayed behind to prepare a good chicken broth.

'We've killed one of the hens specially,' he added, 'and she's made trays of *tagliatelle*, too.'

He bent down to wipe away the tears from Harry's cheeks, who peeped up shyly at his grandfather, thumb in mouth.

Alberto, the barkeeper's son from Badia, worked part-time as a taxi driver and Papà herded us to his gleaming black Aprilia, which Jim greatly admired. Papà insisted Jim travel in the front while he climbed into the back with me and the babies, pulling Harry onto his knee.

'How can Nonno hope to talk to his little grandson if he doesn't know any Italian?' he said, shaking his head at me. 'Eh, Ines? How shall we manage?'

Throughout the car journey up into the mountains, he tried to teach Harry a few simple words in Italian and I hoped Jim wouldn't make a fuss.

'*Motocicletta*,' he pronounced clearly, pointing to one of the many motorbikes spluttering past us along the route. There were far more here in Italy and Harry had fun imitating the revving sounds. Jane slept in my arms while I gazed out of the window at newly constructed houses, neatly tended meadows and my beautiful mountains, seeing them with fresh eyes. When I had left, the landscape had been battle-scarred, desolate. I was proud to see the resilience of my people, how they were resurrecting a new life from nothing.

'We'll stop here for a while and have a drink, and you and the children can freshen up,' said Papà about an hour into the journey.

All I wanted to do was get to the mill quickly to see Mamma again, put my arms around her and share my children; I didn't want the journey held up one moment longer than necessary. But Papà knew the owner of the bar on the road below Pennabilli, and he wanted to introduce us, his grandchildren and his English son-in-law who had travelled so many miles for this return visit. He was so proud of us. The wife of the owner exclaimed what a handsome young man Harry was, and how beautiful and plump the baby.

'But signora,' she said, her hands raised in horror, 'she will catch her death in this cold mountain air! Where are her socks? Where is her vest? Cover her up! Take this shawl and wrap her up warm.'

It was surely not her intention, but she made me feel I was an inadequate mother. In England I always let Jane kick in her pram in our little back garden, her chubby legs bare to the fresh air. But mountain people were wary of spring weather, and waited until July and August to cast off their winter clothing.

Half an hour later we were back in the car and I started to recognise my childhood haunts. My heart beat faster and faster as we passed through Ponte Presale, where the Friday market took place. Then I spied the huge rock studded with fossils in the meadow where our cows used to graze. Next, the baker's, Badia cemetery and the newly built municipal hall with Italian flags fluttering proudly in the breeze, its steps flanked with geraniums spilling from huge urns. And then we were rounding a bend to take the lane down to the mill. This part of the journey seemed to last forever, each bend in the road like a purgatory until, finally, the car turned sharp right down the dirt track towards the mill. There it stood in the afternoon sunshine, perched on its rock above the river. I could hardly wait for the car to stop. Flinging open the door and grabbing hold of the children, I hurried from the car towards the mill steps. With baby Jane in my arms and Harry clinging to my skirt, I climbed the steps.

I shall never forget seeing my poor mother that first time. She stood there, a shadow of herself, tired and grey. In my shock, I nearly dropped the baby.

'Mamma, *Mammina!*' I cried tears as I kissed her, and inside I was thinking, *What have I done to you? It's my fault, isn't it? For going across the sea and leaving. Forgive me, dearest Mammina, forgive me.*

Later on, when we were sitting round the table in the kitchen, having eaten her excellent chicken broth, and Jim and Papà had gone out to drink more wine up in the *osteria* at Rofelle, I asked Mamma if it was my fault she looked so ill.

'Don't be foolish, Ines. The doctor says I have thyroid problems, that's all. I'll soon be right again after I've finished taking his medicines.'

She took Jane from me and hugged her close, then bent down to touch Harry's soft curls and said she didn't want to talk about it any more, she wanted to enjoy the time with me and her grandchildren. *The doctor's telling lies. It's me, it's me, it's me. Far, far away across the sea,* my thoughts whispered to me, teasing me with what I believed was the truth.

In the first days of that holiday, there was a pattern to the reaction from my old neighbours and friends. I had seen the same looks in my parents' eyes too.

'But you're so thin, Ines,' they would say.

That always came after the first embraces, after they'd let me go and stepped back, looking me up and down. Their faces registered shock at the state of me. I knew they were thinking how scrawny I had become, how lifeless my hair was, how my beauty had left for England on the train with me and not come back.

'Don't they feed you in *Inghilterra*, Ines?' commented Lucia from the farm up the road, where we'd been invited to supper one evening.

'Come sit with me and I'll fill your plate. We've made pizza with toppings of courgette flowers and *stracchino* cheese. And roasted hare and boar. Eat, Ines! Give me the baby. Sit and eat.'

And Ida from San Patrignano, she left baskets of eggs, tomatoes on the vine and jars of plum jam on the doorstep at the mill, just like she'd done in the days before our wedding.

Now it was Jim's turn to be the foreigner, and I watched how my people welcomed him, drew him into their warm circle of food and wine and love. Yes, love. That was it. That was what I had been missing back in *Inghilterra*.

*

We stayed for two weeks. Time flew by, and all too soon the day arrived when we had to leave. It was so difficult. I wanted to stay, but how could I? It had been my decision to leave for England with Jim in the first place. How could I even think of leaving him now and staying in Rofelle? In those days, you see, divorce was considered a huge scandal. If the young had the wisdom of the old, then I would have followed what was really in my heart and stayed in Rofelle. I have learned over the years that the answers to all the questions we ask ourselves are already inside us. All we have to do is be quiet and listen.

On the second Sunday of our holiday, I attended Mass in the little stone church where I had made my First Communion and, later, married Jim. I gazed at the cross, muttering my prayers, begging for a miracle to allow me to stay. All I could see in reply were the nails in the hands of Jesus and the blood trickling down his face from his crown of thorns. He seemed to be telling me what I knew already: that life was hard, that everybody had to suffer in some way or other. My trial was Jim, and I had to stay faithful to my marriage vows.

I clung to my mother as we kissed goodbye, as if she were a piece of wreckage and I was drowning in the cold English Channel.

'There's always a place for you here,' she said as she embraced me, pulling me close to her heart. Yes, it was wonderful to arrive but dreadful to leave, and there were tears all round.

And once again the train carried me away across the miles, rocking me with imagined refrains:

I would if I could but I can't.
I would if I could but I can't.
I can't, I can't, I can't, I can't…

Back in England I fell ill and couldn't shake off my sadness. I was constantly tired. My two babies had been born close together, and both labours were long and painful. When I eventually dragged myself to visit the doctor, I wasn't surprised when she diagnosed problems with my thyroid. In a way, I felt it was right that I too should suffer what my own mother was suffering. They were very dark times for me, but my doctor was a kind woman and she urged me to continue to write down my feelings.

And writing did help a little. Talking to Jim didn't. How many promises had he made? How many promises had he broken in our talks?

Far more than he'd kept.

CHAPTER THIRTY

August 1999

At two in the morning, Anna sits, wishing her mother could be sitting next to her on the bed, so she can tell her how much she loves her.

There are only a few pages left of her story but she is struggling to keep her eyes open. Switching off her bedside light, she falls asleep with the pillowcase in her arms.

Without bothering even to make her customary mug of tea next morning, she resumes reading. The date on the next page has jumped nearly twenty years, and she wonders how she can fill in the missing pieces.

Maybe she never will.

30 September 1966

On the pantry shelves of Willow's End there's a regiment of jars of blackberry jam. There's hardly room for more. We shall never get through it all in the coming year, but when the September sun shines like this I have to be outside.

I've hurried through my morning chores, cleared the grate, laid fresh kindling and scrubbed the lino in the hall that looks so much like Italian salami. Before ten o'clock I'm out of the house. The day is mine until Jane returns from school. The curtains twitch at number 23 across the way. The old bag will be wondering where I'm off to again. 'That foreign bit', married to Jim – that's what I've heard her call me. She's complained to him about the smell of garlic wafting from my kitchen, as well. Let her complain! Back home they'd probably have muttered, too, if an English woman had married one of their boys.

This morning is a little fresher than yesterday and I button up my cardigan as I hurry down the footpath. It's one of Freda's old Aran wool cardigans – a little stretched now, but I like wearing it. She was a kind woman, God rest her soul. She was like a mother to me, comforting me when I heard of Mamma's passing away and caring for me when I went through my black moments. I pull the rough wool closer round my middle.

It only takes five minutes to escape from the line of rabbit hutch houses, and when I reach the edge of the cornfields, I stop and breathe in the air, hungry for its scent. If I close my eyes I can almost imagine I'm back in Rofelle. The best blackberries are at the bottom of this field, and as my feet scrunch over the stubble of corn stalks, I can pretend I am back in Tuscany. I can pretend. Especially when the breeze rustles up a dance in the trees at the edge of the field and I look up at the billow of clouds, picturing them like the Apennines soaring above me, enfolding me.

The sun is more diluted than the August sun we enjoyed last month. Jim took us all back to Italy with some of the money Freda left. He couldn't avoid it, for she had stipulated in her will that 'he was duty-bound to take Ines back to her home village for a long-overdue holiday'. In this sheltered corner of the field, the sun does its best to shine a little warmth and I peel off Freda's cardigan.

The breeze is playing with my curls. I'm lucky, I've no grey strands. Papà had a head of black curls until the day he died, and maybe I take after him. A thorn from the brambles tears at my finger and I gasp and suck the wound, blood oozing and mixing with the purple blackberry juice staining my hands. It's the colour of wine at the village *festa* we went to last month. The men clustered round fat flasks of strong red wine, sitting on Farmer Amedeo's cart, slapping each other on the back, using their hands the way we Italians do when we talk. Jim had a good amount to drink. It was free, so he drank it greedily and he had no idea what was going on that evening, the state he was in.

The end of the square outside the town hall was cleared for dancing, chairs and trestle tables arranged under the *loggia* in case it rained. Franco, the butcher, supervised, sliced and shared the succulent *porchetta*. Now, as I think back, my mouth waters at the memory of the sweet meat perfumed with rosemary and garlic. All the women in Rofelle had been busy for days, mixing and cutting yellow ribbons of pasta to go with sauces of wild hare and boar. They let me help, laughing at my fumbling.

'You've forgotten, Ines, you've forgotten how to make *tagliatelle*. What do you cook back in *Inghilterra*? Sandwiches?'

And it's true, I had forgotten. Jim preferred his food the English way, his plate piled with potatoes and meat, swimming in gravy. Nevertheless, my Italian friends let me help and I joined in with their laughter and gossip that evening, and for a while I felt I belonged again. When we had finished cooking, we sat together on hay bales, waiting to be asked to dance polkas and waltzes in the square. The young girls sat modestly, their eyes cast down, peeping every now and then at their sweethearts.

My little hamlet would never feature in glossy guidebooks, but that night Rofelle was a place of magic. Candles and oil lamps glowed in every niche, imbuing old stones with golden warmth. I thought back to myself as a young girl, how I'd turned up my nose at this type of *festa*, at the smallness of the place, the simple goodness and generosity of the people. And I wondered how I could ever have despised it.

Capriolo asked me to dance. The years had been kind to him. He was still lean but his hair was streaked with grey, lending him a distinguished look. The women had filled me in with the gossip, telling me he'd been married for a while to a city girl from Florence, but she'd soon tired of village life and he'd refused to leave his birthplace to go to live with her. He was still active in local politics, but his main job was on the land. I glanced over to where Jim was drinking, surrounded by other men, knocking back tumblers of wine. But he was oblivious to me, his long face shining white in the moonlight. Jane was already on the dance floor, a young man patiently guiding her round to the music. Harry had wandered over to see what his father was up to, and I saw him help himself to a beaker of wine. *Let him*, I thought. *He's nearly nineteen and soon he'll be a man and off to college.*

I settled into Capriolo's arms as he moved me in a waltz to the notes from Beppe's accordion. It was old-fashioned folk music. Pop music by the Beatles and other groups was yet to reach this corner of Italy. The words of the songs came back to me. I sang them softly as he led me round the square, and it was as if I'd never been away. The night was warm and he'd rolled up his shirtsleeves. I could feel the swell of his muscles under my fingers. As he spun me round and round, we stared deep into each other's eyes and the world beyond our space blurred. And it was at that moment I knew I had made the biggest mistake of my life, all those years ago. As he danced, a lock of his unruly hair flopped down over his right eye, the way it always used to when he bent over his schoolbooks in our village classroom. My fingers burned to smooth it back, but I knew the eyes of the villagers, my relations, maybe even Jim and the children would be upon us. At the end of the dance I thanked him and returned to the bales. I watched the shadows of dancers move across the walls of the old stone houses, and suddenly I couldn't watch any more, and I ran and ran and ran.

The road down to the mill where I'd spent my childhood was lit by moonlight but even in the dark I found my way there easily. As I drew nearer, the sounds of water flopping and gurgling over stones grew louder and I leant against a rock, staring downriver towards the mill, wishing with all my heart I had never left.

Footsteps. Capriolo's voice.

'Ines?'

And then his arms were round me and we were kissing and the feel of his lips on mine was like coming home.

'Someone will come along. They'll see us,' I said.

I pulled away. Where we were standing, the full moon shining down on us like daylight, anybody could see us from the bridge.

'Come,' he said, pulling me down the track towards the mill, our feet skidding on the stones in our haste.

He pushed open the door to the barn and, hand in hand, we went in and then I was in his arms again, our kisses deeper, more urgent. We lay down on the hay and for the first time in my life I made love. We made love on the floor of a barn and for those few sad, beautiful moments, I was in paradise. Every part of me sang and afterwards I cried in his arms.

'I should never have let you go, Ines. Maybe if we had done this before you left for England, then you wouldn't have gone away.'

I stopped his words with my kisses and he held me tighter. We kept our eyes open and our gaze never left each other's even at the very height of our lovemaking. I had never felt so complete in all my life.

'Why don't you leave him? Come back here where you belong,' he said as we lay together.

'How can I? How can I leave my children?'

'But we *love* each other. You know, even when I was in bed with my wife, I was thinking of you.'

I felt jealous then. I knew I had no right, but I couldn't help it.

'They told me about her. What was her name?'

'Rita,' he said, raising himself on his elbow, staring down at me where I lay on the straw, 'but she means nothing to me.'

'There were no children, were there? Once there are children, everything changes.'

He shook his head.

'I shouldn't have let you leave,' he said, sitting up abruptly, his back to me. 'But I felt so guilty and ashamed. I didn't deserve you, Ines,' he said.

'Guilty? What do you mean?'

'Your brother was too young to die.'

'I know.'

'It was my fault…' He turned to look down at where I lay on the hay.

'What do you mean, Capriolo?'

His voice was almost a whisper. 'I should have taken Davide with me that day. Instead of telling him to stay in camp. He was angry with me.'

'How can that mean his death was your fault?' I sat up and touched his arm. 'I don't understand.'

'He wanted to prove he was a man. If I'd kept him with me, then he would still be alive, instead of going on a foolhardy one-man mission. It was suicide.'

I pulled him down to me and stroked the curl from his face. He was blaming himself for something that had happened years ago, during the war, with death and destruction all around us. How could Davide's death be his fault? 'Please don't spoil tonight. Just hold me,' I whispered. 'The war's done too much damage to us already. It's over.'

But we had to leave. It was gone midnight. The *festa* was coming to an end and we would be missed. So we dressed and he picked the straw out of my hair, helping me with the buttons on the back of my frock.

And then he smiled and, pulling a penknife from his pocket, he carved our initials in a heart, low down on the wall near to where we had made love.

'You're a boy,' I said, 'a mad, mad boy… what if somebody sees that?'

'The only creatures to see it will be the cattle when they bend to munch on their hay and who will they tell, Ines?'

I laughed and ruffled his hair and he pulled me into his arms again.

'You are still beautiful, even after all this time,' he murmured.

If the clock in the church tower on the hill above in Rofelle hadn't chimed the first notes of midnight, we would have been down in the straw again.

We left separately.

When I reached the square, Jim was being supported by the sons of the owner of the little guest house where we were staying.

'This one will wake up like a bear in the morning. I hope you've strong coffee for his head tomorrow, Ines.'

They helped me carry him up the narrow stairs and when they had gone, I undressed him and climbed into bed beside him.

All night I lay awake.

One week later, we returned to England. Life resumed its routine. Autumn was upon us and I started my crazy blackberry jam-making to keep myself busy. I thought I might go a little mad again, like after Jane was born. But this time, who would look after me?

In the field, the sun hides behind the clouds and I shiver, fastening the old bone buttons on Freda's cardigan again. Just one more branch of blackberries to harvest and I'll return to the house and set the preserving pan on the stove. I pick more fruit, not caring about the thorns, just wanting the sadness to fly away. I won't ever return to Rofelle. I can't. It would cause too much upset to too many people, not least my own children.

My only consolation is of being certain my love for Capriolo is not just a dream. The nausea I've been feeling has now made me sure of the life we started in the barn. I shall tell Jim it happened that night when he was so drunk. But I shall know the truth.

In my heart I long for a son. I picture how he'll lean over his schoolbooks when he's older, a curl of raven-black hair falling in front of his eyes. I picture how I will gently smooth it back from his little forehead and whisper to him in Italian of how he is my special gift.

CHAPTER THIRTY-ONE

Anna counts from August 1966 to May 1967 on the fingers of both her hands: nine months. Ines didn't have a son. She had a baby girl and Anna's own birth date is 15 May 1967.

'You're a good girl, Anna. You're my special gift.'

How often had her mother spoken those words to her in the care home?

Her mind fields thoughts, firing at her one after the other.

Jim wasn't my father. Capriolo was my father. But who was this Capriolo? I am the baby conceived in that barn. What had my mother written? 'This is my inheritance to you. Do with it what you will.'

Her head is spinning. She has to get outside, despite the rain. She pulls on jeans, sweatshirt, a waterproof jacket and walking boots and, slamming the door behind her, she strides down the path to the river. The ground is cloggy underfoot. The river is full but she keeps on walking. And then she remembers the day of the storm and where she sheltered with Alba.

She quickens her pace. At the barn she undoes a rusty piece of wire holding the ramshackle door closed and enters. Rain splashes through the missing roof tiles and it smells musty inside, despite the sun of the past weeks. Kneeling down in the corner near their makeshift picnic table, she finds the heart scratched into the crumbling plaster near the rotten feeding trough.

DS & IS, agosto 1966

She traces the letters with her finger, picturing her mother sitting there, hair undone, blades of straw tangled in her curls, gazing at her lover as he carves their initials. She can see them in the hay, making love, hear their sighs, their groans of passion. Leaving, she pulls the door to and continues walking, not knowing where she is going, just following the course of the river, now more swollen with the steady fall of rain.

As she walks she tries to identify this Capriolo – or *DS*. She frowns with concentration as she racks her brain for any man who might match the initials.

Davide Santini... oh God, no! Ines' own brother!

But then she remembers Uncle Davide had died during the war. Of course it couldn't possibly be him.

The rain has stopped by the time she reaches the waterfall. She sits for a while, willing herself to calm down. The water cascades over the weir with a roar, spewing white foam into the pool below. She watches a couple of fish try to jump back up the waterfall. A grey heron with spindly legs is about to land on a log to fish, but, sensing her presence, he changes course, his large wings cumbersome as he manoeuvres an altered flight. As he soars above her head she hears the whistle of air through his wings.

Dario Starnucci.

The name comes to her, booming in her head like an announcement over a public tannoy. The blood drains from her face; her heartbeat slows almost to a stop.

Dario Starnucci. Francesco has talked about his father often enough. He was a partisan, too. DS must be Dario Starnucci. The father of Francesco and Teresa is also my father.

She feels sick.

She has slept with her brother. The man she loves is her half-brother.

'*Do with it what you will*', her mother had written.

But what is she supposed to do? She walks in a daze back in the direction of her house. Only it isn't even *her* house. It belongs to her half-sister, loaned to her so that she could stay in Italy and be happy. And she has been really happy. But nothing feels right any more.

She lets herself into the house in the square and hauls her suitcase from under the bed, tossing in items: a change of underwear, clean jeans, tops, jacket – it will be colder in England. She checks her passport and credit card are in her handbag. All she wants now is to get away from this place, call a taxi and catch the first available plane to London. She tears a page from one of the children's exercise books on her table, scribbling a note to say she is returning to England for family reasons.

Then she is sick, vomiting again and again down the toilet until she spits bitter bile. She feels ancient and wrung out, and needs to rest for a while on the bed.

When the birds begin to sing hours later, she wakes up. In the early light she gazes at her few possessions scattered around: heart-shaped stones collected by Alba from the riverbed; the little girl's paintings; the bright tablecloth bought from the market, and she thinks they are souvenirs best left behind. She thinks, wryly, that at least Alba will be pleased to see the back of her; she is so jealous of her babbo's time.

Rimini airport is thronging with Russian tourists on a day's shopping trip, their carrier bags crammed with designer clothes and shoes. She nurses a tepid cappuccino at the bar as she waits to go through security. The big Russian women in tight jeans pull out flimsy blouses and bright sandals to show each other. She finds their words harsh and guttural compared with the melody of Italian. Little do they know they've travelled all these air miles to buy goods manufactured especially for them and not for the Italian market, that they've shopped in outlets where Italian women would never set foot.

At a nearby table covered in the paraphernalia of a baby's travel equipment, an exhausted young English mother sits breastfeeding a very young baby while trying to clean a toddler's nose. Anna picks up a toy from the floor for the little dark-haired boy and his mother thanks her, explaining that they are on their way to England to see their sick grandpa.

The air conditioning isn't working and it's hot in the seating area. She watches a couple of *carabinieri* standing to one side, deep in discussion, handsome enough to look as if they have just stepped from the pages of a glossy fashion magazine. Ordinarily Anna enjoys her people watching. Down in the square in Sansepolcro she'd often lingered over a coffee, watching scenes unfold in the Piazza Torre di Berta, observing characters from all walks of life entering from the wings onto a real-life stage. But today she wants to be gone from Italy and for this day to be over so she can escape from her nightmare.

Checking the monitor to see if her flight has been called, she notes the plane from Stansted has not even touched down. There's still an hour to wait before going through to Departures. She knows she should eat something but she's not hungry. Pictures of her and Francesco in bed keep flashing into her mind. She once watched a documentary about incest, late at night on Channel 5. A boy and girl, adopted at different times by the same foster family, had ended up as a couple. They'd justified their love by explaining that nobody had ever told them they were brother and sister. And now she is guilty of the same thing. She shakes her head to free her brain from the images and bends down to talk to the little boy, who is crying for his mother's attention.

'Would you like me to read you a story?' she asks.

At least it will occupy her mind and distract her from thinking of Francesco.

His young mother scrabbles around in her carry-on luggage and produces a tatty, much-thumbed Postman Pat storybook, smiling a thank you to Anna. She starts to read to the child and he pops his thumb into his mouth, leaning against her to look at the pictures.

'Anna?'

Francesco bends over her, touching her arm. She jumps up to leave, excusing herself to the young mother, leaving the little boy crying once again.

Francesco's voice is full of concern as he follows her, clutching hold of her arm.

'What's happened? Stop a minute and talk to me. Has something happened to your brother or sister?'

She shakes her head. She should just pretend, invent a story that Harry is in a coma in intensive care, but instead she stammers, 'Leave me alone.'

'Is it you, then? Are you ill?'

And then she is crying.

He takes her in his arms and despite everything, she sinks into his embrace, sobbing so noisily that a policewoman approaches.

'C'è qualche problema?'

Francesco says no and thanks her politely, leading Anna from the stuffy airport to a bench outside under the shade of a Mediterranean pine. She traces a line of obscene graffiti gouged into the wood, avoiding his gaze.

'We shouldn't be alone like this,' she manages.

'Can you tell me what I've done wrong?'

'It's not you. It's us.'

She looks at him, wishing he didn't have to be so damn special.

'You're not making any sense.'

He tries to take her hand in his but she snatches it away.

'I found out,' she says, 'that you and I... we're related.'

She pauses as he pulls a face. 'You're my brother. My half-brother,' she continues.

He laughs. 'What on earth are you talking about?'

'It's in the diary. Jim wasn't my father. Your father was my father.'

He laughs again. 'Have you been at the *grappa*?'

She raises her voice, telling him not to make light of what she's saying. A couple, topping up their suntan on the dirty patch of grass outside Departures, stare at them and snigger.

'Your father's name was Dario, right?' she asks him. 'Your surname is Starnucci?'

'And so? What does that prove?'

And then she tells him what she has read about her mother's lover and the initials in the barn.

'Don't you see? Capriolo was your father – Dario – and he's my father too.'

Getting up to return to Departures, she says, 'What we've been doing is wrong. I have to go back to England, Francesco. I can't stay here with you.'

'Anna, wait!' He tries to grab her arm but she stiffens.

'All right, all right.' He steps back. 'But I think you're mistaken.'

'I wish that were true.'

She is crying again and sick of feeling sad – for her mother's wretched life and now her own, too.

'Please come back to Rofelle with me,' he continues. 'Just give me twenty-four hours to prove you wrong. I promise I won't touch you – but you can't disappear like this out of all our lives. Please, Anna.'

She can't make up her mind. Would it not just be prolonging the agony to stay, or should she let him try to make things right? The nightmare isn't over yet.

Feeling as if all the stuffing has been knocked out of her, in the end she follows him to his car.

They make the journey out of the busy, scruffy Rimini suburbs and up the Marecchia valley in silence. The sunset is achingly beautiful that evening, with pinks, purples and reds melting into a silken backdrop behind the mountains. Francesco drops her at the door to the little house in the square she thought she would never see again.

'I'll fetch you just before ten tomorrow morning. In the meantime, try to rest,' he says as he waits for her to go in.

Without bothering to wash, she takes off her jeans and T-shirt. Pulling up the covers on her unmade bed, she sinks into the mattress and although it is early, oblivion comes immediately.

CHAPTER THIRTY-TWO

Rain falls again in the morning, a fine drizzle leaving dusty streaks on the vine leaves shading the pergola. A dramatic summer storm develops. Lightning splits the sky, followed by a torrential downpour that lasts for half an hour.

Just after ten, Francesco arrives at her door. '*Buongiorno.* Are you ready?' he asks.

'Where are we going?'

He taps his nose with his index finger.

'All will be revealed,' he replies enigmatically.

'I've had enough of surprises.' She picks up her umbrella as they leave, but he tells her she won't need it, pointing to the blue sky that has replaced the storm clouds. Not for the first time she wonders at the extremes of this country. She follows him outside to his Fiat Panda and he opens the door for her. *Just like old times,* she thinks, *only nothing is the same as before.*

The car bumps up the track to Montebotolino, sometimes skidding where the road still runs with water from the heavy rain. In the sun, glistening raindrops cluster like jewels on spikes of *ginestra* along the verges. Steam rises from the warm earth like a stage effect, and the Mountain of the Moon is purple in the haze.

Francesco parks in the open area near the houses.

'Come,' he says, adding, when she hesitates, 'trust me!'

She follows him for a few metres down a footpath indicated on the side of an outbuilding with a customary red and white waymark. The grass is wet and her unsuitable travel shoes are quickly soaked, but it isn't cold. The rain has refreshed the air, releasing scents of flowers and grass. They stop in front of a tidy vegetable plot terraced into the mountainside, half a dozen beehives in bright colours tucked against the fence. In the far corner an old man is working, staking wayward tomato plants. It is Danilo. Francesco puts his fingers in his mouth and whistles. The old man turns, lifting a hand in recognition.

'What are we doing up here?' asks Anna.

'You told me you wanted to talk to him. Well, now's your chance.'

'It's too late now.'

She turns to retrace her steps but he blocks her way, a smile on his lips. 'Talk to him. I'll wait for you by the car.'

The old man beckons for her to come and sit down. Under an apple tree, an old oak plank supported by two large stones has been made into a crude bench. 'Sit here, signorina. We need to talk.'

He is nervous. His hand is stained green from the tomato plants and she notices, for the first time, his deformed fingers as he rubs his chin. She says, 'I came to talk to you before, about my mother. Twice. You didn't want to listen to me.'

'Francesco told me,' he begins. Followed by, 'I'm listening now.'

'What can you tell me about Dario Starnucci?' she asks.

'That he was my good friend. That he was also a *partigiano*. I can tell you I miss him now he's gone…'

'… And that he loved my mother.'

She finishes his sentence and turns to look at him, but he shakes his head.

'Many boys were in love with your mother. Francesco told me you believe Dario is your father.'

'Yes!'

'Well, you are wrong.'

She experiences a moment of doubt and waits for him to explain, but the old man is gazing into the distance. From his shirt pocket he takes out the photo Anna pushed under his door on her last visit to Montebotolino. The black and white image of her mother stares back, and Anna wishes she'd never bothered to write her diary.

'Your mother was very beautiful. But very stubborn.'

He touches the photo with rough, work-calloused fingers.

'I was always in love with her. Right from when we were small and we used to walk up the track to school together. I loved her when we played in the fields, and later on when I was busy with the *partigiani* and she came to join us in our camp in the mountains. I always loved her.'

He hands Anna the photograph. 'I knew she didn't feel for me in the same way. I was shy with women. Maybe if I'd plucked up courage at that time to tell her what was in my heart, life would have been different.'

'I don't understand.'

Danilo covers her hand with his, squeezes it. 'Your mother was head over heels in love with the *inglese*. She was determined to leave and start a new life. It was hard here in the war. We had *tedeschi* living on top of us, spies everywhere. There wasn't enough food. There was no fun – it was a wretched time… I believe the *inglese* came along when Ines was ripe for romance. I tried to make her think more about what she was doing – leaving her parents, Davide dead…'

'I know all this.'

'Ah, well, you must know what I'm going to tell you next.'

She replies slowly, without conviction, realisation dawning. 'What I said before… that the *inglese* was not my father; that Dario was my father.'

Danilo shakes his head. 'No, he wasn't.' He cups her cheek with his hand, his voice full of emotion. 'I am your father.'

She stares at the old man sitting next to her, feeling as if the whole world has gone mad.

'Everybody calls me by my real name: Starnucci Danilo,' he continues, saying his surname first, according to Italian tradition. 'But during the war, I was known as Capriolo.'

'Then you must be Dario's brother,' she manages to say. 'But why didn't Francesco tell me all this?'

'No, we aren't related, and he didn't know.'

He smiles at her confusion and explains. 'At least, we're not closely related. There are very few family names in the countryside around here, because cousins used to marry cousins all the time in the past. There wasn't a lot of choice.'

She looks at his face, trying to detect something of herself in him, but all she can see are the weathered, lined features of an old man. 'Why are you telling me now? Why didn't you tell me when we first met?'

He shrugs his shoulders. 'It's tricky. I was shocked that day when you turned up in the piazza. At first I thought I'd seen a ghost. You are very like her.'

'But I might never have found out…'

'I was ashamed. In one sense, I could understand why she wouldn't come back to me. I came to England to fetch her, you know.'

'I still don't understand… When did you come?'

'A long time ago, maybe more than thirty years? She told me she didn't want to make any more mistakes and bring more shame on her family. There were three children to consider, and she couldn't take them away from England. She told me to forget about her. And, against what my heart was telling me to do, I thought it best to do as she said.'

'Did you know about me?'

'When I came to England, she didn't want me to come to her house, so we met in the middle of a town. She arrived with a baby in a pushchair. I put two and two together, but I couldn't be certain. In fact, Ines told me the child was Jim's, and that made me even angrier with her.'

'So what made you finally decide to tell me?'

'Francesco came to see me last night. He was confused and upset. He told me what you'd discovered in your mother's diaries and wanted to know if there could have been anything between his father and Ines. I may be a bitter old man, but I couldn't let him believe something that wasn't true. I owed it to his father, as well as to you. Francesco and I talked into the night. And I will tell you now what happened. I have kept it hidden all these years because I am very ashamed. I am the reason your uncle Davide died so young. But make sure you remember my words, because I won't tell my story again.'

He takes her hand again. 'I've had no practice at being a father. It was too late for Rita and me. I hope it's not too late to start now.'

Anna leans forward, her hands clasped tightly as she listens to her father's words flooding her heart, words that are filling in the gaps in her mother's diary that she's been longing to hear ever since she read those first enigmatic lines.

CHAPTER THIRTY-THREE

It was our custom up in the camp on Alpe della Luna to sit around the fire in the evening and talk through our campaign for the following day. One of the Slavs in our group had told us of a bunker he'd heard about on the ridge where the *tedeschi* stored ammunition. I needed to finalise who I'd take with me to detonate it, which route to follow, what time to leave. Normally I used the time before drifting off to sleep to sort out these details, but instead my head was full of Davide. Where was he?

If only I'd not confined him to guard duty in camp. I'd left him, sullen with resentment, slumped against a rock like a moody teenager. *Porca Madonna*, but he *was* a teenager. It was easy to forget, in those unordinary times, that he was only seventeen, too young to be taking part in the bloodbath of those years. He should have been dancing with his girlfriend Carla, hunting for wild boar in the woods with me and his father and cousins, not hunting for men. He should have been an ordinary teenager.

There was nothing for it. Sleep wouldn't come anyway. Before dawn, I crept from my blanket by the fire and pulled on my boots. Somebody had to know where Davide was; I didn't believe he'd wandered far. Maybe he was with Carla up in Montebotolino. The *tedeschi* were occupying her village, so why would they bother to search the houses there? I hoped he was in his girl's arms, or up on the ridge above, maybe hidden in the cave where he and I used to camp, pre-war, on nights before our early-morning bird hunts.

Moonlight glinted off the quartz stones that studded the path I followed, and a bird trilled deep in the woods. Not a nightingale, for they sing in May and June. I stopped still to listen, wondering if it was a guard who'd heard my footsteps in the night, sending a coded warning. But the song was too beautiful. Robins sing when it isn't completely dark, or if there is some disturbance. So I continued on my way, jittery, so that, as I drew nearer the village and a fox ran out in front of me with a stolen chicken in its jaws, I bit back a cry. Further on, I stumbled over a corpse, half buried in the leaves. Turning it over, heart in mouth, I was relieved it wasn't Davide.

In the half-light, I made out the roof of the carpenter's house at the edge of the village. Now it was being used as a guard post. I crouched behind the village fountain to make a plan. If I went to the priest's house, he would give me the low-down. A good man, he'd harboured one of my partisans in his crypt and sent him to us when it was safe. Not all priests could be counted on, but Padre Luca was all right.

Ten metres away a match flared, lighting the faces and hands of two men in German greatcoats, their collars turned up against the cold. They took drags on their cigarettes, laughing at some joke or other. My mother used to say these young men were other mothers' sons, but I stopped thinking that way early on. When you've witnessed the aftermath of a massacre, a baby's bayonetted stomach, the body of a young girl, raped, her skirt above her head, you get on with the job of killing. The enemy is the enemy.

And then I heard a howl. At first I thought it was a wild dog, or a wolf staking out its territory. But this cry was spine-chilling. 'Stop, stop, I've told you, I don't know…' I recognised Davide's voice as he screamed. Light spilled from the school windows, from where the awful cries were coming. The guards moved off and I scurried like a rat along the shadows of the houses towards the school. Climbing onto a pail, I peered inside and then my foot slipped on the frosty surface, the metal container clattering against cobbles. Dogs barked, lights went on in other buildings and I was grabbed fast from behind, dragged to my feet by the guards and taken inside the school.

The image of Davide will be chiselled into my brain until my last day. I won't describe the horror. I can't talk about it. How could I describe what they'd done to him, Anna? War is lunatic. It turns men into lunatics, and some things are not for you to know. Those of us who lived through it all know what was done to us, and what we did or didn't do. I can only tell you I shall forever feel guilty for his death, because although I tried to rescue him, I was too late.

Toni was the man who tortured us. Toni, who had fought with us, lived with us in the camp, shared stories of his youth in London and the Nazi massacres he'd seen in Italy. From the outset, he'd told us a pack of lies so he could infiltrate our group. He wasn't even a barber's son; he'd butchered Davide's hair. The poor boy looked like a shorn convict after he'd taken the scissors to him. That should have sent warning bells to my stupid brain. His father was English, his mother Italian and, yes, he spoke *inglese*, but Toni's mind had been tainted by his fascist blackshirt father, and he'd come to Tuscany to work on the side of the militia.

I have scars on my hands still, but they're nothing compared to the scars on my heart. I couldn't believe Toni's betrayal of us, and I blame myself for that: that I'd harboured a viper in our band and never realised, and placed so many lives in danger. Ezio was one of his henchmen. I'd never doubted him for the weak, misguided weasel he was, but Toni was the big surprise and he taunted me as he inflicted pain, jeering at my stupidity, belittling the courage of our efforts, while all the time he was passing on information to the Nazis. I tried to block him out. I kept my gaze directed on the window. The tips of two cypress trees, silver-black in the dawn light, were me and Ines. As they swayed in the breeze, they were us dancing. I had to escape to be with her, to have a future with the girl I loved. That is what kept me going.

Towards daybreak Toni left us, half-dead, with one guard. He fell asleep. I knew this classroom well. It was where I'd been to school. The bars at the windows were flimsy, ornamental additions. In those days I was very skinny and my days of fighting in the mountains had made me wiry and fit. While the guard snored, I stripped and squeezed myself through the end bar where the gap was wider. I thought my ear would come off, but once my head was through, the rest was easy. My hands were agony, but Toni hadn't made a start on the rest of me. And when you're full of fear, pain is pushed into second place.

The village hadn't stirred, and I hurried back to camp to alert the others. We had to move from that place now we knew Toni had betrayed us, but we were always on the move anyway, and I knew of an abandoned shepherd's refuge near Montelabreve we hadn't yet used. There, we planned our rescue carefully and left it for more than a week, guessing they would be expecting us sooner. But that was another error of judgement. Because when we returned to the school, they'd burnt the place down and shot everyone in the village. Padre Luca's body was flung on top of a pile of old men, women and children. We were too late.

You want to know what happened in the war, Anna. You wonder why we only talk about small, incidental day-to-day matters, what we ate or what we wore; the things that made us laugh. But why would we want to talk about the rest of it? Those events that hurt so much…

Those of us who lived through those years, know what was done. We stand naked in our own sight. You who haven't been there cannot judge us.

Only I can judge myself, and that is for me to live with.

*

Anna can't find the right words for her father, but she puts her arms around the old man and the two of them cling to each other. When he stops shaking, she stands up and gestures to Francesco to come over. The three of them walk in silence to the old man's house. Pushing open his front door, he gestures to them to sit around his kitchen table.

Anna is the first to speak, Danilo still visibly moved. She can see he's fighting hard to control his emotions, and she inches closer to take one of his hands in hers, while murmuring to Francesco, 'So, you heard all this yesterday?'

Francesco nods.

'Babbo,' she says softly, for the first time, and her father touches her face gently.

'I promise I won't ask you about these things again. I know it must be painful, but... I still have questions, pieces of the jigsaw to fit.'

Danilo squeezes her hand and she takes that as permission to continue.

'You mustn't feel bad about Davide. Is that why you didn't pursue my mother, why you wouldn't talk to me when I came to see you?'

He nods. 'Davide is always on my conscience.'

'I don't believe you could have done any more than you did. Davide wasn't a child, you couldn't keep him by your side all the time. And you did all you could to rescue him. I have no idea what living through war is like, but nothing can be normal in times like that.' She turns to Francesco. 'Isn't that right, Francesco?'

'Absolutely. You should stop punishing yourself, Signor Danilo. You need to try to find a place of calm within yourself and stop these ripples of war. And as for Toni… It's over. He's not worth any more of your energy.'

'It's not easy to forget,' the old man says, and then he brings Anna's hand up to his lips and kisses it. 'But I have a reason now to move forward.'

He lets go of her and rises from the table, his chair scraping across the stone floor. '*Su, coraggio*,' he announces. 'No more sad talk, *cara mia*,' he says to Anna. He fetches a bottle of sparkling wine from a corner cupboard. The three of them toast each other, and drink a toast to Davide. The mood is still solemn, but there is hope in the air.

Talk turns to local news, and Anna listens to how Danilo's farming friend has lost another calf to a wolf, how officials from Arezzo don't understand the first thing about the way country people live. She watches the old man with new fondness and admiration as he jokes with Francesco, thumping his hand on the table as he laughs. She senses, despite his joy at finding her, that he's putting on a brave face, trying to turn a page in his life. It will take time to fully comprehend that he is her father, and she hopes they can spend more time together so she can feel closer to him, but they've made a start.

Afterwards, Francesco takes Anna back down the hill. They park outside the village cemetery where the graves are protected by high walls and shaded by tall pines.

'Are you all right, *tesoro?*' he asks, pulling her close. 'You've been through so much in the last few hours.'

She nods. 'As has my poor father. It's been an incredible morning. I still have unanswered questions, but I can't push him. Maybe I'll never know exactly what happened.'

'Maybe some things are not ours to know.' He kisses her gently and she thinks how lucky she is. After a while, he breaks away. 'I brought you here for a reason. I want to show you why it was easy for you to think we were related. Come!'

He turns the key in the metal gate and it creaks as he pushes it open. On the walls are enamelled plaques bearing the names of the dead. Some display photos, taken when they were alive, next to the inscriptions. Some images are of young men in army uniforms from the First and Second World Wars. There are men and women, young and old, dressed in their Sunday best. There are babies and infants. Votive lights flicker red in front of some of the memorials; faded plastic flowers and real flowers are arranged in jars. Two rusted metal crosses protrude from mounds in the grass.

'Look at the surnames,' he says, taking her hand to lead her round the walls. Gori, Valentini, Santini, Starnucci and Butteri are the family names that predominate.

'In villages like ours,' he tells her, 'remote and cut off for so many months in the winter, intermarrying was bound to happen.'

'So we *could* be related,' she says.

'Maybe in the distant, distant past. Anna, come and sit over here with me,' he says, drawing her to a bench set against the cemetery wall.

'Danilo talked a lot about Toni to me yesterday. About his treachery. We talked for hours last night, and he asked me to fill in certain details for you.'

'About Toni? It's so awful… I can understand the truth now of what I've read in Mamma's diary: that people were divided, and it was hard to know whom to trust. When the war was over, how on earth could people live with each other when they'd been such enemies? I mean, Ezio coming to the wedding… how could he dare show his face like that, knowing Dan…' She pauses. 'Oh, Francesco, it's going to take me a while to adjust to calling him Babbo.'

'All in good time, *tesoro*. There are still repercussions, even now. Some families don't have anything to do with each other because of what went on in the war. But as the years pass, there will be less bitterness. The younger generation is too removed from it all to harbour grudges.'

'So much cruelty,' she says as she gets up to walk about the graves, peering at photos until she finds the corner where the Santinis are buried. One bears the photo of a young man, grinning at the camera, and she traces his features with her finger.

'Francesco, come and look.'

The image is of Davide, her uncle.

Francesco joins her and cradles her from behind as they stand. He kisses the top of her head.

'I returned the medal to your father yesterday. I knew you wouldn't mind, Anna. And he told me he didn't deserve it. Those were his words as I placed it in his hands and he immediately stuffed it in his trouser pocket. Then he told me something which I took as a kind of confession.'

'What?'

'He said he'd hunted Toni down after the war. He travelled down to Rome. Apparently, Toni died in an accident. He was knocked off his motorbike by a man driving a lorry. He said he would leave it to my imagination to work out who drove that lorry. He gave me such a strange look and warned me he never wants to talk about it again.'

'And we shall respect his wishes. I won't breathe a word,' Anna replies.

She has a fleeting image of her mother kneeling on the grass next to her, tending her brother's grave, her dark hair falling round her face, arranging greenery in a jam jar. For a vivid moment she senses her presence, hears Ines whisper to her that she must do what her heart tells her. And then the sensation fades and patterns play upon the grass, in dancing shadows cast by the tall pines.

'*Andiamo!* Let's go,' she says, taking Francesco's hand.

CHAPTER THIRTY-FOUR

October 1999

Emerging from the church, they walk beneath an avenue of plane trees to applause from friends and family showering them with handfuls of rice. Alba runs in front, her bridesmaid's dress billowing behind, bubbling with laughter as she throws rose petals into the air above the newlyweds.

Francesco pulls Anna close while they wait for Danilo to catch up. People from the village keep stopping Anna's father to compliment him on his newly discovered family – '*Bravo, Danilo, bravissimo! Auguri!*' – and he beams with pleasure and pride.

Teresa dutifully escorts Anna's brother and sister to the *agriturismo* pick-up truck. Her English family have decided to come at the last minute, curiosity getting the better of them. She doesn't mind; she has enough happiness to share around and defies anybody not to be charmed by her Italian wedding. Anna giggles into her flowers at the sight of a villager giving Jane a helpful push on her ample behind as she clambers into the back of Teresa's truck. The vehicle has been transformed with garlands of greenery and white ribbons. Cynthia clings to Harry's arm, her high heels totally unsuited to the cobbled path, her pink chiffon dress clinging to her, barely hiding her six-month bump, and Harry's smile is like a zip that's been unzipped wide.

Bride and groom drive down the road to the *agriturismo* in Francesco's Fiat that Harry insisted on decorating 'English wedding-style' late last night, attaching old tin cans, balloons and a wellington boot to the bumper. Attracted by the commotion, people come out of their homes to wave handkerchiefs, clap and cheer. '*Auguri, Francesco ed Anna. Complimenti!*'

The railings on the steps to Il Casalone are festooned with laurel branches, garlands of white roses and long strands of ivy. Teresa and her friends from the village have been busy for days in the kitchen, banning Anna from the food preparations. The wedding meal and sharing of food is every bit as important a ritual as the nuptial Mass.

Tables are piled with a feast of colourful, appetising food spread on freshly laundered Busatti linen. A warm, balmy October has followed a wet summer, and so a separate round table is arranged outside on the terrace to hold a whole Parmesan cheese, cut into squares and served with sparkling Prosecco to each guest as they arrive. Teresa and her team have been busy with starters of roast peppers, courgettes and aubergines, pastries with asparagus and artichokes and soft, melting cheeses, home-made *cappelletti* – small hat-shaped *ravioli* stuffed with chicken breast, lean beef, lemon zest and nutmeg – and *tagliatelle*, with Anna's favourite fresh tomato and basil sauce.

And for the main course, Teresa carries in a platter bearing a whole roast suckling pig served with tiny potatoes dug earlier in the year from the *orto*, roasted in olive oil and pungent rosemary. To follow, nasturtiums, borage and marigold petals with young dandelion leaves, wild sorrel and rocket are arranged in a salad, all picked by Teresa and her girlfriends from the meadows around the village. And all this to be washed down with full-bodied local Sangiovese and Chianti Classico.

Jane has insisted on contributing an English tradition to the wedding. At very short notice, for the wedding has been fairly last-minute, she baked a cake before leaving England, and its three tiers of columns and crafted icing draw gasps of astonishment from the female Italian guests. She confided to Anna that on the Channel crossing she slipped down to the car deck to check on the cake's safekeeping and was soundly reprimanded by one of the crew. Before Anna and Francesco cut into the iced concoction, Danilo makes a speech. Pushing back his chair and rising slowly, he taps the side of his glass to gain attention.

'It's not the custom to make speeches at our weddings,' he begins, easing his tie a little further from his starched shirt collar, 'but we all know this is no ordinary wedding. We are here to join in the celebrations of these two lovely people who want to spend their lives together. And I would like also to celebrate finding my family. I hope you will all permit me this selfishness…'

He pauses as the guests applaud; a few stamp their feet and he holds up his hands, waiting for them to quieten down.

When he is ready, he resumes. 'Some of you here today already know a little of my story. My older friends will also remember Ines. Ines Santini.'

There are murmurings among the guests, some of them turning to explain to those next to them. Danilo continues and there are hisses for silence so he can be heard.

'Take a look at my beautiful daughter, and I'm sure you will see Ines' likeness.'

More comments and exclamations follow from the guests, and Anna feels herself blushing as everybody cranes to stare. Francesco plants a kiss on her lips and there are more loud cheers and the traditional ribald shouts of '*Tanti figli maschi*' (may you have many male children).

'The war has been over for more than fifty years now,' continues Danilo. 'Some of you here today lived through that time, although you would probably prefer not to be reminded. I, for one, want to forget. In our school in the village they are preparing a project, and some of the children will ask their grandparents for memories of the war. And I urge you all to be generous with your time.'

He looks over to Francesco and, after clearing his throat, he continues. 'We should not bury all our memories. Some are too painful to share, and so be it. But we made mistakes in those times, which caused anguish...' He pauses and swallows. 'And we need to learn from these mistakes. We fought hard for our freedom, for the freedom of our children.'

More murmurings among the guests.

Then somebody shouts, '*Evviva l'Italia,*' and a few echo him.

Somebody else shouts, '*Evviva l'Inghilterra!*' and there is more enthusiastic applause.

Again Danilo holds up his hands for silence.

'It wasn't my intention to stand up here like the old man I am and talk about the past, or to be political, so let's raise our glasses and make a *brindisi* to Anna and Francesco and wish them both happiness. May they hold onto that happiness, keep it deep within and never let it dwindle. I feel I am the luckiest old man alive today, for somehow my Ines has returned to me. Raise your glasses now, everybody. To Anna and Francesco!'

There are shouts: '*Bravo!*' '*Auguri!*' '*Cin-cin!*'

Anna leans over and, pulling his hand to her cheek, she cups her father's disfigured fingers with her own. He whispers to her, 'I have a gift for you both, but you must wait until after the wedding. Today is not the right time. Come and see me soon in Montebotolino.'

Alba climbs onto his knee. The old man pinches her cheek gently between his second and third fingers and caresses her head. Later, when the tables are pushed back against the walls and the accordionist starts up his music, she even manages to get the old man to dance a polka with her.

*

That night, in bed under the eaves, Francesco strokes Anna's hair, wiping a tear with his thumb as it trickles down her cheek.

'You're weeping for Ines, aren't you?'

She nods. 'And for my father. And my poor Uncle Davide. I'm so happy, and it doesn't seem fair.'

'Life isn't always fair. But Ines led us to each other. That might not have happened if her life had been different.'

She kisses her husband. Tomorrow she will buy a notebook, and will start a diary.

A diary to fill with her own memory pearls.

EPILOGUE

Danilo died four years later, just after his eightieth birthday, but not before he was able to meet all his grandchildren. Davide Danilo Jonathan Starnucci was born in June 2000, at the start of a new millennium, eight months after Francesco and Anna married. Alba was over the moon with her little brother, and just as excited when her twin sisters, Rosanna and Emilia, were born two years later.

Danilo's wedding gift to Anna and Francesco was the ruined watermill along the River Marecchia – *Il Mulino*.

Broken-hearted that she had made a new life in England, and suffering with poor health, Ines' parents had almost completed the sale of the old mill to a local businessman. His plans to knock down the centuries-old building in order to create a holiday park on the site were thwarted by Danilo. He managed to persuade the *Comune* to overthrow the project, pointing out the importance of the listed building, as well as the real danger of flooding in the area located by the river.

Eventually he purchased the old mill himself but never carried out its restoration, and it was in a pitiful state when Anna and Francesco embarked on their project.

Today, after extensive site visits from local architects and planners, geological surveys and successful feasibility studies, Anna and Francesco have fully restored their old watermill. The original millstones have been put back into use and once a week, Francesco produces enough grain to sell to tourists to make home-made bread.

It is also the venue for holidays with a difference, where the real Italy can be sampled. When Anna isn't busy with her growing family, she organises courses in cookery, painting and language. Francesco loves to accompany visitors on walks in the mountains, showing them the rich fauna and flora of the area. He is about to publish a field guide to the butterflies and birds of the Marecchia valley.

Little Davide speaks both Italian and English fluently, and his sisters will be brought up in the same way, encouraged to be proud of their two cultures.

A LETTER FROM ANGELA

Dear reader,

I want to thank you so much for choosing to read *The Tuscan Secret*. Although my book is fiction, much of the story is based on fact and I felt it important to honour the experiences of so many brave people who endured so much in World War II in the corner of Italy I know.

If you would like to keep up to date with all my latest releases and join me on more Tuscan journeys, please sign up by following the link below.

Your email address will never be shared, and you can unsubscribe at any time.

www.bookouture.com/angela-petch

I do hope you enjoyed *The Tuscan Secret*. If you did, I'd be really pleased if you could write a review. I'd love to hear what you thought, and it also helps new readers discover my books. Or perhaps you can recommend it to your family and friends.

I really enjoy hearing from my readers.

You can get in touch with me on my Facebook page, through Twitter, Goodreads or my website.

Thanks so much for your support.
Angela Petch

 AngelaJaneClarePetch

 @Angela_Petch

 angelapetchsblogsite.wordpress.com

 Angela Petch Author Page

ACKNOWLEDGEMENTS

This story was inspired in great part by my amazing Italian mother-in-law, Giuseppina Micheli, who fell in love with Captain Horace Petch of the Royal Artillery of the Eighth Army, when they met in Urbino on 13 October 1944. But I was also told many anecdotes by our Italian friends from Badia Tedalda, Tuscany. This stunning countryside, where I live for half of the year, is situated along the Gothic Line, and history whispers to me along the mule tracks and mountain passes we regularly walk. However, *The Tuscan Secret* is a work of fiction. Any resemblance to real personalities is purely coincidental. I would hate to think anybody might be offended by my imagination. Any mistakes that occur in any historical event that I have drawn on in the story are purely my own.

Thank you, lovely Pina, for sharing your stories and letters. *Grazie* to Fulvio Pieghai at the Tourist Office in Badia Tedalda, for your time and generosity in lending me photos and memoirs written by local folk. Thanks to my lovely editor at Bookouture, Ellen Gleeson, and the whole brilliant team. You have helped me polish up my original story, and I've loved the challenge. I'd also like to thank all my writing friends in the various groups I've belonged to: Liz Minister in Holbrook, who started me off on this writing adventure, The Felixstowe Scribblers, Arun Scribes, Sea Scribes and CHINDI authors. Without you…

Mummy and Daddy – Kenneth and Maureen Sutor (who left us far too early). You are missed each and every day. You took your young family to live in Rome in the early 1960s and kindled a passion for Italy. I love you.

It goes without saying that special love and thanks go to my brilliant family and my husband, Fagiolino, without whom I would be well and truly lost.

BIBLIOGRAPHY

Love and War in the Apennines by Eric Newby

Mander's March on Rome by D'Arcy Mander

Mrs Milburn's Diaries: An Englishwoman's day-to-day reflections, 1939–45 edited by Peter Donnelly

Italy's Sorrow: A Year of War 1944–45 by James Holland

The Art of Falling by Deborah Lawrenson

The Voice of War: The Second World War Told by Those Who Fought It, edited by James Owen and Guy Walters

When the Moon Rises: Escape and Evasion through War-torn Italy by Tony Davies

The Other Italy: The Italian Resistance in World War II by Maria de Blasio Wilhelm

Miracle at Sant' Anna by James McBride

War in Italy: 1943–1945, A Brutal Story by Richard Lamb

L'Appennino del' 44, eccidi e protagonisti sulla linea gotica, a cura di Ivan Tognarini

The King's Dragoon Guards. World War Two, Part 6 http://www. qdg.org.uk/pages/WW2-Part-6-112.php

What Did You Do in the War, Mummy? compiled by Mavis Nicholson